PENGUIN CLASSICS

MENCIUS

ADVISORY EDITOR: BETTY RADICE

Little is known about MENCIUS other than what can be gathered from the book named after him. He was, perhaps, born a century or so after the death of Confucius, and it is likely that he died before the end of the fourth century B.C. In his old age Mencius travelled from one state to another, hoping vainly to convert the feudal princes of the day to his view of man and morality. For a thousand years the *Mencius*, as part of the *Four Books*, was read by every schoolboy. There is no doubt that the influence exerted by Mencius over the development of Confucian thought is second only to Confucius.

D. C. LAU read Chinese at the University of Hong Kong, and, in 1946, he went to Glasgow, where he read philosophy. In 1950 he entered the School of Oriental and African Studies in London to teach Chinese philosophy. After lecturing in Chinese philosophy at the University of London he returned to Hong Kong, where he is a Professor at the Chinese University.

MENCIUS

TRANSLATED WITH
AN INTRODUCTION BY
D. C. LAU

PENGUIN BOOKS

PENGUIN BOOKS

Published by the Penguin Group
Penguin Books Ltd, 27 Wrights Lane, London W8 5TZ, England
Viking Penguin, a division of Penguin Books USA Inc.
375 Hudson Street, New York, New York 10014, USA
Penguin Books Australia Ltd, Ringwood, Victoria, Australia
Penguin Books Canada Ltd, 2801 John Street, Markham, Ontario, Canada L3R 1B4
Penguin Books (NZ) Ltd, 182–190 Wairau Road, Auckland 10, New Zealand

Penguin Books Ltd, Registered Offices: Harmondsworth, Middlesex, England

This translation first published 1970
9 10

Copyright © D. C. Lau, 1970
All rights reserved

Printed in England by Clays Ltd, St Ives plc
Set in Monotype Fournier

Contents

Introduction

Only two Chinese philosophers have the distinction of being known consistently to the West by a latinized name. The first is Confucius. The second is Mencius, whose name is Meng K'e. That Mencius should share the distinction is by no means an insignificant fact, for he is without doubt second only to Confucius in importance in the Confucian tradition, a fact officially recognized in China for over a thousand years. There are various reasons for this. First, the *Analects of Confucius* which forms almost the only reliable source of our knowledge of the thought of Confucius consists of a collection of sayings of the sage, mostly brief and often with little or no context. Hence many ideas are not elaborated upon, leaving a good deal of room for differences in interpretation. The *Mencius*, too, consists of sayings of Mencius and conversations he had with his contemporaries, but these tend to be of greater length and there is often some kind of a context. The ideas are, therefore, more articulate. Thus the *Mencius*, when read side by side with the *Analects of Confucius*, throws a great deal of light on the latter work. Second, Mencius developed some of the ideas of Confucius and at the same time discussed problems not touched on by Confucius. It is not an exaggeration to say that what is called Confucianism in subsequent times contains as much of the thought of Mencius as of Confucius.

The only other great name in early Confucianism is that of Hsün Tzu who was half a century or so later than Mencius. He developed Confucianism in a way radically different from that of Mencius, and we shall have occasion to mention him when we come to discuss the philosophical thought of Mencius. It is perhaps futile to try to decide which of the two was the greater thinker, as the difference between them is due mainly to a difference in philosophical temperament. In William James' famous distinction, Mencius is a 'tender-minded', and Hsün Tzu a 'tough-minded', philosopher. But Hsün Tzu had considerably less influence on subsequent thought than Mencius, and this for two reasons. First,

Mencius was probably the greatest writer amongst ancient philosophers, while Hsün Tzu was, at best, the possessor of an indifferent literary style. When in T'ang times Han Yü raised the banner of the *ku wen* movement,[1] he looked to Mencius as much for his superb style as for his sound philosophy. Second, from the Sung onwards, the philosophy of Mencius became the orthodoxy while Hsün Tzu was almost totally eclipsed. The *Great Learning*, the *Doctrine of the Mean*, the *Analects of Confucius*, together with the *Mencius*, became known as the *Four Books* which, until the present century, were read and memorized by every schoolboy in his first years at school. Thus the position and influence of Mencius were assured.

As with most ancient Chinese thinkers, little is known of the life of Mencius other than what we can glean from the work bearing his name. True, there is a biography[2] in the *Shih chi* (*Records of the Historian*), the first comprehensive history written at the beginning of the first century B.C., but this contains hardly any facts not to be found in the *Mencius* and when Ssu-ma Ch'ien departs from the *Mencius*, as in the case of dates, he goes wrong. There are also some early traditions concerning Mencius and his mother to be found in the *Han shih wai chuan* of the second century B.C. and the *Lieh nü chuan* just over a century later.[3] It is difficult to say how much credence can be given to these traditions, but they attained wide currency and great popularity as cautionary tales.

It is to the *Mencius*, therefore, that we must look if we wish to find out something about Mencius' life. The *Mencius* is divided into seven books, the titles of which are of no significance as they are all simply taken from the opening sentence of the books and, with the exception of the last book, are all names of persons with whom Mencius had conversations. There is no indication that any

1. The movement was so called because it advocated a return to *ku wen*, i.e., the prose style of the ancient period. This came about through a growing dissatisfaction with the parallel prose that had been prevalent since the Six Dynasties.

2. For a translation and a discussion of this biography see Appendix 1.

3. See Appendix 2.

method for the grouping of the sections was followed by the editor, though Book V Part A, for instance, consists solely of questions and answers concerning history. There is, however, one exception, and that is Book I. There the sections are arranged chronologically, and it is this book that furnishes us with some precise dates. In I. A. 5, King Hui of Liang mentions his defeats by Ch'i to the east, by Ch'in to the west, and by Ch'u to the south. The defeat by Ch'i was at Ma Ling in 341 B.C. From that year on-wards, for the next twenty years, Liang suffered a series of defeats at the hands of Ch'in. The humiliation inflicted by Ch'u was in 323 B.C. As King Hui died in 319 B.C., the meeting with Mencius must have fallen within the period, 323 to 319 B.C. With the death of King Hui, King Hsiang succeeded him and I. A. 6 records an interview with the new king. Mencius must have left Liang for Ch'i soon afterwards, finding King Hsiang lacking in the dignity befitting a king. In the next section we find a conversation with King Hsüan of Ch'i who had just succeeded his father, King Wei, in 320. The sections, from I. A. 7 to I. B. 11, are all concerned with King Hsüan, and I. B. 10 and I. B. 11 both deal with the invasion of Yen by Ch'i in 314 B.C. This same event is also dealt with in II. B. 8 and II. B. 9, and this part of Book II seems also to be in chronologi-cal order. In II. B. 14 we find Mencius explaining to a questioner that after his first meeting with the king he had no intention of staying in Ch'i, but 'it so happened that war broke out and I had no opportunity of requesting permission to leave'. This almost certainly refers to the war with Yen, and Mencius must have left shortly after hostilities came to an end. To return to Book I, the remaining chapters of the book record conversations with Duke Mu of Tsou, Duke Wen of T'eng and finally with Duke P'ing of Lu. It seems likely that on leaving Ch'i Mencius was going to Lu, and on his way stopped in Tsou and T'eng. We know nothing of Mencius after this. He probably lived out his last years in retirement in Lu.

There are various events in the *Mencius* with no clear indication of date: for instance, Mencius' return to Lu to bury his mother (II. B. 7), and conversations he had with Duke Wen of T'eng and with his envoys (III. A. 1 to III. A. 3). These, it seems to me, can be fitted into the period 319-314 B.C., for during this period, although Mencius was staying in Ch'i, he made trips abroad from time to time. We know, at least, of one occasion when he was sent as official envoy to the funeral of Duke Ting of T'eng, the father of Duke Wen (II. B. 6). There is no convincing evidence,[1] as far as one can see, for any events recorded in the *Mencius* happening before 319 B.C.

Although we know the dates of the visit to Liang and Ch'i, there is still the question of Mencius' age at that time. There is no direct evidence for a clear answer to this question, but there is some indication that Mencius was an old man. Twice King Hui used the word *sou* (old man) in talking to Mencius. If we bear in mind the fact that the king himself was a man of about seventy, it would seem very unlikely that Mencius was very much younger.

If what we have said so far is accepted, then the *Mencius* covers the last years of Mencius' life. This would mean that the views expressed in the work are his mature views and represent the fruits of a lifetime spent in reflection and teaching. It would also account for the consistency of the work and the authority with which Mencius speaks and, perhaps, for the superb literary skill with which he expresses his ideas.

It is within the fourth century B.C. that the whole of Mencius' life falls, and the fourth century B.C. saw some radical and far-reaching changes in China. The feudal system was gradually replaced by a system of centralized government under which the state was divided into administrative districts. The sale and purchase of land came to be permitted and tax on land was levied in kind. A number of states began to put into practice ideas of Legalist philosophers aimed at strengthening the state. The goal was a highly centralized government with laws applied equally stringently to everyone in the state, and ultimately at a healthy agrarian economy with every peasant able to take up arms in time of war. There is no doubt that the application of these policies brought short-term success, as these states were able, because of their increased military strength, to expand at the expense of their more conservative neighbours. This process culminated in the unification

1. For a discussion of the evidence see Appendix 1.

of China in 221 B.C. by the state of Ch'in which was most thorough-going in its adoption of Legalist ideas. But this was to come. In Mencius' time it meant more frequent wars on an ever-increasing scale. It also meant a growing cynicism towards morality which is implicit in Legalist doctrines based on a view of man as purely egoistic and motivated solely by the thought of reward and punish-ment. With the prevalent atmosphere Mencius was in profound disagreement. In his view man is basically a moral creature. To understand this we must take a brief look at the roots of his thought.

In reading the *Mencius* one cannot but be struck by the admira-tion shown by Mencius for Confucius, and there is no doubt that Mencius' philosophy is essentially based on the teachings of Con-fucius, though in some respects it developed beyond their limits, mainly because philosophical problems had arisen since Confucius of which any serious thinker had to take cognizance.

As Mencius admired Confucius, so did Confucius admire the Duke of Chou. Now when the Chou replaced the Yin as the ruling house of the Empire, they expounded a philosophy as much to instil resignation in the conquered as to inculcate a self-searching vigilance in themselves. To the conquered they had to explain the reason for their loss of the Empire. The Yin believed that they ruled by virtue of the Mandate of Heaven, and because they had held it for so long they had forgotten that this Mandate could be withdrawn. The Chou, by wresting the Empire from the Yin, had shown this to be the case, and they reiterated this truth; this is summed up in a line in the *Book of Odes*,

The Mandate of Heaven is not immutable.[1]

A ruling house could retain the Mandate only so long as it acted morally, that is, acted solely with the good of the people at heart. It would lose it, as indeed the Yin lost it, if the Emperor strayed from the path of virtue. Now this doctrine was double-edged. If it explained the fall of the Yin, it also laid down the conditions which must constantly be fulfilled if the Chou were to retain the Mandate. Hence the Chou Emperors were warned that they had to be constantly vigilant over their own conduct. There is no doubt

1. Ode 235. Mencius quotes this ode in IV. A. 7.

that the Duke of Chou was the architect of this philosophy and it is easy to understand the admiration shown by Confucius.

Confucius' most distinctive contribution to Chinese thought is his exposition of the concepts of *jen* and *yi*. *Jen* has been variously rendered in English as benevolence, human-heartedness, goodness, love, altruism and humanity. Of these I think benevolence is the least objectionable, and as far as Mencius is concerned, has the advantage of echoes of Bishop Butler. For Butler, both benevolence and self-interest are principles as distinct from particular passions, and there is something of this distinction in the thought of Mencius. *Yi* is often rendered as righteousness, but this, though close enough as an equivalent, lacks the versatility of the Chinese word. *Yi* can be applied to an act which is right, to the agent who does what is right and to a duty which an agent ought to do. Although both *jen* and *yi* are of the first importance to Confucius' teaching, *jen* is more basic. It was conceived of as the totality of moral virtues and in this sense we can say that *yi* is rooted in *jen*. As we shall see, both *jen* and *yi* figure prominently in Mencius' teaching and he gave *jen* an important place in his political philosophy.

We have already remarked on the fact that although Mencius thought of himself as a successor to Confucius, nevertheless, because of the changes in the philosophical scene, he had to deal with problems which were either unknown or unimportant in Confucius' day. Mencius' name is, above all, associated with his theory of the goodness of human nature. Now the only remark made by Confucius on the subject is that 'by nature, men are very much the same, it is through practice that they drift apart' (the *Analects of Confucius*, XVII. 2). That there is only one somewhat non-committal remark in the whole of the *Analects of Confucius* on human nature shows at least that human nature was not a prominent issue in the day of Confucius. In contrast, it must already have been a hotly debated topic in Mencius' day. Let us look at the factors contributing to the complexity of the problem.

The concept of *ming*, which in the early Chou was essentially the *mandate* given by Heaven to the ruling house, has meantime undergone development in two ways. Although *ming* had always meant the moral commands of Heaven, so long as it was conceived of as affecting only the fortunes of Empires, there was no need to deal with the relationship between human nature and the mandate of Heaven. But in the course of time the concept of *ming* was extended. The individual, too, has his *ming*. He, too, is enjoined by Heaven to be moral. The question then arises, given his nature, can he obey the commands of Heaven? The answer to this question depends, of course, on the view of human nature one holds. The second development is that *ming* gradually took on the meaning of fate. Already in the *Analects of Confucius* we find examples of this use of the word (e.g. XII. 5). This is even more inimical to moral teachings. If what will be will be, there is hardly room left for human effort, let alone morality. Now by Mencius' time, there was a theory of human nature which must have been widely accepted. According to this theory, the nature of a man consists of his desires and appetites, a view summed up in Kao Tzu's remark, 'Appetite for food and sex is nature' (VI. A. 4). If this were true, man has no other motive to action than the urge to find gratification for his desires, and no matter how much he may wish to comply with the commands of Heaven, it is impossible for him to do so.

It is against this background that we must approach Mencius' theory of human nature. First of all, let us dispose of certain mis-understandings. It has been said by interpreters that Mencius put forth his theory solely with sages in mind, as the sage is the only type of man who possesses unadulterated goodness. This is to restrict the application of Mencius' theory to sages, but as Mencius makes it quite clear that his theory is meant to apply universally to all men, there must be something wrong with the interpretation.

Mencius nowhere contradicted Kao Tzu's statement that 'appetite for food and sex is nature'. He would probably admit that desires and appetites form the greater part of human nature. What he emphatically denied was that human nature consisted *solely* of desires and appetites. According to him, 'Slight is the difference between man and the brutes. The common man loses this distinguishing feature, while the gentleman retains it' (IV. B. 19). To say that the difference between man and the brutes is slight is to imply that they are, for the most part, the same, and if the nature of

animals consists solely of desires and appetites, then these must also
make up the greater part of human nature. There is, however, a
difference, and this, though slight, sets man apart from the animals.
Whether a man is a gentleman or not depends on whether he suc-
ceeds in retaining and, we may say, developing this difference.
But what is this distinguishing feature that the gentleman retains?
The answer is, it is his heart (*hsin*). In IV. B. 28, Mencius says, 'A
gentleman differs from other men in that he retains his heart.'
This 'retaining of the heart' is again mentioned in VII. A. 1. It is
necessary to emphasize the retention of the heart because it is
something very easy to lose. Since the heart is something we pos-
sess originally, it is also referred to as the 'original heart'. Mencius
describes a man who loses his sense of shame and comes to do
things for unworthy motives which he would not, in the first
instance, have done even to escape death as a man who has lost
his 'original heart' (VI. A. 10). Mencius also calls it the 'true heart'.
It is not the case that a man never possessed the benevolent and
righteous heart, but that he has 'let go of his true heart' (VI. A. 8).
We are said to 'let go' of the heart because we possessed it in the
first place. The purpose of learning is 'to go after this strayed
heart' (VI. A. 11).

What, we may ask, is the special function of the heart? The
answer, according to Mencius, is that it is the function of the heart
to think. This marks it off from the other parts of the person,
particularly the senses. These, being unable to think, are drawn
blindly to the objects of their desires. The eyes are attracted by
beautiful sights and the ear to beautiful sounds. This is, in principle,
no different from one inanimate object being attracted by another,
for instance, iron being attracted by a loadstone. Hence man, if
he puts aside his heart, is attracted by outside things as one thing
by another. 'The organs of hearing and sight are unable to think
and can be misled by external things,' says Mencius. 'When one
thing acts on another, all it does is to attract it. The organ of the
heart can think. But it will find the answer only if it does think;
otherwise, it will not find the answer. This is what Heaven has
given me' (VI. A. 15). We can see from this passage why Mencius
attaches the greatest importance to the heart. Without the ability

to think, a living creature is completely determined by its desires and the desires are totally at the mercy of their respective objects. It is the gift from Heaven of a thinking heart that marks human beings off from animals, but, Mencius warns, the mere possession of the heart is not enough, we must in fact think with it. If we fail to make use of the heart, we are still no different from animals.

What did Mencius have in mind when he talked about thinking? He had in mind moral thinking – thinking about moral duties, about priorities, about the purpose and destiny of man and his position in the universe. For Mencius, intellectual thinking forms an insignificant part of thinking. This was a feature common to all ancient Chinese thought. Let us look a little more closely at the objects of thought.

In a group of sections in Book VI Part A, Mencius deals with the problem of relative value. According to this, the various members of the human person are not of equal value. The heart is a greater member while the sense organs are lesser members. A greater member is higher than a lesser member. The difference between a great man and a small man lies in the priorities they give to these members. The great man gets his priorities right, while the small man gets them wrong. The latter is described as 'unthinking to the highest degree' (VI. A. 13).

We can see that the function of the heart being to think, it can make judgements on the relative value of the different members of the human person including itself, and further that it is in fact the heart itself that is of the highest value. This ties up with what Mencius says elsewhere. 'Reason and rightness please my heart in the same way as meat pleases my palate' (VI. A. 7). What pleases the heart is of higher value than what pleases the senses.

Now we are in a better position to appreciate Mencius' objections to the views of human nature current in his day, and also the distinctive feature of his own theory. Though one may admit that man shares with animals the possession of appetites and desires and though one may further admit that these form the greater part of his make-up, nevertheless, one is justified in saying that the desireful nature of man cannot be called human nature, because this fails to distinguish him from animals. What distinguishes him from animals is his heart, for though this forms but a small part of his nature it is both unique to man and the highest amongst his bodily organs.

It is worthwhile at this point to mention one feature of the view of man held by Mencius and, indeed, by Chinese thinkers in general. There is no bifurcation of man into soul and body as in the Western tradition, and so the problem of how the two can interact does not arise. Man, for Mencius, is an organic whole, though in the complex structure which is his person we can distinguish the higher constituents from the lower. It is for this reason that in Mencius' view what is wrong with a man who cares only for his belly is merely that he has got his priorities wrong. If he gets these right, then there is nothing wrong with caring for the belly. He says, 'If a man who cares about food and drink can do so without neglecting any other part of his person, then his mouth and belly are much more than just a foot or an inch of his skin' (VI. A. 14). Again, according to him, a healthy heart in a man 'manifests itself in his face, giving it a sleek appearance. It also shows in his back and extends to his limbs, rendering their message intelligible without words' (VII. A. 21). Finally, he says, 'Our body and complexion are given to us by Heaven. Only a sage can give his body complete fulfilment' (VII. A. 38).

So far we have only seen that the heart is pleased by what is right and reasonable, but the essentially moral nature of the heart is much more deep-seated than that. According to Mencius, there are four incipient tendencies in the heart. These he calls 'the heart of compassion', 'the heart of shame', 'the heart of courtesy and modesty', and 'the heart of right and wrong' (II. A. 6 and VI. A. 6). Mencius further points out that 'the heart of compassion' is the germ of benevolence; 'the heart of shame', the germ of dutifulness; 'the heart of courtesy and modesty', the germ of the observance of the rites; and 'the heart of right and wrong', the germ of wisdom (II. A. 6). Each of these four tendencies has its own significance. The heart of compassion, the finding of suffering in others unbearable, if naturally found in all human beings, will show, according to Mencius, that benevolence has a basis in human nature, and benevolence is the strongest motive to moral action. On the heart of shame Mencius places the greatest emphasis. 'A man,' says Mencius, 'must not be without shame, for the shame of being without shame is shamelessness indeed' (VII. A. 6). Again, he says, 'Great is the use of shame to man. He who indulges in craftiness has no use for shame. If a man is not ashamed of being inferior to other men, how will he ever become their equal?' (VII.A. 7). A man's aspirations to become a morally better man are founded on his feeling of shame. Unless a man realizes his own inferiority, he cannot be expected to make any effort, and not to realize one's own moral inferiority is the greatest obstacle to moral progress. 'When one's finger is inferior to other people's, one has sense enough to resent it, but not when one's heart is inferior. This is known as failure to see that one thing is the same in kind as another' (VI. A. 12). The importance of shame is summed up in the following words: 'Only when a man will not do some things is he capable of doing great things' (IV. B. 8).

'The heart of courtesy and modesty' describes both a man's modesty which does not allow him to claim credit and the courtesy that prompts him to yield precedence to others. This is the basis of rules of conduct in polite society. In a sense, this is a curb on one's natural self-seeking tendencies, and, as we shall see, the clear distinction between morality and self-interest is the corner-stone of Confucian moral theory.

Finally, 'the heart of right and wrong' has a twofold significance. First, it refers to the ability of the heart to distinguish between right and wrong. Second, it can also refer to the approval of the right and the disapproval of the wrong by the heart. Now this ability of the heart is relevant to the understanding of the reasons for Mencius' holding the view that human nature is good. For even when we fail to do what is right we cannot help seeing that what we have failed to do is right and feeling disapproval towards the course of action we have chosen, with its accompanying sense of shame. In this way the statement that human nature is good is given a sense which is completely independent of the way in which human beings in fact behave. Those who think that Mencius, in formulating his theory, had only sages in mind have failed utterly to understand him.

Mencius simply states that there are these four tendencies in man. He does not go on to make any attempt to show that this is so, except in the case of 'the heart of compassion'. In a justly famous passage, he says:

> Suppose a man were, all of a sudden, to see a young child on the verge of falling into a well. He would certainly be moved to compassion, not because he wanted to get in the good graces of the parents, nor because he wished to win the praise of his fellow villagers or friends, nor yet because he disliked the cry of the child. (II. A. 6)

This passage contains a number of points crucial to Mencius' theory, and it is worth looking at it in some detail.

The first point is that the feeling of compassion experienced by the man who saw the child creeping towards the well is completely disinterested. For if his feeling had been motivated by self-interest, he would most likely have acted from one of the motives which Mencius expressly excluded, viz. the hope of getting in the good graces of the child's parents or of winning the praise of his fellow villagers or friends, or even the desire to stop the cry of the child which he found unpleasant. As he had none of these things in mind, he was unlikely to have acted from any other selfish motive. Mencius clinches the argument by deliberately putting in the qualification 'all of a sudden'. The reaction was instantaneous, and therefore spontaneous, as there was no time to reflect, and a reaction which is spontaneous is a true manifestation of a man's nature, because he is caught off his guard.

The second point is that Mencius has taken care not to overstate his case. All men have such a tendency to compassion, but this is literally the germ of benevolence and no more. In order to develop this into full-fledged benevolence, a great deal of nurturing is required. We may notice that the man is only said to experience a feeling of pity. Nothing is said about his taking any action. We are not even told how long the feeling lasted. It may be just a momentary twinge. For as soon as the man gets over the 'suddenness' of the situation his usual habits of thought are liable to re-assert themselves. Indeed, calculating thoughts of self-interest probably arise in his mind and he may raise the question of whether it is worth his while to do anything about the child at all. But whatever happens afterwards, the fact remains that he had no control over the momentary twinge he felt in the first instance and that is all Mencius needs to show that the man has the germ of morality in him. It is for this reason that Mencius says that human nature is good, for no one is completely devoid of such feeling no matter how faint and momentary the experience proves to be. It is also for this reason that Mencius says that the difference between man and animals is slight. It lies in these incipient moral tendencies which are easily lost and such a loss is tantamount to the loss of one's 'original heart'.

At this point it is convenient to compare Mencius' theory of the goodness of human nature with the theory of Hsün Tzu that human nature is bad; for the precise way in which the two philosophers differ has often been misunderstood. It is often assumed that the two theories are contradictory in the same way as, for instance, to say of one and the same thing that it is both white and black. This can be seen from the fact that it is often said that whereas Mencius, in putting forth his theory, had only sages in mind, Hsün Tzu, on the other hand, had in mind only totally wicked men. But to do so is to forget that Mencius and Hsün Tzu shared one common belief, and that is that all men are capable of becoming sages. In other words, Mencius did not think that the failure of men to act morally, at least at times, invalidated his theory, while Hsün Tzu equally did not see any contradiction between his theory together with the fact that few men succeed in becoming sages and his belief that all men are capable of doing so.

What then is Hsün Tzu's theory that human nature is bad? And on what grounds is it based? Hsün Tzu believed that human nature, in concrete terms, consists of certain factors which, in response to outside things, manifest themselves as desires. If every man gives full rein to his desires, the result is certain to be conflict. There are two reasons for this. There are some things which are scarce and will fall short of the quantity necessary to satisfy the desire of all men for them. Even where there is no scarcity, there may still be conflict if more than one man desire one and the same object. Given Hsün Tzu's characterization of human nature, conflict is inevitable, and as conflict is the one thing which, in Hsün Tzu's view, is unquestionably bad, it follows that human nature inevitably leads to a state of affairs which is bad. Whatever necessarily leads to consequences that are bad is itself bad. Hence, concludes Hsün Tzu, human nature is bad.

Hsün Tzu's problem is, then, how to find a way out of this human predicament. His solution is morality, which he conceives of as a system of rules according to which what every man is entitled to is clearly laid down. If one's status does not entitle one to the possession of a thing, even if the thing is in plentiful supply and one has the money, one is still not permitted to possess it.

This solution is purely a theoretical one, and Hsün Tzu has still to show its practicability. First, in Hsün Tzu's view, the solution was arrived at by the ancient sages, but once invented it was obvious to anyone with average intelligence. In this respect it is somewhat like the way Columbus stood his egg on its end. Second, the ancient sages also saw the feasibility of the solution. The basis of the feasibility of the solution lies in habituation. A man can be trained to behave invariably in a way which is contrary to his nature: habit can become second nature. But how can a man make a beginning? This is possible, according to Hsün Tzu, because of the function of the heart. He draws a distinction between the desire for a thing and positive action to go after it. Although Hsün Tzu admits that the heart can never stop a man from desiring a thing, it can, however, make him desist from going after it. One does not go after an object once it is shown to be impossible to secure, a judgement only the heart can make. Similarly, a man can be made by his heart to make an effort to go after a thing when he has no desire for it, or to make a greater effort than is warranted by the strength of his desire.

Now the ancient sages, in inventing morality, saw not only that their solution, once pointed out, would appear to be obviously reasonable to the hearts of all men, but also that all men could be conditioned to become moral against their nature, because the heart has, as we have seen, certain control over action, though not over desires.

An obvious question arises: why does Hsün Tzu exclude the

heart from human nature and so look upon morality as contrary to what is natural? This is due to his definition of 'nature'. In order for a characteristic to count as part of the nature of a thing, it must be inseparable from that thing, impossible to learn to do or learn to do better through application. An example would be the ability of the eye to see. This can be considered part of the nature of the eye, because it cannot be separated from the eye. An eye that cannot see is not, properly speaking, an eye at all. Further, seeing is not something we can learn and we do not improve our ability to see through application.

This is not true of the heart, nor of morality which is the invention of the heart. Not every man but only the ancient sages had the capacity to invent morality, and moral behaviour has to be inculcated into a man. Even then success is far from assured.

We can see now that Mencius and Hsün Tzu took a very different line in the matter of the definition of the nature of a thing. Mencius was looking for what is distinctive while Hsün Tzu was looking for what forms an inseparable part of it. For this reason, desires do not qualify, for Mencius, as a defining characteristic of the nature of man because they are shared with animals. The heart, and in particular the incipient moral tendencies in the human heart, is what distinguishes a man from animals, and as such is a higher organ than his senses. For Hsün Tzu, on the other hand, only what is instinctive can be counted as nature, and the heart with its varying possibilities disqualifies itself.

So far, we have only given an account of the difference between Mencius and Hsün Tzu in terms of the difference in their attitude towards the matter of definition. There are, of course, real differences as well. For Hsün Tzu morality is purely an artificial way of behaviour. True, there must always have existed a possibility, and it is this possibility that prompted the sages to invent morality as a way out of the human predicament. But there is a wide gulf between the possible and the natural. To borrow an illustration from an argument between Mencius and Kao Tzu, it is possible to bend a willow into a cup in the sense that it is impossible to bend a stone. Nevertheless, from Mencius' standpoint, it is not natural for a willow to be bent into a cup in the sense that it is natural for trees to grow on a mountain. Morality is natural in this sense. The incipient moral tendencies are there in human nature originally. They may be weak and easily destroyed, but this does not make them any less natural. According to Hsün Tzu this is not so. Morality is a possible solution to the problem of human conflict but it forms no part of original human nature. This can be shown by the fact that it is separable from man. If we bear in mind that Confucian morality demands of a man his willingness to lay down his life for the sake of morality, we are likely to feel that in the final test the gentleman as conceived by Hsün Tzu may be found wanting. It is doubtful if habit, no matter how strong, will enable a man to walk to the scaffold for the sake of his duty.

To go back to Mencius: the emphasis on a natural moral motive, as distinct from one based on self-interest in the case of the man who sees a child creeping towards a well, touches on a basic tenet of Confucian thought – the distinction between morality and self-interest. The difference between a gentleman and a small man is that the former pursues morality with single-minded dedication while the latter pursues profit with equally single-minded dedication. There is never any doubt in Mencius' mind that when self-interest comes into conflict with morality, it is self-interest that should give way. 'Life is what I want; dutifulness is also what I want. If I cannot have both, I would rather take dutifulness than life' (VI. A. 10). Confucius is also quoted as saying, 'A man whose mind is set on high ideals never forgets that he may end in a ditch; a man of valour never forgets that he may forfeit his head' (II. B. 1 and V. B. 7). This may give the wrong impression that self-interest and morality are necessarily opposed. This is certainly not the Confucian position, which is rather that the two are totally unconnected. It is only when self-interest becomes an obstacle to morality that the former has to be sacrificed, and it is perhaps true that self-interest is the most likely culprit against morality. But nevertheless when self-interest is not in conflict with morality a man has a duty to be prudent. He should not, for instance, stand under a wall on the verge of collapse (VII. A. 2).

There is a difference between self-interest and morality which is relevant to a problem that we touched upon earlier. We pointed out that *ming* gradually took on the meaning of 'fate'. There are examples of the word used in this sense even in the *Analects of Confucius* (see, for example, XII. 5). It should, however, be pointed out that the fatalism that was accepted by the Confucianist was of a limited kind. Only life and death, wealth and position are said to depend on fate. This is to get men to see that it is futile to pursue such ends, ends that most people devote most of their time and energy to. If these things depend on fate, then there is no point in pursuing them. What we ought to pursue is morality which is our proper end. On this matter Mencius has this to say:

> Seek and you will get it; let go and you will lose it. If this is the case, then seeking is of use for getting and what is sought is within yourself. But if there is a proper way to seek it and whether you get it or not depends on destiny, then seeking is of no use to getting and what is sought lies outside yourself. (VII. A. 3)

When whether we are going to get a thing or not depends on fate and our seeking makes no difference to our success or otherwise, then obviously there is no point in seeking it and if we seek it at all, we must do so in accordance with what is right. Mencius seems to intend that all external possessions should come under this head. The only things that are left which we have a duty to seek because seeking makes a difference to our success are internal things. These are our original heart and, more generally, moral ends. In these cases seeking helps because, in a sense, the seeking *is* the getting. Being moral does not depend on successful results but simply on our making the effort. As Confucius put it, 'Is benevolence really far away? As soon as I desire benevolence it is here' (the *Analects of Confucius*, VII. 30). Thus we can see that fatalism of the kind advocated by Confucianists does not constitute an obstacle to obeying Heaven's decree that man should be moral.

Let us return to the subject of incipient moral tendencies. We have seen that, according to Mencius, a man naturally has these tendencies but they are easily smothered and need a great deal of care and cultivation. But how is this done? On this question Mencius has a great deal to say. One great difference between moral philosophers in the Chinese tradition and those in the Western tradition is that the latter do not look upon it as their concern to help people to become sages while the former assume that that is their main concern. Western philosophers deal only with the problem of what morality is. They leave the problem of how to make people better to religious teachers. In China, however, there has never been a strong tradition of religious teaching, and the problem has always fallen within the province of the philosopher.

To understand Mencius' teaching on the matter, it is necessary first to say something about the cosmology prevalent in the fourth century B.C. It was believed that the universe was made up of *ch'i* but this *ch'i* varied in consistency. The grosser *ch'i*, being heavy, settled to become the earth, while the refined *ch'i*, being light, rose to become the sky. Man, being half-way between the two, is a harmonious mixture of the two kinds of *ch'i*. His body consists of grosser *ch'i* while his heart is the seat of the refined *ch'i*. The blood, being neither as solid as the body nor as refined as the breath, lies somewhere in between, but as it is not static and circulates in the body it is more akin to the refined *ch'i*. Hence the term *hsüeh ch'i* (blood and *ch'i*). It is in virtue of the refined *ch'i* that a man is alive and his faculties can function properly. As the heart is the seat of this refined *ch'i*, it is necessary to have a regimen for the heart in order to be healthy and to live to a ripe old age.

Now there seemed to be two schools of thought on this matter. According to one school, though one is born with a fixed fund of *ch'i*, it is possible to acquire further supplies of it, and it is through the apertures that the *ch'i* enters the body. But whether the *ch'i* will stay once it has entered depends on whether the heart is in a fit state for it to take up abode. In order to be a fit abode the heart must be clean, that is, unclouded by desires. The other school believed that the original fund of *ch'i* cannot be augmented, and one dies when it is used up. The possibility of prolonging life lies in good husbandry of what one is endowed with. Every mental activity uses up a certain amount of *ch'i*. Excessive concentration of the heart in thought or the senses on external objects will unnecessarily speed up this expenditure. Hence the slogan of this school is: keep your apertures shut. This is directly opposite to the other school whose object is to let more *ch'i* in and whose slogan is: keep your apertures open.

In a well-known passage in II. A. 2, Mencius describes what he calls the *hao jan chih ch'i* (the flood-like *ch'i*), and it is obvious that this presupposes the prevalent theory we have outlined. For instance, not only does Mencius say of the *ch'i* that it 'fills the body',[1] but it is also impossible to understand his illustration of how the heart is moved by the *ch'i*, that is, how 'stumbling and hurrying affect the *ch'i*, yet in fact palpitations of the heart are produced', unless we understand the '*ch'i*' here as the breath which is supposed to fill the body.

But Mencius did not simply take over the current theory of *ch'i*, he gave it a twist. In place of the physical *ch'i* he puts his own *hao jan chih ch'i* 'which is, in the highest degree, vast and unyielding'. The point of contact between the *hao jan chih ch'i* and physical *ch'i* is courage. Courage is believed to depend on *ch'i*.[2] This no doubt has something to do with the fact that courage is accompanied by a state of heightened tension in the body in which breathing is quickened and the activity of the heart stimulated. But for Mencius genuine courage, instead of being sustained by a state of heightened tension in the body, can only be sustained by the sense of being morally in the right. The *hao jan chih ch'i* 'is a *ch'i* which unites rightness and the Way. Deprive it of these and it will collapse.' As Tseng Tzu put it, 'If, on looking within, one finds oneself to be in the wrong, then even though one's adversary be only a common fellow coarsely clad one is bound to tremble with fear. But if one finds oneself in the right, one goes forward even against men in the thousands.'

In order to become a good man, it is this *hao jan chih ch'i* that one must develop. 'Nourish it with integrity and place no obstacle in its path and it will fill the space between Heaven and Earth.' Elsewhere, Mencius describes the gentleman as being 'in the same

1. This is almost identical with a similar statement in chapter 37 of the *Kuan tzu*, the only differerce being that in the *Kuan tzu*, the word used for 'body' is *shen* instead of *t'i*.

2. The morale of an army is, for instance, called *shih ch'i*, that is, the *ch'i* of the soldiers.

stream as Heaven above and Earth below' (VII. A. 13). If we remember that it is Heaven which planted the moral heart in man, it is hardly surprising that man is in the same stream as Heaven when his heart is cultivated to its utmost possibility.

On the cultivation of one's moral character, there is one important and eloquent passage in which Mencius compares the heart to a mountain:

> There was a time when the trees were luxuriant on the Ox Mountain. As it is on the outskirts of a great metropolis, the trees are constantly lopped by axes. Is it any wonder that they are no longer fine? With the respite they get in the day and in the night, and the moistening by the rain and dew, there is certainly no lack of new shoots coming out, but then the cattle and sheep come to graze upon the mountain. That is why it is as bald as it is. People, seeing only its baldness, tend to think that it never had any trees. But can this possibly be the nature of a mountain? Can what is in man be completely lacking in moral inclinations? A man's letting go of his true heart is like the case of the trees and the axes. When the trees are lopped day after day, is it any wonder that they are no longer fine? If, in spite of the respite a man gets in the day and in the night and of the effect of the morning air on him, scarcely any of his likes and dislikes resemble those of other men, it is because what he does in the course of the day once again dissipates what he has gained. If this dissipation happens repeatedly, then the influence of the air in the night will no longer be able to preserve what was originally in him, and when that happens, the man is not far removed from an animal. Others, seeing his resemblance to an animal, will be led to think that he never had any native endowment. But can that be what a man is genuinely like? Hence, given the right nourishment there is nothing that will not grow, and deprived of it there is nothing that will not wither away. Confucius said, 'Hold on to it and it will remain; let go of it and it will disappear. One never knows the time it comes or goes, neither does one know the direction.' It is perhaps to the heart this refers. (VI. A. 8)

The comparison of the heart to a mountain is more than just an analogy. There is something which the two share in common. Just as it is natural for trees to grow on a mountain, so it is natural for moral shoots in the heart to develop into full-fledged moral tendencies. In the case of the mountain it is the constant lopping of the trees by axes and eating away of young shoots by sheep and cattle that reduce it to a hopeless barrenness. Similarly, it is through pre-occupation with selfish thought and deed that a man's natural tendencies are destroyed. Even then there are moral shoots that come up, just as there are new shoots coming up in the case of the mountain, and it is only when these are repeatedly destroyed that the man is reduced hopelessly to the level of animals. Thus it can be seen that morality is natural to man in the sense that moral shoots spring up naturally when a man is left alone, just as new shoots spring up on the soil when the mountain is left alone. The use of axes and the grazing by sheep and cattle are artificial and accidental to the mountain. Similarly, the selfish desires which destroy a man's moral tendencies do not constitute his essential nature. Furthermore, what gives nourishment to the soil on the mountain is the respite it gets in the night and the moistening by the rain and the dew. Similarly, it is the rest in the night and the reviving power of the air in the night and the early morning which give nourishment to the moral shoots that will spring up naturally if only given the chance. Here Mencius is doing more than giving a metaphorical account of the moral tendencies in a man, he is in fact giving him a practical touchstone for gauging his own moral progress. The freshness and spontaneity a man feels in the morning after a good night's rest constitute the best conditions for preserving and developing his true heart. Perhaps Mencius implies that moral health is inseparable from mental health. Whether this is so or not, a man can see that he is making moral progress in so far as he is able to hold on to this state of mind further and further into the day without its being dissipated by the distraction of selfish thoughts and deeds. It is worth mentioning in this connexion that the Confucian tradition believes in the joy of being a good man. Both Confucius and Mencius repeatedly use the phrase 'delighting in the Way'. Once more this emphasizes the naturalness of morality. Delight and joy are usually experienced when a man pursues a natural activity unimpeded. On this point one can see that Hsün Tzu is not in the true tradition of Confucius, as he looks upon morality as artificial and therefore unnatural. A man, according to him, can only learn to behave morally through incessant habituation

over a lengthy period of time. This may, indeed, change a man
to a moral automaton, but one cannot see how he can feel joy in
pursuing an automatic activity.

Now that we have completed the account of Mencius' theory that
human nature is good, let us go back to the question which
Mencius must have been faced with at the outset: if human nature
is nothing but desires, how can man possibly obey the Decree of
Heaven? The answer, as we have seen, is in two stages. First,
human nature is defined in terms of what is unique to man, viz.,
his heart, rather than in terms of desires which he shares with
animals. Second, the human heart has built-in moral tendencies
which though incipient can be developed, and when fully developed
will enable a man to become a sage. In this way acting morally is
no longer an obedience to an external command, even though the
command may issue from Heaven. Acting in accordance with
Heaven's Decree is something one can do joyfully by looking
inwards and finding the roots of morality within one's own
spiritual make-up. In this way, Mencius broke down the barrier
between Heaven and Man and between the Decree and human
nature. There is a secret passage leading from the innermost part
of a man's person to Heaven, and what pertains to Heaven, instead
of being external to man, turns out to pertain to his truest nature.
In a rather obscure passage, Mencius seems to be explaining just
this point:

> The way the mouth is disposed towards tastes, the eye towards
> colours, the ear towards sounds, the nose towards smells, and the four
> limbs towards ease is human nature, yet therein also lies the Decree.
> That is why the gentleman does not describe it as nature. The way
> benevolence pertains to the relation between father and son, duty to
> the relation between prince and subject, the rites to the relation be-
> tween guest and host, wisdom to the good and wise man, the sage to
> the way of Heaven, is the Decree, but therein also lies human nature.
> That is why the gentleman does not describe it as Decree. (VII. B. 24)

Mencius here begins by agreeing that it is human nature for a man's
sense organs and other parts of the body to seek for their respective
objects of gratification, but what he emphatically denies is that one
can be justified in acting immorally under the pretext that it is

natural to pursue these ends. For the sphere of human action is also the sphere of morality, and we possess a heart which tells us whether we are doing right or not in our pursuit of this gratification. In his way of putting it, therein also lies the Decree. We know that in a conflict, human desires should give way to the Decree because we recognize the human heart as occupying a supreme position in the total nature of man. On the other hand, although there are moral duties arising from various human relationships, we must not describe them simply as Decreed. This is aimed at those who say that these duties may be decreed but it is just not possible to fulfil them. Mencius' point is that there are moral tendencies in human nature which in fact make it possible for man to fulfil these duties. Hence he says, 'therein also lies human nature'. There is one part of human nature which is one with Heaven. The other part which is not one with Heaven is merely that which we share with the animals. And this must not be allowed to stand in the way of a man's realizing his true nature. 'If one makes one's stand on what is of greater importance in the first instance, what is of smaller importance cannot displace it. In this way, one cannot but be a great man' (VI. A. 15).

In upholding the teachings of the Confucian tradition, Mencius was vigorous in combating what he considered heretical views. In particular, he was untiring in his attacks on the Schools of Yang Chu and Mo Ti. The latter persisted as a major school of thought well into the third century B.C., and it is not surprising that it formed one of Mencius' major targets. But the former was hardly a school to be reckoned with by the third century, and it is more difficult to understand why Mencius took it so seriously. It is likely that in the fourth century B.C. the school of Yang Chu was still of considerable influence, and, further, it may have been the precursor of the Taoist philosophers. Viewed in this light, Mencius was by no means mistaken in considering the teachings of Yang Chu as a major menace to the moral teachings of Confucius. Mencius chose a catch phrase from the teachings of each of the two figures for attention. In the case of Mo Tzu, it is the doctrine of love without discrimination (*chien ai*), while in the case of Yang Chu it is that of egoism (*wei wo*). Love without discrimination is indeed the backbone of Mo Tzu's teaching. According to this, a man should love all men equally without discrimination, and Mencius has not misrepresented it. He quotes a Mohist as saying, 'there should be no gradations in love' (III. A. 5). Egoism is equally the central doctrine of Yang Chu's teaching. According to Mencius, 'Yang Tzu chooses egoism. Even if he could benefit the Empire by pulling out one hair he would not do it' (VII. A. 26). In this Mencius is certainly guilty of misrepresentation. This is not quite the point of Yang Chu's egoism. It teaches that the most important possession a man has is his life, and the hedonists are mistaken in concluding that since a man lives only once he should indulge in as much pleasure as possible, for, in so doing, he runs the risk of wearing himself out before his time. Instead, a man should not do anything that can possibly harm his life. Hence in Yang Chu's view one should not give even one hair on one's body in exchange for the possession of the Empire. One hair, though insignificant, constitutes, nevertheless, part of one's body without which one cannot preserve one's life, and the possession of the Empire will almost certainly lead to over-indulgence in one's appetites. It is true that if one refused to give one hair in exchange for the possession of the Empire, *a fortiori* one would refuse to give a hair to benefit the Empire. Mencius' misrepresentation lies in taking what, properly speaking, is only a corollary and presenting it as the basic tenet of Yang Chu's teaching. But this makes no difference to the point of his criticism. His criticism is that 'Yang advocates everyone for himself, which amounts to a denial of one's prince' (III. B. 9). In other words, Yang opted out of his moral obligations to society, obligations that can only be met by taking part in public affairs. Yang's refusal to do so amounts to a 'denial of his prince'. On the other hand, love without discrimination advocated by Mo is a violation of the basic teaching of the Confucian school. One should treat one's fellow human beings with benevolence, but benevolence is based on the love one feels for one's parents: 'The content of benevolence is the serving of one's parents' (IV. A. 27). It is by extending this love to others that one becomes a benevolent man. 'A benevolent man extends his love from those he loves to those he does not love' (VII. B. 1)

'There is just one thing in which the ancients greatly surpassed others, and that is the way they extended what they did' (I. A. 7). As benevolence is an extension of the natural love for one's parents to humanity at large through various degrees of kinship, it would be, according to Confucianists, unnatural to love all men alike. One should love one's parents more than other members of the family, other members of the family more than members of the same village and so on until one reaches humanity at large. Thus to love all men alike is to deny the claim of one's parents to a greater degree of love. Hence Mencius' description of the doctrine of love without discrimination as 'a denial of one's parents'.

Mencius concentrated all his attack on Yang and Mo, paying little attention to his contemporaries. The only group that come in for a certain amount of stricture are those whose teachings are aimed merely at strengthening the state politically and economically without a concomitant improvement in morality.

> Those who are in the service of princes today all say, 'I am able to extend the territory of my prince, and fill his coffers for him.' The good subjects of today would have been looked upon in antiquity as a pest on the people. To enrich a prince who is neither attracted to the Way nor bent upon benevolence is to enrich a Chieh.
>
> Again, they say, 'I am able to gain allies and ensure victory in war for my prince.' The good subjects of today would have been looked upon in antiquity as a pest on the people. To try to make a prince strong in war who is neither attracted to the Way nor bent upon benevolence is to aid a Chieh. (VI. B. 9)

This is not very different from the criticism made by Confucius of one of his disciples quoted by Mencius with approval:

> While he was steward to the Chi family, Jan Ch'iu doubled the yield of taxation without being able to improve their virtue. Confucius said, 'Ch'iu is not my disciple. You, little ones, may attack him to the beating of drums.' (IV. A. 14)

Mencius goes on to comment:

> From this it can be seen that Confucius rejected those who enriched rulers not given to the practice of benevolent government. How much

more would he reject those who do their best to wage war on their behalf. In wars to gain land, the dead fill the plains; in wars to gain cities, the dead fill the cities. This is known as showing the land the way to devour human flesh. Death is too light a punishment for such men. Hence those skilled in war should suffer the most severe punishments; those who secure alliances with other feudal lords come next, and then come those who open up waste lands and increase the yield of the soil.

No doubt Mencius had such reformers as Wu Ch'i and Lord Shang, and scheming politicians like Chang Yi in mind, and his condemnation of them is in no uncertain terms.

On the whole Mencius rarely refers to his contemporaries. During the time he was in Ch'i, Chi Hsia was a great intellectual centre where a number of great thinkers forgathered, yet only two of them – Sung K'eng and Ch'un-yü K'un – are mentioned in the *Mencius* by name. One may, therefore, easily get the impression that Mencius was not conversant with the new ideas current in his time. But this is not altogether justified. Sometimes from the ideas he put forward we can see that he was familiar with what was going on around him. For instance, we have seen this to be the case with his 'flood-like *ch'i*'. Again, sometimes from a turn of phrase he used we can also see the connexion with philosophical problems of the time. An interesting example is what he said when he failed to meet Duke P'ing of Lu. 'When a man goes forward,' said he, 'there is something which urges him on; when he halts, there is something which holds him back. It is not in his power either to go forward or to halt. It is due to Heaven that I failed to meet the Marquis of Lu' (I. B. 16). The sentence 'When a man goes forward, there is something which urges him on' is a translation of *hsing huo shih chih* in which *huo shih chih* literally means 'something causes it'. Chapter 25 of the *Chuang tzu* mentions two theories, Chi Chen's theory of 'nothing does it (*mo wei*)' and Chieh Tzu's theory that 'something causes [it]'. Now we do not know who Chi Chen and Chieh Tzu were, but there is no doubt that these were cosmological theories, according to one of which there is nothing behind the universe while according to the other there is something that causes it to function. That the same phrase *huo shih* (or *huo chih shih*[1]) is used in the *Chuang tzu* shows that the *Mencius* and the *Chuang tzu* are talking about the same thing. Not only is Mencius on the side of there being 'something which causes it', but his further remark shows that this is what he understands by Heaven.

There is one other matter where Mencius shows himself to be conversant with current practice and that is the method of argument he uses. This is of considerable importance to a correct understanding of the *Mencius*. It is not uncommon for a reader of the *Mencius* to get the impression that Mencius was illogical and was unscrupulous towards his opponents. Arthur Waley, for instance, writes about Mencius as a disputant in the following vein:

> As a controversialist he is nugatory. The whole discussion (Book VI) about whether Goodness and Duty are internal or external is a mass of irrelevant analogies, most of which could equally well be used to disprove what they are intended to prove. In other passages, the analogy gets mixed up with the actual point at issue. A glaring example is the discussion (IV. I. XVII) with Shun-yü [this should be Ch'un-yü] K'un, who was shocked by Mencius's reluctance to take office. Shun-yü K'un's argument is as follows: just as in a case of great urgency (despite the taboo on men and women touching hands) a man will give his hand to his sister-in-law to save her from drowning, so in the present emergency of China you ought to put aside the general principles that make you hesitate to take office, and place yourself at the disposal of the government. Mencius's reply is: 'When the world is drowning, it can only be rescued by the Way (of the Former Kings); when a sister-in-law is drowning, she can be rescued with the hand. Do you want me to rescue the world with my hand?'
>
> This is at best a very cheap debating point. The proper answer (which may or may not have been made, but does not occur in *Mencius*) of course is, 'Figuratively, yes. Just as one breaks taboos in an emergency and gives a hand to someone in peril, so I want you in the present political emergency to sacrifice your principles and "give a hand" to public affairs.'[2]

1. *Huo chih shih* in the *Chuang tzu* is the same as *huo shih chih* in the *Mencius* except that in the first the object *chih* is inverted.

2. Arthur Waley, *Three Ways of Thought in Ancient China*, London, 1939, pp. 194–5. For an analysis of the arguments mentioned by Waley, see Appendix 5.

When language as intemperate as this is used of a philosopher, we naturally suspect that there must be a failure of understanding on the part of the critic, but when the philosopher in question happens to be one of the greatest in the ancient period of China, the suspicion cannot easily be dismissed.

The method of argument in common use in the fourth and third centuries B.C. in China is quite different from what we are used to. It consists of the use of analogy. This covers both the use of one thing to throw light on another and the use of one proposition we know to be true to throw light on another of similar form. It is fortunate for us that one of the chapters in the *Mo tzu* gives an account of this method of argument.[1] In using this method one starts with two propositions (1) and (2) which are similar in form and in being true. We argue that as we can derive another proposition (1.1) from (1) which is also true, we can similarly derive a true proposition (2.1) from (2). The *Mo tzu* criticizes this method by showing that it does not always hold. Let us take an example from the *Mo tzu*. We start with a pair of propositions:

(1) This horse's eyes are blind
(2) This horse's eyes are big.

They are identical in form, and let us assume that they are both true. Let us derive two propositions from them:

(1.1) This horse is blind
(2.1) This horse is big.

These are not only similar in form, but bear the same relationship to the original propositions. But we are mistaken if we think that, as the truth of (1.1) follows from that of (1), the truth of (2.1) must also follow from (2). As can be seen, it *follows* from 'this horse's eyes are blind' that 'this horse is blind', but it *does not follow* from 'this horse's eyes are big' that 'this horse is big'.

This is in fact the way analogies work. If we wish to throw light on something which is obscure, we make an analogy with some

1. For a discussion of this see D. C. Lau, 'Some Logical Problems in Ancient China' (*Proceedings of the Aristotelian Society*, Vol. LIII, 1952–3, pp. 189–204).

thing which is clear. Then we try to see whether because we can say something of the latter it follows that we can say something similar of the former. As analogues are rarely perfect, the analogy breaks down sooner or later. There are two points to bear in mind. First, an analogy is at least as instructive, if not more, when it breaks down as when it holds. Second, with subject matter that is obscure, intangible or elusive, analogy is often the only possible tool for probing its nature. And it is by this method that Mencius and his opponents grappled with philosophical problems. As both sides understood the method used, Mencius must have made more impression on his opponents than on the modern reader.

Let us take an example. In VI. A. 3, Kao Tzu begins with the statement

(1) That which is inborn (*sheng*) is what is meant by 'nature (*hsing*)'

and Mencius asks, 'Is that the same as

(2) White is what is meant by "white"?'

Kao Tzu said, 'Yes'.

Now we have good reason to believe that *sheng* (that which is inborn) and *hsing* (nature), being cognate words, were most probably written by the same character in Mencius' time, though they had, in all probability, a slightly different pronunciation. Thus both (1) and (2) are tautologous as written statements and also of exactly the same form.

Having elicited an assent from Kao Tzu, Mencius goes on to produce the proposition

(2.1) The whiteness of white feathers is the same as the whiteness of white snow and the whiteness of white snow is the same as the whiteness of white jade

and Kao Tzu agrees that this is a true proposition.

Then Mencius produces the further proposition

(1.1) The nature of a hound is the same as the nature of an ox and the nature of an ox is the same as the nature of a man.

The silence of Kao Tzu can only be taken to mean that even he was unable to accept this as true.

As the truth of (1.1) does not follow from the truth of (1) while the truth of (2.1) follows from that of (2), though (1.1) and (2.1) are similar in form and (1.1) bears the same relationship to (1) as (2.1) to (2), we can only conclude that 'white is what is meant by "white"' is not a true analogue of 'that which is inborn is what is meant by "nature"', and does not throw any light on it. This is the purpose of Mencius' argument and as this purpose is served, the argument is not taken any further – at least no further stage of the argument is recorded.

If we are interested in the grounds of the argument, we can analyse the two initial propositions and show that they are essentially different. The term 'nature' is a formal, empty term. The expression 'the nature of x' is not informative until x is specified. On the other hand, the term 'white' is not a formal, empty term but a term with a minimum specific content, so that the expression 'the whiteness of x' is informative even when x is not specified. To put it in another way, in the expression 'the nature of x', the term 'nature' is a function of x, while the term 'whiteness' in the expression 'the whiteness of x' is not a function of x.

The difference also comes out in another way. We may notice that in the expression 'the whiteness of white feathers', the term 'white' is repeated before 'feathers', while there is no such repetition in the expression 'the nature of a dog'. This is because 'whiteness' is a contingent character of 'feathers' whereas 'the nature' of a dog is not a contingent character of the dog.

By saying that 'that which is inborn is "nature"', Kao Tzu no doubt meant to say that 'nature is nature' whether it is the nature of an animal or a man. This is connected with his view that 'appetite for food and sex is nature'. If by this is meant simply that appetites are what man has in common with animals, then Mencius would have no quarrel with it, but it is easy to take 'nature is nature' to mean that there is total identity of nature between man and animals. And we have seen that, when this implication was brought out into the open, not even Kao Tzu was willing to go so far as to accept it. If Kao Tzu admits that only part of the nature of man is identical with the nature of animals, then the question would centre on the significance of the distinctively human part of a man's nature. This takes Kao Tzu and Mencius beyond the immediate concern which is the precise implications of the statement 'that which is inborn is "nature"'. The only point established is that the statement 'white is what is meant by "white"' throws no light on the problem as the similarity in form between the two statements is more apparent than real.[1]

Let us turn to Mencius' political philosophy. This is not only consistent with his moral philosophy but is derived from it. Ancient Chinese thinkers all looked upon politics as a branch of morals. More precisely, the relationship between the ruler and the subject was looked upon as a special case of the moral relationship which holds between individuals. Like his moral theory, Mencius' political theory rests on the concept of Heaven. First, Mencius has absolutely no doubt that the ruler is set up by Heaven for the benefit of the people. Hence whether a ruler deserves to remain a ruler depends on whether he carries out this duty or not. If he does not, he should be removed. In a justly celebrated passage, Mencius says:

> The people are of supreme importance; the altars to the gods of earth and grain come next; last comes the ruler.

He goes on to develop this in these words:

> When a feudal lord endangers the altars to the gods of earth and grain he should be replaced. When the sacrificial animals are sleek, the offerings are clean and the sacrifices are observed at due times, and yet floods and droughts come, then the altars should be replaced. (VII. B. 14)

In other words, if a ruler endangers the independence of the state – of which the altars to the gods of earth and grain are the symbol – and so endangers the people, he ought to be replaced. And even the gods of earth and grain are not above replacement if, in spite of the fact that sacrifices are duly offered to them, they fail to

1. For an analysis of further examples of Mencius' arguments, see D. C. Lau, 'On Mencius' Use of the Method of Analogy in Argument' (*Asia Major*, Vol. X, 1963, pp. 173–94), reprinted in Appendix 5.

prevent floods and droughts which harm the people. Thus we can see the full significance of the supremacy of the people.

The removal of the ruler is a subject Mencius touches upon on more than one occasion. When asked about ministers by King Hsüan of Ch'i, Mencius said that ministers of royal blood would not hesitate to depose a ruler who refused repeatedly to listen to admonitions against serious mistakes (v. B. 9). Again, when asked whether it was justified for a good subject to banish a bad ruler, Mencius answered that provided that one had the lofty motives of a Yi Yin it was justified (VII. A. 31). As we can see from this example, the term 'ruler' covers the Emperor as well as rulers of feudal states. In fact the classic examples of the deposition of evil rulers are to be found in the transition of the Three Dynasties. Chieh, the last Emperor of the Hsia Dynasty, and Tchou, the last Emperor of the Shang (or Yin) Dynasty, are bywords for depravity. The former was deposed by T'ang, the founder of the Shang, and the latter by King Wu, the founder of the Chou, by military force. The attitude Mencius takes towards these historical examples is unambiguous:

> King Hsüan of Ch'i asked, 'Is it true that T'ang banished Chieh and King Wu marched against Tchou?'
> 'It is so recorded,' answered Mencius.
> 'Is regicide permissible?'
> 'A man who mutilates benevolence is a mutilator, while one who cripples rightness is a crippler. He who is both a mutilator and a crippler is an "outcast". I have indeed heard of the punishment of the "outcast Tchou", but I have not heard of any regicide.' (I. B. 8)

For Mencius a man who is a mutilator of benevolence and a crippler of rightness is an outcast. That he happens to be an emperor makes no difference. Indeed it makes the situation worse. 'Only the benevolent man is fit to be in high position. For a cruel man to be in high position is for him to disseminate his wickedness among the people' (IV. A. 1). And there is no higher position than that of Emperor.

On one occasion in the Western Han, the question whether in deposing Chieh and Tchou, T'ang and King Wu received the

Mandate of Heaven was debated by two scholars, Yüan-ku Sheng and Huang Sheng, before Emperor Ching (reigned 156-141 B.C.). The former, echoing Mencius' view, said, 'Chieh and Tchou were cruel and disorderly, and the heart of the Empire turned towards T'ang and King Wu who, following the wishes of the Empire, punished Chieh and Tchou. As the people of the Empire no longer obeyed Chieh and Tchou and turned to T'ang and King Wu, they had no alternative but to ascend the throne. If this is not receiving the Mandate, what is?' Huang Sheng, on the other hand, retorted by saying, 'A hat, however well-worn, should only be put on the head, while a shoe, however new, should only be put on the foot. This is because there is a distinction between "above" and "below". Now though Chieh and Tchou no longer followed the Way, they were, nevertheless, rulers above, while T'ang and King Wu, though they were sages, were, nevertheless, subjects below. When an Emperor does anything wrong, and a subject, instead of putting him right by proper advice to safeguard the dignity of the office, puts himself on the throne instead, what is this, if not regicide?' When Yüan-ku cited the example of the overthrow of the Ch'in by the first Emperor of the Han, the debate threatened to get out of hand, and Emperor Ching had to step in with the famous words, 'It is no reflection on one's discerning palate if, in eating meat, one does not wish to try horse's liver. It is no reflection on one's intelligence if, in one's discussions, one keeps off the subject of whether T'ang and King Wu received the Mandate of Heaven.'[1]

Though the unbroken tradition of autocratic rule in China effectively killed Mencius' theory of the right of the people to depose an oppressive ruler, the less radical part of his theory that the Emperor existed for the sake of the people and not the other way round has never been questioned.

Yüan-ku Sheng's view is, indeed, an accurate statement of Mencius' position. In singling out 'the heart of the Empire' he has hit upon its central doctrine. As Mencius puts it,

It was through losing the people that Chieh and Tchou lost the Empire, and through losing the people's hearts that they lost the people.

1. See *Shih chi*, chüan 121, *Han shu*, chüan 88.

> There is a way to win the Empire; win the people and you will win
> the Empire. There is a way to win the people; win their hearts and
> you will win the people. (IV. A. 9)

The emphasis on the heart is firmly based on Mencius' moral
theory. First, the heart is endowed with the ability to judge be-
tween right and wrong, and as the relationship between ruler and
subject is simply one instance of moral relationship, political action
on the part of the ruler is as much subject to moral judgement as any
other kind of action. Second, as we have seen, the human heart con-
stitutes a bridge linking man with Heaven, and there is no more
infallible indication of the will of Heaven than the reaction to the
ruler of the people in their hearts. This problem about the will of
Heaven was raised when Wan Chang asked Mencius how Heaven
was supposed to have given the Empire to Shun. Did Heaven give
detailed and minute instructions to him? No. Heaven did not speak
but revealed itself through its acts and deeds. As the *T'ai shih* had
it, Heaven sees with the eyes of its people; Heaven hears with the
ears of its people (V. A. 5). Behind this talk about Heaven, there
is a firm conviction on Mencius' part that it is impossible, in the
long run, for a ruler to take the people in. If he governs with their
welfare at heart, they will know it, but if he only pretends to do
so, they will see through it. In other words, reduced to its funda-
mentals, moral judgement is something well within the capability
of even the most simple-minded. This is a belief shared by most
moral thinkers of the world, of whatever time and place, because
it is, in fact, a *sine qua non* of the possibility of morality at all.

What is the welfare of the people? This is a question to which
there is a simple answer. The most basic need of the people is a
reasonable and steady livelihood. A man must be able to support
all his family, his parents on the one hand, and his wife and children
on the other. With this end in view, a man must not be taken away
from productive work during busy seasons. Corvée duties should
be kept within manageable limits and to the off seasons. A ruler,
in Mencius' view, is sure to act correctly if he has the right attitude
to his people. He should be both father and mother to them. We
can see, once again, that the relationship between ruler and subject
is looked upon as resting on a personal and moral basis. We can

also see why, for Mencius, the characteristic virtue of the ruler is benevolence, for benevolence is exemplified by the love between parent and child. 'The content of benevolence is the serving of one's parents' (IV. A. 27). 'Loving one's parents is benevolence' (VII. A. 15). The motive behind benevolence is this love between parent and child, and the ruler must feel something of this love for his people before he can become a good ruler. As we have seen, the love a ruler feels for his people is not identical with, but an extension of, the love felt by a parent for his child. This is clearly stated by Mencius in a number of places. For instance, 'A gentleman ... shows benevolence towards the people but is not attached to them. He is attached to his parents but is merely benevolent towards the people' (VII. A. 45). The mistake of the Mohist, in the eyes of the Confucianist, is that he 'believes that a man loves his brother's son no more than his neighbour's newborn babe'[1] (III. A. 5). For the Confucianist, it is natural for a man to love his parent or son, and it is only through pushing this outwards stage by stage that he succeeds in loving all humanity. But as the love for humanity is only an extension of the love for parent or son, it is only natural that one's fellow human beings have less claim on one than one's parent or son.

Thus Mencius' ideal of a state can be summed up by the term 'benevolent government'. So long as the ruler is motivated by benevolence, the people will understand and accept whatever measure he finds it necessary to take. 'If the services of the people were used with a view to sparing them hardship, they would not complain even when hard driven. If people were put to death in pursuance of a policy to keep them alive, they would die bearing no ill-will towards the man who put them to death' (VII. A. 12).

We have already pointed out that for Confucius benevolence was the totality of the moral qualities in man. For Mencius, benevolence was more specifically the virtue that characterizes the relationship between parent and child. By extension, it was the virtue typical of the ruler. The difference between the way Confucius used the term and the way Mencius used it can be seen from the

1. Cf. 'My brother I love, but the brother of a man from Ch'in I do not love.' (VI. A. 4)

fact that the expression 'benevolent government' which forms the cornerstone of Mencius' political philosophy is not to be found at all in the *Analects of Confucius*.

As Mencius believed that the ruler existed for the sake of the people, he had to justify his objection to the proposal by more radical thinkers that the ruler should work side by side with his people in order to justify his existence. Mencius pointed out that for society to function at all there must be people engaged in different kinds of work. A farmer is certainly a man who works for his living, but even a farmer cannot do his own work and, at the same time, engage in making the hundred and one things needed in his daily life. He has to trade the surplus of his produce for the fruits of other people's labour. Why, then, should this not apply to the ruler? The work of government is a good deal more arduous than working in the fields. Why should one expect the ruler to be able to produce his own food and carry on the work of government at the same time?

This may justify the ruler's not working on the land, but the question remains, why should he enjoy a life far above that of the common people in luxury and comfort? The answer is twofold. First, the work of government is so much more important. Any incompetence on the part of the ruler will affect the whole state while an incompetent farmer will ruin only his own plot. Second, the ruler uses his heart, or, as we should say, his mind, while the common man uses his muscles, and it is natural for the latter to be ruled by the former. Here we can see that, for Mencius, the pattern of the body politic is similar to the pattern of the human body. A man's body consists of many parts, and, as we have seen, the importance of the heart as an organ is far greater than that of any other part of the body. It is the master of the whole body. Similarly, the ruler in the body politic is supreme. One can go even further and say that the supreme position of the ruler in the body politic is derived from the fact that the heart is supreme in the body; he uses his heart while the common man uses only his muscles. This is supported by Mencius' use of the terms 'great' and 'small'. As we have seen, according to Mencius the parts of the body vary in importance. Some are of 'greater' importance and some are of 'smaller' importance. He who nurtures the parts of smaller importance is a small man; he who nurtures the parts of greater importance is a great man (VI. A. 14). Again, Mencius says, 'One who is guided by the interests of the parts of his person that are of greater importance is a great man; one who is guided by the interests of the parts of his person that are of smaller importance is a small man' (VI. A. 15). The part of greatest importance is of course the heart. So a man who puts his heart first is a great man, and a man who puts his limbs first is a small man. It cannot be a coincidence that, in describing the distinction between the ruler and the ruled, Mencius uses the same terms. 'There are affairs of great men and there are affairs of small men' (III. A. 4). That the terms are used in the same way is confirmed by the fact that the great men who rule exercise their hearts, while the small men who are ruled exercise their muscles. If this conclusion is correct, then we can say that the pattern of the body politic is not only similar to the pattern of the body but is in fact a projection of it.

Mencius' attitude towards war follows logically from his belief in the supremacy of the people. War brings great suffering to the people as they are the ones who get killed and it is their land that is laid waste. Hence it is something to be abhorred, and should be resorted to only as a desperate remedy. There are two conditions which must be fulfilled before war can be justified. First, it should be used to remove wicked rulers who cannot be removed by any other means. Second, even when directed towards this end, war should only be initiated by someone who has the authority. When these two conditions are fulfilled, the result is what Mencius would call a punitive war. Again, we can see the moral basis of what is political. War is to a state – and so to the ruler – what punishment is to the criminal. When questioned whether he encouraged Ch'i to invade Yen, Mencius replied that he did not. All he did was to say that Yen deserved invasion. As Ch'i was no better than Yen, there was no moral justification for the invasion. In other words, Ch'i had not the moral authority. Only a Heaven-appointed officer had the authority to do so, just as only the Marshal of the Guards had the authority to put a murderer to death (II. B. 8). Elsewhere Mencius says that when the ruler of a state is looked up to even by the people in neighbouring states as their father and mother, he will have no match in the Empire. And he who has no match in the Empire is a Heaven-appointed officer (II. A. 5). So the Heaven-appointed officer turns out to be the ruler who practises benevolent government.

No war other than punitive wars are justified. 'In the Spring and Autumn period there were no just wars,' said Mencius. 'There were only cases of one war not being quite as bad as another. A punitive expedition is a war waged by one in authority against his subordinates. It is not for peers to punish one another by war' (VII. B. 2).

Together with war, Mencius condemned those who were experts at waging war. 'Those skilled in war should suffer the most severe punishment.' For in war enough men are killed to fill the plains and cities which are in dispute. 'This is known as showing the land the way to devour human flesh. Death is too light a punishment' for men 'who do their best to wage war for a prince' (IV. A. 14). If a ruler is benevolent he will have no match in the Empire (VII. B. 4), but if a prince is not benevolent, to extend his territory for him is to be a pest on the people (VI. B. 9). As we have seen, this condemnation is not confined to waging war for the prince. Simply to enrich a prince who is not benevolent is to be a pest on the people.

Let us try to sum up the contributions made by Mencius to Confucian thought. With the passage of time, new developments and new problems arose, and if Confucianism was to hold its own, it had to take cognizance of these new developments and furnish answers to these new problems. First, the problem of human nature which hardly existed in Confucius' day became a hotly debated issue. There were a number of different views. According to some, human nature is neutral: human beings can be made good or bad. According to others, there is neither good nor bad in human nature. According to others again, human nature consists solely of appetites and desires. What Mencius did was to offer his own theory which is not only consistent with, but can furnish a firm basis to, Confucian thought. This is his theory that human nature is good.

Second, the fourth century B.C. can be looked upon as a watershed in the history of Chinese thought in the ancient period. It marks the discovery of the human heart or mind. In the *Analects of Confucius* and the parts of the *Mo tzu* which are earliest in date, although the heart (*hsin*) is actually mentioned, there is no reference to its inner complexities. But by the middle of the fourth century B.C., at the latest, philosophers discovered the complex phenomenon of the human heart and became fascinated by it. This, as we have seen, was initially connected with the theory that *ch'i* was the basic ingredient in the universe. Again, Mencius not only took cognizance of what happened but also produced his own distinctive way of looking at the matter. He produced a moral version of the theory of the heart and *ch'i*.

Finally, in the fourth century B.C. the question was discussed whether there was something behind the universe without which it would cease to function. We have seen that of the two opposing views, 'nothing does it' and 'something causes it', Mencius definitely ranged himself on the side of the second, and this he identified with the earlier belief in Heaven and so related it to the problem of the Mandate or Decree of Heaven.

Mencius brought all these threads together into a complex system. The unique feature of the make-up of a human being is his heart, and so when we speak of human nature we should have in mind, primarily, the human heart. This heart contains incipient moral tendencies which when nurtured with care can enable a man to become a sage. As it is Heaven which is responsible for making morality the unique distinguishing feature of man, his moral nature is that which links him with Heaven. The flood-like *ch'i* which is a manifestation of this nature, when developed to the utmost, fills the space between Heaven and Earth, and when that happens Man is in the same stream as Heaven and Earth. Thus the barrier between the Decree of Heaven and the Nature of Man which some saw as insuperable was shown by Mencius to be non-existent, and there was no obstacle in man's path to a perfect moral character except his own failure to make the effort.

It is a view commonly accepted that the Taoist philosophers Lao Tzu and Chuang Tzu represented mysticism in ancient China.

In my view, the *Tao te ching*, which is supposed to have been written by Lao Tzu, contains ideas that are down-to-earth rather than mystic, as the aim was to help a man pick his way through all the hazards inherent in living in a disorderly age. Chuang Tzu, on the other hand, has a better claim to being a mystic. He had a vision of a universe that transcended values which are, at best, of only limited validity. The purpose of his view of the universe is to foster an attitude of resignation. There was, for Chuang Tzu, no safe recipe for survival. The only thing a man can do is to refuse to recognize the conventional values assigned to life and death. In Chuang Tzu's thought there is a sense of oneness with the universe, and that is what qualifies him as a mystic, but a true mystic, it seems to me, ought to feel that the universe has a purpose, and this is missing in Chuang Tzu. Mencius, on the other hand, is more truly a mystic. Not only does he believe that a man can attain oneness with the universe by perfecting his own moral nature, but he has absolute faith in the moral purpose of the universe. His great achievement is that he not only successfully defended the teachings of Confucius against the corrosive influence of new ideas but, in the process, added to Confucianism a depth that it did not possess before.

D. C. L.

MENCIUS

BOOK I · PART A

1. Mencius went to see King Hui of Liang.[1] 'Sir,' said the King. 'You have come all this distance, thinking nothing of a thousand *li*.[2] You must surely have some way of profiting my state?'

'Your Majesty,' answered Mencius. 'What is the point of mentioning the word "profit"? All that matters is that there should be benevolence and rightness. If Your Majesty says, "How can I profit my state?" and the Counsellors say, "How can I profit my family?" and the Gentlemen[3] and Commoners say, "How can I profit my person?" then those above and those below will be trying to profit at the expense of one another and the state will be imperilled. When regicide is committed in a state of ten thousand chariots, it is certain to be by a vassal with a thousand chariots, and when it is committed in a state of a thousand chariots, it is certain to be by a vassal with a hundred chariots. A share of a thousand in ten thousand or a hundred in a thousand is by no means insignificant, yet if profit is put before rightness, there is no satisfaction short of total usurpation. No benevolent man ever abandons his parents, and no dutiful man ever puts his prince last. Perhaps you will now endorse what I have said, "All that matters is that there should be benevolence and rightness. What is the point of mentioning the word 'profit'?" '

2. Mencius went to see King Hui of Liang. The King was standing over a pond. 'Are such things enjoyed even by a good and wise man?' said he, looking round at his wild geese and deer.

'Only if a man is good and wise,' answered Mencius, 'is he able

1. Names of persons and places are to be found in the Glossary.
2. A little over 400 metres.
3. In the present translation, 'Gentleman' is used to translate *shih* while 'gentleman' is used to translate *chün tzu*. *Shih* was the lowest rank of officials while *chün tzu* denoted either a man of moral excellence or a man in authority. The decision to use the same word for translating both these Chinese terms is not entirely arbitrary, as *shih chün tzu* is a term commonly used in the *Mo tzu* and the *Hsün tzu*.

to enjoy them. Otherwise he would not, even if he had them.

'The *Book of Odes* says,

> He surveyed and began the Sacred Terrace.
> He surveyed it and measured it;
> The people worked at it;
> In less than no time they finished it.
> He surveyed and began without haste;
> The people came in ever increasing numbers.
> The King was in the Sacred Park.
> The doe lay down;
> The doe were sleek;
> The white birds glistened.
> The King was at the Sacred Pond.
> Oh! how full it was of leaping fish![1]

It was with the labour of the people that King Wen built his terrace and pond, yet so pleased and delighted were they that they named his terrace the "Sacred Terrace" and his pond the "Sacred Pond", and rejoiced in his possession of deer, fish and turtles. It was by sharing their enjoyments with the people that men of antiquity were able to enjoy themselves.

'The *T'ang shih* says,

> O Sun,[2] when wilt thou perish?
> We care not if we have to die with thee.[3]

When the people were prepared "to die with" him, even if the tyrant had a terrace and pond, birds and beasts, could he have enjoyed them all by himself?'

3. King Hui of Liang said, 'I have done my best for my state. When crops failed in Ho Nei I moved the population to Ho Tung and the grain to Ho Nei, and reversed the action when crops failed in Ho Tung. I have not noticed any of my neighbours taking as

1. Ode 242.

2. The Sun stands for the tyrant Chieh whom the people did not dare name openly. Chieh was said to have remarked, 'My possession of the Empire is like there being a sun in Heaven. Is there a time when the sun will perish? If the sun perishes, then I shall perish.' (*Han shih wai chuan*, 2/22).

3. See *Shu ching* (*Shih san ching chu shu*, 1815 edition), 8.2b.

much pains over his government. Yet how is it the population of the neighbouring states has not decreased and mine has not increased?'

'Your Majesty is fond of war,' said Mencius. 'May I use an analogy from it? After weapons were crossed to the rolling of drums, some soldiers fled, abandoning their armour and trailing their weapons. One stopped after a hundred paces, another after fifty paces. What would you think if the latter, as one who ran only fifty paces, were to laugh at the former who ran a hundred?'

'He had no right to,' said the King. 'He did not quite run a hundred paces. That is all. But all the same, he ran.'

'If you can see that,' said Mencius, 'you will not expect your own state to be more populous than the neighbouring states.

'If you do not interfere with the busy seasons in the fields, then there will be more grain than the people can eat; if you do not allow nets with too fine a mesh to be used in large ponds, then there will be more fish and turtles than they can eat; if hatchets and axes are permitted in the forests on the hills only in the proper seasons, then there will be more timber than they can use. When the people have more grain, more fish and turtles than they can eat, and more timber than they can use, then in the support of their parents when alive and in the mourning of them when dead, they will be able to have no regrets over anything left undone.[1] This is the first step along the Kingly way.

'If the mulberry is planted in every homestead of five mu[2] of land, then those who are fifty can wear silk; if chickens, pigs and dogs do not miss their breeding season, then those who are seventy can eat meat; if each lot of a hundred mu is not deprived of labour during the busy seasons, then families with several mouths to feed will not go hungry. Exercise due care over the education provided by the village schools, and discipline the people by teaching them the duties proper to sons and younger brothers, and those whose heads have turned grey will not be carrying loads

1. Presumably because they have no lack of food for the support of the living or of timber for coffins in which to bury the dead.

2. As a mu is one nine-hundredth part of a square li, it works out to be somewhat less than 200 square metres.

on the roads. When those who are seventy wear[1] silk and eat meat and the masses are neither cold nor hungry, it is impossible for their prince not to be a true King.

'Now when food meant for human beings is so plentiful as to be thrown to dogs and pigs, you fail to realize that it is time for garnering, and when men drop dead from starvation by the wayside, you fail to realize that it is time for distribution. When people die, you simply say, "It is none of my doing. It is the fault of the harvest." In what way is that different from killing a man by running him through, while saying all the time, "It is none of my doing. It is the fault of the weapon." Stop putting the blame on the harvest and the people of the whole Empire will come to you.'

4. King Hui of Liang said, 'I am ready to listen to what you have to say.'

'Is there any difference,' said Mencius, 'between killing a man with a staff and killing him with a knife?'

'There is no difference.'

'Is there any difference between killing him with a knife and killing him with misrule?'

'There is no difference.'

'There is fat meat in your kitchen and there are well-fed horses in your stables, yet the people look hungry and in the outskirts of cities men drop dead from starvation. This is to show animals the way to devour men. Even the devouring of animals by animals is repugnant to men. If, then, one who is father and mother to the people cannot, in ruling over them, avoid showing animals the way to devour men, wherein is he father and mother to the people?

'When Confucius said, "The inventor of burial figures in human form deserves not to have any progeny," he was condemning him for the use of something modelled after the human form. How, then, can the starving of this very people be countenanced?'

---

1. This passage is found again in I. A. 7 where, instead of 'those who are seventy', the text reads 'the aged' which seems preferable, as 'those who wear silk and eat meat' refers as much to those who are fifty as to those who are seventy.

5. King Hui of Liang said, 'As you know, the state of Chin[1] was second to none in power in the Empire. But when it came to my own time we suffered defeat in the east by Ch'i when my eldest son died, and we lost territory to the extent of seven hundred *li* to Ch'in in the west, while to the south we were humiliated by Ch'u. I am deeply ashamed of this and wish, in what little time I have left in this life, to wash away all this shame. How can this be done?'

'A territory of a hundred *li* square,' answered Mencius, 'is sufficient to enable its ruler to become a true King. If Your Majesty practises benevolent government towards the people, reduces punishment and taxation, gets the people to plough deeply and weed promptly, and if the able-bodied men learn, in their spare time, to be good sons and good younger brothers, loyal to their prince and true to their word, so that they will, in the family, serve their fathers and elder brothers, and outside the family, serve their elders and superiors, then they can be made to inflict defeat on the strong armour and sharp weapons of Ch'in and Ch'u, armed with nothing but staves.

'These other princes take the people away from their work during the busy seasons, making it impossible for them to till the land and so minister to the needs of their parents. Thus parents suffer cold and hunger while brothers, wives and children are separated and scattered. These princes push their people into pits and into water. If you should go and punish such princes, who is there to oppose you? Hence it is said, "The benevolent man has no match." I beg of you not to have any doubts.'

6. Mencius saw King Hsiang of Liang. Coming away, he said to someone, 'When I saw him at a distance he did not look like a ruler of men and when I went close to him I did not see anything that commanded respect. Abruptly he asked me, "Through what can the Empire be settled?"

' "Through unity," I said.

' "Who can unite it?"

' "One who is not fond of killing can unite it," I said.

1. Men of Liang often referred to their own state as Chin.

' "Who can give it to him?" '[1]

' "No one in the Empire will refuse to give it to him. Does Your Majesty not know about young rice plants? Should there be a drought in the seventh or eighth month,[2] these plants will wilt. If clouds begin to gather in the sky and rain comes pouring down, then the plants will spring up again. This being the case, who can stop it? Now in the Empire amongst the shepherds of men there is not one who is not fond of killing. If there is one who is not, then the people in the Empire will crane their necks to watch for his coming. This being truly the case, the people will turn to him like water flowing downwards with a tremendous force. Who can stop it?" '

7. King Hsüan of Ch'i asked, 'Can you tell me about the history of Duke Huan of Ch'i and Duke Wen of Chin?'

'None of the followers of Confucius,' answered Mencius, 'spoke of the history of Duke Huan and Duke Wen. It is for this reason that no one in after ages passed on any accounts, and I have no knowledge of them. If you insist, perhaps I may be permitted to tell you about becoming a true King.'

'How virtuous must a man be before he can become a true King?'

'He becomes a true King by bringing peace to the people. This is something no one can stop.'

'Can someone like myself bring peace to the people?'

'Yes.'

'How do you know that I can?'

'I heard the following from Hu He:

The King was sitting in the upper part of the hall and someone led an ox through the lower part. The King noticed this and

1. For this idea of giving someone the Empire, cf. the sentence in v. A. 5, 6 'Who gave it to him'. Cf. further 'Hence it is easy to give the Empire away but difficult to find the right person for it' (III. A. 4), and 'Following the way of the present day, unless there is a change in the ways of the people, a man could not hold the Empire for the duration of one morning, even if it were given him' (VI. B. 9).

2. This is according to the calendar of the Chou Dynasty. The seventh and eighth months of the Chou calendar are equivalent to the fifth and sixth months of the present lunar calendar which follows that of the Hsia Dynasty.

said, "Where is the ox going?" "The blood of the ox is to be used for consecrating a new bell." "Spare it. I cannot bear to see it shrinking with fear, like an innocent man going to the place of execution." "In that case, should the ceremony be abandoned?" "That is out of the question. Use a lamb instead."

'I wonder if this is true?'

'It is.'

'The heart behind your action is sufficient to enable you to become a true King. The people all thought that you grudged the expense, but, for my part, I have no doubt that you were moved by pity for the animal.'

'You are right,' said the King. 'How could there be such people? Ch'i may be a small state, but I am not quite so miserly as to grudge the use of an ox. It was simply because I could not bear to see it shrink with fear, like an innocent man going to the place of execution, that I used a lamb instead.'

'You must not be surprised that the people thought you miserly. You used a small animal in place of a big one. How were they to know? If you were pained by the animal going innocently to its death, what was there to choose between an ox and a lamb?'

The King laughed and said, 'What was really in my mind, I wonder? It is not true that I grudged the expense, but I *did* use a lamb instead of the ox. I suppose it was only natural that the people should have thought me miserly.'

'There is no harm in this. It is the way of a benevolent man. You saw the ox but not the lamb. The attitude of a gentleman towards animals is this: once having seen them alive, he cannot bear to see them die, and once having heard their cry, he cannot bear to eat their flesh. That is why the gentleman keeps his distance from the kitchen.'

The King said, 'The *Book of Odes* says,

> The heart is another man's,
> But it is I who have surmised it.[1]

This describes you perfectly. For though the deed was mine, when I looked into myself I failed to understand my own heart. You

1. Ode 198.

described it for me and your words struck a chord in me. What made you think that my heart accorded with the way of a true King?'

'Should someone say to you, "I am strong enough to lift a hundred *chün*[1] but not a feather; I have eyes that can see the tip of a fine hair but not a cartload of firewood," would you accept the truth of such a statement?'

'No.'

'Why should it be different in your own case? Your bounty is sufficient to reach the animals, yet the benefits of your government fail to reach the people. That a feather is not lifted is because one fails to make the effort; that a cartload of firewood is not seen is because one fails to use one's eyes. Similarly, that peace is not brought to the people is because you fail to practise kindness. Hence your failure to become a true King is due to a refusal to act, not to an inability to act.'

'What is the difference in form between refusal to act and inability to act?'

'If you say to someone, "I am unable to do it," when the task is one of striding over the North Sea with Mount T'ai under your arm, then this is a genuine case of inability to act. But if you say, "I am unable to do it," when it is one of massaging an elder's joints for him, then this is a case of refusal to act, not of inability. Hence your failure to become a true King is not the same in kind as "striding over the North Sea with Mount T'ai under your arm", but the same as "massaging an elder's joints for him".

'Treat the aged of your own family in a manner befitting their venerable age and extend this treatment to the aged of other families; treat your own young in a manner befitting their tender age and extend this to the young of other families, and you can roll the Empire on your palm.

'The *Book of Odes* says,

> He set an example for his consort
> And also for his brothers,
> And so ruled over the family and the state.[2]

---

1. Just under seven kilogrammes.   2. Ode 240.

In other words, all you have to do is take this very heart here and apply it to what is over there. Hence one who extends his bounty can bring peace to the Four Seas; one who does not cannot bring peace even to his own family. There is just one thing in which the ancients greatly surpassed others, and that is the way they extended what they did. Why is it then that your bounty is sufficient to reach animals yet the benefits of your government fail to reach the people?

'It is by weighing a thing that its weight can be known and by measuring it that its length can be ascertained. It is so with all things, but particularly so with the heart. Your Majesty should measure his own heart.

'Perhaps you find satisfaction only in starting a war, imperilling your subjects and incurring the enmity of other feudal lords?'

'No. Why should I find satisfaction in such acts? I only wish to realize my supreme ambition.'

'May I be told what this is?'

The King smiled, offering no reply.

'Is it because your food is not good enough to gratify your palate, and your clothes not good enough to gratify your body? Or perhaps the sights and sounds are not good enough to gratify your eyes and ears and your close servants not good enough to serve you? Any of your various officials surely could make good these deficiencies. It cannot be because of these things.'

'No. It is not because of these things.'

'In that case one can guess what your supreme ambition is. You wish to extend your territory, to enjoy the homage of Ch'in and Ch'u, to rule over the Central Kingdoms and to bring peace to the barbarian tribes on the four borders. Seeking the fulfilment of such an ambition by such means as you employ is like looking for fish by climbing a tree.'

'Is it as bad as that?' asked the King.

'It is likely to be worse. If you look for fish by climbing a tree, though you will not find it, there is no danger of this bringing disasters in its train. But if you seek the fulfilment of an ambition like yours by such means as you employ, after putting all your heart and might into the pursuit, you are certain to reap disaster in the end.'

'Can I hear about this?'

'If the men of Tsou and the men of Ch'u were to go to war, who do you think would win?'

'The men of Ch'u.'

'That means that the small is no match for the big, the few no match for the many, and the weak no match for the strong. Within the Seas there are nine areas of ten thousand *li* square, and the territory of Ch'i makes up one of these. For one to try to overcome the other eight is no different from Tsou going to war with Ch'u. Why not go back to fundamentals?

'Now if you should practise benevolence in the government of your state, then all those in the Empire who seek office would wish to find a place at your court, all tillers of land to till the land in outlying parts of your realm, all merchants to enjoy the refuge of your market-place, all travellers to go by way of your roads, and all those who hate [*i*] [1] their rulers to lay their complaints before you. This being so, who can stop you from becoming a true King?'

'I am dull-witted,' said the King, 'and cannot see my way beyond this point. I hope you will help me towards my goal and instruct me plainly. Though I am slow, I shall make an attempt to follow your advice.'

'Only a Gentleman can have a constant heart in spite of a lack of constant means of support. The people, on the other hand, will not have constant hearts if they are without constant means. Lacking constant hearts, they will go astray and fall into excesses, stopping at nothing. To punish them after they have fallen foul of the law is to set a trap for the people. How can a benevolent man in authority allow himself to set a trap for the people? Hence when determining what means of support the people should have, a clear-sighted ruler ensures that these are sufficient, on the one hand, for the care of parents, and, on the other, for the support of wife and children, so that the people always have sufficient food in good years and escape starvation in bad; only then does he drive

1. Numbers in square brackets refer to Textual Notes on p. 264.

them towards goodness; in this way the people find it easy to follow him.

'Nowadays, the means laid down for the people are sufficient neither for the care of parents nor for the support of wife and children. In good years life is always hard, while in bad years there is no way of escaping death. Thus simply to survive takes more energy than the people have. What time can they spare for learning about rites and duty?

'If you wish to put this into practice, why not go back to fundamentals? If the mulberry is planted in every homestead of five *mu* of land, then those who are fifty can wear silk; if chickens, pigs and dogs do not miss their breeding season, then those who are seventy can eat meat; if each lot of a hundred *mu* is not deprived of labour during the busy seasons, then families with several mouths to feed will not go hungry. Exercise due care over the education provided by village schools, and discipline the people by teaching them duties proper to sons and younger brothers, and those whose heads have turned grey will not be carrying loads on the roads. When the aged wear silk and eat meat and the masses are neither cold nor hungry, it is impossible for their prince not to be a true King.'

BOOK I · PART B

1. Chuang Pao went to see Mencius. 'The King received me,' he said, 'and told me that he was fond of music. I was at a loss what to say.'

Then he added, 'What do you think of a fondness for music?'

'If the King has a great fondness for music,' answered Mencius, 'then there is perhaps hope for the state of Ch'i.'

Another day, when Mencius was received by the King, he said, 'Is it true that Your Majesty told Chuang Tzu that you were fond of music?'

The King blushed and said, 'It is not the music of the Former Kings that I am capable of appreciating. I am merely fond of popular music.'

'If you have a great fondness for music, then there is perhaps hope for the state of Ch'i. Whether it is the music of today or the music of antiquity makes no difference.'

'Can I hear more about this?'

'Which is greater, enjoyment[1] by yourself or enjoyment in the company of others?'

'In the company of others.'

'Which is greater, enjoyment in the company of a few or enjoyment in the company of many?'

'In the company of many.'

'Let me tell you about enjoyment. Now suppose you were having a musical performance here, and when the people heard the sound of your bells and drums and the notes of your pipes and flutes they all with aching heads and knitted brows said to one another, "In being fond of music, why does our King bring us to such straits that fathers and sons do not see each other, and brothers, wives and children are parted and scattered?" Again,

1. Throughout this passage Mencius is exploiting the fact that the same character is used both for 'music' and 'enjoyment'. It is to be expected that in some cases there is room for a difference of opinion as to whether the character means the one or the other.

suppose you were hunting here, and when the people heard the sound of your chariots and horses and saw the magnificence of your banners they all with aching heads and knitted brows said to one another, "In being fond of hunting, why does our King bring us to such straits that fathers and sons do not see each other, and brothers, wives and children are parted and scattered?" The reason would simply be that you failed to share your enjoyment with the people.

'On the other hand, suppose you were having a musical performance here, and when the people heard the sound of your bells and drums and the notes of your pipes and flutes they all looked pleased and said to one another, "Our King must be in good health, otherwise how could he have music performed?" Again, suppose you were hunting here, and when the people heard the sound of your chariots and horses and saw the magnificence of your banners they all looked pleased and said to one another, "Our King must be in good health, otherwise how could he go hunting?" The reason would again simply be that you shared your enjoyment with the people.

'Now if you shared your enjoyment with the people, you would be a true King.'

2. King Hsüan of Ch'i asked, 'Is it true that the park of King Wen was seventy *li* square?'

'It is so recorded,' answered Mencius.

'Was it really as large as that?'

'Even so, the people found it small.'

'My park is only forty *li* square, and yet the people consider it too big. Why is this?'

'True, King Wen's park was seventy *li* square, but it was open to woodcutters as well as catchers of pheasants and hares. As he shared it with the people, is it any wonder that they found it small?

'When I first arrived at the borders of your state, I inquired about the major prohibitions before I dared enter. I was told that within the outskirts of the capital there was a park forty *li* square in which the killing of a deer was as serious an offence as the killing of a man. This turns the park into a trap forty *li* square in the midst of the state. Is it any wonder that the people consider it too big?'

3. King Hsüan of Ch'i asked, 'Is there a way of promoting good relations with neighbouring states?'

'There is,' answered Mencius. 'Only a benevolent man can submit to a state smaller than his own. This accounts for the submission of T'ang to Ke and King Wen to the K'un tribes. Only a wise man can submit to a state bigger than his own. This accounts for the submission of T'ai Wang to the Hsün Yü and Kou Chien to Wu. He who submits to a state smaller than his own delights in Heaven; he who submits to a state bigger than his own is in awe of Heaven. He who delights in Heaven will continue to enjoy the possession of the Empire while he who is in awe of Heaven will continue to enjoy the possession of his own state. The *Book of Odes* says,

> Being in awe of the majesty of Heaven
> We shall continue to enjoy our territory.'[1]

'Great are your words,' said the King, 'but I have a weakness. I am fond of valour.'[2]

'I beg you not to be fond of small valour. To look fierce, putting your hand on your sword and say, "How dare he oppose me!" is to show the valour of a common fellow which is of use only against a single adversary. You should make it something great.

'The *Book of Odes says*,

> The King blazed in rage
> And marshalled his troops
> To stop the enemy advancing on Chü
> And add to the good fortune of Chou
> In response to the wishes of the Empire.[3]

1. Ode 272.
2. The passage following is similar to two passages in 1. B. 5 beginning 'I have a weakness. I am fond of money' and 'I have a weakness. I am fond of women.' In *Hsin hsü* 3/1 these three passages form, in fact, a continuous whole.
3. Ode 241.

This was the valour of King Wen. In one outburst of rage King Wen brought peace to the people of the Empire.

'The *Book of History* says,

Heaven populated the earth below,
Made the people a lord
And made him their teacher
That he might assist God in loving them.
"In the four quarters, neither the innocent nor the guilty escape my eyes,
Who in the Empire dare be above himself?"[1]

If there was one bully in the Empire, King Wu felt this to be a personal affront. This was the valour of King Wu. Thus he, too, brought peace to the people of the Empire in one outburst of rage. Now if you, too, will bring peace to the people of the Empire in one outburst of rage, then the people's only fear will be that you are not fond of valour.'

4. King Hsüan of Ch'i saw Mencius in the Snow Palace. 'Does even a good and wise man,' asked the King, 'have such enjoyment as this?'

'Should there be a man,[2] answered Mencius, 'who is not given a share in such enjoyment, he would speak ill of those in authority. To speak ill of those in authority because one is not given a share in such enjoyment is, of course, wrong. But for one in authority over the people not to share his enjoyment with the people is equally wrong. The people will delight in the joy of him who delights in their joy, and will worry over the troubles of him who worries over their troubles. He who delights and worries on account of the Empire is certain to become a true King.

'Once, Duke Ching of Ch'i asked Yen Tzu, "I wish to travel to Chuan Fu and Ch'ao Wu, then to follow the Sea south to

1. This is from the *T'ai shih*, one of the lost chapters of the *Book of History*, but has been incorporated into the spurious chapter bearing the same title. See *Shu ching*, 11. 6a.

2. There is doubt as to how this sentence should be construed, as the text is most likely corrupt.

Lang Yeh. What must I do to be able to emulate the travels of the Former Kings?"

'"This is indeed a splendid question!" answered Yen Tzu. "When the Emperor goes to the feudal lords, this is known as 'a tour of inspection'. It is so called because its purpose is to inspect the territories for which the feudal lords are responsible. When the feudal lords go to pay homage to the Emperor, this is known as 'a report on duties'. It is so called because its purpose is to report on duties they are charged with. Neither is undertaken without good reason. In spring the purpose is to inspect ploughing so that those who have not enough for sowing may be given help; in autumn the purpose is to inspect harvesting so that those who are in need may be given aid. As a saying of the Hsia Dynasty puts it:

> If our King does not travel,
> How can we have rest?
> If our King does not go on tour,
> How can we have help?
> Every time he travels
> He sets an example for the feudal lords.

'"This is not so today:

> The army on the march live on dried rice.
> The hungry do not get food;
> The weary do not get rest.
> They look askance and they complain.
> Thus the people begin to go astray.
> The lords misuse the people, going against the Decree.
> Food and drink flow like water.
> Drifting, lingering, rioting and intemperance,
> These excesses amongst the feudal lords are a cause for concern.

By 'drifting' is meant going downstream with no thought of returning; by 'lingering', going upstream with no thought of returning; by 'rioting', being insatiable in the hunt; by 'intemperance', being insatiable in drink. The Former Kings never indulged in any of these excesses. It is for you, my lord, to decide on your course of action."

'Duke Ching was pleased. He made elaborate preparations in the capital and then went to stay in the outskirts.[1] And then he opened up the granaries and gave to those who were needy. He summoned the Grand Musician and told him, "Make me music which expresses the harmony between ruler and subject." The result was the *Chih shao* and *Chüeh shao*. Here is the text,

> What harm is there in curbing the lord?

"To curb the Lord" is "to love him".'[2]

5. King Hsüan of Ch'i asked, 'Everyone advises me to pull down the Hall of Light. Should I or should I not do so?'

'The Hall of Light,' answered Mencius, 'is the hall of a true King. If Your Majesty wished to practise Kingly government, then he should not pull it down.'

'May I hear about Kingly government?'

'Formerly, when King Wen ruled over Ch'i,[3] tillers of land were taxed one part in nine;[4] descendants of officials received hereditary emoluments; there was inspection but no levy at border stations and market places; fish-traps were open for all to use; punishment did not extend to the wife and children of an offender. Old men without wives, old women without husbands, old people without children, young children without fathers – these four types of people are the most destitute and have no one to turn to for help. Whenever King Wen put benevolent measures into effect, he always gave them first consideration. The *Book of Odes* says,

> Happy are the rich;
> But have pity on the helpless.[5]

1. i.e., he made preparations for giving help to the needy and marked the solemnity of the occasion by leaving the comforts of his palace.

2. Mencius is here playing on the fact that the word meaning 'to curb' and the word meaning 'to love' were near homophones in his time.

3. This is different from the state of Ch'i which figures so largely in this part of the book, though the romanization of the two names happens to be identical.

4. i.e., the method of *chu* was used, by which eight families help to cultivate the public land. Cf. III. A. 3.

5. Ode 192.

'Well spoken,' commented the King.

'If you consider my words well spoken, then why do you not put them into practice?'

'I have a weakness. I am fond of money.'

'In antiquity Kung Liu was fond of money too. The *Book of Odes* says,

> He stocked and stored;
> He placed provisions
> In bags and sacks.
> He brought harmony and so glory to his state.
> On full display were bows and arrows,
> Spears, halberds and axes.
> Only then did the march begin.[1]

It was only when those who stayed at home had full granaries and those who went forth to war had full sacks that the march could begin. You may be fond of money, but so long as you share this fondness with the people, how can it interfere with your becoming a true King?'

'I have a weakness,' said the King. 'I am fond of women.'

'In antiquity, T'ai Wang was fond of women, and loved his concubines. The *Book of Odes* says,

> Ku Kung Tan Fu[2]
> Early in the morning galloped on his horse
> Along the banks of the river in the West
> Till he came to the foot of Mount Ch'i.
> He brought with him the Lady Chiang,
> Looking for a suitable abode.[3]

At that time, there were neither girls pining for a husband nor men without a wife. You may be fond of women, but so long as you share this fondness with the people, how can it interfere with your becoming a true King?'

6. Mencius said to King Hsüan of Ch'i, 'Suppose a subject of Your Majesty's, having entrusted his wife and children to the care of

---

1. Ode 250.　　　2. i.e., T'ai Wang.　　　3. Ode 237.

a friend, were to go on a trip to Ch'u, only to find, upon his return, that his friend had allowed his wife and children to suffer cold and hunger, then what should he do about it?'

'Break with his friend.'

'If the Marshal of the Guards was unable to keep his guards in order, then what should be done about it?'

'Remove him from office.'

'If the whole realm within the four borders was ill-governed, then what should be done about it?'

The King turned to his attendants and changed the subject.

7. Mencius went to see King Hsüan of Ch'i. 'A "state of established traditions",' said he, 'is so called not because it has tall trees but because it has ministers whose families have served it for generations. You no longer have trusted ministers. Those you promoted yesterday have all disappeared today without your even being aware of it.'

'How could I have known,' said the King, 'that they lacked ability and so avoided making the appointments in the first instance?'

'When there is no choice, the ruler of a state, in advancing good and wise men, may have to promote those of low position over the heads of those of exalted rank and distant relatives over near ones. Hence such a decision should not be taken lightly. When your close attendants all say of a man that he is good and wise, that is not enough; when the Counsellors all say the same, that is not enough; when everyone says so, then have the case investigated. If the man turns out to be good and wise, then and only then should he be given office. When your close attendants all say of a man that he is unsuitable, do not listen to them; when the Counsellors all say the same, do not listen to them; when everyone says so, then have the case investigated. If the man turns out to be unsuitable, then and only then should he be removed from office. When your close attendants all say of a man that he deserves death, do not listen to them; when the Counsellors all say the same, do not listen to them; when everyone says so, then have the case investigated. If the man turns out to deserve death, then and only then should he be put to death. In this way, it will be said, "He was put to death by the whole country." Only by acting in this manner can one be father and mother to the people.'

8. King Hsüan of Ch'i asked, 'Is it true that T'ang banished Chieh and King Wu marched against Tchou?'[1]

'It is so recorded,' answered Mencius.

'Is regicide permissible?'

'A man who mutilates benevolence is a mutilator, while one who cripples rightness is a crippler. He who is both a mutilator and a crippler is an "outcast". I have indeed heard of the punishment of the "outcast Tchou", but I have not heard of any regicide.'

9. Mencius went to see King Hsüan of Ch'i. 'To build a big house,' said he, 'one has to ask the master carpenter to search for huge pieces of timber. If the master carpenter succeeds in finding such timber, the King will be pleased and consider him equal to his task. If the carpenter spoils this timber by whittling it away, the King will be angry and consider him a bungler. A man, having spent his childhood in acquiring knowledge, naturally wishes to put this knowledge to use when he grows up. Now what would happen if the King were to say to him, "Just put aside what you have learned and do as I tell you"? Suppose we have here a piece of uncut jade. Even if its value is equivalent to ten thousand yi[2] of gold, you will still have to entrust its cutting to a jade-cutter. But when it comes to the government of your state, you say, "Just put aside what you have learned and do as I tell you." In what way is this different from teaching the jade-cutter his job?'

10. Ch'i attacked and defeated Yen. King Hsüan said, 'Some advise me against annexing Yen while others urge me to do so. The occupation of a state of ten thousand chariots by another of equal

1. It so happens that the name of the last emperor of the Shang Dynasty and the name of the dynasty which succeeded it come out in identical romanization. To avoid unnecessary confusion I have decided arbitrarily to use 'Tchou' for the tyrant, reserving 'Chou' for the dynasty.

2. Just under 300 grammes.

strength in a matter of fifty days is a feat which could not have been brought about by human agency alone. If I do not annex Yen, I am afraid Heaven will send down disasters. What would you think if I decided on annexation?'

'If in annexing Yen,' answered Mencius, 'you please its people, then annex it. There are examples of men in antiquity following such a course of action. King Wu was one. If in annexing Yen you antagonize its people, then do not annex it. There are also examples of men in antiquity following such a course. King Wen was one. When it is a state of ten thousand chariots attacking another of equal strength and your army is met by the people bringing baskets of rice and bottles of drink, what other reason can there be than that the people are fleeing from water and fire? Should the water become deeper and the fire hotter, they would have no alternative but to turn elsewhere for succour.'

11. Ch'i attacked and annexed Yen. The feudal lords deliberated how they might go to the aid of Yen. King Hsüan said, 'Most of the feudal lords are thinking of going to war with me. What measure should I take to meet the threat?'

'I have heard,' answered Mencius, 'of one who gained ascendancy over the Empire from the modest beginning of seventy *li* square. Such a one was T'ang. I have never heard of anyone ruling over a thousand *li* being frightened of others.

'The *Book of History* says,

> In his punitive expeditions T'ang began with Ke.[1]

With this he gained the trust of the Empire, and when he marched on the east, the western barbarians complained, and when he marched on the south, the northern barbarians complained. They all said, "Why does he not come to us first?"[2] The people longed for his coming as they longed for a rainbow in time of severe drought. Those who were going to market did not stop; those who were ploughing went on ploughing. He punished the rulers

---

1. It is possible that this quotation is from the *T'ang cheng* ('Punitive Expeditions of T'ang'), one of the lost chapters of the *Book of History*.
2. Cf. VII. B. 4.

and comforted the people, like a fall of timely rain, and the people greatly rejoiced.[1]

'The *Book of History* says,

We await our Lord. When he comes we will be revived.[2]

'Now when you went to punish Yen which practised tyranny over its people, the people thought you were going to rescue them from water and fire, and they came to meet your army, bringing baskets of rice and bottles of drink. How can it be right for you to kill the old and bind the young, destroy the ancestral temples and appropriate the valuable vessels? Even before this, the whole Empire was afraid of the power of Ch'i. Now you double your territory without practising benevolent government. This is to provoke the armies of the whole Empire. If you hasten to order the release of the captives, old and young, leave the valuable vessels where they are, and take your army out after setting up a ruler in consultation with the men of Yen, it is still not too late to halt the armies of the Empire.'

12. There was a border clash between Tsou and Lu. Duke Mu of Tsou asked, 'Thirty-three of my officials died, yet none of my people would sacrifice their lives for them. If I punish them, there are too many to be punished. If I do not punish them, then there they were, looking on with hostility at the death of their superiors without going to their aid. What do you think is the best thing for me to do?' [2]

'In years of bad harvest and famine,' answered Mencius, 'close on a thousand of your people suffered, the old and the young being abandoned in the gutter, the able-bodied scattering in all directions, yet your granaries were full and there was failure on the part of your officials to inform you of what was happening. This shows how callous those in authority were and how cruelly they treated the people. Tseng Tzu said, "Take heed! Take heed!

1. This passage, starting from 'With this he gained', seems also to be a quotation, though probably not from the *Book of History*.

2. Probably also from the *T'ang cheng*. For this whole passage, starting from the previous quotation from the *Book of History*, cf. III. B. 5.

What you mete out will be paid back to you." It is only now that the people have had an opportunity of paying back what they received. You should not bear them any grudge. Practise benevolent government and the people will be sure to love their superiors and die for them.'

13. Duke Wen of T'eng asked, 'T'eng is a small state, wedged between Ch'i and Ch'u. Should I be subservient to Ch'i or should I be subservient to Ch'u?'

'This is a question that is beyond me,' answered Mencius. 'If you insist, there is only one course of action I can suggest. Dig deeper moats and build higher walls and defend them shoulder to shoulder with the people. If they would rather die than desert you, then all is not lost.'

14. Duke Wen of T'eng asked, 'Ch'i is going to fortify Hsüeh. I am greatly perturbed. What is the best thing for me to do?'

'In antiquity,' answered Mencius, 'T'ai Wang was in Pin. The Ti tribes invaded Pin and he left and went to settle at the foot of Mount Ch'i. He did this, not out of choice but because he had no alternative. If a man does good deeds, then amongst his descendants in future generations there will rise one who will become a true King. All a gentleman can do in starting an enterprise is to leave behind a tradition which can be carried on. Heaven alone can grant success. What can you do about Ch'i? You can only try your best to do good.'

15. Duke Wen of T'eng said, 'T'eng is a small state. If it tries with all its might to please the large states, it will only bleed itself white in the end. What is the best thing for me to do?'

'In antiquity,' answered Mencius, 'when T'ai Wang was in Pin, the Ti tribes invaded the place. He tried to buy them off with skins and silks; he tried to buy them off with horses and hounds; he tried to buy them off with pearls and jade; but all to no avail. Then he assembled the elders and announced to them, "What the Ti tribes want is our land. I have heard that a man in authority never turns what is meant for the benefit of men into a source of harm

to them. It will not be difficult for you, my friends, to find another
lord. I am leaving." And he left Pin, crossed the Liang Mountains
and built a city at the foot of Mount Ch'i and settled there. The
men of Pin said, "This is a benevolent man. We must not lose him."
They flocked after him as if to market.

'Others expressed the view, "This is the land of our for-
bears. It is not a matter for us to decide. Let us defend it to the
death."

'You will have to choose between these two courses.'

16. Duke P'ing of Lu was about to go out. A favourite by the
name of Tsang Ts'ang asked, 'My lord, on previous occasions
when you went out you always gave instructions to the officials
as to where you were going. Now the carriage is ready and the
officials have not been told of your destination. May I be told
about it?'

'I am going to see Mencius,' said the Duke.

'I am amazed! Is it because you think him a good and wise man
that you lower yourself in taking the initiative towards a meeting
with a common fellow? The good and wise man is the source of
the rites and what is right, yet with Mencius the funeral on the
later occasion [when his mother died] was more splendid than that
on the earlier occasion [when his father died]. My lord, I beg of
you not to go to see him.'

'As you wish.'

Yüeh-cheng Tzu went in and asked, 'My lord, why did you not
go to see Meng K'e?'

'Someone told me that with Mencius the funeral on the later
occasion [when his mother died] was more splendid than that on
the earlier occasion [when his father died]. It was for that reason
that I did not go.'

'I am amazed! Is it because on the later occasion the style was
that appropriate to a mourner with the status of a Counsellor while
on the earlier occasion it was that appropriate to one with the status
of only a Gentleman that you use the expression "more splendid"?
Or is it because on the later occasion five tripods of offerings were
used while on the earlier occasion three only were used?'

'No. I had in mind the superior quality of the coffins[1] and the clothes.'

'That is not a matter of being "more splendid". It is simply a matter of being in more comfortable circumstances.'

Yüeh-cheng Tzu saw Mencius. 'I mentioned you to the prince,' said he, 'and he was to have come to see you. Amongst his favourites is one Tsang Ts'ang who dissuaded him. That is why he failed to come.'

'When a man goes forward, there is something which urges him on; when he halts, there is something which holds him back. It is not in his power either to go forward or to halt. It is due to Heaven that I failed to meet the Marquis of Lu. How can this fellow Tsang be responsible for my failure?'

1. Cf. II. B. 7.

BOOK II · PART A

1. Kung-sun Ch'ou asked, 'If you, Master, were to hold the reins of government in Ch'i, could a repetition of the success of Kuan Chung and Yen Tzu be predicted?'

'You are very much a native of Ch'i,' said Mencius. 'You know only of Kuan Chung and Yen Tzu.

'Someone once asked Tseng Hsi,[1] "My good sir, how do you compare with Tzu-lu?"

'"Even my late father held him in awe," answered Tseng Hsi, with an air of embarrassment.

'"In that case, how do you compare with Kuan Chung?"

'This time Tseng Hsi looked offended. "Why do you compare me with such a man as Kuan Chung?" he asked. "Kuan Chung enjoyed the confidence of his prince so exclusively and managed all his affairs for so long, and yet his achievements were so insignificant. Why do you compare me with such a man?"'

Mencius then added, 'If it was beneath even Tseng Hsi to become a Kuan Chung, are you saying that I would be willing?'

'Kuan Chung made his prince leader of the feudal lords, and Yen Tzu made his illustrious. Are they not good enough for you to emulate?'

'To make the King of Ch'i a true King is as easy as turning over one's hand.'

'If that is the case, then I am more perplexed than ever. Virtuous as King Wen was, he did not succeed in extending his influence over the whole Empire when he died at the age of a hundred. It was only after his work was carried on by King Wu and the Duke of Chou that that influence prevailed. Now you talk as if becoming a true King were an easy matter. In that case, do you find King Wen an unworthy example?'

1. This Tseng Hsi was the younger son of Tseng Tzu, disciple of Confucius, not to be confused with the Tseng Hsi mentioned in IV. A. 19, VII. B. 36 and VII. B. 37 who was Tseng Tzu's father. The Chinese names behind the apparent identity in romanization are quite different.

'How can I stand comparison with King Wen? From T'ang to Wu Ting, there were six or seven wise or sage kings, and the Empire was for long content to be ruled by the Yin. What has gone on for long is difficult to change. Wu Ting commanded the homage of the feudal lords and maintained the possession of the Empire as easily as rolling it on his palm.

'Tchou was not far removed in time from Wu Ting. There still persisted traditions of ancient families and fine government measures handed down from earlier times. Furthermore, there were the Viscount of Wei, Wei Chung, Prince Pi Kan, the Viscount of Chi and Chiao Ke, all fine men, who assisted Tchou. That is why it took him such a long time to lose the Empire. There was not one foot of land which was not his territory, nor a single man who was not his subject. On the other hand, King Wen was just rising from a territory of only one hundred *li* square. That is why it was so difficult.

'The people of Ch'i have a saying,

> You may be clever,
> But it is better to make use of circumstances;
> You may have a hoe
> But it is better to wait for the right season.

The present is, however, an easy time.

'Even at the height of their power, the Hsia, Yin and Chou never exceeded a thousand *li* square in territory, yet Ch'i has the requisite territory. The sound of cocks crowing and dogs barking can be heard all the way to the four borders. Thus Ch'i has the requisite population. For Ch'i no further extension of its territory or increase of its population is necessary. The King of Ch'i can become a true King just by practising benevolent government, and no one will be able to stop him.

'Moreover, the appearance of a true King has never been longer overdue than today; and the people have never suffered more under tyrannical government than today. It is easy to provide food for the hungry and drink for the thirsty. Confucius said,

> The influence of virtue spreads
> Faster than an order transmitted through posting stations.

'At the present time, if a state of ten thousand chariots were to practise benevolent government, the people would rejoice as if they had been released from hanging by the heels. Now is the time when one can, with half the effort, achieve twice as much as the ancients.'

2. Kung-sun Ch'ou said, 'If you, Master, were raised to a position above the Ministers in Ch'i and were able to put the Way into practice, it would be no surprise if through this you were able to make the King of Ch'i a leader of the feudal lords or even a true King. If this happened, would it cause any stirring in your heart?'

'No,' said Mencius. 'My heart has not been stirred since the age of forty.'

'In that case you far surpass Meng Pin.'

'That is not difficult. Kao Tzu succeeded in this at an even earlier age than I.'

'Is there a way to develop a heart that cannot be stirred?'

'Yes, there is. The way Po-kung Yu cultivated his courage was by never showing submission on his face or letting anyone out-stare him. For him, to yield the tiniest bit was as humiliating as to be cuffed in the market place. He would no more accept an insult from a prince with ten thousand chariots than from a common fellow coarsely clad. He would as soon run a sword through the prince as through the common fellow. He had no respect for persons, and always returned whatever harsh tones came his way.

'Meng Shih-she said this about the cultivation of his courage. "I look upon defeat as victory. One who advances only after sizing up the enemy, and joins battle only after weighing the chances of victory is simply showing cowardice in face of superior numbers. Of course I cannot be certain of victory. All I can do is to be without fear."

'Meng Shih-she resembled Tseng Tzu while Po-kung Yu re-sembled Tzu-hsia. It is hard to say which of the two was superior, but Meng Shih-she had a firm grasp of the essential.

'Tseng Tzu once said to Tzu-hsiang, "Do you admire courage? I once heard about supreme courage from the Master.[1] If, on

1. i.e., Confucius.

looking within, one finds oneself to be in the wrong, then even though one's adversary be only a common fellow coarsely clad one is bound [3] to tremble with fear. But if one finds oneself in the right, one goes forward even against men in the thousands." Meng Shih-she's firm hold on his *ch'i*[1] is inferior to Tseng Tzu's firm grasp of the essential.'

'I wonder if you could tell me something about the heart that cannot be stirred, in your case and in Kao Tzu's case?'

'According to Kao Tzu, "If you fail to understand words, do not worry about this in your heart; and if you fail to understand in your heart, do not seek satisfaction in your *ch'i*." It is right that one should not seek satisfaction in one's *ch'i* when one fails to understand in one's heart. But it is wrong to say that one should not worry about it in one's heart when one fails to understand words.

'The will is commander over the *ch'i* while the *ch'i* is that which fills the body. The *ch'i* halts where the will arrives. Hence it is said, "Take hold of your will and do not abuse your *ch'i*."'

'As you have already said that the *ch'i* rests where the will arrives, what is the point of going on to say, "Take hold of your will and do not abuse your *ch'i*"?'

'The will, when blocked, moves the *ch'i*. On the other hand, the *ch'i*, when blocked, also moves the will. Now stumbling and hurrying affect the *ch'i*,[2] yet in fact palpitations of the heart are produced.'[3]

'May I ask what your strong points are?'

'I have an insight into words. I am good at cultivating my "flood-like *ch'i*".'

'May I ask what this "flood-like *ch'i*" is?'

'It is difficult to explain. This is a *ch'i* which is, in the highest degree, vast and unyielding. Nourish it with integrity and place no obstacle in its path and it will fill the space between Heaven and Earth. It is a *ch'i* which unites rightness and the Way. Deprive it

1. For a discussion of this term see Introduction p. 24ff.

2. The *ch'i* here is the breath.

3. This seems to be the end of this passage, the rest of the section constituting a separate section.

of these and it will collapse. It is born of accumulated rightness and cannot be appropriated by anyone through a sporadic show of rightness. Whenever one acts in a way that falls below the standard set in one's heart, it will collapse. Hence I said Kao Tzu never understood rightness because he looked upon it as external.[1] You must work at it and never let it out of your mind.[4] At the same time, while you must never let it out of your mind, you must not forcibly help it grow either. You must not be like the man from Sung.[2] There was a man from Sung who pulled at his rice plants because he was worried about their failure to grow. Having done so, he went on his way home, not realizing what he had done. "I am worn out today," said he to his family. "I have been helping the rice plants to grow." His son rushed out to take a look and there the plants were, all shrivelled up. There are few in the world who can resist the urge to help their rice plants grow. There are some who leave the plants unattended, thinking that nothing they can do will be of any use. They are the people who do not even bother to weed. There are others who help the plants grow. They are the people who pull at them. Not only do they fail to help them but they do the plants positive harm.'

'What do you mean by "an insight into words"?'

'From biased words I can see wherein the speaker is blind; from immoderate words, wherein he is ensnared; from heretical words, wherein he has strayed from the right path; from evasive words, wherein he is at his wits' end. What arises in the mind will interfere with policy, and what shows itself in policy will interfere with practice. Were a sage to rise again, he would surely agree with what I have said.'[3]

'Tsai Wo and Tzu-kung excelled in rhetoric; Jan Niu, Min Tzu and Yen Hui excelled in the exposition of virtuous conduct.[4] Confucius excelled in both and yet he said, "I am not versed in rhetoric." In that case you, Master, must already be a sage.'

1. Cf. VI. A. 4.

2. In the writings of the Warring States period the man from Sung was a byword for stupidity.

3. The last part of this passage is found also in III. B. 9.

4. Cf. the *Analects of Confucius*, XI. 2.

'What an extraordinary thing for you to say of me! Tzu-kung once asked Confucius, "Are you, Master, a sage?" Confucius replied, "I have not succeeded in becoming a sage. I simply never tire of learning nor weary of teaching." Tzu-kung said, "Not to tire of learning is wisdom; not to weary of teaching is benevolence. You must be a sage to be both wise and benevolent.[1]" A sage is something even Confucius did not claim to be. What an extraordinary thing for you to say of me!'

'I have heard that Tzu-hsia, Tzu-yu and Tzu-chang each had one aspect of the Sage while Jan Niu, Min Tzu and Yen Hui were replicas of the Sage in miniature. Which would you rather be?'

'Let us leave this question for the moment.'

'How about Po Yi and Yi Yin?'

'They followed paths different from that of Confucius. Po Yi was such that he would only serve the right prince and rule over the right people, took office when order prevailed and relinquished it when there was disorder. Yi Yin was such that he would serve any prince and rule over any people, would take office whether order prevailed or not. Confucius was such that he would take office, or would remain in a state, would delay his departure or hasten it, all according to circumstances.[2] All three were sages of old. I have not been able to emulate any of them, but it is my hope and wish to follow the example of Confucius.'

'Were Po Yi and Yi Yin as much an equal of Confucius as that?'

'No. Ever since man came into this world, there has never been another Confucius.'

'Was there anything in common to all of them?'

'Yes. Were they to become ruler over a hundred *li* square, they would have been capable of winning the homage of the feudal lords and taking possession of the Empire; but had it been necessary to perpetrate one wrongful deed or to kill one innocent man in order to gain the Empire, none of them would have consented to it. In this they were alike.'

'In what way were they different?'

'Tsai Wo, Tzu-kung and Yu Jo were intelligent enough to

1. Cf. ibid., VII. 33. The version there seems less complete.
2. Cf. V. B. I.

appreciate the Sage.[1] They would not have stooped so low as to show a bias in favour of the man they admired. Tsai Wo said, "In my view, the Master surpassed greatly Yao and Shun." Tzu-kung said, "Through the rites of a state he could see its government; through its music, the moral quality of its ruler. Looking back over a hundred generations he was able to appraise all the kings, and no one has ever been able to show him to be wrong in a single instance. Ever since man came into this world, there has never been another like the Master." Yu Jo said, "It is true not only of men. The unicorn is the same in kind as other animals, the phoenix as other birds; Mount T'ai is the same as small mounds of earth; the Yellow River and the Sea are no different from water that runs in the gutter. The Sage, too, is the same in kind as other men.

> Though one of their kind
> He stands far above the crowd.

Ever since man came into this world, there has never been one greater than Confucius." '

3. Mencius said, 'One who uses force while borrowing from benevolence will become leader of the feudal lords,[2] but to do so he must first be the ruler of a state of considerable size. One who puts benevolence into effect through the transforming influence of morality will become a true King, and his success will not depend on the size of his state. T'ang began with only seventy li square, and King Wen with a hundred. When people submit to force they do so not willingly but because they are not strong enough. When people submit to the transforming influence of morality they do so sincerely, with admiration in their hearts. An example of this is the submission of the seventy disciples to Confucius. The Book of Odes says,

> From east, from west,
> From north, from south,
> There was none who did not submit.[3]

This describes well what I have said.'

1. i.e., Confucius.   2. Cf. VII. A. 30.   3. Ode 244.

4. Mencius said, 'Benevolence brings honour; cruelty, disgrace. Now people who dwell in cruelty while disliking disgrace are like those who are content to dwell in a low-lying place while disliking dampness. If one dislikes disgrace, one's best course of action is to honour virtue and to respect Gentlemen. If, when good and wise men are in high office and able men are employed, a ruler takes advantage of times of peace to explain the laws to the people, then even large states will certainly stand in awe of him. The *Book of Odes* says,

> While it has not yet clouded over and rained,
> I take the bark of the mulberry
> And bind fast the windows.
> Now none of the people below
> Will dare treat me with insolence.[1]

Confucius' comment was: "The writer of this poem must have understood the Way. If a ruler is capable of putting his state in order, who would dare treat him with insolence?"

'Now a ruler who takes advantage of times of peace to indulge in pleasure and indolence is courting disaster. There is neither good nor bad fortune which man does not bring upon himself. The *Book of Odes* says,

> Long may he be worthy of Heaven's Mandate
> And seek for himself much good fortune.[2]

The *T'ai Chia* says,

> When Heaven sends down calamities,
> There is hope of weathering them;
> When man brings them upon himself,
> There is no hope of escape.[3]

This describes well what I have said.'

1. Ode 155. This ode is entitled *Ch'ih hsiao* ('Kite-owl') and is written in the first person, representing a bird persecuted by the kite-owl.

2. Ode 235.

3. The *T'ai Chia* is one of the lost chapters of the *Book of History*. This quotation has been incorporated into the spurious chapter of the same title in the present text. See *Shu ching*, 8. 21a.

5. Mencius said, 'If you honour the good and wise and employ the able so that outstanding men are in high position, then Gentlemen throughout the Empire will be only too pleased to serve at your court. In the market-place, if goods are exempted when premises are taxed, and premises exempted when the ground is taxed, then the traders throughout the Empire will be only too pleased to store their goods in your market-place. If there is inspection but no duty at the border stations, then the travellers throughout the Empire will be only too pleased to go by way of your roads. If tillers help in the public fields but pay no tax on the land, then farmers throughout the Empire will be only too pleased to till the land in your realm. If you abolish the levy in lieu of corvée and the levy in lieu of the planting of the mulberry, then all the people of the Empire will be only too pleased to come and settle in your state. If you can truly execute these five measures, the people of your neighbouring states will look up to you as to their father and mother; and since man came into this world no one has succeeded in inciting children against their parents. In this way, you will have no match in the Empire. He who has no match in the Empire is a Heaven-appointed officer, and it has never happened that such a man failed to become a true King.'

6. Mencius said, 'No man is devoid of a heart sensitive to the suffering of others. Such a sensitive heart was possessed by the Former Kings and this manifested itself in compassionate government. With such a sensitive heart behind compassionate goverment, it was as easy to rule the Empire as rolling it on your palm.

'My reason for saying that no man is devoid of a heart sensitive to the suffering of others is this. Suppose a man were, all of a sudden, to see a young child on the verge of falling into a well. He would certainly be moved to compassion, not because he wanted to get in the good graces of the parents, nor because he wished to win the praise of his fellow villagers or friends, nor yet because he disliked the cry of the child. From this it can be seen that whoever is devoid of the heart of compassion is not human, whoever is devoid of the heart of shame is not human, whoever is devoid of the heart of courtesy and modesty is not human, and whoever is devoid of the heart of right and wrong is not human. The heart of compassion is the germ of benevolence; the heart of shame, of dutifulness; the heart of courtesy and modesty, of observance of the rites; the heart of right and wrong, of wisdom. Man has these four germs just as he has four limbs. For a man possessing these four germs to deny his own potentialities is for him to cripple himself; for him to deny the potentialities of his prince is for him to cripple his prince. If a man is able to develop all these four germs that he possesses, it will be like a fire starting up or a spring coming through. When these are fully developed, he can take under his protection the whole realm within the Four Seas, but if he fails to develop them, he will not be able even to serve his parents.'

7. Mencius said, 'Is the maker of arrows really more unfeeling than the maker of armour? He is afraid lest he should fail to harm people, whereas the maker of armour is afraid lest he should fail to protect them. The case is similar with the sorcerer-doctor and the coffin-maker. For this reason one cannot be too careful in the choice of one's calling.

'Confucius said, "The best neighbourhood is where benevolence is to be found. Not to live in such a neighbourhood when one has the choice cannot by any means be considered wise."[1] Benevolence is the high honour bestowed by Heaven and the peaceful abode of man. Not to be benevolent when nothing stands in the way is to show a lack of wisdom. A man neither benevolent nor wise, devoid of courtesy and dutifulness, is a slave. A slave ashamed of serving is like a maker of bows ashamed of making bows, or a maker of arrows ashamed of making arrows. If one is ashamed, there is no better remedy than to practise benevolence. Benevolence is like archery: an archer makes sure his stance is correct before letting fly the arrow, and if he fails to hit the mark, he does not hold it against his victor. He simply seeks the cause within himself.'

8. Mencius said, 'When anyone told him that he had made a mistake, Tzu-lu was delighted. When he heard a fine saying, Yü

1. Cf. the *Analects of Confucius*, IV. 1.

bowed low before the speaker. The Great Shun went even further. He was ever ready to fall into line with others, giving up his own ways for theirs, and glad to take from others that by which he could do good. From the time he was a farmer, a potter and a fisherman to the time he became Emperor, there was nothing he did that he did not take from others. To take from others that by which one can do good is to help them do good. Hence there is nothing more important to a gentleman than helping others do good.'

9. Mencius said, 'Po Yi would serve only the right prince and be-friend only the right man. He would not take his place at the court of an evil man, nor would he converse with him. For him to do so would be like sitting in mud and pitch wearing a court cap and gown. He pushed his dislike for evil to the extent that, if a fellow-villager in his company had his cap awry, he would walk away without even a backward look, as if afraid of being defiled. Hence even when a feudal lord made advances in the politest language, he would repel them. He repelled them simply because it was beneath him to go to the feudal lord.

'Liu Hsia Hui, on the other hand, was not ashamed of a prince with a tarnished reputation, neither did he disdain a modest post. When in office, he did not conceal his own talent, and always acted in accordance with the Way. When he was passed over he harboured no grudge, nor was he distressed even in straitened circumstances. That is why he said,[1] "You are you and I am I. Even if you were to be stark naked by my side, how could you defile me?" Consequently, he was in no hurry to take himself away, and looked perfectly at ease in the other man's company, and would stay when pressed. He stayed when pressed, simply because it was beneath him to insist on leaving.'

Mencius added, 'Po Yi was too straight-laced; Liu Hsia Hui was not dignified enough. A gentleman would follow neither extreme.'

1. In place of 'that is why he said,' the parallel passage in v. b. 1 has the sentence 'when he was with a fellow-villager he simply could not tear himself away'. In the present passage, this sentence must have dropped out by mistake, as without it what follows becomes quite unintelligible.

BOOK II · PART B

1. Mencius said, 'Heaven's favourable weather is less important than Earth's advantageous terrain, and Earth's advantageous terrain is less important than human unity.[1] Suppose you laid siege to a city with inner walls measuring, on each side, three *li* and outer walls measuring seven *li*, and you failed to take it. Now in the course of the siege, there must have been, at one time or another, favourable weather, and in spite of that you failed to take the city. This shows that favourable weather is less important than advantageous terrain. Sometimes a city has to be abandoned in spite of the height of its walls and depth of its moat, the quality of arms and abundance of food supplies. This shows that advantageous terrain is less important than human unity.

'Hence it is said, It is not by boundaries that the people are confined, it is not by difficult terrain that a state is rendered secure, and it is not by superiority of arms that the Empire is kept in awe. One who has the Way will have many to support him; one who has not the Way will have few to support him. In extreme cases, the latter will find even his own flesh and blood turning against him while the former will have the whole Empire at his behest. Hence either a gentleman does not go to war or else he is sure of victory, for he will have the whole Empire at his behest, while his opponent will have even his own flesh and blood turning against him.'

2. Mencius was about to go to court to see the King when a messenger came from the King with the message, 'I was to have come to see you, but I am suffering from a chill and cannot be exposed to the wind. In the morning I shall, however, be holding court. I wonder if I shall have the opportunity of seeing you then.' To this Mencius replied, 'Unfortunately, I too am ill and shall be unable to come to court.'

1. Mencius is here claiming for Man an importance greater even than Heaven and Earth.

The next day, Mencius went on a visit of condolence to the Tung-kuo family. Kung-sun Ch'ou said, 'Yesterday you excused yourself on the ground of illness, yet today you go on a visit of condolence. This is, perhaps, ill-advised.'

'I was ill yesterday, but I am recovered today. Why should I not go on a visit of condolence?'

The King sent someone to inquire after Mencius' illness; and a doctor came. Meng Chung-tzu in reply to the inquiry said, 'Yesterday when the King's summons came, Mencius was ill and was unable to go to court. Today he is somewhat better and has hastened to court. But I am not sure if, in his condition, he will get there.'

Then several men were sent to waylay Mencius with the message, 'Do not, under any circumstances, come home but go straight to court.'

Mencius was forced to go and spend the night with the Ching-ch'ou family.

'Within the family,' said Ching Tzu, 'the relationship between father and son is the most important, while outside, it is that between prince and subject. The former exemplifies love, the latter respect. I have seen the King show you respect, but I have yet to see you show the King respect.'

'What a thing to say! No one in Ch'i talks to the King about benevolence and rightness. Do you think it is because they do not think these beautiful? It is simply because, in their hearts, they say to themselves something to this effect, "How can we talk to *him* about benevolence and rightness?" There is nothing more lacking in respect than that. I have never dared put before the King anything short of the way of Yao and Shun. That is why no man from Ch'i respects the King as much as I.'

'No,' said Ching Tzu. 'That is not what I had in mind. According to the rites, "When summoned by one's father, one should not answer, I am coming.[1] When summoned by one's prince, one should not wait for the horses to be harnessed." You were, in the first instance, about to go to court, but on being summoned by the King you changed your mind. This would seem to be contrary to the rites.'

1. But go immediately.

'Is that what you meant? Tseng Tzu said, "The wealth of Chin and Ch'u cannot be rivalled. They may have their wealth, but I have my benevolence; they may have their exalted rank, but I have my integrity. In what way do I suffer in the comparison?" If this is not right, Tseng Tzu would not have said it. It must be a possible way of looking at the matter. There are three things which are acknowledged by the world to be exalted: rank, age and virtue. At court, rank is supreme; in the village, age; but for assisting the world and ruling over the people it is virtue. How can a man, on the strength of the possession of one of these, treat the other two with condescension? Hence a prince who is to achieve great things must have subjects he does not summon. If he wants to consult them, he goes to them. If he does not honour virtue and delight in the Way in such a manner, he is not worthy of being helped towards the achievement of great things. Take the case of Yi Yin. T'ang had him first as a tutor and only afterwards did he treat him as a minister. As a result, T'ang was able to become a true King without much effort. Again, take the case of Kuan Chung. Duke Huan treated him in exactly the same way and, as a result, was able to become a leader of the feudal lords without much effort. Today there are many states, all equal in size and virtue, none being able to dominate the others. This is simply because the rulers are given to employing those they can teach rather than those 'from whom they can learn. T'ang did not dare summon Yi Yin, nor did Duke Huan dare summon Kuan Chung. Even Kuan Chung could not be summoned, much less someone who would not be a Kuan Chung.'[1]

3. Ch'en Chen asked, 'The other day in Ch'i the King presented you with a hundred *yi* of gold of superior quality and you refused, but in Sung you were presented with seventy *yi* and you accepted; in Hsüeh you likewise accepted fifty *yi*. If your refusal in the first instance was right, then your acceptance on subsequent occasions must be wrong; on the other hand, if your acceptance was right, your refusal must be wrong. You cannot escape one or the other of these two alternatives.'

1. Cf. II. A. I.

'Both refusal and acceptance were right,' said Mencius. 'When I was in Sung, I was about to go on a long journey, and for a traveller there is always a parting gift. The accompanying note said, "Presented as a parting gift." Why then should I have refused? In Hsüeh, I had to take precautions for my safety. The message accompanying the gift said, "I hear that you are taking precautions for your safety. This is a contribution towards the expenses of acquiring arms." Again, why should I have refused? But in the case of Ch'i I had no justification for accepting a gift. To accept a gift without justification is tantamount to being bought. Surely a gentleman should never allow himself to be bought.'

4. Mencius went to P'ing Lu. 'Would you or would you not,' said he to the governor, 'dismiss a lancer who has failed three times in one day to report for duty?'

'I would not wait for the third time.'

'But you yourself have failed to report for duty many times. In years of famine close on a thousand of your people suffered, the old and the young being abandoned in the gutter, the able-bodied scattered in all directions.'[1]

'It was not within my power to do anything about this.'

'Supposing a man were entrusted with the care of cattle and sheep. Surely he ought to seek pasturage and fodder for the animals. If he found that this could not be done, should he return his charge to the owner or should he stand by and watch the animals die?'

'In this I am at fault.'

On another day Mencius saw the King. 'Of the officials who are in charge of your provinces,' said he, 'I know five. The only one who realizes his own fault is K'ung Chü-hsin. May I repeat our conversation for you.'

'In this I am really the one at fault,' said the King.

5. Mencius said to Ch'ih Wa, 'When you gave up the governorship of Ling Ch'iu and requested to be made Marshal of the Guards

1. Cf. I. B. 12, where this is given as the reason for the cold antipathy shown by the people towards those in authority.

your decision seemed right, as your new position offered opportunity for giving advice. That was several months ago. Have you not found an opportunity to speak yet?'

Ch'ih Wa offered advice to the King and tendered his resignation when this was not followed.

'Mencius gave splendid advice to Ch'ih Wa,' said the men of Ch'i, 'but we have yet to hear of him giving as good advice to himself.'

Kung-tu Tzu reported this to Mencius. 'I have heard,' said Mencius, 'that one who holds an office will resign it if he is unable to discharge his duties, and one whose responsibility is to give advice will resign if he is unable to give it. I hold no office, neither have I any responsibility for giving advice. Why should I not have plenty of scope when it comes to the question of staying or leaving?'

6. When Mencius was a Minister of Ch'i he went on a mission of condolence to T'eng. The King of Ch'i made Wang Huan, the governor of Ke, his deputy. Wang Huan went to see Mencius morning and evening, but throughout the journeys to and from T'eng, Mencius never discussed official business with him.

'Your position as Minister of Ch'i,' asked Kung-sun Ch'ou, 'is by no means insignificant, and the distance between Ch'i and T'eng is by no means short, yet throughout the journeys between the two states you never discussed official business with Wang Huan. Why was that?'

'He has managed the whole affair. What was there for me to say?'

7. Mencius returned from Ch'i to Lu for the burial [of his mother], and, on his way back to Ch'i, he put up at Ying.

'Some days ago,' ventured Ch'ung Yü, 'you did not think me unworthy and entrusted me with the task of overseeing the carpenters. As the work was urgent, there was something I dared not ask about. May I ask about it now? The wood seemed to be excessively fine in quality.'[1]

1. This same criticism was used by Mencius' enemies to discredit him. See I. B. 16.

'In high antiquity, there were no regulations governing the inner and outer coffins. In middle antiquity,[1] it was prescribed that the inner coffin was to be seven inches thick with the outer coffin to match. This applied to all conditions of men, from Emperor to Commoner. This is not simply for show. It is only in this way that one can express fully one's filial love. However, if such wood is not available, one cannot have the satisfaction of using it; neither can one if one is unable to afford the cost. When both conditions are fulfilled, the ancients always used wood of fine quality. Why should I alone be an exception? Furthermore, does it not give one some solace to be able to prevent the earth from coming into contact with the dead who is about to decompose? I have heard it said that a gentleman would not for all the world skimp expenditure on his parents.'

8. Shen T'ung asked on his own account, 'Is it all right to march on Yen?'

'Yes,' answered Mencius. 'Tzu-k'uai had no right to give Yen[2] to another; neither had Tzu-chih any right to accept it from Tzu-k'uai. Supposing there were a Gentleman here whom you liked and you were to take it upon yourself to give him your emolument and rank without informing the King, and he, for his part, were to accept these from you without royal sanction. Would this be permissible? The case of Yen is no different from this.'

Ch'i marched on Yen.

'Is it true,' someone asked Mencius, 'that you encouraged Ch'i to march on Yen?'

'No. When Shen T'ung asked me, "Is it all right to march on Yen?" I answered, "Yes." And they marched on Yen. Had he asked, "Who has the right to march on Yen?" I would have

1. According to K'ung Kuang-sen, 'middle antiquity' should be taken to refer to a time before the Duke of Chou, as the different classes came under different regulations according to the rites of the Chou.

2. In 315 B.C. King K'uai of Yen abdicated in favour of his prime minister Tzu-chih. This sparked off an armed conflict in Yen, and it was at this point that King Hsüan of Ch'i intervened. Apart from this and the next section, I. B. 10 and I. B. 11 also refer to this affair.

answered, "A Heaven-appointed officer has the right to do so."
Suppose a man killed another, and someone were to ask, "Is it
all right to kill the killer?" I would answer, "Yes." But if he further
asked, "Who has the right to kill him?" I would answer, "The
Marshal of the Guards has the right to kill him." As it is, it is just
one Yen marching on another Yen. Why should I have encouraged
such a thing?'

9. The people of Yen rose in rebellion. The King of Ch'i said,
'I am very much ashamed to face Mencius.'

'You should not let this affair worry you,' said Ch'en Chia.
'Which do you think a wiser and more benevolent man, the Duke
of Chou or yourself?'

'What a thing to ask!'

'The Duke of Chou made Kuan Shu overlord of Yin and Kuan
Shu used it as a base to stage a rebellion. If the Duke of Chou
sent Kuan Shu knowing what was going to happen, then he was
not benevolent; if he sent him for lack of foresight, then he was
unwise. Even the Duke of Chou left something to be desired in the
way of benevolence and wisdom. How much more in the case of
Your Majesty. May I be permitted to go and disabuse Mencius'
mind?'

He went to see Mencius. 'What sort of a man,' he asked, 'was
the Duke of Chou?'

'A sage of antiquity.'

'Is it true that he made Kuan Shu overlord of Yin and Kuan
Shu used it to stage a rebellion?'

'Yes.'

'Did the Duke send him, knowing that he was going to stage
a rebellion?'

'No. He did not.'

'In that case even a sage makes mistakes.'

'The Duke of Chou was the younger brother of Kuan Shu. Is
it not natural for him to have made such a mistake? Furthermore,
when he made a mistake, the gentleman of antiquity would make
amends, while the gentleman of today persists in his mistakes.
When the gentleman of antiquity made a mistake it was there

to be seen by all the people, like the eclipse of the sun and the
moon; and when he made amends the people looked up to him.[1]
The gentleman of today not only persists in his mistakes but tries
to gloss over them.'

10. Mencius was returning home, having resigned from office. The
King went to see him. 'Previously,' said the King, 'I wished in
vain to meet you. Then I had the opportunity of attending you
in the same court, much to my delight. Now you abandon me and
go home. I wonder if I shall have further opportunities of seeing
you?'

'That is just what I should wish,' answered Mencius, 'though
I did not dare make the suggestion.'

On another day, the King said to Shih Tzu. 'I wish to give
Mencius a house in the most central part of my capital and a pension
of ten thousand measures of rice for the support of his disciples, so
that my officials and my people will have an example to look up
to. Why do you not sound him out for me?'

Shih Tzu informed Mencius of this through Ch'en Tzu. When
Mencius heard Shih Tzu's message through Ch'en Tzu, he said,
'I see. But then Shih Tzu cannot be expected to realize that this
cannot be done. Do you think that I am after wealth? If I were,
would I give up a hundred thousand measures and accept ten
thousand instead?

'Chi Sun once said, "How odd Tzu-shu Yi was! His advice was
not followed while he was in office. This did not prevent him from
getting the younger members of his family into high office. Who
is there that does not want wealth and rank? But he was the only
one that had his own 'vantage point' therein." In antiquity, the
market was for the exchange of what one had for what one lacked.
The authorities merely supervised it. There was, however, a des-
picable fellow who always looked for a vantage point and, going
up on it, gazed into the distance to the left and to the right in order
to secure for himself all the profit there was in the market. The
people all thought him despicable, and, as a result, they taxed him.
The taxing of merchants began with this despicable fellow.'

1. Cf. the *Analects of Confucius*, XIX. 21.

11. Mencius left Ch'i and on his way put up at Chou. There was a man who wished to persuade Mencius to stay on behalf of the King. He sat upright and began to speak, but Mencius made no reply and lay down, leaning against the low table.

The visitor was displeased. 'Only after observing a day's fast,' said he, 'dare I speak. You, Master, simply lie down and make no effort to listen to me. I shall never dare present myself again.'

'Be seated. I shall speak to you plainly. In the time of Duke Mu of Lu, if he did not have one of his own men close to Tzu-ssu he could not have kept Tzu-ssu happy. On the other hand, Hsieh Liu and Shen Hsiang remained secure only by having one of their own friends close to the Duke. You, my son, are trying to arrange things on my behalf, yet you fall short of following the example of Tzu-ssu. Are you refusing to have anything to do with me, or am I refusing to have anything to do with you?'

12. After Mencius left Ch'i, Yin Shih said to someone, 'If he did not realize that the King could not become a T'ang or a King Wu he was blind, but if he came realizing it, he was simply after advancement. He came a thousand *li* to see the King, and left because he met with no success. It took him three nights to go beyond Chou. Why was he so long about it? I for one find this most distasteful.'

Kau Tzu[1] told Mencius of this. 'How little,' said Mencius, 'does Yin Shih understand me. I came a thousand *li* to see the King because I wanted to. Having met with no success, I am leaving, not because I want to but because I have no alternative. True, it took me three nights to go beyond Chou. But even then I felt that I had not taken long enough. I had hoped against hope that the King would change his mind. I was sure he would recall me if this happened. It was only when I went beyond Chou and the King made no attempt to send after me that the desire to go home

1. There are at least three people whose names come out in romanization as 'Kao Tzu'. To avoid confusion, I have decided arbitrarily to reserve 'Kao Tzu' for the philosopher who discusses the problem of human nature with Mencius in Book VI. For the others I use the spelling 'Kau'. The 'Kau Tzu' here is probably the same as the 'Kau Tzu' who appears in VII. B. 21 and VII. B. 22, while the 'Kau Tzu' who figures in VI. B. 3 seems to be an older man and so a different person.

surged up in me. Even then it was not as if I had abandoned the King. The King is still capable of doing good. If the King had employed me, it would not simply be a matter of bringing peace to the people of Ch'i, but of bringing peace to the people of the whole Empire as well. If only the King would change his mind: that is what I hope for every day. I am not like those petty men who, when their advice is rejected by the prince, take offence and show resentment all over their faces, and, when they leave, travel all day before they would put up for the night.'

Yin Shih, on hearing this, said, 'I am indeed a petty man.'

13. When Mencius left Ch'i, on the way Ch'ung Yü asked, 'Master, you look somewhat unhappy. I heard from you the other day that a gentleman reproaches neither Heaven nor man.'

'This is one time; that was another time. Every five hundred years a true King should arise, and in the interval there should arise one from whom an age takes its name. From Chou to the present, it is over seven hundred years. The five hundred mark is passed; the time seems ripe. It must be that Heaven does not as yet wish to bring peace to the Empire. If it did, who is there in the present time other than myself? Why should I be unhappy?'

14. Mencius left Ch'i and stayed at Hsiu. Kung-sun Ch'ou asked, 'Is it ancient practice to take office without accepting pay?'

'No. In Ch'ung after I had my first audience with the King, I already had the intention of leaving. It was because I did not want to have to change my mind subsequently that I did not accept pay in the first place. It so happened that war broke out and I had no opportunity of requesting permission to leave. It never was my intention to remain long in Ch'i.'

1. Duke Wen of T'eng, while still crown prince, was once going to Ch'u. While passing through Sung, he saw Mencius who talked to him about the goodness of human nature, always citing as his authorities Yao and Shun.

On the way back from Ch'u the crown prince again saw Mencius.

'Does Your Highness doubt my words?' asked Mencius. 'There is one Way and one only. Ch'eng Chien said to Duke Ching of Ch'i, "He is a man and I am a man. Why should I be in awe of him?" Similarly, Yen Hui said, "What sort of a man was Shun? And what sort of a man am I? Anyone who can make anything of himself will be like that." Kung-ming Yi said, "When he said that he modelled himself on King Wen, the Duke of Chou was only telling the truth."

'Now if you reduce T'eng to a regular shape, it would have a territory of almost fifty *li* square. It is big enough for you to do good.[1] [5]

'The *Book of History* says,

If the medicine does not make the head swim, the illness will not be cured.'[2]

2. Duke Ting of T'eng died. The crown prince said to Jan Yu, 'I have never been able to forget what Mencius once said to me in Sung. Now that I have had the misfortune to lose my father, I want you to go and ask Mencius' advice before making funeral arrangements.'

Jan Yu went to Tsou to ask Mencius' advice.

'Splendid,' said Mencius. 'The funeral of a parent is an occasion

1. Omitting the word *kuo*. Otherwise the translation would be, 'It is big enough to be a good state.'

2. This saying is also to be found in the *Kuo yü* (*Ch'u yü I*) where it is said to be from the *Book of Wu Ting*. It has been incorporated into the spurious *Yüeh Ming I* of the present *Shu ching* (10. 3a).

for giving of one's utmost.[1] Tseng Tzu said, "Serve your parents in accordance with the rites during their lifetime; bury them in accordance with the rites when they die; offer sacrifices to them in accordance with the rites; and you deserve to be called a good son."[2] I am afraid I am not conversant with the rites observed by the feudal lords. Still, I have heard something about funeral rites. Three years as the mourning period, mourning dress made of rough hemp with a hem, the eating of nothing but rice gruel – these were observed in the Three Dynasties by men of all conditions alike, from Emperor to Commoner.'

Jan Yu reported this to the crown prince, and it was decided to observe the three-year mourning period. The elders and all the officials were opposed to this and said, 'The ancestral rulers of the eldest branch of our house in Lu never observed this; neither did our own ancestral rulers. When it comes to you, you go against our accepted practice. This is perhaps ill-advised. Furthermore, the *Records* say, "In funeral and sacrifice, one follows the practice of one's ancestors ...", "I have authority for what I do".

The crown prince said to Jan Yu, 'In the past I have never paid much attention to studies, caring only for riding and fencing. Now the elders and all my officials do not think too highly of me, and I am afraid they may not give of their best in this matter. Go and consult Mencius for me.'

Jan Yu went once again to Tsou to ask Mencius for advice.

'I see,' said Mencius. 'But in this matter the solution cannot be sought elsewhere. Confucius said, "When the ruler dies the heir entrusts his affairs to the steward[3] and sips rice gruel, showing a deep inky colour on his face. He then takes his place and weeps, and none of his numerous officials dare show a lack of grief. This is because he sets the example. When someone above shows a preference for anything, there is certain to be someone below who will outdo him. The gentleman's virtue is like wind; the virtue of the common people is like grass. Let the wind sweep over the

1. Cf. the *Analects of Confucius*, XIX. 17
2. Cf. ibid, II. 5, where the saying is attributed to Confucius.
3. Cf. ibid., XIV. 41.

grass, and the grass is sure to bend."[1] It rests with the crown prince.'

Jan Yu reported on his mission.

'That is so,' said the crown prince. 'It does, indeed, rest with me.'

For five months he stayed in his mourning hut, issuing no orders or prohibitions. The officials and his kinsmen approved of his actions and thought him well-versed in the rites. When it was time for the burial ceremony, people came from all quarters to watch. He showed such a grief-stricken countenance and wept so bitterly that the mourners were greatly delighted.

3. Duke Wen of T'eng asked about government.

'The business of the people,' said Mencius, 'must be attended to without delay. The *Book of Odes* says,

> In the day time they go for grass;
> At night they make it into ropes.
> They hasten to repair the roof;
> Then they begin sowing the crops.[2]

This is the way of the common people. Those with constant means of support will have constant hearts, while those without constant means will not have constant hearts. Lacking constant hearts, they will go astray and get into excesses, stopping at nothing. To punish them after they have fallen foul of the law is to set a trap for the people. How can a benevolent man in authority allow himself to set a trap for the people?[3] Hence a good ruler is always respectful and thrifty, courteous and humble, and takes from the people no more than is prescribed. Yang Hu said, "If one's aim is wealth one cannot be benevolent; if one's aim is benevolence one cannot be wealthy."

'In the Hsia Dynasty, each family was given fifty *mu* of land, and the "*kung*" method of taxation was used; in the Yin, each family was given seventy *mu* and the "*chu*" method was used;

1. Cf. ibid., XII. 19.
2. Ode 154.
3. This passage is also found in I. A. 7.

in the Chou, each family was given a hundred *mu* and the "*ch'e*" method was used. In fact, all three amounted to a taxation of one in ten. "*Ch'e*" means "commonly practised"; "*chu*" means "to lend help". Lung Tzu said, "In administering land, there is no better method than *chu* and no worse than *kung*." With the *kung* method, the payment due is calculated on the average yield over a number of years. In good years when rice is so plentiful that it goes to waste, the people are no more heavily taxed, though this would mean no hardship; while in bad years, when there is not enough to spare for fertilizing the fields, the full quota is insisted upon. If he who is father and mother to the people makes it necessary for them to borrow because they do not get enough to minister to the needs of their parents in spite of having toiled incessantly all the year round, and causes the old and young to be abandoned in the gutter, wherein is he father and mother to the people?

'Hereditary emolument as a matter of fact is already practised in T'eng.

'The *Book of Odes* says,

> The rain falls on our public land,
> And so also on our private land.[1]

There is "public land" only when *chu* is practised. From this we see that even the Chou practised *chu*.[2]

' "*Hsiang*", "*hsü*", "*hsüeh*" and "*hsiao*" were set up for the purpose of education. "*Hsiang*" means "rearing", "*hsiao*" means "teaching" and "*hsü*" means "archery".[3] In the Hsia Dynasty it was called "*hsiao*", in the Yin "*hsü*" and in the Chou "*hsiang*", while "*hsüeh*" was a name common to all the Three Dynasties. They all serve to make the people understand human relationships.[4] When it is clear that those in authority understand

1. Ode 212.

2. Although he said earlier on that they used the *ch'e* method. On this point cf. I. B. 5, 'Formerly, when King Wen ruled over Ch'i, tillers of land were taxed one part in nine; descendants of officials received hereditary emoluments.'

3. These are phonetic glosses, being near homophones of the words glossed.

4. For the importance of understanding human relationships, cf., for instance, IV. B. 19, 'Shun understood the way of things and had a keen insight into human relationships.' and III. A. 4.

human relationships, the people will be affectionate. Should a true King arise, he is certain to take this as his model. Thus he who practises this will be tutor to a true King.

'The *Book of Odes* says,

> Though Chou is an old state,
> Its Mandate is new.[1]

This refers to King Wen. If you can put heart into your practice you would also be able to renew your state.'

The Duke sent Pi Chan to ask about the well-field system.

'Your prince,' said Mencius, 'is going to practise benevolent government and has chosen you for this mission. You must do your best. Benevolent government must begin with land demarcation. When boundaries are not properly drawn, the division of land according to the well-field system and the yield of grain used for paying officials cannot be equitable. For this reason, despotic rulers and corrupt officials always neglect the boundaries. Once the boundaries are correctly fixed, there will be no difficulty in settling the distribution of land and the determination of emolument.

'T'eng is limited in territory. Nevertheless, there will be men in authority and there will be the common people. Without the former, there would be none to rule over the latter; without the latter, there would be none to support the former. I suggest that in the country the tax should be one in nine, using the method of *chu*, but in the capital it should be one in ten, to be levied in kind. From Ministers downwards, every official should have fifty *mu* of land for sacrificial purposes. In ordinary households, every extra man is to be given another twenty-five *mu*. Neither in, burying the dead, nor in changing his abode, does a man go beyond the confines of his village. If those who own land within each *ching*[2] befriend one another both at home and abroad, help each other

---

1. Ode 235.

2. As can be seen from the sequel, when a piece of land is divided into nine parts, it looks like the Chinese character *ching* 井 . Hence the system is known as *ching*-fields. The common translation of the term as 'well-fields', being based on the accident that the word *ching* means 'a well', is somewhat misleading, but I have kept it as it has become the standard translation.

to keep watch, and succour each other in illness, they will live in love and harmony. A *ching* is a piece of land measuring one *li* square, and each *ching* consists of 900 *mu*. Of these, the central plot of 100 *mu* belongs to the state, while the other eight plots of 100 *mu* each are held by eight families who share the duty of caring for the plot owned by the state. Only when they have done this duty dare they turn to their own affairs. This is what sets the common people apart.

'This is a rough outline. As for embellishments, I leave them to your prince and yourself.'

4. There was a man by the name of Hsü Hsing who preached the teachings of Shen Nung.[1] He came to T'eng from Ch'u, went up to the gate and told Duke Wen, 'I, a man from distant parts, have heard that you, my lord, practise benevolent government. I wish to be given a place to live and become one of your subjects.'

The Duke gave him a place.

His followers, numbering several score, all wore unwoven hemp, and lived by making sandals and mats.

Ch'en Hsiang and his brother Hsin, both followers of Ch'en Liang, came to T'eng from Sung, carrying ploughs on their backs. 'We have heard,' said they, 'that you, my lord, practise the government of the sages. In that case you must yourself be a sage. We wish to be the subjects of a sage.'

Ch'en Hsiang met Hsü Hsing and was delighted with his teachings, so he abjured what he had learned before and became a follower of Hsü Hsing.

Ch'en Hsiang saw Mencius and cited the words of Hsü Hsing. 'The prince of T'eng is a truly good and wise ruler. However, he has never been taught the Way. To earn his keep a good and wise ruler shares the work of tilling the land with his people. He rules while cooking his own meals. Now T'eng has granaries and treasuries. This is for the prince to inflict hardship on the people in order to keep himself. How can he be a good and wise prince?'

'Does Hsü Tzu only eat grain he has grown himself?' asked Mencius.

1. The legendary Emperor credited with the invention of agriculture.

'Yes.'

'Does Hsü Tzu only wear cloth he has woven himself?'

'No. He wears unwoven hemp.'

'Does Hsü Tzu wear a cap?'

'Yes.'

'What kind of cap does he wear?'

'Plain raw silk.'

'Does he weave it himself?'

'No. He trades grain for it.'

'Why does Hsü Tzu not weave it himself?'

'Because it interferes with his work in the fields.'

'Does Hsü Tzu use an iron pot and an earthenware steamer for cooking rice and iron implements for ploughing the fields?'

'Yes.'

'Does he make them himself?'

'No. He trades grain for them.'

'To trade grain for implements is not to inflict hardship on the potter and the blacksmith. The potter and the blacksmith, for their part, also trade their wares for grain. In doing this, surely they are not inflicting hardship on the farmer either. Why does Hsü Tzu not be a potter and a blacksmith as well so that he can get everything he needs from his own house? Why does he indulge in such multifarious trading with men who practise the hundred crafts? Why does Hsü Tzu put up with so much bother?'

'It is naturally impossible to combine the work of tilling the land with that of a hundred different crafts.'

'Now, is ruling the Empire such an exception that it can be combined with the work of tilling the land? There are affairs of great men, and there are affairs of small men. Moreover, it is necessary for each man to use the products of all the hundred crafts. If everyone must make everything he uses, the Empire will be led along the path of incessant toil. Hence it is said, "There are those who use their minds and there are those who use their muscles. The former rule; the latter are ruled. Those who rule are supported by those who are ruled." This is a principle accepted by the whole Empire.

'In the time of Yao, the Empire was not yet settled. The Flood[1] still raged unchecked, inundating the Empire; plants grew thickly; birds and beasts multiplied; the five grains did not ripen; birds and beasts encroached upon men, and their trail criss-crossed even the Central Kingdoms. The lot fell on Yao to worry about this situation. He raised Shun to a position of authority to deal with it. Shun put Yi in charge of fire. Yi set the mountains and valleys alight and burnt them, and the birds and beasts went into hiding. Yü dredged the Nine Rivers, cleared the courses of the Chi and the T'a to channel the water into the Sea, deepened the beds of the Ju and the Han, and raised the dykes of the Huai and the Ssu to empty them into the River. Only then were the people of the Central Kingdoms able to find food for themselves. During this time Yü spent eight years abroad and passed the door of his own house three times without entering. Even if he had wished to plough the fields, could he have done it?

'Hou Chi taught the people how to cultivate land and the five kinds of grain. When these ripened, the people multiplied. This is the way of the common people: once they have a full belly and warm clothes on their back they degenerate to the level of animals if they are allowed to lead idle lives, without education and discipline. This gave the sage King further cause for concern, and so he appointed Hsieh as the Minister of Education whose duty was to teach the people human relationships: love between father and son, duty between ruler and subject, distinction between husband and wife, precedence of the old over the young, and faith between friends. Fang Hsün[2] said,

> Encourage them in their toil,
> Put them on the right path,
> Aid them and help them,
> Make them happy in their station,
> And by bountiful acts further relieve them of hardship.

The Sage worried to this extent about the affairs of the people. How could he have leisure to plough the fields? Yao's only

1. Cf. p. 113 and Appendix 4.
2. i.e., Yao.

worry was that he should fail to find someone like Shun, and Shun's only worry was that he should fail to find someone like Yü and Kao Yao. He who worries about his plot of a hundred *mu* not being well cultivated is a mere farmer.

'To share one's wealth with others is generosity; to teach others to be good is conscientiousness; to find the right man for the Empire is benevolence. Hence it is easier to give the Empire away than to find the right man for it.

'Confucius said, "Great indeed was Yao as a ruler! Heaven alone is great, and it was Yao who modelled himself on Heaven. So great was he that the people could not find a name for him. What a ruler Shun was! He was so lofty that while in possession of the Empire he held aloof from it."[1]

'It is not true that Yao and Shun did not have to use their minds to rule the Empire. Only they did not use their minds to plough the fields.

'I have heard of the Chinese converting barbarians to their ways, but not of their being converted to barbarian ways. Ch'en Liang was a native of Ch'u. Being delighted with the way of the Duke of Chou and Confucius, he came north to study in the Central Kingdoms. Even the scholars in the north could not surpass him in any way. He was what one would call an outstanding scholar. You and your brother studied under him for scores of years, and now that your teacher is dead, you turn your back on him.

'When Confucius died and the three-year mourning period had elapsed, his disciples packed their bags and prepared to go home. They went in and bowed to Tzu-kung and facing one another they wept until they lost their voices before setting out for home. Tzu-kung went back to build a hut in the burial grounds and remained there on his own for another three years before going home. One day, Tzu-hsia, Tzu-chang and Tzu-yu wanted to serve Yu Jo as they had served Confucius because of his resemblance to the Sage. They tried to force Tseng Tzu to join them, but Tseng Tzu said, "That will not do. Washed by the River and the river Han, bleached by the autumn sun, so immaculate was he that his whiteness could not be surpassed."

1. Cf. the *Analects of Confucius*, VIII. 18, 19.

'Now you turn your back on the way of your teacher in order to follow the southern barbarian with the twittering tongue, who condemns the way of the Former Kings. You are indeed different from Tseng Tzu. I have heard of coming out of the dark ravine to settle on a tall tree, but not of forsaking the tall tree to descend into the dark ravine. The *Lu sung* says,

> It was the barbarians that he attacked;
> It was Ching and Shu that he punished.[1]

It is these people the Duke of Chou was going to punish and you want to learn from. That is not a change for the better, is it?'

'If we follow the way of Hsü Tzu there will only be one price in the market, and dishonesty will disappear from the capital. Even if you send a mere boy to the market, no one will take advantage of him. For equal lengths of cloth or silk, for equal weights of hemp, flax or raw silk, and for equal measures of the five grains, the price will be the same; for shoes of the same size, the price will also be the same.'

'That things are unequal is part of their nature. Some are worth twice or five times, ten or a hundred times, even a thousand and ten thousand times, more than others. If you reduce them to the same level, it will only bring confusion to the Empire. If a roughly finished shoe sells at the same price as a finely finished one, who would make the latter? If we follow the way of Hsü Tzu, we will be showing one another the way to being dishonest. How can one govern a state in this way?'

5. Yi Chih, a Mohist, sought to meet Mencius through the good offices of Hsü Pi. 'I wish to see him too,' said Mencius, 'but at the moment I am not well. When I get better, I shall go to see him. There is no need for him to come here.'

Another day, he sought to see Mencius again. Mencius said, 'Now I can see him. If one does not put others right, one cannot hold the Way up for everyone to see. I shall put him right. I have heard that Yi Tzu is a Mohist. In funerals, the Mohists follow the way of frugality. Since Yi Tzu wishes to convert the Empire to

1. Ode 300.

frugality, it must be because he thinks it the only honourable way. But then Yi Tzu gave his parents lavish burials. In so doing, he treated his parents in a manner he did not esteem.'

Hsü Tzu reported this to Yi Tzu.

'The Confucians,' said Yi Tzu, 'praised the ancient rulers for acting "as if they were tending a new-born babe."[1] What does this saying mean? In my opinion, it means that there should be no gradations in love, though the practice of it begins with one's parents.'

Hsü Tzu reported this to Mencius.

'Does Yi Tzu truly believe,' said Mencius, 'that a man loves his brother's son no more than his neighbour's new-born babe? He is singling out a special feature in a certain case: when the new-born babe creeps towards a well it is not its fault.[2] Moreover, when Heaven produces things, it gives them a single basis, yet Yi Tzu tries to give them a dual one.[3] This accounts for his belief.

'Presumably there must have been cases in ancient times of people not burying their parents. When the parents died, they were thrown in the gullies. Then one day the sons passed the place and there lay the bodies, eaten by foxes and sucked by flies. A sweat broke out on their brows, and they could not bear to look. The sweating was not put on for others to see. It was an outward expression of their innermost heart. They went home for baskets and spades. If it was truly right for them to bury the remains of their parents, then it must also be right for all dutiful sons and benevolent men to do likewise.'

Hsü Tzu repeated this to Yi Tzu who looked lost for quite a while and replied, 'I have taken his point.'

1. This saying is to be found in the *K'ang kao* chapter of the *Book of History*. (*Shu ching*, 14. 6b.)

2. This seems to be a reference to the example given in II. A. 6 of a new-born babe creeping towards a well.

3. By a dual basis, Mencius is presumably referring to the incompatibility between the denial of gradations of love and the insistence on its practice beginning with one's parents.

BOOK III · PART B

1. Ch'en Tai said, 'When you refused even to see them, the feudal lords naturally appeared insignificant to you. Now that you have seen them, they are either kings or, at least, leaders of the feudal lords. Moreover, it is said in the *Records*, "Bend the foot in order to straighten the yard." That seems worth doing.'

'Once,' said Mencius, 'Duke Ching of Ch'i went hunting and summoned his gamekeeper with a pennon.[1] The gamekeeper did not come, and the Duke was going to have him put to death. "A man whose mind is set on high ideals never forgets that he may end in a ditch; a man of valour never forgets that he may forfeit his head." What did Confucius find praiseworthy in the gamekeeper? His refusal to answer to a form of summons to which he was not entitled.[2] What can one do about those who go without even being summoned? Moreover, the saying "Bend the foot in order to straighten the yard" refers to profit. If it is for profit, I suppose one might just as well bend the yard to straighten the foot.

'Once, Viscount Chien of Chao sent Wang Liang to drive the chariot for his favourite, Hsi. In the whole day they failed to catch one single bird. Hsi reported to his master, "He is the worst charioteer in the world." Someone told Wang Liang of this. Liang asked, "May I have another chance?" It was with difficulty that Hsi was persuaded, but in one morning they caught ten birds. Hsi reported to his master, "He is the best charioteer in the world." "I shall make him drive for you," said Viscount Chien. He asked Wang Liang, but Wang Liang refused. "I drove for him according to the proper rules," said he, "and we did not catch a single bird all day. Then I used underhand methods, and we caught ten birds in one morning. The *Book of Odes* says,

1. For this incident see the *Tso chuan*, Duke Chao 20. Cf pp. 157–8 where the appropriate means of summons are explained.
2. Cf. v. b. 7.

> He never failed to drive correctly,
> And his arrows went straight for the target.[1]

I am not used to driving for small men. May I be excused?"

'Even a charioteer is ashamed to be in league with an archer. When doing so means catching enough birds to pile up like a mountain, he would still rather not do it. What can one do about those who bend the Way in order to please others? You are further mistaken. There has never been a man who could straighten others by bending himself.'

2. Ching Ch'un said, 'Were not Kung-sun Yen and Chang Yi great men? As soon as they showed their wrath the feudal lords trembled with fear, and when they were still the Empire was spared the conflagration of war.'

'How can they be thought great men?' said Mencius. 'Have you never studied the rites? When a man comes of age his father gives him advice.[2] When a girl marries, her mother gives her advice, and accompanies her to the door with these cautionary words, "When you go to your new home, you must be respectful and circumspect. Do not disobey your husband." It is the way of a wife or concubine to consider obedience and docility the norm.

'A man lives in the spacious dwelling, occupies the proper position, and goes along the highway of the Empire.[3] When he achieves his ambition he shares these with the people; when he fails to do so he practises the Way alone. He cannot be led into excesses when wealthy and honoured or deflected from his purpose when poor and obscure, nor can he be made to bow before superior force. This is what I would call a great man.'

3. Chou Hsiao asked, 'Did the gentlemen in ancient times take office?'

1. Ode 179.
2. Judging by the context, the advice given by the father should be quoted as a contrast to that given by the mother. Otherwise, there seems little point in just mentioning the father's advice. The present text is probably defective.
3. Cf. 'Benevolence is man's peaceful abode and rightness his proper path' (IV. A. 10).

'Yes,' said Mencius. 'The *Records* say, "When Confucius was not in the service of a lord for three months, he became agitated. When he left for another state, he always took a present for the first audience with him." Kung-ming Yi said, "In ancient times when a man was not in the service of a lord for three months he was offered condolences."'

'Does this not show an unseemly haste?'

'A Gentleman losing his position is like a feudal lord losing his state. The *Rites* say, "A feudal lord takes part in the ploughing to supply the grain for sacrificial offerings. His wife takes part in sericulture to provide the material for sacrificial dresses. When the sacrificial animals are not fat, the grain not clean and the items of dress not ready, he dare not perform the sacrifice. In the case of a Gentleman, if he has no land, he does not offer sacrifice. When the vessels used for killing the animals and the items of dress are not ready, he dare neither offer sacrifices nor hold banquets." Is this not serious enough for condolences to be offered?'

'Why did Confucius always take a present with him when he left for another state?'

'A Gentleman takes office as a farmer cultivates his land. Does a farmer leave his farming tools behind just because he is leaving for another state?'

'People here in Chin take office as in any other state, but I have never heard of such haste. If taking office is such an urgent matter, why does a Gentleman find it so hard to take office?'

'When a man is born his parents wish that he may one day find a wife, and when a woman is born they wish that she may find a husband. Every parent feels like this. But those who bore holes in the wall to peep at one another, and climb over it to meet illicitly, waiting for neither the command of parents nor the good offices of a go-between, are despised by parents and fellow-countrymen alike. In ancient times men were indeed eager to take office, but they disliked seeking it by dishonourable means, for all [6] those who do so are no different from the men and women who bore holes in the wall.'

4. P'eng Keng asked, 'Is it not excessive to travel with a retinue of hundreds of followers in scores of chariots, and to live off one feudal lord after another?'

'If it is not in accordance with the Way,' answered Mencius, 'one should not accept even one basketful of rice from another person. On the other hand, Shun accepted the Empire from Yao without considering it excessive, when it was in accordance with the Way. Or perhaps you consider even this excessive?'

'No. But it is not right for a Gentleman not to earn his keep.'

'If people cannot trade the surplus of the fruits of their labours to satisfy one another's needs, then the farmer will be left with surplus grain and the women with surplus cloth. If things are exchanged, you can feed the carpenter and the carriage-maker. Here is a man. He is obedient to his parents at home and respectful to his elders abroad and acts as custodian of the way of the Former Kings for the benefit of future students. In spite of that, you say he ought not to be fed. Why do you place more value on the carpenter and the carriage-maker than on a man who practises morality?'

'It is the intention of the carpenter and the carriage-maker to make a living. When a Gentleman pursues the Way, is it also his intention to make a living?'

'What has intention got to do with it? If he does good work for you then you ought to feed him whenever possible. Moreover, do you feed people on account of their intentions or on account of their work?'

'Their intentions.'

'Here is a man who makes wild movements with his trowel, ruining the tiles. Would you feed him because his intention is to make a living?'

'No.'

'Then you feed people on account of their work, not on account of their intentions.'

5. Wan Chang asked, 'If Sung, a small state, were to practise Kingly government and be attacked by Ch'i and Ch'u for doing so, what could be done about it?'

'When T'ang was in Po,' answered Mencius, 'his territory

adjoined the state of Ke. The Earl of Ke was a wilful man who neglected his sacrificial duties. T'ang sent someone to ask, "Why do you not offer sacrifices?" "We have no suitable animals." T'ang sent gifts of oxen and sheep to the Earl of Ke, but he used them for food and continued to neglect his sacrificial duties. T'ang once again sent someone to ask, "Why do you not offer sacrifices?" "We have no suitable grain." T'ang sent the people of Po to help in the ploughing and also sent the aged and young with gifts of food. The Earl of Ke led his people out and waylaid those who were bringing wine, food, millet and rice, trying to take these things from them by force. Those who resisted were killed. A boy bearing millet and meat was killed and the food taken. The *Book of History* says,

> The Earl of Ke treated those who brought food as enemies.

That is the incident to which this refers. When an army was sent to punish Ke for killing the boy, the whole Empire said, "This is not coveting the Empire but avenging common men and common women."

> T'ang began his punitive expeditions with Ke.[1]

In eleven expeditions he became matchless in the Empire. When he marched on the east, the western barbarians complained, and when he marched on the south, the northern barbarians complained. They all said, "Why does he not come to us first?"[2] The people longed for his coming as they longed for rain in time of severe drought. Those who were going to market did not stop; those who were weeding went on weeding. He punished the rulers and comforted the people, like a fall of timely rain, and the people rejoiced greatly. The *Book of History* says,

> We await our Lord. When he comes we will suffer no more.

The state of Yu did not submit. The King went east to punish it, bringing peace to men and women. They put bundles of black and

1. For this quotation and the whole of the passage following, see the parallel passage in I. B. 11.
2. Cf. also VII. B. 4.

yellow silk into baskets as gifts, seeking the honour of an audience
with the King of Chou, and declared themselves subjects of the great
state of Chou.[1]

The gentlemen filled baskets with black and yellow silk to bid the
gentlemen welcome; the common people brought baskets of food
and bottles of drink to bid the common people welcome. The
King of Chou rescued the people from water and fire and took
captive only their cruel masters. The *T'ai shih* says,

> We show our military might and attack the territory of Yü, taking
> captive their cruel rulers. Our punitive acts are glorious. In this we
> surpass even T'ang.[2]

It is all a matter of failing to practise Kingly government. If you
should practise Kingly government, all within the Four Seas
would raise their heads to watch for your coming, desiring you as
their ruler. Ch'i and Ch'u may be big in size, but what is there to be
afraid of?'

6. Mencius said to Tai Pu-sheng, 'Do you wish your King[3] to be
good? I shall speak to you plainly. Suppose a Counsellor of Ch'u
wished his son to speak the language of Ch'i. Would he have a
man from Ch'i to tutor his son? Or would he have a man from
Ch'u?'

'He would have a man from Ch'i to tutor his son.'

'With one man from Ch'i tutoring the boy and a host of Ch'u
men chattering around him, even though you caned him every
day to make him speak Ch'i, you would not succeed. Take him
away to some district like Chuang and Yüeh[4] for a few years,
then even if you caned him every day to make him speak Ch'u,

1. This quotation about the state of Yu is presumably also from a lost
chapter of the *Book of History*, though it has been incorporated into the
spurious *Wu ch'eng* of the present text. See *Shu ching*, 11. 23b.

2. From the lost *T'ai shih*, though in the present *Book of History*, this has
again been incorporated into the spurious chapter bearing the same name. See
ibid., 11. 10a.

3. This is Yen, the King of Sung.

4. It is possible that these are names of streets in Ch'i.

you would not succeed. You have placed Hsüeh Chü-chou near the King because you think him a good man. If everyone around the King, old or young, high or low, is a Hsüeh Chü-chou, then who will help the King to do evil? But if no one around the King is a Hsüeh Chü-chou, then who will help the King to do good? What difference can one Hsüeh Chü-chou make to the King of Sung?'

7. Kung-sun Ch'ou asked, 'What is the significance of your not trying to see the feudal lords?'

'In ancient times,' said Mencius, 'one did not try to see a feudal lord unless one held office under him. Tuan-kan Mu climbed over a wall to avoid a meeting;[1] Hsieh Liu bolted his door and refused admittance.[2] Both went too far. When forced, one may see them.

'Yang Hu wanted to see Confucius, but disliked acting in a manner contrary to the rites. When a Counsellor made a gift to a Gentleman, the Gentleman, if he was not at home to receive it, had to go to the Counsellor's home to offer his thanks. Yang Hu waited until Confucius was out before presenting him with a steamed piglet. But Confucius also waited until Yang Hu went out before going to offer his thanks.[3] At that time if Yang Hu had taken the initiative in showing courtesy to Confucius, how could Confucius have refused to see him? Tseng Tzu said, "It is more fatiguing to shrug one's shoulders and smile ingratiatingly than to work on a vegetable plot in the summer." Tzu-lu said, "To concur while not in agreement and to show this by blushing is quite beyond my understanding." From this it is not difficult to see what it is a gentleman cultivates in himself.'

8. Tai Ying-chih said, 'We are unable in the present year to change over to a tax of one in ten and to abolish custom and market duties. What would you think if we were to make some reductions and wait till next year before putting the change fully into effect?'

'Here is a man,' said Mencius, 'who appropriates one of his

---

1. With the lord of Wei.
2. To the Duke of Lu.
3. Cf. the *Analects of Confucius*, XVII. 1.

neighbour's chickens every day. Someone tells him, "This is not how a gentleman behaves." He answers, "May I reduce it to one chicken every month and wait until next year to stop altogether?"

'When one realizes that something is morally wrong, one should stop it as soon as possible. Why wait for next year?'

9. Kung-tu Tzu said, 'Outsiders all say that you, Master, are fond of disputation. May I ask why?'

'I am not fond of disputation,' answered Mencius. 'I have no alternative. The world has existed for a long time, now in peace, now in disorder. In the time of Yao, the water reversed its natural course, flooding the central regions, and the reptiles made their homes there, depriving the people of a settled life. In low-lying regions, people lived in nests; in high regions, they lived in caves. The *Book of History* says,

> The Deluge was a warning to us.[1]

By the "Deluge" was meant the "Flood". Yü was entrusted with the task of controlling it. He led the flood water into the seas by cutting channels for it in the ground, and drove the reptiles into grassy marshes. The water, flowing through the channels, formed the Yangtse, the Huai, the Yellow River and the Han. Obstacles receded and the birds and beasts harmful to men were annihilated. Only then were the people able to level the ground and live on it.

'After the death of Yao and Shun, the way of the Sages declined, and tyrants arose one after another. They pulled down houses in order to make ponds, and the people had nowhere to rest. They turned fields into parks, depriving the people of their livelihood. Moreover, heresies and violence arose. With the multiplication of parks, ponds and lakes, arrived birds and beasts. By the time of the tyrant Tchou, the Empire was again in great disorder. The Duke of Chou helped King Wu to punish Tchou. He waged war on Yen for three years and punished its ruler; he drove Fei Lien to the edge of the sea and executed him. He annexed fifty states. He drove tigers, leopards, rhinoceroses and elephants to the distant wilds, and the Empire rejoiced. The *Book of History* says,

1. From a lost chapter.

Lofty indeed were the plans of King Wen!
Great indeed were the achievements of King Wu!
Bless us and enlighten us, your descendants,
So that we may act correctly and not fall into error.[1]

'When the world declined and the Way fell into obscurity,
heresies and violence again arose. There were instances of regicides
and parricides. Confucius was apprehensive and composed the
Spring and Autumn Annals. Strictly speaking, this is the Emperor's
prerogative. That is why Confucius said, "Those who understand
me will do so through the *Spring and Autumn Annals*; those who
condemn me will also do so because of the *Spring and Autumn
Annals*."

'No sage kings have appeared since then. Feudal lords do as
they please; people with no official position are uninhibited in the
expression of their views,[2] and the words of Yang Chu and Mo
Ti fill the Empire. The teachings current in the Empire are those of
either the school of Yang or the school of Mo. Yang advocates
everyone for himself, which amounts to a denial of one's prince;
Mo advocates love without discrimination,[3] which amounts to a
denial of one's father. To ignore one's father on the one hand,
and one's prince on the other, is to be no different from the beasts.
Kung-ming Yi said, "There is fat meat in your kitchen and there
are well-fed horses in your stables, yet the people look hungry and
in the outskirts of cities men drop dead from starvation. This
is to show animals the way to devour men."[4] If the way of Yang
and Mo does not subside and the way of Confucius is not proclaimed,
the people will be deceived by heresies and the path of morality
will be blocked. When the path of morality is blocked, then we
show animals the way to devour men, and sooner or later it will
come to men devouring men. Therefore, I am apprehensive. I
wish to safeguard the way of the former sages against the on-

1. From a lost chapter but incorporated into the spurious *Chün ya* chapter
(*Shu ching*, 19. 12a–b).
2. Cf. IV. A. 22.
3. Cf. VII. A. 26.
4. This saying is also found in I. A. 4 though there it is not attributed to
Kung-ming Yi.

slaughts of Yang and Mo and to banish excessive views. Then
advocates of heresies will not be able to rise. For what arises in
the mind will interfere with policy, and what shows itself in
policy will interfere with practice. Were there once more a sage,
he would surely agree with what I have said.[1]

'In ancient times Yü controlled the Flood and brought peace to
the Empire; the Duke of Chou subjugated the northern and
southern barbarians, drove away the wild animals, and brought
security to the people; Confucius completed the *Spring and Autumn
Annals* and struck terror into the hearts of rebellious subjects
and undutiful sons. The *Book of Odes* says,

> It was the barbarians that he attacked.
> It was Ching and Shu that he punished.
> "There was none who dared stand up to me."[2]

The Duke of Chou wanted to punish those who ignored father and
prince. I, too, wish to follow in the footsteps of the three sages in
rectifying the hearts of men, laying heresies to rest, opposing
extreme action, and banishing excessive views. I am not fond of
disputation. I have no alternative. Whoever can, with words,
combat Yang and Mo is a true disciple of the sages.'

10. K'uang Chang said, 'Is Ch'en Chung-tzu not truly a man of
scruples? When he was in Wu Ling, he went without food for
three days and as a result could neither hear with his ears nor see
with his eyes. By the well was a plum tree, more than half of whose
plums were worm-eaten. He crept up, took one and ate it. Only
after three mouthfuls was he able to hear with his ears and see with
his eyes.'

'I count Chung-tzu as the finest among Gentlemen in the
state of Ch'i,' said Mencius. 'Even so, how can he pass for a man
of scruples? Pushed to its utmost limits, his way of life would only
be possible for an earthworm which eats the dry earth above and
drinks from the yellow spring below. Was the house where Chung-
tzu lived built by Po Yi? Or was it built by the Bandit Chih? Was

1. For these two sentences cf. II. A. 2.
2. Ode 300.

the millet he ate grown by Po Yi? Or was it grown by the Bandit Chih? The answer cannot be known.'

'What does it matter? He himself made sandals and his wife made hemp and silk thread to barter for these things.'

'Chung-tzu came from an old family. His elder brother Tai had an income of ten thousand bushels, but he considered his brother's income ill-gotten and refused to benefit from it, and he considered his brother's house ill-gotten and refused to live in it. He lived in Wu Ling apart from his brother and mother. One day when he came home for a visit and found that his brother had been given a present of a live goose, he knitted his brow and said, "What does one want this honking creature for?" Another day, his mother killed the goose and gave it to him to eat. His brother came home and said, "This is the meat of that honking creature." He went out and vomited it all up. He ate what his wife provided but not what his mother provided. He lived in Wu Ling but not in his brother's house. Did he think that he had succeeded in pushing his principle to the utmost limits? Pushed to the utmost limits, his way of life would only be possible if he were an earthworm.'

BOOK IV · PART A

1. Mencius said, 'Even if you had the keen eyes of Li Lou and the skill of Kung-shu Tzu, you could not draw squares or circles without a carpenter's square or a pair of compasses; even if you had the acute ears of Shih K'uang, you could not adjust the pitch of the five notes correctly without the six pipes; even if you knew the way of Yao and Shun, you could not rule the Empire equitably except through benevolent government. Now there are some who, despite their benevolent hearts and reputations, succeed neither in benefiting the people by their benevolence nor in setting an example for posterity. This is because they do not practise the way of the Former Kings. Hence it is said,

> Goodness alone is not sufficient for government;
> The law unaided cannot make itself effective.

The *Book of Odes* says,

> Do not swerve to one side, do not overlook anything;
> Follow established rules in everything you do.[1]

No one ever erred through following the example of the Former Kings.

'The sage, having taxed his eyes to their utmost capacity, went on to invent the compasses and the square, the level and the plumb-line, which can be used endlessly for the production of squares and circles, planes and straight lines, and, having taxed his ears to their utmost capacity, he went on to invent the six pipes which can be used endlessly for setting the pitch of the five notes, and, having taxed his heart to its utmost capacity, he went on to practise government that tolerated no suffering, thus putting the whole Empire under the shelter of his benevolence. Hence it is said, "To build high one should always take advantage of hills, to dig deep one should always take advantage of rivers and marshes." Can one be deemed wise if, in governing the people, one fails to

1. Ode 249.

take advantage of the way of the Former Kings? Hence, only the benevolent man is fit to be in high position. For a cruel man to be in high position is for him to disseminate his wickedness among the people. When those above have no principles and those below have no laws, when courtiers have no faith in the Way and craftsmen have no faith in measures, when gentlemen offend against the right and common people risk punishment, then it is good fortune indeed if a state survives. Hence it is said, "When the city walls are not intact and arms are not abundant, it is no disaster for a state. When waste land is not brought under cultivation and wealth is not accumulated, this, too, is no disaster for the state. But when those above ignore the rites, those below ignore learning, and lawless people arise, then the end of the state is at hand." The *Book of Odes* says,

> Heaven is about to stir,
> Do not chatter so.[1]

"To chatter" is "to talk too much". To ignore dutifulness in serving one's ruler, to disregard the rites in accepting and relinquishing office, and yet to make calumnious attacks on the way of the Former Kings is what is meant by "talking too much". Hence it is said, "To take one's prince to task is respect; to discourse on the good and keep out heresies is reverence; to say 'My prince will never be capable of doing it' is to cripple him.'"

2. Mencius said, 'The compasses and the carpenter's square are the culmination of squares and circles; the sage is the culmination of humanity. If one wishes to be a ruler, one must fulfil the duties proper to a ruler; if one wishes to be a subject, one must fulfil the duties proper to a subject. In both cases all one has to do is to model oneself on Yao and Shun. Not to serve one's prince in the way Shun served Yao is not to respect one's prince; not to govern the people in the way Yao governed his is to harm one's people. Confucius said, "There are two ways and two only: benevolence and cruelty." If a ruler ill-uses his people to an extreme degree, he will be murdered and his state annexed; if he does it to a lesser

1. Ode 254.

degree, his person will be in danger and his territory reduced. Such rulers will be given the posthumous names of "Yu" and "Li",[1] and even dutiful sons and grandsons will not be able to have them revoked in a hundred generations. The *Book of Odes* says,

> The lesson for the Yin was not far to seek:
> It lay with the age of the Hsia.[2]

This sums up what I have said.'

3. Mencius said, 'The Three Dynasties won the Empire through benevolence and lost it through cruelty. This is true of the rise and fall, survival and collapse, of states as well. An Emperor cannot keep the Empire within the Four Seas unless he is benevolent; a feudal lord cannot preserve the altars to the gods of earth and grain unless he is benevolent; a Minister or a Counsellor cannot preserve his ancestral temple unless he is benevolent; a Gentleman or a Commoner cannot preserve his four limbs unless he is benevolent. To dislike death yet revel in cruelty is no different from drinking beyond your capacity despite your dislike of drunkenness.'

4. Mencius said, 'If others do not respond to your love with love, look into your own benevolence; if others fail to respond to your attempts to govern them with order, look into your own wisdom; if others do not return your courtesy, look into your own respect. In other words, look into yourself whenever you fail to achieve your purpose. When you are correct in your person, the Empire will turn to you. The *Book of Odes* says,

> Long may he be worthy of Heaven's Mandate,
> And seek for himself much good fortune.[3]

1. i.e., 'benighted' and 'tyrannical'. These names which imply extreme condemnation were, as a matter of fact, given to Emperors of the Chou Dynasty and these are mentioned in VI. A. 6.
2. Ode 255.
3. Ode 235.

5. Mencius said, 'There is a common expression, "The Empire, the state, the family". The Empire has its basis in the state, the state in the family, and the family in one's own self.'

6. Mencius said, 'It is not difficult to govern. All one has to do is not to offend the noble families. Whatever commands the admiration of the noble families will command the admiration of the whole state; whatever commands the admiration of a state will command the admiration of the Empire. Thus moral influence irresistibly fills to overflowing the whole Empire within the Four Seas.'

7. Mencius said, 'When the Way prevails in the Empire men of small virtue serve men of great virtue, men of small ability serve men of great ability. But when the Way is in disuse, the small serve the big, the weak serve the strong. Both are due to Heaven. Those who are obedient to Heaven are preserved; those who go against Heaven are annihilated. Duke Ching of Ch'i said, "Since, on the one hand, we are not in a position to dictate, and on the other, we refuse to be dictated to, we are destined to be exterminated." With tears he gave his daughter to Wu as a bride. Now the small states emulate the big states yet feel ashamed of being dictated to by them. This is like disciples feeling ashamed of obeying their masters. If one is ashamed, the best thing is to take King Wen as one's model. He who models himself on King Wen will prevail over the whole Empire, in five years if he starts with a big state, and in seven if he starts with a small state. The *Book of Odes* says,

> The descendants of Shang
> Exceed a hundred thousand in number,
> But because God so decreed,
> They submit to Chou.
> They submit to Chou
> Because the Mandate of Heaven is not immutable.
> The warriors of Yin are handsome and alert.
> They assist at the libations in the Chou capital.[1]

1. Ode 235.

Confucius said, "Against benevolence there can be no superiority in numbers. If the ruler of a state is drawn to benevolence, he will be matchless in the Empire." Now to wish to be matchless in the Empire by any means but benevolence is like holding something hot and refusing to cool one's hand with water. The *Book of Odes* says,

> Who can hold something hot
> And not cool his hand with water?"[1]

8. Mencius said, 'How can one get the cruel man to listen to reason? He dwells happily amongst dangers, looks upon disasters as profitable and delights in what will lead him to perdition. If the cruel man listened to reason, there would be no annihilated states or ruined families. There was a boy who sang,

> If the blue water is clear
> It is fit to wash my chin-strap.
> If the blue water is muddy
> It is only fit to wash my feet.

Confucius said, "Listen to this, my little ones. When clear the water washes the chin-strap, when muddy it washes the feet. The water brings this difference in treatment upon itself." Only when a man invites insult will others insult him. Only when a family invites destruction will others destroy it. Only when a state invites invasion will others invade it. The *T'ai chia* says,

> When Heaven sends down calamities,
> There is hope of weathering them;
> When man brings them upon himself,
> There is no hope of escape.[2]

This describes well what I have said.'

9. Mencius said, 'It was through losing the people that Chieh and Tchou lost the Empire, and through losing the people's hearts that they lost the people. There is a way to win the Empire; win the people and you will win the Empire. There is a way to win the

1. Ode 257.
2. This passage from the lost *T'ai chia* is again quoted in II. A. 4.

people; win their hearts and you will win the people. There is a way to win their hearts; amass what they want for them; do not impose what they dislike on them. That is all. The people turn to the benevolent as water flows downwards or as animals head for the wilds. Thus the otter drives the fish to the deep; thus the hawk drives birds to the bushes; and thus Chieh and Tchou drove the people to T'ang and King Wu. Now if a ruler in the Empire is drawn to benevolence, all the feudal lords will drive the people to him. He cannot but be a true King. In the present day, those who want to be king are like a man with an illness that has lasted seven years seeking *ai*[1] that has been stored for three years. If one has not the foresight to put by such a thing, one will not be able to find it when the need arises. If one does not aim steadfastly at benevolence, one will suffer worry and disgrace all one's life and end in the snare of death. The *Book of Odes* says,

> How can they be good?
> They only lead one another to death by drowning.[2]

This describes well what I have said.'

10. Mencius said, 'It is not worth the trouble to talk to a man who has no respect for himself, and it is not worth the trouble to make a common effort with a man who has no confidence in himself. The former attacks morality; the latter says, "I do not think I am capable of abiding by benevolence or of following rightness." Benevolence is man's peaceful abode and rightness his proper path. It is indeed lamentable for anyone not to live in his peaceful abode and not to follow his proper path.'

11. Mencius said, 'The Way lies at hand yet it is sought afar off; the thing lies in the easy yet it is sought in the difficult. If only

---

1. *Ai* is a herb of the genus Artemisia. In a dried form it is burned close to the skin as a treatment for certain ailments. The method is known as *chiu* in Chinese, but is generally known in the West as moxibustion, a term derived from the word moxa which, in turn, is an Anglicized form of the Japanese word *mokusa*, the meaning of which is *moegusa* (burned herb).
2. Ode 257.

everyone loved his parents and treated his elders with deference, the Empire would be at peace.'

12. Mencius said, 'If a man in a subordinate position fails to win the confidence of his superiors, he cannot hope to govern the people. There is a way for him to win the confidence of his superiors. If his friends do not trust him, he will not win the confidence of his superiors. There is a way for him to win the trust of his friends. If in serving his parents he fails to please them, he will not win the trust of his friends. There is a way for him to please his parents. If upon looking within he finds that he has not been true to himself, he will not please his parents. There is a way for him to become true to himself. If he does not understand goodness he cannot be true to himself. Hence being true is the Way of Heaven; to reflect upon this is the Way of man. There has never been a man totally true to himself who fails to move others. On the other hand, one who is not true to himself can never hope to move others.'

13. Mencius said, 'Po Yi fled from Tchou and settled on the edge of the North Sea. When he heard of the rise of King Wen he stirred and said, "Why not go back? I hear that Hsi Po[1] takes good care of the aged." T'ai Kung fled from Tchou and settled on the edge of the East Sea. When he heard of the rise of King Wen he stirred and said, "Why not go back? I hear that Hsi Po takes good care of the aged."[2] These two were the grand old men of the Empire, and they turned to him. In others words, the fathers of the Empire turned to him. When the fathers of the Empire turned to him, where could the sons go? If any feudal lord practises the government of King Wen he will certainly be ruling over the Empire within seven years.'

14. Mencius said, 'While he was steward to the Chi family, Jan Ch'iu doubled the yield of taxation without being able to improve their virtue. Confucius said, "Ch'iu is not my disciple. You,

1. i.e., King Wen.
2. This passage is found also in VII. A. 22.

little ones, may attack him to the beating of drums."[1] From this it can be seen that Confucius rejected those who enriched rulers not given to the practice of benevolent government. How much more would he reject those who do their best to wage war on their behalf. In wars to gain land, the dead fill the plains; in wars to gain cities, the dead fill the cities. This is known as showing the land the way to devour human flesh. Death is too light a punishment for such men. Hence those skilled in war should suffer the most severe punishments; those who secure alliances with other feudal lords come next, and then come those who open up waste lands and increase the yield of the soil.'

15. Mencius said, 'There is in man nothing more ingenuous than the pupils of his eyes. They cannot conceal his wickedness. When he is upright within his breast, a man's pupils are clear and bright; when he is not, they are clouded and murky. How can a man conceal his true character if you listen to his words and observe the pupils of his eyes?'

16. Mencius said, 'He who is respectful does not insult others; he who is frugal does not rob others. The one fear of rulers who insult and rob others is that the people will not be docile. How can they be respectful and frugal? Can an unctuous voice and a smiling countenance pass for respectfulness and frugality?'

17. Ch'un-yü K'un said, 'Is it prescribed by the rites that, in giving and receiving, man and woman should not touch each other?'

'It is,' said Mencius.

'When one's sister-in-law is drowning, does one stretch out a hand to help her?'

'Not to help a sister-in-law who is drowning is to be a brute. It is prescribed by the rites that, in giving and receiving, man and woman should not touch each other, but in stretching out a helping hand to the drowning sister-in-law one uses one's discretion.'

1. Cf. the *Analects of Confucius*, XI. 16.

'Now the Empire is drowning. Why do you not help it?'

'When the Empire is drowning, one helps it with the Way; when a sister-in-law is drowning, one helps her with one's hand. Would you have me help the Empire with my hand?'

18. Kung-sun Ch'ou said, 'Why does a gentleman not take on the teaching of his own sons?'

'Because in the nature of things,' said Mencius, 'it will not work. A teacher necessarily resorts to correction, and if correction produces no effect, he will end by losing his temper. When this happens, father and son will hurt each other instead. "You teach me by correcting me, but you yourself are not correct." So father and son hurt each other, and it is bad that such a thing should happen. In antiquity people taught one another's sons. Father and son should not demand goodness from each other.[1] To do so will estrange them, and there is nothing more inauspicious than estrangement between father and son.'

19. Mencius said, 'What is the most important duty? One's duty towards one's parents. What is the most important thing to watch over? One's own character. I have heard of a man who, not having allowed his character to be morally lost, is able to discharge his duties towards his parents; but I have not heard of one morally lost who is able to do so. There are many duties one should discharge, but the fulfilment of one's duty towards one's parents is the most basic. There are many things one should watch over, but watching over one's character is the most basic.

'Tseng Tzu, in looking after Tseng Hsi,[2] saw to it that he always had meat and drink, and, on clearing away the food, always asked to whom it should be given. When asked whether there was any food left, he always replied in the affirmative. After Tseng Hsi's death, when Tseng Yüan looked after Tseng Tzu, he, too, saw to it that he always had meat and drink, but, on clearing away

---

1. Cf. 'It is for friends to demand goodness from each other. For father and son to do so seriously undermines the love between them.' (IV. B. 30)

2. This is the father of Tseng Tzu, not to be confused with the Tseng Hsi who was Tseng Tzu's younger son. See note to II. A. 1.

the food, never asked to whom it should be given. When asked whether there was any food left, he always replied in the negative. He did this so that the left-over food could be served up again. This can only be described as looking after the mouth and belly. Someone like Tseng Tzu can truly be said to be solicitous of the wishes of his parent. One does well if one can emulate the way Tseng Tzu treated his parent.'

20. Mencius said, 'The people in power are not worth our censure; their government is not worth condemnation. The great man alone can rectify the evils in the prince's heart. When the prince is benevolent, everyone else is benevolent; when the prince is dutiful, everyone else is dutiful; when the prince is correct, everyone else is correct. Simply by rectifying the prince one can put the state on a firm basis.'

21. Mencius said, 'There is unexpected praise; equally, there is perfectionist criticism.'

22. Mencius said, 'He who opens his mouth lightly does so simply because he has no responsibilities of office.'[1] [7]

23. Mencius said, 'The trouble with people is that they are too eager to assume the role of teacher.'

24. Yüeh-cheng Tzu came to Ch'i in the retinue of Tzu-ao.[2] He went to see Mencius, who said, 'It is very gracious of you to come to see me.'

'Why do you say such a thing, sir?'

'How many days is it since you arrived?'

'I arrived yesterday.'

'In that case, am I not justified in my remark?'

'I had not found a place to lodge.'

1. Cf. 'People with no official positions are uninhibited in the expression of their views' (III. B. 9). The traditional interpretation of this saying is: 'A man opens his mouth lightly because he has never been taken to task for saying the wrong thing.'

2. i.e., Wang Huan who appears in II. B. 6 and IV. B. 27.

'Where did you learn that one should only visit one's elders after finding a place to lodge?'

'I am guilty.'

25. Mencius said to Yüeh-cheng Tzu, 'Have you come in the retinue of Tzu-ao solely for the sake of food and drink? I never thought that you would put the way of antiquity that you studied to such a use.'

26. Mencius said, 'There are three ways of being a bad son. The most serious is to have no heir. Shun married without telling his father for fear of not having an heir. To the gentleman, this was as good as having told his father.'[1]

27. Mencius said, 'The content of benevolence is the serving of one's parents; the content of dutifulness is obedience to one's elder brothers; the content of wisdom is to understand these two and to hold fast to them; the content of the rites is the regulation and adornment of them; the content of music is the joy that comes of delighting in them. When joy arises how can one stop it? And when one cannot stop it, then one begins to dance with one's feet and wave one's arms without knowing it.'

28. Mencius said, 'Shun alone was able to look upon the fact that the Empire, being greatly delighted, was turning to him, as of no more consequence than trash. When one does not please one's parents, one cannot be a man; when one is not obedient to one's parents, one cannot be a son. Shun did everything that was possible to serve his parents, and succeeded, in the end, in pleasing the Blind Man.[2] Once the Blind Man was pleased, the Empire was transformed. Once the Blind Man was pleased, the pattern for the relationship between father and son in the Empire was set. This is the supreme achievement of a dutiful son.'

1. Cf. v. A. 2.   2. Shun's father.

1. Mencius said, 'Shun was an Eastern barbarian; he was born in Chu Feng, moved to Fu Hsia, and died in Ming T'iao. King Wen was a Western barbarian; he was born in Ch'i Chou and died in Pi Ying. Their native places were over a thousand *li* apart, and there were a thousand years between them. Yet when they had their way in the Central Kingdoms, their actions matched like the two halves of a tally. The standards of the two sages, one earlier and one later, were identical.'

2. When the administration of the state of Cheng was in his hands, Tzu-ch'an used his own carriage to take people across the Chen and the Wei.

'He was a generous man,' commented Mencius, 'but he did not know how to govern. If the footbridges are built by the eleventh month and the carriage bridges by the twelfth month[1] every year, the people will not suffer the hardship of fording. A gentleman, when he governs properly, can clear his path of people when he goes out. How can he find the time to take each man across the river? Hence if a man in authority has to please every one separately, he will not find the day long enough.'

3. Mencius said to King Hsüan of Ch'i, 'If a prince treats his subjects as his hands and feet, they will treat him as their belly and heart. If he treats them as his horses and hounds, they will treat him as a stranger. If he treats them as mud and weeds, they will treat him as an enemy.'

'According to the rites,' said the King, 'there is provision for wearing mourning for a prince one has once served. Under what circumstances will this be observed?'

'When a subject whose advice has been adopted to the benefit of the people has occasion to leave the country, the prince sends

1. Equivalent to the ninth and tenth months of the present lunar calendar. See note to I. A. 6.

someone to conduct him beyond the border, and a messenger is sent ahead to prepare the way. Only if, after three years, he decides not to return does the prince take over his land. This is known as the three courtesies. If the prince behaves in this way then it is the subject's duty to wear mourning for him. Today when a subject whose advice has been rejected to the detriment of the people has occasion to leave, the prince puts him in chains, makes things difficult for him in the state he is going to and takes his land the day he leaves. This is what is meant by "enemy". What mourning is there for an enemy?'

4. Mencius said, 'When an innocent Gentleman is put to death, a Counsellor is justified in leaving; when innocent people are killed, a Gentleman is justified in going to live abroad.'

5. Mencius said, 'When the prince is benevolent, everyone else is benevolent; when the prince is dutiful, everyone else is dutiful.'[1]

6. Mencius said, 'A great man will not observe a rite that is contrary to the spirit of the rites, nor will he perform a duty that goes against the spirit of dutifulness.'

7. Mencius said, 'Those who are morally well-adjusted look after those who are not; those who are talented look after those who are not. That is why people are glad to have good fathers and elder brothers. If those who are morally well-adjusted and talented abandon those who are not, then scarcely an inch will separate the good from the depraved.'

8. Mencius said, 'Only when a man will not do some things is he capable of doing great things.'

9. Mencius said, 'Think of the consequences before you speak of the shortcomings of others.'

10. Mencius said, 'Confucius was a man who never went beyond reasonable limits.'

1. This saying forms part of IV. A. 20.

11. Mencius said, 'A great man need not keep his word nor does he necessarily see his action through to the end. He aims only at what is right.'

12. Mencius said, 'A great man is one who retains the heart of a new-born babe.'

13. Mencius said, 'Keeping one's parents when they are alive is not worth being described as of major importance; it is treating them decently when they die that is worth such a description.'

14. Mencius said, 'A gentleman steeps himself in the Way because he wishes to find it in himself. When he finds it in himself, he will be at ease in it; when he is at ease in it, he can draw deeply upon it; when he can draw deeply upon it, he finds its source wherever he turns. That is why a gentleman wishes to find the Way in himself.'

15. Mencius said, 'Learn widely and go into what you have learned in detail so that in the end you can return to the essential.'

16. Mencius said, 'You can never succeed in winning the allegiance of men by trying to dominate them through goodness. You can only succeed by using this goodness for their welfare. You can never gain the Empire without the heart-felt admiration of the people in it.'

17. Mencius said, 'Words without reality are ill-omened, and the reality of the ill-omened will befall those who stand in the way of good people.'

18. Hsü Tzu said, 'More than once Confucius expressed his admiration for water by saying, "Water! Oh, water!"[1] What was it he saw in water?'

'Water from an ample source,' said Mencius, 'comes tumbling down, day and night without ceasing, going forward only after

1. Cf. the *Analects of Confucius*, IX. 17.

all the hollows are filled,[1] and then draining into the sea. Anything that has an ample source is like this. What Confucius saw in water is just this and nothing more. If a thing has no source, it is like the rain water that collects after a downpour in the seventh and eighth months.[2] It may fill all the gutters, but we can stand and wait for it to dry up. Thus a gentleman is ashamed of an exaggerated reputation.'

19. Mencius said, 'Slight is the difference between man and the brutes. The common man loses this distinguishing feature, while the gentleman retains it. Shun understood the way of things and had a keen insight into human relationships. He followed the path of morality. He did not just put morality into practice.'

20. Mencius said, 'Yü disliked delicious wine but was fond of good advice. T'ang held to the mean, and adhered to no fixed formula in the selection of able men. King Wen treated the people as if he were tending invalids, and gazed at the Way as if he had never seen it before. King Wu never treated those near him with familiarity, nor did he forget those who were far away. The Duke of Chou sought to combine the achievements of the Three Dynasties and the administrations of the Four Kings. Whenever there was anything he could not quite understand, he would tilt his head back and reflect, if need be through the night as well as the day. If he was fortunate enough to find the answer, he would sit up to await the dawn.'

21. Mencius said, 'When the wooden clappers[3] [8] of the true King fell into disuse, songs were no longer collected. When songs were no longer collected, the *Spring and Autumn Annals* were written. The *Sheng* of Chin, the *T'ao U* of Ch'u and the *Spring and Autumn Annals* of Lu are the same kind of work. The events recorded concern Duke Huan of Ch'i and Duke Wen of Chin, and the style

1. Cf. VII. A. 24.
2. Equivalent to the fifth and sixth months in the present lunar calendar. See note to I. A. 6.
3. Used by officials who went round collecting ballads.

is that of the official historian. Confucius said, "I have appropriated the didactic principles therein." '

22. Mencius said, 'The influence of both the gentleman and the small man ceases to be felt after five generations. I have not had the good fortune to have been a disciple of Confucius. I have learned indirectly from him through others.'

23. Mencius said, 'When it is permissible both to accept and not to accept, it is an abuse of integrity to accept. When it is permissible both to give and not to give, it is an abuse of generosity to give. When it is permissible both to die and not to die, it is an abuse of valour to die.'

24. P'eng Meng learned archery from Yi, and, having learned everything Yi could teach, thought to himself that in all the world Yi was the only archer better than himself. Thereupon he killed Yi.

'Yi,' commented Mencius, 'was also to blame.'

'Kung-ming Yi said, "He seems blameless." '

'All Kung-ming Yi meant was that the blame was slight, but how can Yi be said to be blameless? The men of Cheng sent Tzu-chuo Ju-tzu to invade Wei, and Wei sent Yü Kung chih Ssu to pursue him. Tzu-chuo Ju-tzu said, "I have an attack of an old complaint today and cannot hold my bow. I suppose I am as good as dead." He then asked his driver, "Who is pursuing me?" His driver said, "Yü Kung chih Ssu." "Then I shall not die." His driver said, "Yü Kung chih Ssu is the best archer in Wei. Why do you say, 'Then I shall not die'?" "Yü Kung chih Ssu learned archery from Yin Kung chih T'uo who learned it from me. Yin Kung chih T'uo is an upright man and I have no doubt that he chooses only upright men as his friends." Yü Kung chih Ssu came up and said, "Master, why have you not taken up your bow?" "I have an attack of an old complaint today and cannot hold my bow." "I learned archery from Yin Kung chih T'uo who learned it from you. It distresses me to harm you by your own art. Nevertheless, today I am charged with the affair of my prince. I dare not neglect it." He drew his arrows, knocked their tips off against the wheel, and let fly a set of four arrows before he retired.'

25. Mencius said, 'If the beauty Hsi Shih is covered with filth, then people will hold their noses when they pass her. But should an ugly[1] man fast and cleanse himself, he would be fit to offer sacrifices to God.'

26. Mencius said, 'In talking about human nature people in the world merely follow former theories. They do so because these theories can be explained with ease. What they dislike in clever men is that they bore their way through. If clever men could act as Yü did in guiding the flood waters, then there would be nothing to dislike in them. Yü guided the water by imposing nothing on it that was against its natural tendency. If clever men can also do this, then great indeed will their cleverness be. In spite of the height of the heavens and the distance of the heavenly bodies, if one seeks out former instances, one can calculate the solstices of a thousand years hence without stirring from one's seat.'

27. Kung-hang Tzu lost a son, and Wang Huan, the *yu shih*,[2] went to offer his condolences. As he entered, people went up to greet him, and, as he sat down, others came over to speak to him. Mencius did not speak to him and Wang Huan was displeased. 'All the gentlemen present spoke to me,' said he, 'with the sole exception of Mencius. He showed me scant courtesy.'

Mencius, on hearing of this, said, 'According to the rites, at court one should not step across seats to speak to others, neither should one step across steps to bow to them. All I wished was to observe the rites, and Tzu-ao thought I was showing him scant courtesy. Is that not extraordinary?'

28. Mencius said, 'A gentleman differs from other men in that he retains his heart. A gentleman retains his heart by means of

1. Mencius is here playing on the fact that the word *e* means 'evil' as well as 'ugly'.

2. An official post in the state of Ch'i. It is not clear what its functions were.

benevolence and the rites. The benevolent man loves others, and the courteous man respects others. He who loves others is always loved by them; he who respects others is always respected by them. Suppose a man treats one in an outrageous manner. Faced with this, a gentleman will say to himself, "I must be lacking in benevolence and courtesy, or how could such a thing happen to me?" When, looking into himself, he finds that he has been benevolent and courteous, and yet this outrageous treatment continues, then the gentleman will say to himself, "I must have failed to do my best for him." When, on looking into himself, he finds that he has done his best and yet this outrageous treatment continues, then the gentleman will say, "This man does not know what he is doing. Such a person is no different from an animal. One cannot expect an animal to know any better." Hence while a gentleman has perennial worries, he has no unexpected vexations. His worries are of this kind: Shun was a man; I am also a man. Shun set an example for the Empire worthy of being handed down to posterity, yet here am I, just an ordinary man. That is something worth worrying about. If one worries about it, what should one do? One should become like Shun. That is all. On the other hand, the gentleman is free from vexations. He never does anything that is not benevolent; he does not act except in accordance with the rites. Even when unexpected vexations come his way, the gentleman refuses to be perturbed by them.'

29. In a period of peace, Yü and Chi passed their own door three times without entering.[1] Confucius praised them for it. In an age of disorder, Yen Hui lived in a mean dwelling, subsisting on a bowlful of rice and a ladleful of water, and remained happy in a life whose hardship would have been beyond the endurance of others. Confucius also praised him for it.[2]

'The way followed by Yü, Chi and Yen Hui,' commented Mencius, 'was the same. Yü looked upon himself as responsible for

1. Yü was the one who passed his door three times without entering. Chi is mentioned here only because his name is often coupled with that of Yü. See, for instance, III. A. 4.
2. Cf. the *Analects of Confucius*, VI. 11.

anyone in the Empire who drowned; Chi looked upon himself as responsible for anyone in the Empire who starved.[1] That is why they went about their tasks with such a sense of urgency. Had Yü, Chi and Yen Hui changed places they would not have acted differently.

'Now if a fellow-lodger is involved in a fight, it is right for you to rush to his aid with your hair hanging down and your cap untied. But it would be misguided to do so if it were only a fellow-villager. There is nothing wrong with bolting your door.'

30. Kung-tu Tzu said, 'K'uang Chang is dubbed an undutiful son by the whole country. Why do you, Master, not only associate with him but treat him with courtesy?'

'What the world commonly calls undutiful in a son falls under five heads,' said Mencius. 'First, the neglect of one's parents through laziness of limb. Second, the neglect of one's parents through indulgence in the games of *po* and *yi* and fondness for drink. Third, the neglect of one's parents through miserliness in money matters and partiality towards one's wife. Fourth, indulgence in sensual pleasures to the shame of one's parents. Fifth, a quarrelsome and truculent disposition that jeopardizes the safety of one's parents. Has Chang Tzu a single one of these failings? In his case father and son are at odds from taxing each other over a moral issue. It is for friends to demand goodness from each other. For father and son to do so seriously undermines the love between them.[2] Do you think that Chang Tzu does not want to be with his wife and sons? Because of his offence, he is not allowed near his father. Therefore, he sent his wife and sons away and refused to allow them to look after him. To his way of thinking, unless he acted in this way, his offence would be greater. That is Chang Tzu for you.'[3]

---

1. Because Yü was entrusted with the task of dealing with the Flood and Chi with the task of teaching the people the art of cultivating the crops. Again, see III. A. 4.

2. Cf. IV. A. 18.

3. It is not clear what transpired between K'uang Chang and his father. In the *Chan kuo ts'e* (*Ch'i ts'e* 1/13) there is an account of one Chang Tzu whose

31. Tseng Tzu lived in Wu Ch'eng. Invaders came from Yüeh. Someone said, 'Invaders are coming. Why do you not leave?'

'Do not let anyone,' said Tseng Tzu, 'live in my house or do damage to my trees.'

When the invaders left, Tseng Tzu again said, 'Repair the walls and roof of my house. I shall return presently.'

After the invaders had left, Tseng Tzu returned. His attendants said, 'The Master has been shown every respect and everything possible is done for him. Perhaps it was not right that when we were invaded he should have taken the lead in leaving and only returned after the invaders left.'

Shen-yu Hsing said, 'This is beyond your comprehension. At one time, I had trouble in my place with a man by the name of Fu Ch'u, but none of the Master's seventy followers were involved in the incident.'

Tzu-ssu lived in Wei. There were invaders from Ch'i. Someone said, 'Invaders are coming. Why do you not leave?'

'If I leave,' answered Tzu-ssu, 'who will help the prince defend the state?'

'The way followed by Tseng Tzu and Tzu-ssu,' commented Mencius, 'was the same. Tseng Tzu was a teacher, an elder; Tzu-ssu was a subject in an insignificant position. Had Tseng Tzu and Tzu-ssu changed places they would not have acted differently.'

32. Ch'u Tzu said, 'The King sent someone to spy on you to see whether you were at all different from other people.'

'In what way,' said Mencius, 'should I be different from other people? Even Yao and Shun were the same as anyone else.'

---

father killed his mother and buried her under the stables. Chang Tzu wanted to have his mother re-buried but felt unable to do so as his father died without leaving instructions for it. Although this account has been related to the dispute referred to here by Mencius, it does not seem justified, as in the *Chan kuo ts'e* there is in fact no mention of any dispute between father and son during the time when the father was alive. It is likely that the Chang Tzu in the *Chan kuo ts'e* is not the same as the K'uang Chang here. For a discussion of this problem see Appendix 1, p. 211ff.

33. A man from Ch'i lived with his wife and concubine. When the good man went out, he always came back full of food and drink. His wife asked about his companions, and they all turned out to be men of wealth and consequence. His wife said to the concubine, 'When our husband goes out, he always comes back full of food and drink. When I asked about his companions, they all turned out to be men of wealth and consequence, yet we never have had a distinguished visitor. I shall find out where he really goes.'

She got up early and followed her husband everywhere he went. Not a single person in the city stopped to talk to him. In the end he went to the outskirts on the east side of the city amongst the graves. He went up to someone who was offering sacrifices to the dead and begged for what was left over. This not being enough, he looked around and went up to another. This was how he had his food and drink.

His wife went home and said to the concubine, 'A husband is someone on whom one's whole future depends, and ours turns out like this.' Together they reviled their husband and wept in the courtyard. The husband, unaware of all this, came swaggering in to show off to his womenfolk.

In the eyes of the gentleman, few of all those who seek wealth and position fail to give their wives and concubines cause to weep with shame.

BOOK V · PART A

1. Wan Chang asked, 'While toiling in the fields, Shun wept and wailed, calling [9] upon merciful Heaven. Why did he weep and wail?'

'He was complaining and yearning at the same time,' answered Mencius.

' "When one is loved by one's parents, though pleased, one must not forget oneself; when one is disliked by them, though distressed, one must not bear them any grudge."[1] Are you saying that Shun bore a grudge against his parents?'

'Ch'ang Hsi said to Kung-ming Kao, "That Shun toiled in the fields I now understand, but that he should have wept and wailed, calling [9] upon merciful Heaven and calling [9] upon father and mother, I have not understood." Kung-ming Kao said, "That is something beyond your comprehension." Now Kung-ming Kao did not think that a son could be so complacent as to say, all that is required of me is that I should do my best in tilling the fields and discharge the duties of a son, and if my parents do not love me, what is that to me? The Emperor[2] sent his nine sons, and two daughters, together with the hundred officials, taking with them the full quota of cattle and sheep and provisions, to serve Shun in the fields. Most of the Gentlemen of the Empire placed themselves under him, and the Emperor was about to hand the Empire over to him. But because he was unable to please his parents, Shun was like a man in extreme straits with no home to go back to. Every man wants to please the Gentlemen of the Empire, yet this was not sufficient to deliver him from anxiety; beautiful women are also something every man desires, yet the bestowal of the Emperor's two daughters on Shun as wives was not sufficient to deliver him from anxiety; wealth is something every man wants, yet the wealth of possessing the whole Empire was not sufficient to deliver him

1. This seems to be a saying of Tseng Tzu's. It is to be found in chapter 24 of the *Li chi* and chapter 52 of the *Ta Tai li chi*.
2. i.e., Yao.

from anxiety; rank is something every man wants, yet the supreme rank of Emperor was not sufficient to deliver him from anxiety. None of these things was sufficient to deliver him from anxiety which the pleasure of his parents alone could relieve. When a person is young he yearns for his parents; when he begins to take an interest in women, he yearns for the young and beautiful; when he has a wife, he yearns for his wife; when he enters public life he yearns for his prince and becomes restless if he is without one. A son of supreme dutifulness yearns for his parents all his life. In Shun I have seen an example of a son who, even at the age of fifty, yearned for his parents.'

2. Wan Chang asked, 'The *Book of Odes* says,

> How does one take a wife?
> By first telling one's parents.[1]

If that were truly so, it would seem that Shun's example was not to be followed. Why did Shun marry without telling his parents?'

'Because he would not have been allowed to marry if he had told them. A man and woman living together is the most important of human relationships. If he had told his parents, he would have to put aside the most important of human relationships and this would result in bitterness against his parents. That is why he did not tell them.'

'The reason why Shun married without telling his parents is now clear to me. But why did the Emperor give Shun his daughters in marriage without telling Shun's parents?'

'The Emperor was also aware that telling them would have prevented the marriage from taking place.'

'Shun's parents sent him to repair the barn. Then they removed the ladder and the Blind Man set fire to the barn. They sent Shun to dredge the well, set out after him and blocked up the well over him. Hsiang[2] said, "The credit for plotting against the life of Shun goes to me. The cattle and sheep go to you, father and mother, and the granaries as well. But the spears go to me, and the lute and the *ti* bow as well. His two wives should also be made to look

1. Ode 101.   2. Shun's younger brother.

after my quarters." Hsiang went into Shun's house and there Shun was, seated on the bed playing on the lute. Hsiang, in some embarrassment, said, "I was thinking of you." Shun said, "I am thinking of my subjects. You can help me in the task of government." I wonder if Shun was unaware of Hsiang's intention to kill him.'

'How could he be unaware? He was worried when Hsiang was worried, and pleased when Hsiang was pleased.'

'In that case did Shun just pretend to be pleased?'

'No. Once, someone presented a live fish to Tzu-ch'an of Cheng. Tzu-ch'an told his fish-keeper to keep it in the pond. But the keeper cooked the fish and came back to report to Tzu-ch'an. "When I first let go of it," said he, "it was still sickly, but after a while it came to life and swam away into the distance." "It is in its element! It is in its element!" said Tzu-ch'an. On coming out, the keeper said, "Who says that Tzu-ch'an is wise? I cooked and ate the fish and he said, 'It is in its element! It is in its element!' " That only goes to show that a gentleman can be taken in by what is reasonable, but cannot be easily hoodwinked by the wrong method. He, Hsiang, came as a loving brother, and so Shun honestly believed him and was pleased. What need was there for pretence?'

3. Wan Chang said, 'Hsiang devoted himself every day to plotting against Shun's life. Why did Shun only banish him when he became Emperor?'

'He enfeoffed him,' said Mencius. 'Some called this banishment.'

'Shun banished Kung Kung to Yu Chou,' said Wan Chang, 'and Huan Tou to Mount Ch'ung; he banished San Miao to San Wei and killed Kun on Mount Yü. On these four culprits being punished, the people in the Empire bowed to his will with admiration in their hearts. That was because he punished the wicked. Hsiang was the most wicked of them all, yet he was enfeoffed in Yu Pi. What wrong had the people of Yu Pi done? Is that the way a benevolent man behaves? Others he punishes, but when it comes to his own brother he enfeoffs him instead.'

'A benevolent man never harbours anger or nurses a grudge against a brother. All he does is to love him. Because he loves him, he wishes him to enjoy rank; because he loves him, he wishes him to enjoy wealth. To enfeoff him in Yu Pi was to let him enjoy wealth and rank. If as Emperor he were to allow his brother to be a nobody, could that be described as loving him?'

'May I ask what you meant by saying that some called this banishment?'

'Hsiang was not allowed to take any action in his fief. The Emperor appointed officials to administer the fief and to collect tributes and taxes. For this reason it was described as banishment. Hsiang was certainly not permitted to ill-use the people. Shun frequently wanted to see him and so there was an endless flow of tributes streaming in.

> When it was time for tribute,
> Yu Pi was received on account of affairs of state.[1]

This describes what happened.'

4. Hsien-ch'iu Meng asked, 'As the saying goes,

> A man of abundant virtue
> Cannot be treated as a subject by the prince,
> Nor can he be treated as a son by his father.

Shun stood facing south, while Yao stood facing north,[2] at the head of the feudal lords, paying homage to him. The Blind Man likewise stood facing north, paying homage to him. Shun saw the Blind Man and a distressed look came over his face. Confucius commented, "At that moment the Empire was precariously balanced." I wonder if this was really so?'

'No,' said Mencius. 'These are not the words of a gentleman but of a rustic from Eastern Ch'i.

'When Yao was old, Shun acted as regent. The *Yao tien* says,

After twenty-eight years, Fang Hsün[3] died. It was as if the people had lost their fathers and mothers. For three years all musical instruments were silenced.[4]

1. It is possible that this quotation is from one of the lost chapters of the *Book of History*.
2. The sovereign faces south while his subjects face north.
3. Yao's name.   4. The *Shu ching*, 3. 18b.

According to Confucius, "There cannot be two kings for the people just as there cannot be two suns in the heavens." If Shun had already become Emperor, then for him to lead the feudal lords in the observance of three years' mourning for Yao would have meant two emperors.'

'That Shun did not treat Yao as a subject,' said Hsien-ch'iu Meng, 'is now clear to me. But the *Book of Odes* says,

> There is no territory under Heaven
> Which is not the king's;
> There is no man on the borders of the land
> Who is not his subject.[1]

Now after Shun became Emperor, if the Blind Man was not his subject, what was he [10]?'

'This is not the meaning of the ode, which is about those who were unable to minister to the needs of their parents as a result of having to attend to the king's business. They were saying, "None of this is not the king's business. Why are we alone over-burdened?" Hence in explaining an ode, one should not allow the words to obscure the sentence, nor the sentence to obscure the intended meaning. The right way is to meet the intention of the poet with sympathetic understanding. If one were merely to take the sentences literally, then there is the ode *Yün han* which says,

> Of the remaining multitudes of Chou
> Not a single man survived.[2]

If this is taken to be literal truth, it would mean that not a single Chou subject survived.

'The greatest thing a dutiful son can do is to honour his parents, and the greatest thing he can do to honour his parents is to let them enjoy the Empire. To be the father of the Emperor is the highest possible honour. To give him the enjoyment of the Empire is to give him the greatest enjoyment. The *Book of Odes* says,

> He was always filial,
> And, being filial, he was a model to others.[3]

This describes well what I have said.

1. Ode 205.   2. Ode 258.   3. Ode 243.

'The *Book of History* says

> He went to see the Blind Man in the most respectful frame of mind, in fear and trembling, and the Blind Man, for his part, became amenable.[1]

Can this be described as "Nor can he be treated as a son by his father"?'

5. Wan Chang said, 'Is it true that Yao gave the Empire to Shun?'

'No,' said Mencius. 'The Emperor cannot give the Empire to another.'

'In that case who gave the Empire to Shun?'

'Heaven gave it him.'

'You say Heaven gave it him. Does this mean that Heaven gave him detailed and minute instructions?'

'No. Heaven does not speak but reveals itself through its acts and deeds.'

'How does Heaven do this?'

'The Emperor can recommend a man to Heaven but he cannot make Heaven give this man the Empire; just as a feudal lord can recommend a man to the Emperor but he cannot make the Emperor bestow a fief on him, or as a Counsellor can recommend a man to a feudal lord but cannot make the feudal lord appoint him a Counsellor. In antiquity, Yao recommended Shun to Heaven and Heaven accepted him; he presented him to the people and the people accepted him. Hence I said, "Heaven does not speak but reveals itself by its acts and deeds." '

'May I ask how he was accepted by Heaven when recommended to it and how he was accepted by the people when presented to them?'

'When he was put in charge of sacrifices, the hundred gods enjoyed them. This showed that Heaven accepted him. When he was put in charge of affairs, they were kept in order and the people were content. This showed that the people accepted him. Heaven gave it to him, and the people gave it to him. Hence I

1. From a lost chapter.

said, "The Emperor cannot give the Empire to another." Shun
assisted Yao for twenty-eight years. This is something which
could not be brought about by man, but by Heaven alone. Yao
died, and after the mourning period of three years, Shun withdrew
to the south of Nan Ho, leaving Yao's son in possession of the
field, yet the feudal lords of the Empire coming to pay homage
and those who were engaged in litigation went to Shun, not to
Yao's son, and ballad singers sang the praises of Shun, not of
Yao's son. Hence I said, "It was brought about by Heaven."
Only then did Shun go to the Central Kingdoms and ascend the
Imperial throne. If he had just moved into Yao's palace and ousted
his son, it would have been usurpation of the Empire, not receiving
it from Heaven. The *T'ai shih* says,

> Heaven sees with the eyes of its people. Heaven hears with the ears
> of its people.[1]

This describes well what I meant.'

6. Wan Chang asked, 'It is said by some that virtue declined with
Yü who chose his own son to succeed him, instead of a good and
wise man. Is this true?'.

'No,' said Mencius. 'It is not. If Heaven wished to give the
Empire to a good and wise man, then it should be given to a good
and wise man. But if Heaven wished to give it to the son, then it
should be given to the son. In antiquity, Shun recommended Yü
to Heaven, and died seventeen years later. When the mourning
period of three years was over, Yü withdrew to Yang Ch'eng,
leaving Shun's son in possession of the field, yet the people of the
Empire followed him just as, after Yao's death, the people followed
Shun instead of Yao's son. Yü recommended Yi to Heaven, and
died seven years later. When the mourning period of three years
was over, Yi withdrew to the northern slope of Mount Ch'i,
leaving Yü's son in possession of the field. Those who came to
pay homage and those who were engaged in litigation went to

---

1. From the lost chapter of the *Book of History* though incorporated into
the spurious *T'ai shih* of the present text. (*Shu ching*, 11. 10a)

Ch'i[1] instead of Yi, saying, "This is the son of our prince."
Ballad singers sang the praises of Ch'i instead of Yi, saying, "This
is the son of our prince." Tan Chu[2] was depraved, as was the son
of Shun. Over a period of many years Shun assisted Yao, and Yü
assisted Shun. Thus the people enjoyed their bounty for a long
time. Ch'i was good and capable, and able to follow in the footsteps
of Yü. Yi assisted Yü for only a few years, and the people had not
enjoyed his bounty for long. Shun and Yü differed from Yi greatly
in the length of time they assisted the Emperor, and their sons
differed as radically in their moral character. All this was due to
Heaven and could not have been brought about by man. When a
thing is done though by no one, then it is the work of Heaven;
when a thing comes about though no one brings it about, then
it is decreed.

  'A common man who comes to possess the Empire must not
only have the virtue of a Shun or a Yü but also the recommendation
of an Emperor. That is why Confucius never possessed the Empire.
On the other hand, he who inherits the Empire is only put aside by
Heaven if he is like Chieh or Tchou. That is why Yi, Yi Yin and
the Duke of Chou never came to possess the Empire. T'ang came to
rule over the Empire through the assistance of Yi Yin. When T'ang
died, T'ai Ting did not succeed to the throne.[3] Wai Ping ruled for
two years, and Chung Jen for four. Then T'ai Chia upset the laws
of T'ang, and Yi Yin banished him to T'ung. After three years,
T'ai Chia repented and reproached himself, and, while in T'ung,
reformed and became a good and dutiful man. After another three
years, since he heeded the instruction of Yi Yin, he was allowed to
return to Po. That the Duke of Chou never came to possess the
Empire is similar to the case of Yi in Hsia and that of Yi Yin in Yin.
Confucius said, "In T'ang and Yü[4] succession was through abdica-
tion, while in Hsia, Yin and Chou it was hereditary. The basic
principle was the same." '

----

  1. Yü's son.   2. Yao's son.
  3. Through an early death.
  4. T'ang is here the name of Yao's dynasty, not to be confused with the
founder of the Yin or Shang dynasty, while Yü is here the name of Shun's
dynasty, not to be confused with the founder of the Hsia dynasty.

7. Wan Chang asked, 'It is said by some that Yi Yin tried to attract the attention of T'ang by his culinary abilities. Is this true?'

'No,' said Mencius. 'It is not. Yi Yin worked in the fields in the outskirts of Yu Hsin, and delighted in the way of Yao and Shun. If it was contrary to what was right or to the Way, were he given the Empire he would have ignored it, and were he given a thousand teams of horses he would not have looked at them. If it was contrary to what was right or to the Way, he would neither give away a mite nor accept it. When T'ang sent a messenger with presents to invite him to court, he calmly said, "What do I want T'ang's presents for? I much prefer working in the fields, delighting in the way of Yao and Shun." Only after T'ang sent a messenger for the third time did he change his mind and say, "Is it not better for me to make this prince a Yao or a Shun than to remain in the fields, delighting in the way of Yao and Shun? Is it not better for me to make the people subjects of a Yao or a Shun? Is it not better for me to see this with my own eyes? Heaven, in producing the people, has given to those who first attain understanding the duty of awakening those who are slow to understand; and to those who are the first to awaken the duty of awakening those who are slow to awaken. I am among the first of Heaven's people to awaken. I shall awaken this people by means of this Way. If I do not awaken them, who will do so?" When he saw a common man or woman who did not enjoy the benefit of the rule of Yao and Shun, Yi Yin felt as if he had pushed him or her into the gutter. This is the extent to which he considered the Empire his responsibility.[1] So he went to T'ang and persuaded him to embark upon a punitive expedition against the Hsia to succour the people. I have never heard of anyone who can right others by bending himself,[2] let alone someone who can right the Empire by bringing disgrace upon himself. The conduct of sages is not always the same. Some live in retirement, others enter the world; some withdraw, others stay on; but it all comes to keeping their integrity intact. I have heard that Yi Yin attracted the attention of T'ang by the way of Yao and Shun, but I have never heard that he did it by his culinary abilities. The *Yi hsün*[3] says,

---

1. Cf. v. b. 1.   2. Cf. iii. a. 1.
3. A lost chapter of the *Book of History*.

The punishment of Heaven began in the Mu Palace of Chieh.
I came on the scene only at the city of Po.'

8. Wan Chang asked, 'According to some, when he was in Wei
Confucius' host was Yung Chü, and in Ch'i the royal attendant
Chi Huan. Is this true?'

'No,' said Mencius. 'It is not. These were fabrications by people
with nothing better to do. In Wei, Confucius' host was Yen Ch'ou-
yu. The wife of Mi Tzu was a sister of the wife of Tzu-lu. Mi Tzu
said to Tzu-lu, "If Confucius will let me act as host to him, the
office of Minister in Wei is his for the asking." Tzu-lu reported
this to Confucius who said, "There is the Decree."[1] Confucius
went forward in accordance with the rites and withdrew in accord-
ance with what was right, and in matters of success or failure said,
"There is the Decree." If, in spite of this, he accepted Yung Chü
and the royal attendant Chi Huan as hosts, then he would be
ignoring both what is right and the Decree.

'When Confucius met with disfavour in Lu and Wei, there was
the incident of Huan Ssu-ma of Sung who was about to waylay and
kill him, and he had to travel through Sung in disguise. At that
time Confucius was in trouble, and he had as host Ssu-ch'eng
Chen-tzu and took office with Chou, Marquis of Ch'en.

'I have heard that one judges courtiers who are natives of the
state by the people to whom they act as host, and those who have
come to court from abroad by the hosts they choose. If Confucius
had chosen Yung Chü and the royal attendant Chi Huan as hosts,
he would not have been Confucius.'

9. Wan Chang asked, 'Some say that Po-li Hsi sold himself to a
keeper of cattle in Ch'in for five sheep skins, and tended cattle to
attract the attention of Duke Mu of Ch'in. Is this true?'

'No,' said Mencius. 'It is not. These were fabrications by people
who had nothing better to do. Po-li Hsi was a native of Yü. Chin
offered the jade of Ch'ui Chi and the horses of Ch'ü in exchange

1. 'When a thing is done though by no one, then it is the work of
Heaven; when a thing comes about though no one brings it about, then it is
decreed.' (v. A. 6)

for permission to send troops through the territory of Yü to attack Kuo. Kung chih Ch'i advised against accepting the gift while Po-li Hsi remained silent. He knew that the ruler of Yü was beyond advice and left for Ch'in. He was seventy then. If at that age he did not know that it was undignified to secure a chance to speak to Duke Mu of Ch'in through feeding cattle, could he be called wise? Yet can he be called unwise when he remained silent, knowing that advice would be futile? He certainly was not unwise when he left in advance, knowing the ruler of Yü to be heading for disaster. Again, can he be said to be unwise when, after being raised to office in Ch'in, he decided to help Duke Mu, seeing in him a man capable of great achievement? When prime minister of Ch'in, he was responsible for the distinction his prince attained in the Empire, and posterity has found him worthy of being remembered. Was this the achievement of a man with no ability? To sell oneself into slavery in order to help one's prince towards achievement is what even a self-respecting villager would not do. Are you saying that it is the act of a good and wise man?'

1. Mencius said, 'Po Yi would neither look at improper sights with his eyes nor listen to improper sounds with his ears. He would only serve the right prince and rule over the right people. He took office when order prevailed and relinquished it when there was disorder.[1] He could not bear to remain in a place where the government took outrageous measures and unruly people were to be found. To be in company with a fellow-villager was, for him, just like sitting in mud or pitch while wearing a court cap and gown.[2] He happened to live during the time of Tchou, and he retired to the edge of the North Sea[3] to wait for the troubled waters of the Empire to return to limpidity. Hence, hearing of the way of Po Yi, a covetous man will be purged of his covetousness and a weak man will become resolute.[4]

'Yi Yin said, "I serve any prince; I rule over any people. I take office whether order prevails or not."[5] Again, he said, "Heaven, in producing the people, has given to those who first attain understanding the duty of awakening those who are slow to understand; and to those who are the first to awaken the duty of

---

1. Cf. II. A. 2.

2. It is difficult to see why Po Yi should object to the company of a fellow-villager as such. This passage is found also in II. A. 9 where the text reads, 'Po Yi . . . would not take his place at the court of an evil man, nor would he converse with him. For him to do so would be like sitting in mud or pitch wearing a court cap and gown. He pushed this dislike for evil to the extent that, if a fellow-villager in his company had his cap awry, he would walk away without even a backward look, as if afraid of being defiled.' We can see that the text in the present section is corrupt, with the result that it is wrong on three counts. First, it was being at the court of an evil man and conversing with him that was for Po Yi like sitting in mud or pitch while wearing court cap and gown. Second, he only objected to the company of a fellow-villager who had his cap awry. Third, all he did was walk away in disgust.

3. Cf. IV. A. 13 and VII. A. 22.

4. For this remark about the effect of Po Yi on certain types of people and for a similar remark about Liu Hsia Hui further on, cf. VII. B. 15.

5. Cf. II. A. 2.

awakening those who are slow to awaken. I am amongst the first of Heaven's people to awaken. I shall awaken this people by means of this Way." When he saw a common man or woman who did not enjoy the benefit of the rule of Yao and Shun, Yi Yin felt as if he had pushed him or her into the gutter. This is the extent to which he considered the Empire his responsibility.[1] [11]

'Liu Hsia Hui was not ashamed of a prince with a tarnished reputation, neither did he disdain a modest post.[2] When in office, he did not conceal his own talent, and always acted in accordance with the Way. When he was passed over he harboured no grudge, nor was he distressed even in straitened circumstances. When he was with a fellow-villager he simply could not tear himself away. "You are you and I am I. Even if you were to be stark naked by my side, how could you defile me?"[3] Hence hearing of the way of Liu Hsia Hui, a narrow-minded man will become tolerant and a mean man generous.

'When he left Ch'i, Confucius started after emptying the rice from the steamer, but when he left Lu he said, "I proceed as slowly as possible." This is the way to leave the state of one's father and mother.[4] He was the sort of man who would hasten his departure or delay it, would remain in a state, or would take office, all according to circumstances.'[5]

Mencius added, 'Po Yi was the sage who was unsullied; Yi Yin was the sage who accepted responsibility; Liu Hsia Hui was the sage who was easy-going; Confucius was the sage whose actions were timely. Confucius was the one who gathered together all that was good. To do this is to open with bells and conclude with jade tubes.[6] To open with bells is to begin in an orderly fashion; to conclude with jade tubes is to end in an orderly fashion. To begin in an orderly fashion is the concern of the wise while to end in an orderly fashion is the concern of a sage. Wisdom is like skill, shall I say, while sageness is like strength. It is like

1. This passage is also found in v. A. 7. The last sentence of the present section is defective and has been emended in the light of v. A. 7.

2. Cf. VI. B. 6.   3. Cf. II. A. 9.
4. Cf. VII. B. 17.   5. Cf. II. A. 2.
6. This refers to music.

shooting from beyond a hundred paces. It is due to your strength that the arrow reaches the target, but it is not due to your strength that it hits the mark.'

2. Po-kung Ch'i asked, 'What was the system of rank and income like under the House of Chou?'

Mencius answered, 'This cannot be known in detail, for the feudal lords destroyed the records, considering the system to be detrimental to themselves. But I have heard a brief outline of it.

'The Emperor, the duke, the marquis and the earl each constituted one rank, while the viscount and the baron shared the same rank, thus totalling five grades. The ruler, the Minister, the Counsellor, the Gentlemen of the First, the Second and the Third Grades each constituted one rank, totalling six grades.

'The territory under the direct jurisdiction of the Emperor was a thousand *li* square, under a duke or a marquis one hundred *li* square, under an earl seventy *li* square, while under a viscount or a baron it was fifty *li* square, totalling four grades. Those who held territories under fifty *li* square had no direct access to the Emperor. They had to affiliate themselves to a feudal lord and were known as "dependencies".

'The Minister of the Emperor enjoyed a territory comparable to a marquis; the Counsellor of the Emperor enjoyed a territory comparable to an earl; the Senior Gentleman of the Emperor enjoyed a territory comparable to a viscount or a baron.

'The territory of a large state was a hundred *li* square, and its ruler enjoyed an income ten times that of a Minister, a Minister four times that of a Counsellor, a Counsellor twice that of a Gentleman of the First Grade, a Gentleman of the First Grade twice that of a Gentleman of the Second Grade, a Gentleman of the Second Grade twice that of a Gentleman of the Third Grade, and a Gentleman of the Third Grade the same as a Commoner who was in public service, in other words, an income in place of what he would get from cultivating the land.

'The territory of a medium state was seventy *li* square, and its ruler enjoyed an income ten times that of a Minister, a Minister three times that of a Counsellor, a Counsellor twice that of a

Gentleman of the First Grade, a Gentleman of the First Grade twice that of a Gentleman of the Second Grade, a Gentleman of the Second Grade twice that of a Gentleman of the Third Grade, and a Gentleman of the Third Grade the same as a Commoner who was in public service, in other words, an income in place of what he would get from cultivating the land.

'The territory of a small state was fifty *li* square, and its ruler enjoyed an income ten times that of a Minister, a Minister twice that of a Counsellor, a Counsellor twice that of a Gentleman of the First Grade, a Gentleman of the First Grade twice that of a Gentleman of the Second Grade, a Gentleman of the Second Grade twice that of a Gentleman of the Third Grade, and a Gentleman of the Third Grade the same as a Commoner who was in public service, in other words, an income in place of what he would get from cultivating the land.

'What a farmer got was what he reaped from a hundred *mu* of land, the allocation of each man. With an allocation [12] of a hundred *mu*, a farmer could feed nine persons, eight persons, seven persons, six persons, or five persons, according to his grading as a farmer. The salary of a Commoner who was in public service was also graded accordingly.'

3. Wan Chang asked, 'May I ask about friendship?'

'In making friends with others,' said Mencius, 'do not rely on the advantage of age, position or powerful relations. In making friends with someone you do so because of his virtue, and you must not rely on any advantages you may possess.

'Meng Hsien Tzu was a noble with a hundred chariots. He had five friends, including Yüeh-cheng Ch'iu and Mu Chung – the names of the other three I have forgotten. Hsien Tzu had these five as friends because they lacked his position. If these five had had his position, they would not have accepted him as a friend. This applies not only to a noble with a hundred chariots, but also to rulers of small states. Duke Hui of Pi said, "Tzu-ssu I treat as a teacher; Yen Pan I treat as a friend; as for Wang Shun and Ch'ang Hsi, they are men who serve me." Not only does this apply to rulers of small states, but sometimes also to rulers of large states.

Take Duke P'ing of Chin and Hai T'ang for instance. He entered when Hai T'ang said "Enter", sat down when Hai T'ang said "Sit down", and ate when Hai T'ang said "Eat", and he ate his fill even when the fare was unpolished rice and vegetable broth, because he did not dare do otherwise. But Duke P'ing went no further than this. He did not share with Hai T'ang his position, his duties, or his revenue – all given to him by Heaven. This is the honouring of good and wise men by a Gentleman, not the honouring of good and wise men by kings and dukes.

'Shun went to see the Emperor, who placed his son-in-law in a separate mansion. He entertained Shun but also allowed himself to be entertained in return. This is an example of an Emperor making friends with a common man.

'For an inferior to show deference to a superior is known as "honouring the honoured"; for a superior to show deference to an inferior is known as "honouring the good and wise". These two derive, in fact, from the same principle.'

4. Wan Chang asked, 'In social intercourse, what, may I ask, is the correct attitude of mind?'

'A respectful attitude of mind,' said Mencius.

'Why is it said, "Too insistent a refusal constitutes a lack of respect"?'

'When a superior honours one with a gift, to accept it only after one has asked the question "Did he or did he not come by it through moral means?" is to show a lack of respect. That is why one does not refuse.'

'Cannot one refuse, not in so many words, but in one's heart? Thus while saying to oneself, "He has taken this from the people by immoral means," one offers some other excuse for one's refusal.'

'When the superior makes friends with one in the correct way and treats one with due ceremony, under such circumstances even Confucius would have accepted a gift.'

'Suppose a man waylays other men outside the gates to the capital. Can one accept the loot when the robber makes friends with one in the correct way and treats one with due ceremony?'

'No. The *K'ang kao* says,

He who murders and robs and is violent and devoid of the fear of
death is detested by the people.[1]

One can punish such a person without first attempting to re-
form him. This is a practice which the Yin took over from the
Hsia and the Chou from the Yin without question. Such robbery
flourishes more than ever today. How can it be right to accept
the loot?'

'Now the way feudal lords take from the people is no different
from robbery. If a gentleman accepts gifts from them so long as
the rites proper to social intercourse are duly observed, what is the
justification?'

'Do you think that if a true King should arise he would line up
all the feudal lords and punish them? Or do you think he would
try reforming them first before resorting to punishment? To say
that taking anything that does not belong to one is robbery is
pushing moral principles to the extreme. When Confucius held
office in Lu, the people of Lu were in the habit of fighting over the
catch in a hunt to use as sacrifice, and Confucius joined in the
fight. If even fighting over the catch is permissible, how much
more the acceptance of a gift.'

'In that case, did not Confucius take office in order to further
the Way?'

'Yes. He did.'

'If he did, why did he join in the fight over the catch?'

'The first thing Confucius did was to lay down correct rules
governing sacrificial vessels, ruling out the use of food acquired
from the four quarters in such vessels.'

'Why did he not resign his office?'

'He wanted to make a beginning. When this showed that a ban
was practicable, and in spite of this it was not put into effect, he
resigned. In this way Confucius never remained at any court for
as long as three years. Confucius took office sometimes because
he thought there was a possibility of practising the Way, sometimes
because he was treated with decency, and sometimes because the

1. See *Shu ching*, 14. 8b.

prince wished to keep good people at his court. That he took office with Chi Huan Tzu was an example of the first kind; with Duke Ling of Wei, the second kind; and with Duke Hsiao of Wei, of the last kind.'

5. Mencius said, 'Poverty does not constitute grounds for taking office, but there are times when a man takes office because of poverty. To have someone to look after his parents does not constitute grounds for marriage, but there are times when a man takes a wife for the sake of his parents. A man who takes office because of poverty chooses a low office in preference to a high one, an office with a small salary to one with a large salary. In such a case, what would be a suitable position to choose? That of a gate-keeper or of a watchman. Confucius was once a minor official in charge of stores. He said, "All I have to do is to keep correct records." He was once a minor official in charge of sheep and cattle. He said, "All I have to do is to see to it that the sheep and cattle grow up to be strong and healthy." To talk about lofty matters when in a low position is a crime. But it is equally shameful to take one's place at the court of a prince without putting the Way into effect.'

6. Wan Chang said, 'Why is it a Gentleman does not place himself under the protection of a feudal lord?'

'He does not presume to do so,' said Mencius. 'According to the rites, only a feudal lord who has lost his state places himself under the protection of another. It would be contrary to the rites for a Gentleman to place himself under the protection of a feudal lord.'

'But if the ruler gives him rice,' said Wan Chang, 'would he accept it?'

'Yes.'

'On what principle does he accept it?'

'A prince naturally gives charity to those who have come from abroad to settle.'

'Why is it that one accepts charity but refuses what is bestowed on one?'

'One does not dare presume.'

'Why does one not dare presume?'

'A gate-keeper or a watchman accepts his wages from the authorities because he has regular duties. For one who has no regular duties to accept what is bestowed on him is for him to show a lack of gravity.'

'If it is permissible to accept gifts from the ruler, I wonder if one could count on their continuance?'

'Duke Mu frequently sent messengers to ask after Tzu-ssu, every time making gifts of meat for the tripod. Tzu-ssu was displeased and in the end ejected the messenger from the front door, faced north, knocked his head twice on the ground and refused, saying, "Now I realize that the prince treats me in the way he treats his horses and hounds." Presumably it was only after this [13] that no more gifts were made. If, in spite of one's claim to like good and wise men, one is able neither to raise them to office nor to take care of them, can one be truly said to like such men?'

'If the ruler of a state wishes to take care of good and wise men, how should this be done?'

'Gifts are made at the outset in the name of the prince, and the recipient accepts them after knocking his head twice on the ground. After this is done, the granary keeper presents grain and the cook presents meat, and these gifts are no longer made in the name of the prince. In Tzu-ssu's view, to make him bob up and down rendering thanks for the gift of meat for the tripod was hardly the right way to take care of a gentleman. In the case of Yao, he sent his nine sons to serve Shun and gave him his two daughters as wives. After this, the hundred officials provided Shun with cattle and sheep and granaries for his use while he worked in the fields. And then Yao raised Shun to high office. Hence the phrase, "the honouring of the good and wise by kings and dukes".'[1]

7. Wan Chang said, 'May I ask on what grounds does one refuse to meet feudal lords?'

'Those who live in the capital,' said Mencius, 'are known as "subjects of the market place", while those who live in the out-

1. Cf. v. b. 3.

skirts are known as "subjects in the wilds". In both cases the reference is to Commoners. According to the rites, a Commoner does not dare present himself to a feudal lord unless he has handed in his token of allegiance.'

'When a Commoner,' said Wan Chang, 'is summoned to corvée he goes to serve. Why then should he refuse to go when he is summoned to an audience?'

'It is right for him to go and serve, but it is not right for him to present himself. Moreover, for what reason does the prince wish to see him?'

'For the reason that he is well-informed or that he is good and wise.'

'If it is for the reason that he is well-informed, even the Emperor does not summon his teacher, let alone a feudal lord. If it is for the reason that he is a good and wise man, then I have never heard of summoning such a man when one wishes to see him. Duke Mu frequently went to see Tzu-ssu. "How did kings of states with a thousand chariots in antiquity make friends with Gentlemen?" he asked. Tzu-ssu was displeased. "What the ancients talked about," said he, "was serving them, not making friends with them." The reason for Tzu-ssu's displeasure was surely this. "In point of position, you are the prince and I am your subject. How dare I be friends with you? In point of virtue, it is you who ought to serve me. How can you presume to be friends with me?" If the ruler of a state with a thousand chariots cannot even hope to be friends with him, how much less can he hope to summon such a man. Duke Ching of Ch'i went hunting and summoned his game-keeper with a pennon. The gamekeeper did not come, and the Duke was going to have him put to death. "A man whose mind is set on high ideals never forgets that he may end in a ditch; a man of valour never forgets that he may forfeit his head." What did Confucius find praiseworthy in the gamekeeper? His refusal to answer to a form of summons to which he was not entitled.'[1]

'May I ask with what should a gamekeeper be summoned?'

'With a leather cap. A Commoner should be summoned with a bent flag, a Gentleman with a flag with bells and a Counsellor with

1. Cf. III. B. 1.

a pennon. When the gamekeeper was summoned with what was appropriate only to a Counsellor, he would rather die than answer the summons. How would a Commoner dare to answer when he is summoned with what is appropriate only to a Gentleman? How much more would this be the case when a good and wise man is summoned with what is appropriate only to one who is neither good nor wise! To wish to meet a good and wise man while not following the proper way is like wishing him to enter while shutting the door against him. Rightness is the road and the rites are the door. Only a gentleman can follow this road and go in and out through this door. The *Book of Odes* says,

> The highway is like a grindstone.
> Its straightness is like an arrow.
> It is walked on by the gentleman
> And looked up to by the small man.'[1]

Wan Chang said, 'Confucius, when summoned by the prince, did not wait for the carriage to be harnessed.[2] In that case was Confucius wrong in what he did?'

'Confucius was in office and had specific duties, and he was summoned in his official capacity.'

8. Mencius said to Wan Chang, 'The best Gentleman of a village is in a position to make friends with the best Gentlemen in other villages; the best Gentleman in a state, with the best Gentlemen in other states; and the best Gentleman in the Empire, with the best Gentlemen in the Empire. And not content with making friends with the best Gentlemen in the Empire, he goes back in time and communes with the ancients. When one reads the poems and writings of the ancients, can it be right not to know something about them as men? Hence one tries to understand the age in which they lived. This can be described as "looking for friends in history".'

9. King Hsüan of Ch'i asked about ministers.

1. Ode 203.
2. Cf. II. B. 2 where this is quoted as part of a ritual text.

'What kind of ministers,' said Mencius, 'is Your Majesty asking about?'

'Are there different kinds of ministers?'

'Yes. There are ministers of royal blood and those of families other than the royal house.'

'What about ministers of royal blood?'

'If the prince made serious mistakes, they would remonstrate with him, but if repeated remonstrations fell on deaf ears, they would depose him.'

The King blenched at this.

'Your Majesty should not be surprised by my answer. Since you asked me, I dared not give you anything but the proper answer.'

Only after he had regained his composure did the King ask about ministers of families other than the royal house.

'If the prince made mistakes, they would remonstrate with him, but if repeated remonstrations fell on deaf ears, they would leave him.'

1. Kao Tzu said, 'Human nature is like the *ch'i* willow. Dutifulness is like cups and bowls. To make morality out of human nature is like making cups and bowls out of the willow.'

'Can you,' said Mencius, 'make cups and bowls by following the nature of the willow? Or must you mutilate the willow before you can make it into cups and bowls? If you have to mutilate the willow to make it into cups and bowls, must you, then, also mutilate a man to make him moral? Surely it will be these words of yours men in the world will follow in bringing disaster upon morality.'

2. Kao Tzu said, 'Human nature is like whirling water. Give it an outlet in the east and it will flow east; give it an outlet in the west and it will flow west. Human nature does not show any preference for either good or bad just as water does not show any preference for either east or west.'

'It certainly is the case,' said Mencius, 'that water does not show any preference for either east or west, but does it show the same indifference to high and low? Human nature is good just as water seeks low ground. There is no man who is not good; there is no water that does not flow downwards.

'Now in the case of water, by splashing it one can make it shoot up higher than one's forehead, and by forcing it one can make it stay on a hill. How can that be the nature of water? It is the circumstances being what they are. That man can be made bad shows that his nature is no different from that of water in this respect.'

3. Kao Tzu said, 'The inborn is what is meant by "nature".'

'Is that,' said Mencius, 'the same as "white is what is meant by 'white' "?' [1]

1. In '*sheng chih wei hsing*' ('the inborn is what is meant by "nature"'), the two words '*sheng*' and '*hsing*', though slightly different in pronunciation, were probably written by the same character in Mencius' time. This would

'Yes.'

'Is the whiteness of white feathers the same as the whiteness of white snow and the whiteness of white snow the same as the whiteness of white jade?'

'Yes.'

'In that case, is the nature of a hound the same as the nature of an ox and the nature of an ox the same as the nature of a man?'

4. Kao Tzu said, 'Appetite for food and sex is nature. Benevolence is internal, not external; rightness is external, not internal.'

'Why do you say,' said Mencius, 'that benevolence is internal and rightness is external?'

'That man there is old and I treat him as elder. He owes nothing of his elderliness to me, just as in treating him as white because he is white I only do so because of his whiteness which is external to me. That is why I call it external.'

'The case of rightness is different from that of whiteness. "Treating as white" is the same whether one is treating a horse as white [14] or a man as white. But I wonder if you would think that "treating as old" is the same whether one is treating a horse as old or a man as elder? Furthermore, is it the one who is old that is dutiful, or is it the one who treats him as elder that is dutiful?'

'My brother I love, but the brother of a man from Ch'in I do not love. This means that the explanation [15] lies in me. Hence I call it internal. Treating an elder of a man from Ch'u as elder is no different from treating an elder of my own family as elder. This means that the explanation [15] lies in their elderliness. Hence I call it external.'

'My enjoyment of the roast provided by a man from Ch'in is no different from my enjoyment of my own roast. Even with inanimate things we can find cases similar to the one under discussion. Are we, then, to say that there is something external even in the enjoyment of roast?'

---

make the statement at least tautological in written form and so parallel to '*pai chih wei pai*' ('white is what is meant by "white"').

5. Meng Chi-tzu asked Kung-tu Tzu, 'Why do you say that rightness is internal?'

'It is the respect in me that is being put into effect. That is why I say it is internal.'

'If a man from your village is a year older than your eldest brother, which do you respect?'

'My brother.'

'In filling their cups with wine, which do you give precedence to?'

'The man from my village.'

'The one you respect is the former; the one you treat as elder is the latter. This shows that it is in fact external, not internal.'

Kung-tu Tzu was unable to find an answer and gave an account of the discussion to Mencius.

Mencius said, '[Ask him,] "Which do you respect, your uncle or your younger brother?" He will say, "My uncle." "When your younger brother is impersonating an ancestor at a sacrifice, then which do you respect?" He will say, "My younger brother." You ask him, "What has happened to your respect for your uncle?" He will say, "It is because of the position my younger brother occupies." You can then say, "[In the case of the man from my village] it is also because of the position he occupies. Normal respect is due to my elder brother; temporary respect is due to the man from my village." '

When Meng Chi-tzu heard this, he said, 'It is the same respect whether I am respecting my uncle or my younger brother. It is, as I have said, external and does not come from within.'

'In winter,' said Kung-tu Tzu, 'one drinks hot water, in summer cold. Does that mean that even food and drink can be a matter of what is external?'

6. Kung-tu Tzu said, 'Kao Tzu said, "There is neither good nor bad in human nature," but others say, "Human nature can become good or it can become bad, and that is why with the rise of King Wen and King Wu, the people were given to goodness, while with the rise of King Yu and King Li, they were given to cruelty."

Then there are others who say, "There are those who are good by nature, and there are those who are bad by nature. For this reason, Hsiang could have Yao as prince, and Shun could have the Blind Man as father, and Ch'i, Viscount of Wei and Prince Pi Kan could have Tchou as nephew as well as sovereign."[1] Now you say human nature is good. Does this mean that all the others are mistaken?'

'As far as what is genuinely in him is concerned, a man is capable of becoming good,' said Mencius. 'That is what I mean by good. As for his becoming bad, that is not the fault of his native endowment. The heart of compassion is possessed by all men alike; likewise the heart of shame, the heart of respect, and the heart of right and wrong. The heart of compassion pertains to benevolence, the heart of shame to dutifulness, the heart of respect to the observance of the rites, and the heart of right and wrong to wisdom.[2] Benevolence, dutifulness, observance of the rites, and wisdom are not welded on to me from the outside; they are in me originally. Only this has never dawned on me. That is why it is said, "Seek and you will find it; let go and you will lose it."[3] There are cases where one man is twice, five times or countless times better than another man, but this is only because there are people who fail to make the best of their native endowment. The *Book of Odes* says,

> Heaven produces the teeming masses,
> And where there is a thing there is a norm.
> If the people held on to their constant nature,
> They would be drawn to superior virtue.[4]

Confucius commented, "The author of this poem must have had knowledge of the Way." Thus where there is a thing there is a norm, and because the people hold on to their constant nature they are drawn to superior virtue.'

1. According to the *Shih chi* (*Records of the Historian*) the Viscount of Wei was an elder brother of Tchou, and son of a concubine of low rank. For this reason, it has been pointed out that the description of having Tchou as nephew applies only to Pi Kan. Cf. the coupling of the name of Chi with that of Yü in IV. B. 29.

2. Cf. II. A. 6.   3. Cf. VII. A. 3.   4. Ode 260.

7. Mencius said, 'In good years the young men are mostly lazy, while in bad years they are mostly violent. Heaven has not sent down men whose endowment differs so greatly. The difference is due to what ensnares their hearts. Take the barley for example. Sow the seeds and cover them with soil. The place is the same and the time of sowing is also the same. The plants shoot up and by the summer solstice they all ripen. If there is any unevenness, it is because the soil varies in richness and there is no uniformity in the fall of rain and dew and the amount of human effort devoted to tending it. Now things of the same kind are all alike. Why should we have doubts when it comes to man? The sage and I are of the same kind. Thus Lung Tzu said, "When someone makes a shoe for a foot he has not seen, I am sure he will not produce a basket." All shoes are alike because all feet are alike. All palates show the same preferences in taste. Yi Ya was simply the man first to discover what would be pleasing to my palate. Were the nature of taste to vary from man to man in the same way as horses and hounds differ from me in kind, then how does it come about that all palates in the world follow the preferences of Yi Ya? The fact that in taste the whole world looks to Yi Ya shows that all palates are alike. It is the same also with the ear. The whole world looks to Shih K'uang, and this shows that all ears are alike. It is the same also with the eye. The whole world appreciates the good looks of Tzu-tu; whoever does not is blind. Hence it is said: all palates have the same preference in taste; all ears in sound; all eyes in beauty. Should hearts prove to be an exception by possessing nothing in common? What is common to all hearts? Reason and rightness. The sage is simply the man first to discover this common element in my heart. Thus reason and rightness please my heart in the same way as meat pleases my palate.'

8. Mencius said, 'There was a time when the trees were luxuriant on the Ox Mountain. As it is on the outskirts of a great metropolis, the trees are constantly lopped by axes. Is it any wonder that they are no longer fine? With the respite they get in the day and in the night, and the moistening by the rain and dew, there is certainly no lack of new shoots coming out, but then the cattle and sheep

come to graze upon the mountain. That is why it is as bald as it is. People, seeing only its baldness, tend to think that it never had any trees. But can this possibly be the nature of a mountain? Can what is in man be completely lacking in moral inclinations? A man's letting go of his true heart is like the case of the trees and the axes. When the trees are lopped day after day, is it any wonder that they are no longer fine? If, in spite of the respite a man gets in the day and in the night and of the effect of the morning air on him, scarcely any of his likes and dislikes resemble those of other men, it is because what he does in the course of the day once again dissipates what he has gained. If this dissipation happens repeatedly, then the influence of the air in the night will no longer be able to preserve what was originally in him, and when that happens, the man is not far removed from an animal. Others, seeing his resemblance to an animal, will be led to think that he never had any native endowment. But can that be what a man is genuinely like? Hence, given the right nourishment there is nothing that will not grow, and deprived of it there is nothing that will not wither away. Confucius said, "Hold on to it and it will remain; let go of it and it will disappear. One never knows the time it comes or goes, neither does one know the direction." It is perhaps to the heart this refers.'

9. Mencius said, 'Do not be puzzled by the King's lack of wisdom. Even a plant that grows most readily will not survive if it is placed in the sun for one day and exposed to the cold for ten. It is very rarely that I have an opportunity of seeing the King, and as soon as I leave, those who expose him to the cold arrive on the scene. What can I do with the few new shoots that come out? Now take *yi*,[1] which is only an art of little consequence. Yet if one does not give one's whole mind to it, one will never master it. Yi Ch'iu is the best player in the whole country. Get him to teach two people to play, one of whom concentrates his mind on the game and listens only to what Yi Ch'iu has to say, while the other, though he listens,

1. The ancient name for the game of *wei ch'i*, better known in the West by the name *go* which is simply the Japanese pronunciation of the Chinese word *ch'i*. This game is also mentioned in IV. B. 30.

dreams of an approaching swan and wants to take up his bow and corded arrow to shoot at it. Now even though this man shares the lessons with the first, he will never be as good. Is this because he is less clever? The answer is, "No." '

10. Mencius said, 'Fish is what I want; bear's palm is also what I want. If I cannot have both, I would rather take bear's palm than fish. Life is what I want; dutifulness is also what I want. If I cannot have both, I would rather take dutifulness than life. On the one hand, though life is what I want, there is something I want more than life. That is why I do not cling to life at all costs. On the other hand, though death is what I loathe, there is something I loathe more than death. That is why there are troubles I do not avoid. If there is nothing a man wants more than life, then why should he have scruples about any means, so long as it will serve to keep him alive? If there is nothing a man loathes more than death, then why should he have scruples about any means, so long as it helps him to avoid trouble? Yet there are ways of remaining alive and ways of avoiding death to which a man will not resort. In other words, there are things a man wants more than life and there are also things he loathes more than death. This is an attitude not confined to the moral man but common to all men. The moral man simply never loses it.

'Here is a basketful of rice and a bowlful of soup. Getting them will mean life; not getting them will mean death. When these are given with abuse, even a wayfarer would not accept them; when these are given after being trampled upon, even a beggar would not accept them. Yet when it comes to ten thousand bushels of grain one is supposed to accept without asking if it is in accordance with the rites or if it is right to do so. What benefit are ten thousand bushels of grain to me? [Do I accept them] for the sake of beautiful houses, the enjoyment of wives and concubines, or for the sake of the gratitude my needy acquaintances will show me? What I would not accept in the first instance when it was a matter of life and death I now accept for the sake of beautiful houses; what I would not accept when it was a matter of life and death I now accept for the enjoyment of wives and concubines; what I would not accept when it was a matter of life and death I now accept for the sake of the gratitude my needy acquaintances will show me. Is there no way of putting a stop to this? This way of thinking is known as losing one's original heart.'

11. Mencius said, 'Benevolence is the heart of man, and rightness his road. Sad it is indeed when a man gives up the right road instead of following it and allows his heart to stray without enough sense to go after it. When his chickens and dogs stray, he has sense enough to go after them, but not when his heart strays.[1] The sole concern of learning is to go after this strayed heart. That is all.'

12. Mencius said, 'Now if one's third finger is bent and cannot stretch straight, though this neither causes any pain nor impairs the use of the hand, one would think nothing of the distance between Ch'in and Ch'u if someone able to straighten it could be found. This is because one's finger is inferior to other people's. When one's finger is inferior to other people's, one has sense enough to resent it, but not when one's heart is inferior. This is known as failure to see that one thing is the same in kind as another.'

13. Mencius said, 'Even with a *t'ung* or a *tzu* tree one or two spans thick, anyone wishing to keep it alive will know how it should be tended, yet when it comes to one's own person, one does not know how to tend it. Surely one does not love one's person any less than the *t'ung* or the *tzu*. This is unthinking to the highest degree.'

14. Mencius said, 'A man loves all parts of his person without discrimination. As he loves them all without discrimination, he nurtures them all without discrimination. If there is not one foot or one inch of his skin that he does not love, then there is not one

1. As quoted in the *Han shih wai chuan* 4/27, this goes on as follows: 'Does he think less of his heart than of his chickens and dogs? This is an extreme case of failure to see that one thing is the same in kind as another. How sad! In the end such a man is sure only to perish.' This further passage must have dropped out of the present text by accident.

foot or one inch that he does not nurture. Is there any other way of telling whether what a man does is good or bad than by the choice he makes? The parts of the person differ in value and importance. Never harm the parts of greater importance for the sake of those of smaller importance, or the more valuable for the sake of the less valuable. He who nurtures the parts of smaller importance is a small man; he who nurtures the parts of greater importance is a great man. Now consider a gardener. If he tends the common trees while neglecting the valuable ones, then he is a bad gardener. A man who takes care of one finger to the detriment of his shoulder and back without realizing his mistake is a muddled man. A man who cares only about food and drink is despised by others because he takes care of the parts of smaller importance to the detriment of the parts of greater importance. If a man who cares about food and drink can do so without neglecting any other part of his person, then his mouth and belly are much more than just a foot or an inch of his skin.'

15. Kung-tu Tzu asked, 'Though equally human, why are some men greater than others?'

'He who is guided by the interests of the parts of his person that are of greater importance is a great man; he who is guided by the interests of the parts of his person that are of smaller importance is a small man.'

'Though equally human, why are some men guided one way and others guided another way?'

'The organs of hearing and sight are unable to think and can be misled by external things. When one thing acts on another, all it does is to attract it. The organ of the heart can think. But it will find the answer only if it does think; otherwise, it will not find the answer. This is what Heaven has given me. If one makes one's stand on what is of greater importance in the first instance, what is of smaller importance cannot displace it. In this way, one cannot but be a great man.'

16. Mencius said, 'There are honours bestowed by Heaven, and there are honours bestowed by man. Benevolence, dutifulness,

conscientiousness, truthfulness to one's word, unflagging delight in what is good, – these are honours bestowed by Heaven. The position of a Ducal Minister, a Minister, or a Counsellor is an honour bestowed by man. Men of antiquity bent their efforts towards acquiring honours bestowed by Heaven, and honours bestowed by man followed as a matter of course. Men of today bend their efforts towards acquiring honours bestowed by Heaven in order to win honours bestowed by man, and once the latter is won they discard the former. Such men are deluded to the extreme, and in the end are sure only to perish.'

17. Mencius said, 'All men share the same desire to be exalted. But as a matter of fact, every man has in him that which is exalted. The fact simply never dawned on him. What man exalts is not truly exalted. Those Chao Meng exalts, Chao Meng can also humble. The *Book of Odes* says,

> Having filled us with drink,
> Having filled us with virtue, . . .[1]

The point is that, being filled with moral virtue, one does not envy other people's enjoyment of fine food and, enjoying a fine and extensive reputation, one does not envy other people's fineries.'

18. Mencius said, 'Benevolence overcomes cruelty just as water overcomes fire. Those who practise benevolence today are comparable to someone trying to put out a cartload of burning firewood with a cupful of water. When the fire fails to be extinguished, they say water cannot overcome fire. For a man to do this is for him to place himself on the side of those who are cruel to the extreme, and in the end he is sure only to perish.'

19. Mencius said, 'The five types of grain are the best of plants, yet if they are not ripe they are worse than the wild varieties. With benevolence the point, too, lies in seeing to its being ripe.'

1. Ode 247.

20. Mencius said, 'In teaching others archery, Yi naturally aims at drawing the bow to the full, and the student naturally also aims at drawing the bow to the full. In teaching others, the master carpenter naturally does so by means of compasses and square, and the student naturally also learns by means of compasses and square.'

BOOK VI · PART B

1. A man from Jen asked Wu-lu Tzu, 'Which is more important, the rites or food?'

'The rites.'

'Which is more important, the rites or sex?'

'The rites.'

'Suppose you would starve to death if you insisted on the observance of the rites, but would manage to get something to eat if you did not. Would you still insist on their observance? Again, suppose you would not get a wife if you insisted on the observance of *ch'in ying*,[1] but would get one if you did not. Would you still insist on its observance?'

Wu-lu Tzu was unable to answer. The following day he went to Tsou and gave an account of the discussion to Mencius.

'What difficulty is there,' said Mencius, 'in answering this? If you bring the tips to the same level without measuring the difference in the bases, you can make a piece of wood an inch long reach a greater height than a tall building. In saying that gold is heavier than feathers, surely one is not referring to the amount of gold in a clasp and a whole cartload of feathers? If you compare a case where food is important with a case where the rite is inconsequential, then the greater importance of food is not the only absurd conclusion you can draw. Similarly with sex. Go and reply to the questioner in this way, "Suppose you would manage to get something to eat if you took the food from your elder brother by twisting his arm, but would not get it if you did not. Would you twist his arm? Again, suppose you would get a wife if you climbed over the wall of your neighbour on the east side and dragged away the daughter of the house by force, but would not if you did not. Would you drag her away by force?"'

1. This is the part of the marriage rites where the groom goes to the home of the bride to fetch her.

2. Ts'ao Chiao asked, 'Is it true that all men are capable of becoming a Yao or a Shun?'

'Yes,' said Mencius.

'I heard that King Wen was ten foot[1] tall, while T'ang was nine. Now I am a little more than nine foot four inches, yet all I can do is to eat rice. What should I do?'

'What difficulty is there? All you have to do is to make an effort. Here is a man who cannot lift a chicken. He is, indeed, a weak man. Now if he were to lift a ton, then he would, indeed, be a strong man. In other words, whoever can lift the same weight as Wu Huo[2] is himself a Wu Huo. The trouble with a man is surely not his lack of sufficient strength, but his refusal to make the effort. One who walks slowly, keeping behind his elders, is considered a well-mannered younger brother. One who walks quickly, overtaking his elders, is considered an ill-mannered younger brother. Walking slowly is surely not beyond the ability of any man. It is simply a matter of his not making the effort. The way of Yao and Shun is simply to be a good son and a good younger brother. If you wear the clothes of Yao, speak the words of Yao and behave the way Yao behaved, then you *are* a Yao. On the other hand, if you wear the clothes of Chieh, speak the words of Chieh and behave the way Chieh behaved, then you *are* a Chieh. That is all.'

'If the ruler of Tsou receives me and I am given a place to lodge, then I should like to stay and be a disciple of yours.'

'The Way is like a wide road. It is not at all difficult to find. The trouble with people is simply that they do not look for it. You go home and look for it and there will be teachers enough for you.'

3. Kung-sun Ch'ou said, 'According to Kau Tzu, the *Hsiao p'an*[3] is the poem of a petty man.'

'Why did he say so?'

'Because there is a plaintive note.'

1. The Chinese foot in this period was, needless to say, much shorter than the English foot.

2. A byword for a strong man.   3. Ode 197.

'How rigid was old Master Kau in his interpretation of poetry! Here is a man. If a man from Yüeh bends his bow and takes a shot at him, one can recount the incident in a light-hearted manner. The reason is simply that one feels no concern for the man from Yüeh. If it had been one's own elder brother who did this, then one would be in tears while recounting the incident. The reason for the difference is simply that one feels concern for one's brother. The plaintive note is due to the poet's feeling of intimate concern for his parent. To feel this is benevolence. How rigid was old Master Kau in his interpretation of poetry!'

'Why is there no plaintive note in the *K'ai feng*?'[1]

'The *K'ai feng* deals with a minor wrong committed by the parent while the *Hsiao p'an* deals with a major wrong. Not to complain about a major wrong committed by one's parent is to feel insufficient concern; on the other hand, to complain about a minor wrong is to react too violently. Insufficient concern and too violent a reaction are both actions of a bad son. Confucius said, "Shun was the highest example of a good son. At the age of fifty, he still yearned for his parents." '[2]

4. Sung K'eng was on his way to Ch'u. Mencius, meeting him at Shih Ch'iu, asked him, 'Where are you going, sir?'

'I heard that hostilities had broken out between Ch'in and Ch'u. I am going to see the king of Ch'u and try to persuade him to bring an end to them. If I fail to find favour with the king of Ch'u I shall go to see the king of Ch'in and try to persuade him instead. I hope I shall have success with one or other of the two kings.'

'I do not wish to know the details, but may I ask about the gist of your argument? How are you going to persuade the kings?'

'I shall explain to them the unprofitability of war.'

'Your purpose is lofty indeed, but your slogan is wrong. If you place profit before the kings of Ch'in and Ch'u, and they call off their armies because they are drawn to profit, then it means that the soldiers in their armies retire because they are drawn to profit. If a subject, in serving his prince, cherished the profit motive, and a

1. Ode 32.   2. Cf. v. A. 1.

son, in serving his father, and a younger brother, in serving his elder brother, did likewise, then it would mean that in their mutual relations, prince and subject, father and son, elder brother and younger brother, all cherished the profit motive to the total exclusion of morality. The prince of such a state is sure to perish. If, on the other hand, you placed morality before the kings of Ch'in and Ch'u and they called off their armies because they were drawn to morality, then it would mean that the soldiers in their armies retired because they were drawn to morality. If a subject, in serving his prince, cherished morality, and a son, in serving his father, and a younger brother, in serving his elder brother, did likewise, then it would mean that in their mutual relations, prince and subject, father and son, elder brother and younger brother, all cherished morality to the exclusion of profit. The prince of such a state is sure to become a true King. What is the point of mentioning the word "profit"?'

5. When Mencius was staying in Tsou, Chi Jen, who was acting for the Lord of Jen, sought his friendship by sending a gift. Mencius accepted it without any gesture in return. When Mencius was in P'ing Lu, Ch'u Tzu, who was a minister of Ch'i, also sought his friendship by sending a gift. Mencius, again, accepted it without any gesture in return. Subsequently, when Mencius went to Jen from Tsou he went to see Chi Tzu, but when he went to Ch'i from P'ing Lu he did not go to see Ch'u Tzu. Wu-lu Tzu was overjoyed and said, 'At last I have found an opening.' He asked Mencius, 'Master, you went to see Chi Tzu when you went to Jen but did not go to see Ch'u Tzu when you went to Ch'i. Is this because the latter is only a minister?'

'No. The *Book of History* says,

In a gift what counts is the politeness. If the thing outstrips the politeness, that is tantamount to not making the gift. This is because the gift fails to embody the good will of the giver.[1]

That is to say, there is something wanting in the gift.'

Wu-lu Tzu was pleased. Someone questioned him, and he replied,

1. See *Shu ching*, 15. 19b.

'Chi Tzu was unable to go to Tsou, but Ch'u Tzu could have gone to P'ing Lu.'

6. Ch'un-yü K'un said, 'He who puts reputation and real achievement first is a man who tries to benefit others; he who puts reputation and real achievement last is a man who tries to benefit himself. You are numbered among the three Ministers yet you fail to make any reputation and real achievement either in your services to your prince or in your services to the people. Is that all that one can expect of a benevolent man?'

'Even when in a low position,' said Mencius, 'a man was not willing, as a good man, to serve a bad ruler. Such was Po Yi. Another went five times to T'ang and five times to Chieh. Such was Yi Yin. Yet another was not ashamed of a prince with a tarnished reputation, nor was he disdainful of a modest post.[1] Such was Liu Hsia Hui. These three followed different paths, but their goal was one. What is meant by "one"? The answer is, "Benevolence". All that is to be expected of a gentleman is benevolence. Why must he be exactly the same as other gentlemen?'

'In the time of Duke Mu of Lu, Kung-yi Tzu was in charge of affairs of state, and Tzu-liu and Tzu-ssu were in office, yet Lu dwindled in size even more rapidly than before. Are good and wise men of so little benefit to a state?'

'Yü was annexed for failing to employ Po-li Hsi, while Duke Mu of Ch'in, by employing him, became leader of the feudal lords.[2] A state which fails to employ good and wise men will end by suffering annexation. How can it hope to suffer no more than a reduction in size?'

'Formerly, when Wang Pao settled on the River Ch'i, the district to the west of the Yellow River came to be known for song; when Mien Chü settled in Kao T'ang, the right part of Ch'i likewise came to be known for song. The wives of Hua Chou and Ch'i Liang, being supreme in the way they wept for their husbands, transformed the practice of a whole state. When one has something within, it necessarily shows itself without. I have not seen anyone

1. Cf. II. A. 9 and V. B. I.
2. Cf. V. A. 9.

who devotes himself to any pursuit without some achievement to
show for it. Hence there cannot be any good and wise men, other-
wise I am bound to know of them.'

'Confucius was the police commissioner of Lu, but his advice
was not followed. He took part in a sacrifice, but, afterwards, was
not given a share of the meat of the sacrificial animal. He left the
state without waiting to take off his ceremonial cap. Those who
did not understand him thought he acted in this way because of
the meat, but those who understood him realized that he left
because Lu failed to observe the proper rites. For his part Confucius
preferred to be slightly at fault in thus leaving rather than to leave
with no reason at all. The doings of a gentleman are naturally
above the understanding of the ordinary man.'

7. Mencius said, 'The Five Leaders of the feudal lords were
offenders against the Three Kings; the feudal lords of today are
offenders against the Five Leaders of the feudal lords; the Coun-
sellors of today are offenders against the feudal lords of today.

'When the Emperor goes to the feudal lords, this is known as
"a tour of inspection". When the feudal lords go to pay homage
to the Emperor, this is known as "a report on duties". In spring
the purpose is to inspect ploughing so that those who have not
enough for sowing may be given help; in autumn the purpose is
to inspect the harvesting so that those who are in need may be
given aid.[1] When the Emperor enters the domain of a feudal lord,
if the land is opened up and the fields are well cultivated, the old
are cared for and the good and wise honoured, and men of dis-
tinction are in positions of authority, then that feudal lord is re-
warded – rewards taking the form of land. On the other hand, on
entering the domain of a feudal lord, if he finds the land is neglected,
the old are forgotten and the good and wise overlooked, and grasp-
ing men are in positions of power, then there is reprimand.

'If a feudal lord fails to attend court, he suffers a loss in rank for
a first offence, and is deprived of part of his territory for a second
offence, and for a third offence the Six Armies will move into his
state.

1. Cf. 1. B. 4.

'Hence the Emperor punishes but does not attack, while a feudal lord attacks but does not punish. The Five Leaders of the feudal lords intimidated feudal lords into joining them in their attacks on other feudal lords. That is why I said, "The Five Leaders of the feudal lords were offenders against the Three Kings."

'Of the Five Leaders, Duke Huan of Ch'i was the most illustrious. In the meeting of K'uei Ch'iu, the feudal lords bound the animals, placed the text of the pledge on record, but did not sip the blood of the animals. The first item of the pledge was, "Sons who are not dutiful are to be punished; heirs should not be put aside; concubines should not be elevated to the status of wives." The second was, "Honour good and wise men and train the talented so as to make known the virtuous." The third was, "Respect the aged and be kind to the young; do not forget the guest and the traveller." The fourth was, "Gentlemen should not hold office by heredity; different offices should not be held concurrently by the same man; the selection of Gentlemen should be appropriate; a feudal lord should not exercise sole authority in the execution of a Counsellor." The fifth was, "Dykes should not be diverted; the sale of rice to other states should not be prohibited; any fief given should be reported." The text went on to say, "All those who have taken part in this pledge should, after the event, come to an amicable understanding." The feudal lords of today all violate these five injunctions. That is why I said, "The feudal lords of today are offenders against the Five Leaders of the feudal lords."

'The crime of encouraging a ruler in his evil deeds is small compared to that of pandering to his unspoken evil desires. The Counsellors of today all do wrong in order to please their prince. That is why I said, "The Counsellors today are offenders against the feudal lords of today."'

8. Lu wanted to make Shen Tzu commander of the army. Mencius said, 'To send the people to war before they are trained is to bring disaster upon them. One who brings disaster upon the people would not have been tolerated in the days of Yao and Shun. Even

if Ch'i could be defeated in one battle and Nan Yang annexed, it would still not be permissible . . .'

Shen Tzu, looking displeased, said, 'This is something I do not understand.'

'I shall tell you plainly. The domain of the Emperor is a thousand *li* square, for anything less will not be sufficient to enable him to receive the feudal lords. The domain of a feudal lord is a hundred *li* square, for with anything less he will not be able to safeguard the archives of the ancestral temple. When the Duke of Chou was enfeoffed in Lu, his domain was a hundred *li* square. There was no shortage of land, but the fief he was given did not exceed a hundred *li*. When T'ai Kung was enfeoffed in Ch'i, his domain was a hundred *li* square. There was no shortage of land, but the fief he was given did not exceed a hundred *li*. Today Lu is five times a hundred *li* square. If a true King arises, do you think Lu will be one of the states he will enlarge or one of the states he will reduce? A benevolent man would not even take from one man to give to another, let alone seek territory at the cost of human lives. In serving his lord, a gentleman has only one aim and that is to put him on the right path and set his mind on benevolence.'

9. Mencius said, 'Those who are in the service of princes today all say, "I am able to extend the territory of my prince, and fill his coffers for him." The good subject of today would have been looked upon in antiquity as a pest on the people. To enrich a prince who is neither attracted to the Way nor bent upon benevolence is to enrich a Chieh.

'Again, they say, "I am able to gain allies and ensure victory in war for my prince." The good subject of today would have been looked upon in antiquity as a pest on the people. To try to make a prince strong in war who is neither attracted to the Way nor bent upon benevolence is to aid a Chieh.

'Following the practice of the present day, unless there is a change in the ways of the people, a man could not hold the Empire for the duration of one morning, even if it were given to him.'

10. Po Kuei said, 'I should like to fix the rate of taxation at one in twenty. What do you think of it?'

'Your way,' said Mencius, 'is that of the Northern barbarians. In a city of ten thousand households, would it be enough to have a single potter?'

'No. There will be a shortage of earthenware.'

'In the land of the Northern barbarians, the five grains do not grow. Millet is the only crop that grows. They are without city walls, houses, ancestral temples or the sacrificial rites. They do not have diplomacy with its attendant gifts and banquets, nor have they the numerous offices and officials. That is why they can manage on a tax of one in twenty. Now in the Central Kingdoms, how can human relationships and men in authority be abolished? The affairs of a city cannot be conducted when there is a shortage even of potters. How much more so if the shortage is of men in authority? Those who wish to reduce taxation to below the level laid down by Yao and Shun are all, to a greater or less degree, barbarians; while those who wish to increase it are all, to a greater or less degree, Chiehs.'

11. Po Kuei said, 'In dealing with water I am better than Yü.'

'You are mistaken,' said Mencius. 'In dealing with water, Yü followed the natural tendency of water. Hence he emptied the water into the Four Seas. Now you empty the water into the neighbouring states. When water goes counter to its course, it is described as a "deluge", in other words, a "flood", and floods are detested by the benevolent man. You are mistaken, my good sir.'

12. Mencius said, 'Other than by adherence to his word, in what respect can a gentleman be guilty of inflexibility?'[1]

13. Lu wished to entrust the government to Yüeh-cheng Tzu.

'When I heard this,' said Mencius, 'I was so happy that I could not sleep.'

1. Cf. 'A great man need not keep his word nor does he necessarily see his action through to the end. He aims only at what is right.' (IV. B. 11)

'Has Yüeh-cheng Tzu,' asked Kung-sun Ch'ou, 'great strength
of character?'

'No.'

'Is he a man of thought and foresight?'

'No.'

'Is he widely informed?'

'No.'

'Then why were you so happy that you could not sleep?'

'He is a man who is drawn to the good.'

'Is that enough?'

'To be drawn to the good is more than enough to cope with the
Empire, let alone the state of Lu. If a man is truly drawn to the
good, then, within the Four Seas, men will come, thinking nothing
of the distance of a thousand *li*, to bring to his notice what is good.
On the other hand, if he is not drawn to the good, then men will
say of him, "He seems to say 'I know it all'." The way one says
"I know it all" with its accompanying look of complacence will
repel men a thousand *li* away. If Gentlemen stay a thousand *li*
away, then the flatterers will arrive. Can one succeed in one's wish
to govern a state properly when one is surrounded by flatterers?'

14. Ch'en Tzu said, 'Under what condition would a gentleman in
antiquity take office?'

'There are three conditions,' said Mencius, 'under each of which
he would take office; equally, there are three conditions under
each of which he would relinquish it.

'First, when he was sent for with the greatest respect, in accord-
ance with the proper rites, and told that his advice would be put into
practice, he would go. But when his advice was not put into prac-
tice, he would leave, even though the courtesies were still observed.

'Second, when he was sent for with the greatest respect, in
accordance with the proper rites, he would go, though his advice
was not put into practice. But he would leave when the courtesies
were no longer meticulously observed.

'Third, when he could no longer afford to eat either in the morn-
ing or in the evening, and was so weak from hunger that he could
no longer go out of doors, then he could accept charity from the

prince who, hearing of his plight, gave to him out of kindness, saying, "As I have failed, in the first instance, to put into practice the way he taught, and then failed to listen to his advice, it will be to my shame if he dies of hunger in my domain." But the purpose of this acceptance is merely to ward off starvation.'[1]

15. Mencius said, 'Shun rose from the fields; Fu Yüeh was raised to office from amongst the builders; Chiao Ke from amidst the fish and salt; Kuan Chung from the hands of the prison officer; Sun Shu-ao from the sea and Po-li Hsi from the market. That is why Heaven, when it is about to place a great burden on a man, always first tests his resolution, exhausts his frame and makes him suffer starvation and hardship, frustrates his efforts so as to shake him from his mental lassitude, toughen his nature and make good his deficiencies. As a rule, a man can mend his ways only after he has made mistakes. It is only when a man is frustrated in mind and in his deliberations that he is able to innovate. It is only when his intentions become visible on his countenance and audible in his tone of voice that others can understand him. As a rule, a state without law-abiding families and reliable Gentlemen on the one hand, and, on the other, without the threat of foreign invasion, will perish. Only then do we learn the lesson that we survive in adversity and perish in ease and comfort.'

16. Mencius said, 'There are more ways than one of instructing others. My disdain to instruct a man is itself one way of instructing him.'

1. Cf. v. b. 5 and v. b. 6.

BOOK VII · PART A

1. Mencius said, 'For a man to give full realization to his heart is for him to understand his own nature, and a man who knows his own nature will know Heaven. By retaining his heart and nurturing his nature he is serving Heaven. Whether he is going to die young or to live to a ripe old age makes no difference to his steadfastness of purpose. It is through awaiting whatever is to befall him with a perfected character that he stands firm on his proper destiny.'

2. Mencius said, 'Though nothing happens that is not due to destiny, one accepts willingly only what is one's proper destiny. That is why he who understands destiny does not stand under a wall on the verge of collapse. He who dies after having done his best in following the Way dies according to his proper destiny. It is never anyone's proper destiny to die in fetters.'

3. Mencius said, 'Seek and you will get it; let go and you will lose it. If this is the case, then seeking is of use to getting and what is sought is within yourself.[1] But if there is a proper way to seek it and whether you get it or not depends on destiny, then seeking is of no use to getting and what is sought lies outside yourself.'[2]

4. Mencius said, 'All the ten thousand things are there in me. There is no greater joy for me than to find, on self-examination, that I am true to myself. Try your best to treat others as you would wish to be treated yourself, and you will find that this is the shortest way to benevolence.'

5. Mencius said, 'The multitude can be said never to understand what they practise, to notice what they repeatedly do, or to be aware of the path they follow all their lives.'

1. This refers to one's true heart. The opening sentence is also to be found in VI. A. 6.
2. This refers to external possessions like wealth and position.

6. Mencius said, 'A man must not be without shame, for the shame of being without shame is shamelessness indeed.'

7. Mencius said, 'Great is the use of shame to man. He who indulges in craftiness has no use for shame. If a man is not ashamed of being inferior to other men, how will he ever become their equal?'

8. Mencius said, 'Wise kings in antiquity devoted themselves to goodness, forgetting their own exalted position. How should wise Gentlemen in antiquity be any different? They delighted in the Way, forgetting the exalted position of others. That is why kings and dukes could not get to see them often except by showing them due respect and observing due courtesy. If just to see them often was so difficult, how much more so to induce them to take office.'

9. Mencius said to Sung Kou-chien, 'You are fond of travelling from state to state, offering advice. I shall tell you how this should be done. You should be content whether your worth is recognized by others or not.'
   'What must a man be before he can be content?'
   'If he reveres virtue and delights in rightness, he can be content. Hence a Gentleman never abandons rightness in adversity, nor does he depart from the Way in success. By not abandoning rightness in adversity, he finds delight in himself; by not departing from the Way in success, he does not disappoint the people. Men of antiquity made the people feel the effect of their bounty when they realized their ambition, and, when they failed to realize their ambition, were at least able to show the world an exemplary character. In obscurity a man makes perfect his own person, but in prominence he makes perfect the whole Empire as well.'

10. Mencius said, 'Those who make the effort only when there is a King Wen are ordinary men. Outstanding men make the effort even without a King Wen.'

11. Mencius said, 'To look upon oneself as deficient even though the possessions of the families of Han and Wei be added to one's own is to surpass other men by a long way.'

12. Mencius said, 'If the services of the common people were used with a view to sparing them hardship, they would not complain even when hard driven. If the common people were put to death in pursuance of a policy to keep them alive, they would die bearing no ill-will towards the man who put them to death.'

13. Mencius said, 'The people under a leader of the feudal lords are happy; those under a true King are expansive and content. They bear no ill-will when put to death, neither do they feel any gratitude when profited. They move daily towards goodness without realizing who it is that brings this about. A gentleman transforms where he passes, and works wonders where he abides. He is in the same stream as Heaven above and Earth below. Can he be said to bring but small benefit?'

14. Mencius said, 'Benevolent words do not have as profound an effect on the people as benevolent music. Good government does not win the people as does good education. He who practises good government is feared by the people; he who gives the people good education is loved by them. Good government wins the wealth of the people; good education wins their hearts.'

15. Mencius said, 'What a man is able to do without having to learn it is what he can truly do; what he knows without having to reflect on it is what he truly knows. There are no young children who do not know loving their parents, and none of them when they grow up will not know respecting their elder brothers. Loving one's parents is benevolence; respecting one's elders is rightness. What is left to be done is simply the extension of these to the whole Empire.'

16. Mencius said, 'When Shun lived in the depth of the mountains, he lived amongst trees and stones, and had as friends deer and pigs. The difference between him and the uncultivated man of the mountains then was slight. But when he heard a single good word, witnessed a single good deed, it was like water causing a breach

in the dykes of the Yangtse or the Yellow River. Nothing could withstand it.'

17. Mencius said, 'Do not do what others do not choose to do; do not desire what others do not desire. That is all.'

18. Mencius said, 'It is often through adversity that men acquire virtue, wisdom, skill and cleverness. The estranged subject or the son of a concubine, because he conducts himself with the greatest of caution and is constantly on the watch out for possible disasters, succeeds where others would have failed.'

19. Mencius said, 'There are men whose purpose is to serve a prince. They will try to please whatever prince they are serving. There are men whose aim is to bring peace to the state. They achieve satisfaction through bringing this about. There are the subjects of Heaven. They practise only what could be extended to the whole Empire. There are the great men. They can rectify others by rectifying themselves.'

20. Mencius said, 'A gentleman delights in three things, and being ruler over the Empire is not amongst them. His parents are alive and his brothers are well. This is the first delight. Above, he is not ashamed to face Heaven; below, he is not ashamed to face man. This is the second delight. He has the good fortune of having the most talented pupils in the Empire. This is the third delight. A gentleman delights in three things and being ruler over the Empire is not amongst them.'

21. Mencius said, 'An extensive territory and a vast population are things a gentleman desires, but what he delights in lies elsewhere. To stand in the centre of the Empire and bring peace to the people within the Four Seas is what a gentleman delights in, but that which he follows as his nature lies elsewhere. That which a gentleman follows as his nature is not added to when he holds sway over the Empire, nor is it detracted from when he is reduced to straitened circumstances. This is because he knows his allotted

station. That which a gentleman follows as his nature, that is to say, benevolence, rightness, the rites and wisdom, is rooted in his heart, and manifests itself in his face, giving it a sleek appearance. It also shows in his back and extends to his limbs, rendering their message intelligible without words.'

22. Mencius said, 'Po Yi fled from Tchou and settled on the edge of the North Sea. When he heard of the rise of King Wen he stirred and said, "Why not go back? I hear that Hsi Po[1] takes good care of the aged." T'ai Kung fled from Tchou and settled on the edge of the East Sea. When he heard of the rise of King Wen he stirred and said, "Why not go back? I hear that Hsi Po takes good care of the aged."[2] When there is someone in the Empire who takes good care of the aged, benevolent men will look upon him as their refuge.

'If the mulberry is planted at the foot of the walls in every homestead of five *mu* of land and the woman of the house keeps silkworms, then the aged can wear silk. If there are five hens and two sows, and these do not miss their breeding season, then the aged will not be deprived of meat. If a man tills a hundred *mu* of land, there will be enough for his family of eight mouths not to go hungry.[3]

'When Hsi Po was said to "take good care of the aged", what was meant is this. He laid down the pattern for the distribution of land, taught the men the way to plant trees and keep animals, and showed their womenfolk the way to care for the aged. A man needs silk for warmth at fifty and meat for sustenance at seventy. To have neither warm clothes nor a full belly is to be cold and hungry. The people under King Wen had no old folk who were cold and hungry.'

23. Mencius said, 'Put in order the fields of the people, lighten their taxes, and the people can be made affluent. If one's consump-

---

1. i.e. King Wen.
2. Cf. IV. A. 13.
3. Cf. I. A. 3 and I. A. 7. The wording, however, is slightly different in the present passage.

tion of food is confined to what is in season and one's use of other
commodities is in accordance with the rites, then one's resources
will be more than sufficient. The common people cannot live
without water and fire, yet one never meets with a refusal when
knocking on another's door in the evening to beg for water or
fire. This is because these are in such abundance. In governing
the Empire, the sage tries to make food as plentiful as water and
fire. When that happens, how can there be any amongst his people
who are not benevolent?'

24. Mencius said, 'When he ascended the Eastern Mount, Con-
fucius felt that Lu was small, and when he ascended Mount T'ai,
he felt that the Empire was small. Likewise it is difficult for water
to come up to the expectation of someone who has seen the Sea,
and it is difficult for words to come up to the expectation of some-
one who has studied under a sage. There is a way to judge water.
Watch for its ripples. When the sun and moon shine, the light
shows up the least crack that will admit it. Flowing water is such
that it does not go further forward until it has filled all the hollows.[1]
A gentleman, in his pursuit of the Way, does not get there unless
he achieves a beautiful pattern.'

25. Mencius said, 'He who gets up with the crowing of the cock
and never tires of doing good is the same kind of man as Shun; he
who gets up with the crowing of the cock and never tires of
working for profit is the same kind of man as Chih.[2] If you wish
to understand the difference between Shun and Chih, you need
look no further than the gap separating the good and the profit-
able.'

26. Mencius said, 'Yang Tzu chooses egoism. Even if he could
benefit the Empire by pulling out one hair he would not do it.[3] Mo

1. Cf. IV. B. 18.
2. A byword for robbers.
3. This is almost certain to be a distortion of Yang Chu's doctrine. What he
taught was rather that one should not give a hair on one's body in exchange
for the enjoyment of the Empire.

Tzu advocates love without discrimination. If by shaving his head and showing his heels he could benefit the Empire, he would do it. Tzu-mo holds on to the middle, half way between the two extremes. Holding on to the middle is closer to being right, but to do this without the proper measure is no different from holding to one extreme. The reason for disliking those who hold to one extreme is that they cripple the Way. One thing is singled out to the neglect of a hundred others.'

27. Mencius said, 'A hungry man finds his food delectable; a thirsty man finds his drink delicious. Both lack the proper measure of food and drink because hunger and thirst interfere with his judgement. The palate is not the only thing which is open to interference by hunger and thirst. The human heart, too, is open to the same interference. If a man can prevent hunger and thirst from interfering with his heart, then he does not need to worry about being inferior to other men.'

28. Mencius said, 'Liu Hsia Hui would not have compromised on his integrity for the sake of the three ducal offices.'

29. Mencius said, 'To try to achieve anything is like digging a well. You can dig a hole nine fathoms deep, but if you fail to reach the source of water, it is just an abandoned well.'

30. Mencius said, 'Yao and Shun had it as their nature. T'ang and King Wu embodied it.[1] The Five Leaders of the feudal lords borrowed it.[2] But if a man borrows a thing and keeps it long enough, how can one be sure that it will not become truly his?'

31. Kung-sun Ch'ou said, 'Yi Yin banished T'ai Chia to T'ung, saying, "I do not wish to be close to one who is intractable", and the people were greatly pleased. When T'ai Chia became good, Yi Yin restored him to the throne, and the people, once again,

1. Cf. VII. B. 33.
2. Cf. II. A. 3. The 'it' here would seem to refer to benevolence.

were pleased. When a prince is not good, is it permissible for a good and wise man who is his subject to banish him?'

'It is permissible,' said Mencius, 'only if he had the motive of a Yi Yin; otherwise, it would be usurpation.'

32. Kung-sun Ch'ou said, 'The *Book of Odes* says,

> [A gentleman] enjoys only food he has earned.

Why, then, does a gentleman eat food when he does not share in the work of tilling the land?'

'When a gentleman stays in a state,' said Mencius, 'if he is employed he can make the prince secure, rich and honoured, and, if the young men come under his influence, he can make them dutiful to their parents and elders, conscientious in their work and faithful to their word. Is there a truer case of "enjoying only food he has earned"?'

33. Prince Tien asked, 'What is the business of a Gentleman?'

'To set his mind on high principles.'

'What do you mean by this?'

'To be moral. That is all. It is contrary to benevolence to kill one innocent man; it is contrary to rightness to take what one is not entitled to. Where is one's dwelling? In benevolence. Where is one's road? In rightness. To dwell in benevolence and to follow rightness constitute the sum total of the business of a great man.'

34. Mencius said, 'Everyone believes that Ch'en Chung would refuse the state of Ch'i were it offered to him against the principles of rightness. But what he calls rightness is merely the rightness which refuses a basketful of rice and a bowlful of soup.[1] No one considers the neglect of parents and the denial of relationships between prince and subject and between superior and inferior as laudable.[2] How, then, can we take on trust his conduct on

[1] For Ch'en Chung see III. B. 10, and for the refusal of a basketful of rice and a bowlful of soup see VI. A. 10.

[2] The translation of this sentence is tentative as the text is exceedingly obscure.

important issues simply on the strength of his conduct in minor matters?'

35. T'ao Ying asked, 'When Shun was Emperor and Kao Yao was the judge, if the Blind Man killed a man, what was to be done?'

'The only thing to do was to apprehend him.'

'In that case, would Shun not try to stop it?'

'How could Shun stop it? Kao Yao had his authority from which he received the law.'

'Then what would Shun have done?'

'Shun looked upon casting aside the Empire as no more than discarding a worn shoe. He would have secretly carried the old man on his back and fled to the edge of the Sea and lived there happily, never giving a thought to the Empire.'

36. Mencius went to Ch'i from Fan. When he saw the son of the King of Ch'i from a distance, he sighed and said, 'A man's surroundings transform his air just as the food he eats changes his body. Great indeed are a man's surroundings. Otherwise, are we not all the son of some man or another?'

He added, 'The house, carriage, horses and dress of the prince are not so different from those of other people, yet the prince is so different. This is because of the surroundings. How much more if one were to live in the loftiest of dwellings[1] in the Empire.

'The lord of Lu went to Sung, and called in front of the Tieh Tse Gate. The keeper said, "This is not my lord, yet how like is the voice to that of my lord." The reason is simply that both princes came from similar surroundings.'

37. Mencius said, 'To feed a man without showing him love is to treat him like a pig; to love him without showing him respect is to keep him like a domestic animal. Respect is but a gift that is not yet presented. Respect that is without reality will not take a gentleman in merely by its empty show.'

1. i.e. benevolence. Cf. VII. A. 33; also IV. A. 11. The term is also found in III. B. 2.

38. Mencius said, 'Our body and complexion are given to us by Heaven. Only a sage can give his body complete fulfilment.'

39. King Hsüan of Ch'i wanted to cut short the period of mourning. Kung-sun Ch'ou commented, 'Is it not better to observe a year's mourning than not to observe any mourning at all?'

'This is the same,' said Mencius, 'as saying to someone who is twisting his elder brother's arm, "Do it gently". What you ought to do is simply to teach him the duties of a son and a younger brother.'

There was a prince whose mother died. His tutor requested, on his behalf, permission to observe mourning for a number of months. Kung-sun Ch'ou asked, 'How about this?'

'This is a case where the man has no hope of realizing his wish to observe the full period of mourning. Under such circumstances, even to prolong the period by a single day is better than not to prolong it at all. What I said the other day referred to those who failed to act even when there were no obstacles.'

40. Mencius said, 'A gentleman teaches in five ways. The first is by a transforming influence like that of timely rain. The second is by helping the student to realize his virtue to the full. The third is by helping him to develop his talent. The fourth is by answering his questions. And the fifth is by setting an example others not in contact with him can emulate. These five are the ways in which a gentleman teaches.'

41. Kung-sun Ch'ou said, 'The Way is indeed lofty and beautiful, but to attempt it is like trying to climb up to Heaven which seems beyond one's reach. Why not substitute for it something which men have some hopes of attaining so as to encourage them constantly to make the effort?'

'A great craftsman,' said Mencius, 'does not put aside the plumb-line for the benefit of the clumsy carpenter. Yi did not compromise on his standards of drawing the bow for the sake of the clumsy archer.[1] A gentleman is full of eagerness when he has

1. Cf. VI. A. 20.

drawn his bow, but before he lets fly the arrow, he stands in the middle of the path, and those who are able to do so follow him.'

42. Mencius said, 'When the Way prevails in the Empire, it goes where one's person goes; when the Way is eclipsed, one's person goes where the Way has gone. I have never heard of making the Way go where other people are going.'

43. Kung-tu Tzu said, 'When T'eng Keng was studying under you, he appeared to deserve your courtesy; yet you never answered his questions. Why was that?'

'I never answer any questioner,' said Mencius, 'who relies on the advantage he possesses of position, capability, age,[1] merit or status as an old friend. T'eng Keng was guilty on two of these counts.'

44. Mencius said, 'He who stops where he ought not to will always stop wherever he may be. He who treats badly those he ought to treat well will always treat other people badly whoever they may be. He who advances sharply falls back rapidly.'

45. Mencius said, 'A gentleman is sparing with things but shows no benevolence towards them; he shows benevolence towards the people but is not attached to them. He is attached to his parents but is merely benevolent towards the people; he is benevolent towards the people but is merely sparing[2] with things.'

46. Mencius said, 'A wise man knows everything, but he considers urgent only that which demands attention. A benevolent man loves everyone, but he devotes himself to the close association with good and wise men. Even Yao and Shun did not use their wisdom on all things alike; this is because they put first things first. Nor did they use their benevolence to love everyone; this is because they considered urgent the close association with good

1. Cf. v. b. 3.
2. Throughout this passage Mencius is exploiting the fact that the word *ai* means both 'to love' and 'to be sparing, to be frugal'.

and wise men. For a man to observe meticulously three or five months' mourning while failing to observe three years' mourning, or for him to ask whether he is guilty of breaking the food with his teeth while bolting down his food and drink is for him to show an ignorance of priorities.'

BOOK VII · PART B

1. Mencius said, 'How ruthless was King Hui of Liang! A bene-volent man extends his love from those he loves to those he does not love. A ruthless man extends his ruthlessness from those he does not love to those he loves.'

'What do you mean?' asked Kung-sun Ch'ou.

'King Hui of Liang sent his people to war, making pulp of them, for the sake of gaining further territory. He suffered a grave defeat and when he wanted to go to war a second time he was afraid he would not be able to win, so he herded the young men he loved to their death as well. This is what I meant when I said he extended his ruthlessness from those he did not love to those he loved.'

2. Mencius said, 'In the *Spring and Autumn Annals* there were no just wars. There were only cases of one war not being quite as bad as another. A punitive expedition is a war waged by one in authority against his subordinates. It is not for peers to punish one another by war.'

3. Mencius said, 'If one believed everything in the *Book of History*, it would have been better for the *Book* not to have existed at all. In the *Wu ch'eng* chapter[1] I accept only two or three strips.[2] A benevolent man has no match in the Empire. How could it be that "the blood spilled was enough to carry staves along with it", when the most benevolent waged war against the most cruel?'[3]

4. Mencius said, 'There are people who say, "I am expert at military formations; I am expert at waging war." This is a grave crime. If

1. One of the lost chapters of the *Book of History*. The chapter by the same name in the present text of the *Book of History* is spurious.

2. In ancient China books were written on narrow bamboo strips which were bound together by leather thongs or cords so that they could be rolled up when not in use.

3. The *Wu ch'eng* gives an account of the war waged by King Wu against the tyrant Tchou.

the ruler of a state is drawn to benevolence he will have no match in the Empire. "When he marched on the south, the northern barbarians complained; when he marched on the east, the western barbarians complained. They all said, 'Why does he not come to us first?' "[1]

'When King Wu marched on Yin, he had three hundred war chariots and three thousand brave warriors. He said, "Do not be afraid. I come to bring you peace, not to wage war on the people." And the sound of the people knocking their heads on the ground was like the toppling of a mountain. To wage a punitive war is to rectify.[2] There is no one who does not wish himself rectified. What need is there for war?'

5. Mencius said, 'A carpenter or a carriage-maker can pass on to another the rules of his craft, but he cannot make him skilful.'

6. Mencius said, 'When Shun lived on dried rice and wild vege-tables, it was as though he was going to do this for the rest of his life. But when he became Emperor, clad in precious robes, playing on his lute, with the two daughters [of Yao] in attendance, it was as though this was what he had been used to all his life.'

7. Mencius said, 'Only now do I realize how serious it is to kill a member of the family of another man. If you killed his father, he would kill your father; if you killed his elder brother, he would kill your elder brother. This being the case, though you may not have killed your father and brother with your own hands, it is but one step removed.'

8. Mencius said, 'In antiquity, a border station was set up as a precaution against violence. Today it is set up to perpetrate vio-lence.'

9. Mencius said, 'If you do not practise the Way yourself, you cannot expect it to be practised even by your own wife and children.

1. For this quotation see I. B. 11.
2. The two verbs in Chinese are cognate.

If you do not impose work on others in accordance with the Way, you cannot expect obedience even from your own wife and children.'

10. Mencius said, 'He who never misses a chance for profit cannot be killed by a bad year; he who is equipped with every virtue cannot be led astray by a wicked world.'

11. Mencius said, 'A man who is out to make a name for himself will be able to give away a state of a thousand chariots, but reluctance would be written all over his face if he had to give away a basketful of rice and a bowlful of soup when no such purpose was served.'

12. Mencius said, 'If the benevolent and the good and wise are not trusted, the state will only be a shell; if the rites and rightness are absent, the distinction between superior and inferior will not be observed; if government is not properly regulated, the state will not have enough resources to meet expenditure.'

13. Mencius said, 'There are cases of a ruthless man gaining possession of a state, but it has never happened that such a man gained possession of the Empire.'

14. Mencius said, 'The people are of supreme importance; the altars to the gods of earth and grain come next; last comes the ruler. That is why he who gains the confidence of the multitudinous people will be Emperor; he who gains the confidence of the Emperor will be a feudal lord; he who gains the confidence of a feudal lord will be a Counsellor. When a feudal lord endangers the altars to the gods of earth and grain[1] he should be replaced. When the sacrificial animals are sleek, the offerings are clean and the sacrifices are observed at due times, and yet floods and droughts come, then the altars should be replaced.'

1. The symbol of independence of the state.

15. Mencius said, 'The sage is teacher to a hundred generations. Such were Po Yi and Liu Hsia Hui. Hence hearing of the way of Po Yi, a covetous man will be purged of his covetousness and a weak man will become resolute; hearing of the way of Liu Hsia Hui, a mean man will become generous and a narrow-minded man tolerant.[1] Can these two, if they were not sages, have inspired by their example all those who come a hundred generations after them? How much more inspiring they must have been to those who were fortunate enough to have known them personally!'

16. Mencius said, ' "Benevolence" means "man".[2] When these two are conjoined, the result is "the Way".'

17. Mencius said, 'When he left Lu, Confucius said, "I proceed as slowly as possible." This is the way to leave the state of one's father and mother. When he left Ch'i he started after emptying the rice from the steamer.[3] This is the way to leave a foreign state.'

18. Mencius said, 'That the gentleman[4] was in difficulties in the region of Ch'en and Ts'ai was because he had no friends at court.'

19. Mo Chi said, 'I am not much of a speaker.'
'There is no harm in that,' said Mencius. 'A Gentleman dislikes those who speak too much. The *Book of Odes* says,

> I am sad and silent,
> For I am hated by the small men.[5]

Such a one was Confucius.

> He neither dispelled the dislike of others
> Nor did he lose his own reputation.[6]

Such a one was King Wen.'

1. Cf. v. b. 1.
2. This is not a simple phonetic gloss based on identical pronunciations, as the two words are in fact cognate.
3. Cf. v. b. 1.   4. i.e. Confucius.
5. Ode 26.   6. Ode 237.

20. Mencius said, 'A good and wise man helps others to understand clearly by his own clear understanding. Nowadays, men try to help others understand by their own benighted ignorance.'

21. Mencius said to Kau Tzu, 'A trail through the mountains, if used, becomes a path in a short time, but, if unused, becomes blocked by grass in an equally short time. Now your heart is blocked by grass.'

22. Kau Tzu said, 'The music of Yü surpassed that of King Wen.'
'What makes you say that?' said Mencius.
'It is the bell-rope. It is almost worn through.'
'That is not sufficient as evidence. Do you imagine that the rut through the city gates was made by a single pair of horses?'

23. There was a famine in Ch'i. Ch'en Chen said, 'The people all thought that you, Master, were going to bring about another distribution of grain from the T'ang granary. I suppose there is no hope of that happening?'
'To do this,' said Mencius, 'is to do a "Feng Fu". There was a man in Chin by the name of Feng Fu. He was an expert at seizing tigers with his bare hands, but in the end he became a good Gentleman. It happened that he went to the outskirts of the city, and there was a crowd pursuing a tiger. The tiger turned at bay and no one dared go near it. On seeing Feng Fu, the people hastened to meet him. Feng Fu rolled up his sleeves and got off his carriage. The crowd was delighted, but those who were Gentlemen laughed at him.'

24. Mencius said, 'The way the mouth is disposed towards tastes, the eye towards colours, the ear towards sounds, the nose towards smells, and the four limbs towards ease is human nature, yet therein also lies the Decree. That is why the gentleman does not describe it as nature. The way benevolence pertains to the relation between father and son, duty to the relation between prince and subject, the rites to the relation between guest and host, wisdom to the good and wise man, the sage to the way of Heaven, is the Decree, but

therein also lies human nature. That is why the gentleman does not describe it as Decree.'

25. Hao-sheng Pu-hai asked, 'What sort of a man is Yüeh-cheng Tzu?'

'A good man,' said Mencius. 'A true man.'

'What do you mean by "good" and "true"?'

'The desirable is called "good". To have it in oneself is called "true". To possess it fully in oneself is called "beautiful", but to shine forth with this full possession is called "great". To be great and be transformed by this greatness is called "sage"; to be sage and to transcend the understanding is called "divine". Yüeh-cheng Tzu has something of the first two qualities but has not quite reached the last four.'

26. Mencius said, 'Those who desert the Mohist school are sure to turn to that of Yang; those who desert the Yang school are sure to turn to the Confucianist. When they turn to us we simply accept them. Nowadays, those who debate with the followers of Yang and Mo behave as if they were chasing strayed pigs. They are not content to return the pigs to the sty, but go on to tie their feet up.'

27. Mencius said, 'There is taxation levied in cloth, in grain, and in labour. A gentleman employs one to the full while relaxing the other two. If two are employed to the full, there would be death from starvation amongst the people, and if all three are so employed, father will be separated from son.'

28. Mencius said, 'The feudal lords have three treasures: land, people and government. Those who treasure pearls and jade are sure to suffer the consequences in their own lifetime.'

29. P'en-ch'eng K'uo took office in Ch'i. Mencius said, 'He is certain to meet his death.'

P'en-ch'eng K'uo was killed and Mencius' disciples asked, 'How did you, Master, know that he was going to be killed?'

'He was a man with limited talent who had never been taught the great way of the gentleman. That was just enough to cost him his life.'

30. Mencius went to T'eng and put up at the Shang Kung. There was a pair of unfinished sandals on the window-sill. The men in the hostelry looked for them in vain. Someone asked Mencius, 'Are your followers so deceitful in appearance?'

'Do you think that they have come with the express purpose of stealing the sandals?'

'Is that not so?'

'In setting myself [16] up as a teacher, I do not go after anyone who leaves, nor do I refuse anyone who comes. So long as he comes with the right attitude of mind, I accept him. That is all.'[1]

31. Mencius said, 'For every man there are things he cannot bear. To extend this to what he can bear is benevolence.[2] For every man there are things he is not willing to do. To extend this to what he is willing to do is rightness. If a man can extend to the full his natural aversion to harming others, then there will be an overabundance of benevolence. If a man can extend his dislike for boring holes and climbing over walls,[3] then there will be an overabundance of rightness. If a man can extend his unwillingness to suffer the actual humiliation of being addressed as "thou" and "thee", then wherever he goes he will not do anything that is not right.

'To speak to a Gentleman who cannot be spoken to is to use speech as a bait; on the other hand, not to speak to one who could be spoken to is to use silence as a bait.[4] In either case, the action is of the same kind as that of boring holes and climbing over walls.'

1. Mencius' attitude towards those who came to study under him is reminiscent of the attitude of Confucius. Cf. the *Analects of Confucius*, VII. 29.

2. Cf. VII. B. 1.

3. Cf. 'those who bore holes in the wall to peep at one another, and climb over it to meet illicitly' (III. B. 3).

4. Cf. the *Analects of Confucius*, XV. 8.

32. Mencius said, 'Words near at hand but with far-reaching import are good words. The way of holding on to the essential while giving it wide application is a good way. The words of a gentleman never go as far as below the sash, yet in them is to be found the Way. What the gentleman holds on to is the cultivation of his own character, yet this brings order to the Empire. The trouble with people is that they leave their own fields to weed the fields of others. They are exacting towards others but indulgent towards themselves.'

33. Mencius said, 'Yao and Shun had it as their nature; T'ang and King Wu returned to it.[1] To be in accord with the rites in every movement is the highest of virtue. When one mourns sorrowfully over the dead it is not to impress the living. When one follows unswervingly the path of virtue it is not to win advancement. When one invariably keeps one's word it is not to establish the rectitude of one's actions. A gentleman merely follows the norm and awaits his destiny.'[2]

34. Mencius said, 'When speaking to men of consequence it is necessary to look on them with contempt and not be impressed by their lofty position. Their hall is tens of feet high; the capitals are several feet broad. Were I to meet with success, I would not indulge in such things. Their tables, laden with food, measure ten feet across, and their female attendants are counted in the hundreds. Were I to meet with success, I would not indulge in such things. They have a great time drinking, driving and hunting, with a retinue of a thousand chariots. Were I to meet with success I would not indulge in such things. All the things they do I would not do, and everything I do is in accordance with ancient institutions. Why, then, should I cower before them?'

35. Mencius said, 'There is nothing better for the nurturing of the heart than to reduce the number of one's desires. When a man has but few desires, even if there is anything he fails to retain in

1. Cf. VII. A. 30. The 'it' here must also be referring to benevolence.
2. Cf. VII. A. 1.

himself, it cannot be much; but when he has a great many desires, then even if there is anything he manages to retain in himself, it cannot be much.'[1]

36. Because Tseng Hsi[2] was fond of eating jujubes, Tseng Tzu could not bring himself to eat them. Kung-sun Ch'ou asked, 'Which is more tasty, mince and roast or jujubes?'

'Minces and roast, of course,' said Mencius.

'In that case why did Tseng Tzu eat mince and roast, but not jujubes?'

'Mince and roast were a taste shared by others, but not jujubes. A personal name is tabooed but not a surname, because a surname is shared while a personal name is not.'

37. Wan Chang asked, 'When Confucius was in Ch'en, he exclaimed, "Let us go home. The young men of my school are wild and unconventional, rushing forward while not forgetting their origins."[3] As Confucius was in Ch'en, what made him think of the wild Gentlemen of Lu?'

Mencius answered, 'Confucius [said], "If one fails to find those who follow the middle way as associates, one can only fall back on the wild and the squeamish. The wild rush forward, while the squeamish find certain things beneath them."[4] Of course Confucius wanted those who followed the middle way, but he could not be sure of finding such men. Hence he thought of the second best.'

'May I ask what sort of a person will be described as "wild"?'

'Men like Ch'in Chang, Tseng Hsi and Mu P'i were what Confucius described as "wild".'

'Why were they called "wild"?'

'They had great ambition and were always saying "The ancients! The ancients!" and yet, when one examines their conduct,

1. Cf. IV. B. 28, 'A gentleman differs from other men in that he retains his heart. A gentleman retains his heart by means of benevolence and the rites.'
2. Tseng Tzu's father.
3. Cf. the *Analects of Confucius*, V. 20.
4. Cf. ibid., XIII. 21.

it did not always fall within prescribed limits. When even the "wild" could not be found, Confucius wished to find for associates Gentlemen who were aloof. These are the squeamish, and they are one step further down. Confucius said, "The only people who pass my house by without causing me regret are perhaps the 'village honest men'. The village honest man is the enemy of virtue." [1]

'What sort of a man will be described as a "village honest man"?'

'[The man who says] "What is the point of having such great ambition? Their words and deeds take no notice of each other, and yet they keep on saying, 'The ancients! The ancients!' Why must they walk along in such solitary fashion? Being in this world, one must behave in a manner pleasing to this world. So long as one is good, it is all right." He tries in this way cringingly to please the world. Such is the village honest man.'

'If a man is praised for his honesty in his village,' said Wan Tzu, 'then he is an honest man wherever he goes. Why did Confucius consider such a man an enemy of virtue?'

'If you want to censure him, you cannot find anything; if you want to find fault with him, you cannot find anything either. He shares with others the practices of the day and is in harmony with the sordid world. He pursues such a policy and appears to be conscientious and faithful, and to show integrity in his conduct. He is liked by the multitude and is self-righteous. It is impossible to embark on the way of Yao and Shun with such a man. Hence the name "enemy of virtue". Confucius said, "I dislike what is specious. I dislike weeds for fear they might be confused with the rice plant; I dislike flattery for fear it might be confused with what is right; I dislike glibness for fear it might be confused with the truthful; I dislike the music of Cheng for fear it might be confused with proper music; I dislike purple for fear it might be confused with vermilion; I dislike the village honest man for fear he might be confused with the virtuous." [2] A gentleman goes back to the norm. That is all. When the norm is properly set then the common

1. Cf. ibid., XVII. 13.
2. Cf. ibid., XVII. 18.

people will be roused; when the common people are roused then heresy and aberration will disappear.'

38. Mencius said, 'From Yao and Shun to T'ang it was over five hundred years. Men like Yü and Kao Yao knew Yao and Shun personally, while those like T'ang knew them only by reputation. From T'ang to King Wen it was over five hundred years. Men like Yi Yin and Lai Chu knew T'ang personally, while those like King Wen knew him only by reputation. From King Wen to Confucius it was over five hundred years. Men such as T'ai Kung Wang and San-yi Sheng knew King Wen personally, while those like Confucius knew him only by reputation. From Confucius to the present it is over a hundred years. In time we are so near to the age of the sage while in place we are so close to his home, yet if there is no one who has anything of the sage, well then, there is no one who has anything of the sage.'

Appendix 1

THE DATING OF EVENTS IN THE
LIFE OF MENCIUS

The earliest account of the life of Mencius is to be found in the *Shih chi* (*Records of the Historian*), the earliest general history of China, written at the beginning of the first century B.C. by Ssu-ma Ch'ien:

> Meng K'e (Mencius) was a man from the state of Tsou. He studied under a disciple of Tzu Ssu,[1] and when he had mastered the Way he travelled to Ch'i where he took office at the court of King Hsüan who, however, was unable to entrust him with affairs of state. He then went to Liang. King Hui of Liang found Mencius' views, before he had fully listened to them, to be impracticable and remote from actuality.
>
> At that time, Ch'in had put Lord Shang into power, greatly enhancing the wealth and military power of the state; Ch'u and Wei in turn entrusted Wu Ch'i with the government of the state and were able to be victorious in war, weakening their enemies; while King Wei and King Hsüan of Ch'i made the feudal lords turn east and pay homage to Ch'i by employing Sun Tzu, T'ien Chi and others. When the Empire, busily engaged now in vertical, and now in horizontal, alliances, valued only military prowess, Meng K'e preached the virtuous tradition of T'ang, Yü and the Three Dynasties. For this reason he never secured a sympathetic hearing no matter where he went. He then retired and, together with Wan Chang and others, wrote the *Mencius* in seven books, giving an exposition of the *Odes* and the *History* and developing the ideas of Confucius. (*Shih chi*, chüan 74)

This account differs on one important point from the *Mencius*. Here Mencius is said to have visited Ch'i before he went to Liang whereas in the *Mencius* he visited Liang first. Now the chronology of the Warring States period in the *Shih chi* is inaccurate in many

---

1. Grandson of Confucius.

places. Where Mencius is concerned the mistakes in the dates of King Hui of Liang and King Hsüan of Ch'i are particularly important. According to the *Shih chi*, the reign periods of the Liang kings from 370 to 296 B.C. are as follows: King Hui 370–335; King Hsiang 334–319; King Ai 318–296. But the correct dates established with the help of the *Bamboo Annals*[1] are as follows: King Hui 370-319; King Hsiang 318-296. There are circumstances which render the mistakes in the *Shih chi* understandable. King Hui was originally Ying, the Marquis of Wei, but in 334, he and King Wei of Ch'i had a meeting at Hsü Chou where they agreed to recognize each other as king. To mark this event, King Hui initiated a new reign period. Ssu-ma Ch'ien mistook this as marking the beginning of the reign of his successor, King Hsiang. Having done this, it is natural for him to make the further mistake of treating the death of King Hui in 319 as the death of King Hsiang. He was then left with the period 318-296 without a king and King Ai was invented to fill the gap. But even this invention is not altogether without foundation in fact. It is very likely that King Hsiang's full title was King Ai Hsiang, though he was generally known only as King Hsiang. This is, to a certain extent, supported by the fact that there was also a King Ai Hsiang in Han. What Ssu-ma Ch'ien did was to make two kings out of one.

The reign periods of the Ch'i kings from 378 to 284 B.C. are given in the *Shih chi* as follows: King Wei 378-343; King Hsüan 342-324; King Min 323-284. The correct dates, again established with the help of the *Bamboo Annals*, are as follows: King Wei 357-320; King Hsüan 319-301; King Min 300-284.[2]

1. The *Bamboo Annals* were discovered in 281 A.D. and were still extant in T'ang times. They were then lost and the present work bearing that title is a reconstitution and, as such, not altogether reliable. But there are numerous quotations from it in early sources and these have proved invaluable for rectifying the mistakes in the *Shih chi* chronology of the Warring States period. It is interesting that the *Bamboo Annals* were, in fact, the annals of Wei (or Liang) and recorded events up to the time of King Hsiang who is referred to as 'the present ruler'.

2. For detailed discussions of these problems see Ch'ien Mu, *Hsien Ch'in chu tzu hsi nien*, revised and enlarged edition, Hong Kong, 1956, and Yang K'uan, *Chan kuo shih*, Shanghai, 1955.

To go back to the difference between the *Shih chi* and the *Mencius* on the order of the visits to Liang and Ch'i. One may easily think that the putting of the visit to Ch'i before the visit to Liang in the *Shih chi* is due to the mistakes in the chronology, but this is not so. For though King Hui is made to die sixteen years earlier in 335, so, too, is King Hsüan made to succeed his father twenty-three years earlier in 342, and as Ssu-ma Ch'ien, knowing that Mencius visited Liang a year before King Hui's death, placed Mencius' visit to Liang in 336 (when it should, of course, have been in 320), it would still have been possible for him to place Mencius' visit to Liang before his visit to Ch'i. Thus the mistaken chronology is not really responsible for Ssu-ma Ch'ien's mistake. While this is true, nevertheless, if he had got his chronology right he would have seen that it was impossible for Mencius to have visited Ch'i in 319, stayed for several years and then to visit Liang before the death of King Hui.

Now the correct dates of King Hui of Liang were well known to scholars for a very long time. The *Tzu chih t'ung chien*, the monumental chronological history of China covering the period from 403 B.C. to 959 A.D., completed in 1085 by Ssu-ma Kuang, already gave the correct dates. But the correct dates of King Hsüan of Ch'i were less well known. The *Mencius* mentions more than once the invasion of Yen by Ch'i. In I. B. 10 and I. B. 11, King Hsüan is mentioned by name, while in II. B. 8 and II. B. 9 the text only says 'the King of Ch'i', but in II. B. 8 Tzu-k'uai and Tzu-chih are mentioned. Now the abdication of Tzu-k'uai in favour of Tzu-chih, we know, from a number of sources, took place in 315 or 314. For those who accepted the dates of King Hsüan of Ch'i as given in the *Shih chi*, there is the problem of reconciling the fact that King Hsüan was supposed to have died in 324 with the fact that the invasion of Yen after Tzu-k'uai's abdication was known to have taken place in 314.[1] Two solutions have been proposed, neither of which is satisfactory. According to the first, since King Hsüan died before the invasion which took place in 314 but is

1. The *Tzu chih t'ung chien* arbitrarily moved the reign of King Hsüan forward ten years to 332–314 simply to bring the invasion of Yen just within his lifetime.

mentioned in connexion with an invasion in Book I, there must
have been two invasions. The invasion referred to in Book I took
place in 333 while the one mentioned in Book II in connexion with
Tzu-k'uai's abdication indeed took place in 314, but the unnamed
king involved was King Min and not King Hsüan.[1] This solution
has at least the merit of respecting the text of the *Mencius*. The
second solution is nothing if not drastic. According to this, the only
king in Ch'i Mencius ever saw was King Min. The numerous places
in the present text where the name of King Hsüan is to be found are
all due to the tampering with the text by editors.[2]

But from the eighteenth century onwards, there has been no
lack of scholars who saw that the problem was due to a mistake
in the chronology of the Ch'i kings in the *Shih chi*. Ts'ui Shu
(1740-1816) pointed out that the difficulty arose because Ssu-ma
Ch'ien moved the reigns of King Wei and King Hsüan back
twenty years as a result of having left out two earlier rulers.[3]
Apart from Ts'ui Shu, Lin Ch'un-p'u (1775-1861)[4] and Wei Yuan
(1794-1856)[5] both arrived at the same conclusion.[6]

There are two other rulers mentioned in the *Mencius* whose
dates are given incorrectly in the *Shih chi*. The first is Duke P'ing
of Lu, the dates of whose reign are given as 314-297 when they
should be 322-303. The second is Yen, King of Sung (posthumous
name King K'ang) the dates of whose reign are given as 328-286
when they should be 337-286. The year 328 was the year he assumed

1. This suggestion is recorded by Huang Chen in his *Huang shih jih ch'ao*,
quoted by Lin Ch'un-p'u, *Meng tzu shih shih nien piao huo shuo* (*Chu po shan
fang shih wu chung* edition), 1816, pp. 4b-6a.

2. This theory is quoted with approval by no less an authority than Ch'ien
Ta-hsin (1728-1804). See his *Shih chia chai yang hsin lu* (Basic Sinological
Series edition), 1935, pp. 54-5.

3. Ts'ui Shu, *Meng tzu shih shih lu* (*K'ao hsin lu, Wan yu wen k'u* edition),
1937, p. 672.

4. Lin Ch'un-p'u, loc. cit.

5. Wei Yuan, *Meng tzu nien piao*, 2.25 (*Ku wei t'ang nei wai chi* edition,
1878).

6. Amongst Western scholars Henri Maspero was the first to write on the
problem of the chronology of the Ch'i kings. See his *La chronologie des rois
de Ts'i au IVe siècle avant notre ère* (*T'oung Pao*, Vol. XXV, 1928, pp. 367-
86).

the title of king and not the date of his accession as Ssu-ma Ch'ien took it to be.[1]

We have seen that there is no reason to doubt the order of events implicit in Book I of the *Mencius* and where the *Shih chi* disagrees with the *Mencius* it is the *Shih chi* that is at fault. But there still remains one question concerning the dating of the events in Mencius' life. Book I covers the period from 320 to some time after the end of the invasion of Yen by Ch'i begun in 314. The question is: are there any events recorded in the *Mencius* which can be shown definitely to date from before the year 320? There are a number of events which, some scholars have argued, must have taken place before 320. It is then further argued from this that Mencius must have made another visit to Ch'i before the time of King Hsüan and this earlier visit must have been in the time of King Wei. It is, therefore, worth while examining the evidence to see if it is, in fact, sound.

(1) There are two related passages which we shall take together. According to II. B. 7, while in Ch'i Mencius made a visit to Lu for the burial of his mother. In I. B. 16, Duke P'ing of Lu was dissuaded by Tsang Ts'ang, a favourite of his, from going to see Mencius on the grounds that he gave a more splendid funeral to his mother than to his father who died earlier. There are two questions concerning these two passages. The first is, was it before 319 that Mencius returned to Lu from Ch'i to bury his mother? The second is, did the incident with Duke P'ing occur during Mencius' return to Lu to bury his mother? Mr Ch'ien Mu, for instance, answers both questions in the affirmative. He starts from the assumption that the position of Mencius throughout his stay in Ch'i from 319 was that of a Minister (*ch'ing*). He, then, goes on to make two points. First, at the time of the burial, Mencius' official position was that of a Counsellor (*ta fu*) as was stated by Yüeh-cheng Tzu. Since his position in Ch'i in the time of King Hsüan was that of a Minister, his return to Lu must have been during a previous visit in the time of King Wei. Second, Tsang Ts'ang referred to Mencius as 'a common fellow'. This would be inconceivable if Mencius

1. See Ch'ien Mu, op cit., p. 339 and p. 274.

was in fact a Minister. Hence the incident involving Duke P'ing
must also date from before 319.[1] It seems to me that Mr Ch'ien's
process of reasoning is rather odd, to say the least. Let us take his
second point first. That Mencius' position was that of a Counsellor
at the time of the burial is not in dispute. If Tsang Ts'ang's remark
was made soon afterwards, he was calling him 'a common fellow'
in spite of the fact that he was a Counsellor. Why, then, should
he not have done so even if Mencius had been a Minister? If it is
seriously suggested that Tsang Ts'ang could have called Mencius
'a common fellow' only if he was without any official rank, then
this would, in fact, be an argument in favour of this having been
done when Mencius visited Lu after his final departure from Ch'i
some time after 314, for he would then be indeed without official
position of any kind, whereas he would have been a Counsellor
if the remark was made during his return to bury his mother. But
I do not think that the remark 'a common fellow' can be used
as serious evidence at all. It was simply a term of abuse and nothing
more. Now the argument that Mencius must have returned to Lu
from Ch'i to bury his mother before 319 rests solely on the assump-
tion that from 319 onwards Mencius was a Minister. But there is
no firm evidence that this was the case. True, in II. B. 6 and VI. B. 6,
it is said that Mencius was a Minister in Ch'i, but as his whole stay
lasted at least five or six years, all we can be sure of is that *at some
stage* he was made a Minister. We cannot rule out the possibility
that he was only a Counsellor in the initial period of his stay. There
seems, therefore, no reason why we should not place Mencius'
return to Lu after 319. As to the incident with Duke P'ing, the fact
that the section is placed at the end of Book I Part B seems to imply
that it was after Mencius' final departure from Ch'i.

(2) There are the three passages which refer to Sung. In II. B. 3,
we find Ch'en Chen questioning Mencius on why he accepted in
Sung a gift of gold, having refused previously a gift in Ch'i. This
clearly shows that Mencius visited Sung after he had been in Ch'i.
The question is, does this refer to his visit to Ch'i in 319? In III. B. 6,
we find Mencius talking to Tai Pu-sheng who, it is clear from the
context, was an official at the court of the king of Sung. In III. B. 5,

1. op. cit., pp. 349–50.

Wan Chang asked Mencius, 'If Sung, a small state, were to prac-
tise Kingly government and be attacked by Ch'i and Ch'u for
doing so, what could be done about it?' Now there is no doubt
that the king of Sung during this period was Yen, because, as
we have seen, he reigned from 337-286. But as Yen assumed the
title of king in 328, Mr Ch'ien Mu argues that it must be soon after
he assumed the title of king that he wished to practise Kingly
government. It is concluded from this that Mencius' visit to Sung
must be in 328 or shortly after, and the visit to Ch'i which preceded
this must have been before 319 in the time of King Wei.[1] This
again seems to me hardly convincing as an argument. Though Yen
assumed the title of king in 328, as he reigned for over forty years,
one can hardly insist that it must have been shortly after he assumed
the title of king that he decided to practise Kingly government.
Moreover, Wan Chang's question is, on my interpretation, couched
in a hypothetical form and has no actual reference to any particular
period of his reign. Finally, even if he started practising Kingly
government in 328, this was likely to have gone on for a good
many years and there is no reason to think that Mencius must
have arrived on the scene shortly after 328. Once again, there is
no evidence to show that the visit to Sung could not have taken
place after Mencius' final departure from Ch'i.

(3) There is Mencius' friendship with K'uang Chang. In IV. B. 30,
when questioned why he not only befriended K'uang Chang but
treated him with courtesy, Mencius answered that K'uang Chang
had none of the failings commonly regarded as undutiful in a son.
He went on to describe what happened in his case between him
and his father:

In his case father and son are at odds through taxing each other over
a moral issue. It is for friends to demand goodness from each other.
For father and son to do so seriously undermines the love between
them. Do you think that Chang Tzu does not want to be with his
wife and sons? Because of his offence, he is not allowed near his
father. Therefore, he sent his wife and sons away and refused to allow
them to look after him. To his way of thinking, unless he acted in

1. op. cit., p. 314.

this way, his offence would be the greater. That is Chang Tzu for you.'

It is rather tantalizing that Mencius does not tell us what the moral issue is between K'uang Chang and his father. In an effort to throw some light on this obscure topic, some commentators relate this passage of the *Mencius* to a passage in the *Chan kuo ts'e*. This gives an account of King Wei of Ch'i sending a man called Chang Tzu to lead the army against the invading forces from Ch'in. When some one reported that Chang Tzu had gone over to the enemy, King Wei expressed his firm faith in Chang Tzu by saying:

> Ch'i, the mother of Chang Tzu, offended his father and he killed her and had her buried beneath the stables. In giving the command to Chang Tzu, I said to him, by way of encouragement, 'If with your prowess you bring the troops safely home, I promise you I shall have your mother re-buried.' He answered, 'It is not that I am unable to re-bury her. Ch'i, my mother, offended my father and my father died without leaving instructions. If I should re-bury my mother in spite of the fact that my father left no instructions, this is taking advantage of my father because he is dead. That is why I have not dared do so.' If a man would not, as a son, take advantage of his dead father, is he likely, as a subject, to take advantage of his living prince? (*Ch'i ts'e*, 1/13)

This account, it is believed, explains why K'uang Chang was dubbed an undutiful son by the whole country. It is then further argued that as King Wei must have had Chang Tzu's mother re-buried after the campaign, he would no longer be dubbed an undutiful son, so Mencius' remarks must have been made before this happened. As the campaign took place in the time of King Wei, it follows that Mencius must have visited Ch'i in the time of King Wei when he befriended K'uang Chang.[1] There seems to me to be a major flaw in this argument. The justification for relating the *Chan kuo ts'e* passage to the *Mencius* passage is that it throws light on the latter. But there is, in fact, no point of contact between the two passages. In the *Mencius*, K'uang Chang was dubbed an undutiful son because he was at odds with his father, and although we

1. Ch'ien Mu, op. cit., p. 316.

do not know the nature of the issue between them we do know that this happened during the lifetime of his father, and that he was not allowed near his father. In the *Chan kuo ts'e*, Chang Tzu is said not to be able to re-bury his mother because his father died without leaving instructions. This concerns his relationship with his dead father and there is no mention of any dispute between him and his father when his father was alive. Thus this throws no light on the *Mencius* passage at all. This being the case, it is not unreasonable to question whether the Chang Tzu in the *Chan kuo ts'e* is the same as the K'uang Chang in the *Mencius*. While it is true that Mencius referred to K'uang Chang as Chang Tzu, it does not follow that anyone referred to as Chang Tzu must be K'uang Chang. Again, the *Chan kuo ts'e* is not always reliable as history, and this invasion of Ch'i by Ch'in has never been definitely identified and supported by other sources. We cannot be sure even of the correctness of the reference to King Wei. Once more, we see that there is no real evidence to show that Mencius must have visited Ch'i before 319.

Although the results we have arrived at in our examination of the purported evidence for events in the *Mencius* having taken place before 320 are negative, this at least shows that there is no real evidence against the apparent chronological order in which the sections of Book I of the *Mencius* are arranged, neither is there any event in the whole work which can be shown to date definitely from a date before the year 320 B.C.

EARLY TRADITIONS ABOUT MENCIUS

There are certain traditions about Mencius to be found in two works of the Western Han, the *Han shih wai chuan* of the second century B.C. and the *Lieh nü chuan* just over a century later. It is difficult to know how much credence is to be given to these traditions but they are of some interest in their own right because of the wide currency they attained as cautionary tales.

(A) HAN SHIH WAI CHUAN

1. When Mencius was a boy, he was repeating his lessons while his mother was weaving. He stopped abruptly and then went on again. His mother knew that he could not remember the text. She called him to her and asked, 'Why did you stop?' He answered, 'I lost the thread, but I picked it up again.' His mother drew a knife and cut what she had woven, to drive home the lesson that he must not repeat his mistake again. From then on, Mencius never again forgot his lessons.

When Mencius was a boy, the neighbour on the east side once slaughtered a piglet. He asked his mother, 'Why does our neighbour on the east side slaughter a piglet?' 'Why, in order to offer you some pork to eat, of course,' answered his mother. She then regretted what she had said. 'When I was carrying this boy, I would not sit when the mat was not in position;[1] nor would I eat when the meat was not cut in regular shapes,' said she to herself. 'This is because it was the way of pre-natal education. Now he has just reached the age of understanding and I have told him an untruth. This is to teach him to be dishonest.' So she bought some pork from the neighbour and gave it to Mencius to eat, to show that she had not been dishonest with him.

1. Read *cheng* for *chih*.

The *Book of Odes* says,

> It is only to be expected that your sons and grandsons should be
> prudent,[1]

meaning that a good and wise mother will make her son good and
wise as well. (9/1)

2. Mencius' wife was alone and she was sitting with her knees up,
Mencius entered the room, stared at her and went to tell his mother.
'My wife is lacking in manners. Please send her away.' 'What has
happened?' asked his mother. 'She is sitting with her knees up.'
'How did you know?' 'I saw her with my own eyes.' 'It is not
your wife but you who are lacking in manners. Do the *Rites* not
prescribe,

> On entering the gate of the house,
> Ask which members of the family are still alive;[2]
> On ascending the hall,
> Raise your voice;
> On entering the door of a room,
> Lower your eyes.

This is to avoid catching people unawares. Now you went to her
private chamber and failed to raise your voice on entering so that
you found her sitting with her knees up and you stared at her. It is
not your wife but you who are lacking in manners.'

Thereupon Mencius blamed himself and dared not send his wife
away.

The *Book of Odes* says,

> When gathering turnips
> Pay no heed to the roots.[3] (9/15)

(B) LIEH NÜ CHUAN

1. The mother of Meng K'e of Tsou was known as Mother Meng.
Her house was near a graveyard, and the boy Mencius played at
grave-digging and was most energetic at building and interring.

---

1. Ode 5.
2. This line has been inserted on the authority of the parallel in the *Lieh nü
chuan* passage. See below.   3. Ode 35.

'This is no place for my child,' said Mother Meng, so she moved to live next to the market. Mencius played he was a hawker hawking his goods. Once more Mother Meng said, 'This is no place for my child.' Once again she moved to live near a school. Mencius played at sacrificial and ceremonial rituals. 'This is truly a place for my son,' said Mother Meng and she settled there. When Mencius became a man, he studied the six arts and became known as a great Confucianist.

In the opinion of the gentleman, Mother Meng knew the method of gradual transformation. The *Book of Odes* says,

> That docile boy,
> What should one give him?[1]

This is a case in point.

2. When Mencius was a boy, he came home one day from school. Mother Meng who was weaving asked him, 'Where have you got to in your lessons?' 'The same place as I got to before,' answered Mencius. With her knife Mother Meng cut what she had woven. This frightened Mencius and he asked why she had done it. 'Your neglecting your lessons is just like my cutting this fabric. Now a gentleman studies in order to make a name and to make his knowledge extensive. For this reason, when he stays at home he will be safe and when he is abroad no harm will come near him. Now you neglect your lessons. This means that you will escape neither servitude nor disaster. What difference is there between this and abandoning half way one's weaving and spinning on which one's livelihood depends? How can one clothe one's husband and avoid shortage of food for long? A woman who gives up her means of livelihood or a man who is indolent in the cultivation of his virtue will either become a thief or a slave.' This frightened Mencius. He studied with industry incessantly day and night and became a disciple of Tzu Ssu. In the end he became a Confucianist known throughout the Empire.

In the opinion of the gentleman, Mother Meng knew how to be a mother. The *Book of Odes* says,

1. Ode 53.

> That docile boy,
> What should one tell him?[1]

This is a case in point.

3. After Mencius was married, one day when he was just about to enter his private chamber, he found his wife scantily clad, Mencius was displeased and left without entering. His wife took leave of Mother Meng and asked to be allowed to go. 'I have heard', she said, 'that ceremony between husband and wife does not extend to the private chamber. Just now I was relaxing in my room and my husband, seeing me, showed anger in his face. This is treating me as a visitor. It is not right for a woman to stay overnight as a visitor. I beg to be allowed to return to my parents.' So Mother Meng summoned Mencius and told him, 'According to the *Rites*,

> On entering the gate of a house,
> Ask which members of the family are still alive.

This is in order to pay one's respects.

> On ascending the hall,
> Raise your voice.

This is in order to give warning.

> On entering the door of a room,
> Lower your eyes.

This is for fear of seeing others at fault.

'Now you expect others to conform to the *Rites* while failing yourself to see their import. Is this not wide of the mark?'

Mencius apologized and kept his wife. In the opinion of the gentleman, Mother Meng understood the *Rites* and knew how to be a mother-in-law.

4. When Mencius was in Ch'i, he looked worried. On seeing this, Mother Meng said, 'You seem to be worried. What is the matter?' 'Nothing,' said Mencius.

On another day, when he was not doing anything, Mencius put

1. loc. cit.

his arms round a pillar and sighed. On seeing this, Mother Meng said, 'Some time ago, I saw you looking worried, but you said, "Nothing". Now you put your arms round a pillar and sigh. What is the matter?' 'I have heard,' answered Mencius, 'that a gentleman takes a position that is commensurate with his person. He does not accept a reward he does not deserve; nor does he covet honour and wealth. When a feudal lord does not listen to his views, he will not allow his name to be placed before the authorities. When a feudal lord listens to his views but will not have them put into practice, he will not set foot in his court. Now as the Way is not put into practice in Ch'i, I wish to leave, but you, mother, are advanced in years. That is what is worrying me.' 'Now according to the *Rites*, all a woman has to do is to be good at the five kinds of cooked rice, to cover up the drinks with a cloth, to minister to the needs of the father and mother of her husband, and to sew. Hence she should be concerned with the orderly running of the household and not with affairs beyond the boundary.

'The *Book of Changes* says,

> It lies in feeding the family.
> There is no taking upon herself of affairs.[1]

The *Book of Odes* says,

> Neither wrong nor right
> But only wine and food are her concern.[2]

In other words, it is not for a woman to take on herself the making of decisions; her guiding principle is the "three submissions". In youth, she submits to her parents; after marriage, to her husband; after the death of her husband, to her son. This is in accordance with the rites. Now you are a grown man and I am old. You do what is right for you and I act according to the rites which apply to me.'

In the opinion of the gentleman, Mother Meng understood the way of a woman. The *Book of Odes* says,

1. Hexagram 37.
2. Ode 189.

> Gentle and smiling,
> Neither angry nor eager to correct.[1]

Mother Meng is a case in point (chüan 1).

1. Ode 299. There is a difference in the last line between the quotation and the present text of the Mao school which reads, 'Correcting without being angry.'

Appendix 3

THE TEXT OF THE *MENCIUS*

There are two theories concerning the composition of the *Mencius*. The first is that the work was written by Mencius himself. The second is that it was produced by some of his disciples or, perhaps, by the disciples of his disciples. There are certain arguments in favour of the second theory. The feudal lords who appear in the work are referred to by their posthumous titles, but some of these must have survived Mencius and their posthumous titles could not have been known to him. Hence the *Mencius* must have, at least, undergone some editing after the death of Mencius. Again, most of the disciples of Mencius are referred to as *tzu* with the exception of Wan Chang and Kung-sun Ch'ou. If Mencius had written the work himself, it would be strange for him to show them the deference implicit in this appellation, and even more strange, if he decided to do so, to make an exception of Wan Chang and Kung-sun Ch'ou. Again, this seems obviously the work of some editor and what appears to be strange will become quite natural if Wan Chang and Kung-sun Ch'ou were two of the editors. If this were so, can we assume that the editors compiled the *Mencius* out of the notes taken by a number of disciples rather than just out of their own notes of the sayings and conversations of the Master? There is one feature of the work which may have some bearing on this point. In the *Mencius* there are a dozen or so cases of the same passage appearing in more than one section. This in itself is nothing surprising. Thinkers of the Warring States period were in the habit of having a ready stock of illustrations and homilies to be used on appropriate occasions, and Mencius was no exception. But there are two or three cases which do not seem to fall within this category. For instance, I. B. 13 and I. B. 14, taken together, seem just to be a variant version of I. B. 15. Again, V. B. 1, apart from the final comment, consists solely of passages to be found elsewhere in the work, and VII. B. 17 is simply a duplication of one of these passages without even affording a fresh context. If Mencius actually wrote the *Mencius*, it would be odd that he should have left such repetitions in. On the other hand, if the *Mencius* was compiled by an editor from notes taken down by Mencius' disciples, then it is not surprising that some repetitions should have escaped the editing. In this connexion, a passage quoting the words of Yi Yin which is found both in v. B. 1 and v. A. 7 is particularly interesting. The text is identical in the two sections except for the use of the two particles *ssu* and *tz'u* – both meaning 'this'; where v. B. 1 has *ssu* v. A. 7 has *tz'u* and vice versa. This is not difficult to understand if the two versions of the same passages represent notes taken down by two disciples.

If we accept the hypothesis that the *Mencius* was compiled from notes taken by his disciples, does this detract from its authoritativeness? The answer is, No. The notes must have been verbatim notes for there is rarely any divergence in the text where the same passage is found more than once. The words of the Master were, as is to be expected, sacrosanct in the eyes of the disciples, and the greatest care must have been taken to preserve them as they were spoken by him. Thus the question whether Mencius actually wrote the *Mencius* becomes one of little significance. While Mencius may not have composed the work, the words contained in it are his very words, or as near to being his very words as to make little difference, and carry with them the same authority as if he had written them himself.

The text of the *Mencius* as we have it has come down to us through Chao Ch'i (d. A.D. 201). Not only was Chao Ch'i one of the earliest commentators on the *Mencius* but his commentary is the only early commentary to have come down to us and, as such, is of considerable value to the understanding of the text. Chao Ch'i mentions that, apart from the seven inner books, there were four outer books which he decided to expunge because 'these books, lacking in width and depth, bear no resemblance to the inner books and are likely to be the spurious work of a later age rather than the authentic work of Mencius.' The question naturally arises: was Chao Ch'i right in expunging the outer books? To this one can only return a tentative answer, as the outer books are lost to us –

the extant work bearing the title *The Outer Books of Mencius* being
a late forgery. There are quotations from the *Mencius* in various
works which are not to be found in the present text, and these
taken together have some relevance to our question. Fortunately for
us, there are two collections of such quotations. The first was by
Li T'iao-yüan (1734-1803) and the second by Ma Kuo-han (1794-
1857).[1] The first has eighteen items while the second has thirty-two,
with a certain amount of overlapping. If we confine ourselves to
works before Chao Ch'i's time or contemporary with him, the
number of such quotations is no more than a dozen. None of these
quotations are significant in content. Again, if we should take the
T'ai p'ing yü lan, the famous encyclopaedia compiled between A.D.
977 and 984 and based on earlier encyclopaedias, there are only
four out of more than 180 quotations from the *Mencius* that are
not to be found in the present text. We do not know, of course,
whether these quotations which are not found in the present text
come from the outer books or from the inner books. Even if, for
argument's sake, we were to assume that they all came from the
outer books, it would only show that there was little worth quoting
in them. On the other hand, if we assumed that the quotations came
from the inner books we can see that, as the quotations are so few
in number, our present text is pretty sound. In fact considering
that works from the Warring States period tend to abound in
textual corruptions, one's impression of the *Mencius* is that the
text is extraordinarily well preserved. Here and there there is a
possibility of textual corruption,[2] but these are few and far between.
There are, of course, variant readings, but again there are few
that are significant. It is no exaggeration to say that in the *Mencius*
we have one of the best preserved texts from the Warring State
period. In this we are, indeed, fortunate, for Mencius, besides being
one of the greatest thinkers, happens to be one of the greatest
stylists in the whole history of Chinese literature.

1. See Li T'iao-yüan, *Yi Meng tzu* (*Han hai*, t'ao 25) and Ma Kuo-han, *Yi
Meng tzu* (*Yü han shan fang chi yi shu*, *Mu keng t'ieh hsü pu*, *Ching pien*, *Meng
tzu lei*).
2. See V. B. 1 and VI. A. 11.

Appendix 4

ANCIENT HISTORY AS UNDERSTOOD
BY MENCIUS

Chinese thinkers were in the habit of appealing to examples in history, and each school had its own favourites amongst the ancient kings. For the Confucianists these were Yao and Shun, Yü, T'ang, King Wen and King Wu. Mencius, for instance, frequently cites the authority of Yao and Shun, but ancient history was for Mencius something more than an authority for occasional citation. Its significance is twofold. First, ancient personages were made concrete embodiments of moral qualities. On the one hand, Yao was the embodiment of kingly virtue, and Shun, besides being a sage king, was also the embodiment of filial virtue. On the other, Chieh and Tchou were bywords for wickedness in a ruler. Second, these idealized personages are envisaged in actual situations and these are discussed in detail and in all earnestness. For instance, after Shun became Emperor, what would he have done if his recalcitrant father, the Blind Man, were to commit murder? This serves the same purpose as the artificially contrived examples some Western philosophers use. It is to give concrete shape to abstract moral problems. The above example raises the problem of the conflict between the duty of a good son and the duty of a good Emperor.

Thus we can see that a knowledge of ancient history is not only necessary as a general background to the *Mencius* but is in fact something without which a good deal of the work would be unintelligible. The reader who has the patience can piece together a good deal of ancient history from passages scattered in the *Mencius*, but this is a tedious task. To save him this trouble, in what follows passages in the *Mencius* concerning ancient history are collected together and arranged in chronological order, supplemented where necessary from other sources. It is fortunate for us that the Confucianist version of ancient history is based on the *Shu ching* (*Book of History*) and the account in the *Shih chi* (*Records of the*

Historian) also follows this tradition and thus can be used to supplement the accounts found in the *Mencius*.

It is, perhaps, not out of place to emphasize that the Confucianist version was only one version of ancient history and that there were other traditions. For instance, according to the Confucianist version, Yao abdicated in favour of Shun while Ch'i, the son of Yü, succeeded his father as Emperor because the common people turned to him instead of to Yi. But according to the *Bamboo Annals*, Shun imprisoned Yao and Ch'i put Yi to death. Again, according to the Confucianist version, Yi Yin banished T'ai Chia because he upset the laws of T'ang but restored him to the throne when he reformed (v. A. 6). But according to the *Bamboo Annals*, Yi Yin banished T'ai Chia and usurped the throne, only to be killed by T'ai Chia who returned secretly. It is futile to try to decide which is the true version as we cannot even be sure whether Yao and Shun existed or not. The reader should, therefore, take the account of ancient history that follows simply as an aid to the understanding of the *Mencius*.

(A) THE FIVE EMPERORS

Traditionally there were Emperors earlier than the Five Emperors. One of these, Shen Nung, is, indeed, mentioned in the *Mencius*, but he is only mentioned in connexion with a man called Hsü Hsing who preached his doctrines, and has no significance for Mencius. There are also various ways of counting the Five Emperors, but the way they differ does not concern us either, as only the last two, Yao and Shu, appear in the *Mencius*.

Yao was the Emperor whose dynasty is known as T'ang. Of his early life nothing is said in the *Mencius*. It is in connexion with the Flood that Yao is first mentioned:

> In the time of Yao, the Empire was not yet settled. The Flood still raged unchecked, inundating the Empire; plants grew thickly; birds and beasts multiplied; the five grains did not ripen; birds and beasts encroached upon men, and their trail criss-crossed even the Central Kingdoms. The lot fell on Yao to worry about this situation. (III. A. 4)

Kun was recommended to Yao as capable of dealing with the Flood. After nine years he met with no success. Then after seventy years as Emperor, Yao wanted a successor and Shun was recommended to him. Yao gave Shun his two daughters as wives (v. A. 1, v. B. 6, VII. B. 6). Though Shun was still a Commoner, Yao treated him as equal:

> Shun went to see the Emperor, who placed his son-in-law in a separate mansion. He entertained Shun but also allowed himself to be entertained in return. This is an example of an Emperor making friends with a common man. (v. B. 3)

Then Shun was raised to a position of authority (v. B. 6), and after a number of years he was made regent (v. A. 4).

During his regency Shun punished the four most wicked men in the Empire. He 'banished Kung Kung to Yu Chou and Huan Tou to Mount Ch'ung; he banished San Miao to San Wei and killed Kun [presumably for his failure to deal successfully with the Flood] on Mount Yü' (v. A. 3).

On Yao's death the *Yao tien* has this to say:

> After twenty-eight years, Fang Hsün died. It was as if the people had lost their fathers and mothers. For three years all musical instruments were silenced. (v. A. 4)

Shun succeeded Yao as Emperor because, as Mencius puts it, 'Yao recommended Shun to Heaven and Heaven accepted him; he presented him to the people and the people accepted him.'

> Yao died, and after the mourning period of three years, Shun withdrew to the south of Nan Ho, leaving Yao's son in possession of the field, yet the feudal lords of the Empire coming to pay homage and those who were engaged in litigation went to Shun, not to Yao's son, and ballad singers sang the praises of Shun, not of Yao's son..... Only then did Shun go to the Central Kingdoms and ascend the Imperial throne. (v. A. 5)

Shun was said to be an Eastern barbarian who was born in Chu Feng, moved to Fu Hsia and died in Ming T'iao (IV. B. 1). He came from very humble circumstances. According to Mencius, 'he rose from the fields' (VI. B. 15), and had also been a fisherman, and a potter (II. A. 8).

Shun's father, known as the Blind Man, was a most perverse man, his mother was stupid, and his younger brother Hsiang took after his father. When Yao wanted to give his two daughters to Shun as wives, he had to do so without letting the Blind Man know or he would have prevented the marriage (V. A. 2, IV. A. 26). Even after Shun married the daughters of the Emperor, the Blind Man and Hsiang were constantly plotting against his life:

> Shun's parents sent him to repair the barn. Then they removed the ladder and the Blind Man set fire to the barn. They sent Shun to dredge the well, and then set out after him and blocked up the well over him. (V. A. 2)

It is said that Shun escaped on the first occasion by flying down from the barn, using two bamboo hats as wings, and on the second by getting out through some hidden opening. After the attempt on Shun's life when he thought Shun dead,

> Hsiang said, 'The credit for plotting against the life of Shun goes to me. The cattle and sheep go to you, father and mother, and the granaries as well. But the spears go to me, and the lute and the *ti* bow as well. His two wives should also be made to look after my quarters.' Hsiang went into Shun's house and there Shun was, seated on the bed playing on the lute. Hsiang looking awkward said, 'I was thinking of you.' Shun said, 'I am thinking of my subjects. You can help me in the task of government.' (loc. cit.)

While he was regent, 'Shun put Yi in charge of fire. Yi set the mountains and valleys alight and burnt them, and the birds and beasts went into hiding.' Shun gave Yü the task of controlling the Flood, and Ch'i that of teaching the people cultivation of the five grains, and made Hsieh the Minister of Education (III. A. 4), and Kao Yao the judge (VII. A. 35).

When Shun became Emperor the dynasty was known as Yü. Even as Emperor he continued to behave towards his father in a manner befitting a son (V. A. 4). He also enfeoffed Hsiang in Yu Pi (V. A. 3). For Mencius, Shun was the symbol of a perfectly good son. After years of striving, he was able in the end to please his father. 'Once the Blind Man was pleased, the pattern for the relationship between father and son in the Empire was set' (IV. A. 28). In the eyes of Mencius, Shun also furnished incontrovertible evidence of the goodness of human nature. He was an ordinary man in whom the incipient moral tendencies were strong.

> When Shun lived in the depth of the mountains, he lived amongst trees and stones, and had as friends deer and pigs. The difference between him and the uncultivated man of the mountains was slight. But when he heard a single good word, witnessed a single good deed, it was like water causing a breach in the dykes of the Yangtse or the Yellow River. Nothing could withstand it. (VII. A. 16)

Yü helped Shun to govern the Empire for seventeen years before Shun died.

> When the mourning period of three years was over, Yü withdrew to Yang Ch'eng, leaving Shun's son in possession of the field, yet the people of the Empire followed him just as, after Yao's death, the people followed Shun instead of Yao's son. (V. A. 6)

(B) THE THREE DYNASTIES

Yü became the first Emperor of the Hsia Dynasty which, according to tradition, ended after 471 years when Chieh was overthrown by T'ang. Yü is known in history for his success in controlling the Flood. There are two accounts of this in the *Mencius*. In III. A. 4, we have:

> Yü dredged the Nine Rivers, cleared the courses of the Chi and the T'a to channel the water into the Sea, deepened the beds of the Ju and the Han, and raised the dykes of the Huai and Ssu to empty them into the River. Only then were the people of the Central Kingdoms able to find food for themselves. During this time Yü spent eight years abroad and passed the door of his own house three times without entering.

In III. B. 9, we have:

> In the time of Yao, the water reversed its natural course, flooding the central regions, and the reptiles made their homes there, depriving the people of a settled life. In low-lying regions, people lived in

nests; in high regions, they lived in caves. . . . Yü was entrusted with
the task of controlling it. He led the flood water into the seas by
cutting channels for it in the ground, and drove the reptiles into
grassy marshes. The water, flowing through the channels, formed
the Yangtse, the Huai, the Yellow River and the Han. Obstacles re-
ceded and the birds and beasts harmful to men were annihilated. Only
then were the people able to level the ground and live on it.

In controlling the Flood, Yü is said to have worked until there
was no hair left on his thighs and shins (*Han fei tzu*, ch. 49). It is
perhaps for this reason that Yü acquired the reputation of an
ascetic. In the *Analects of Confucius*, he is said to spend little on
clothes, food and houses, but lavishly on sacrifices to the gods
and on drainage (VIII. 21), while Mencius also says that he 'disliked
delicious wine but was fond of good advice' (IV. B. 20), so much
so that 'when he heard a fine saying, Yü bowed low before the
speaker' (II. A. 8).

Yü recommended Yi to Heaven as his successor. When he died
seven years later, after

> the mourning period of three years was over, Yi withdrew to the
> northern slope of Mount Ch'i, leaving Yü's son in possession of the
> field. Those who came to pay homage and those who were engaged
> in litigation went to Ch'i [Yü's son] instead of Yi, saying, 'This is
> the son of our prince.' Ballad singers sang the praise of Ch'i instead
> of Yi, saying 'This is the son of our prince.' (V. A. 6)

The question why Yü was succeeded by his son while he him-
self and Shun before him came to the throne through abdication
of their predecessors is an important one for Mencius. Was it, as
Wan Chang put it, because virtue declined with Yü? Mencius'
answer was, No. There were two reasons for the difference. First,
Yi assisted Yü for only seven years, while Shun assisted Yao for
twenty-eight, and Yü assisted Shun for seventeen. Second, Ch'i,
Yü's son, was a good man while Tan Chu, the son of Yao, and
the son of Shun were both depraved.

The last Emperor of the Hsia was Chieh. Although he became for
posterity a byword for depravity, even in the *Shih chi* none of his
depraved deeds are recorded. His rule was intolerable for the com-

mon people, but he was so sure of the immutability of the Mandate of Heaven that he said, 'My possession of the Empire is like there being a sun in Heaven. Is there a time when the sun will perish? If the sun perishes, then I shall perish' (*Han shih wai chuan* 2/22). Mencius quotes the *T'ang Shih* as saying,

> O Sun, when wilt thou perish?
> We care not if we have to die with thee. (I. A. 2)

It is in the *Han shih wai chuan* that accounts of his depravity are to be found, and it is perhaps ironical that a descendant of Yü who disliked delicious wine should be said to have made a lake of wine big enough for boats and for three thousand people to drink from it like cattle (4/2).

When T'ang was in Po he began punitive campaigns against the feudal lords, and the first to be punished was the Earl of Ke. There are two accounts of this in the *Mencius* (I. B. 11, III. B. 5). The account in III. B. 5 is more detailed,

> When T'ang was in Po his territory adjoined the state of Ke. The Earl of Ke was a wilful man who neglected his sacrificial duties. T'ang sent someone to ask, 'Why do you not offer sacrifices?' 'We have no suitable animals.' T'ang sent gifts of oxen and sheep to the Earl of Ke, but he used them for food and continued to neglect his sacrificial duties. T'ang once again sent someone to ask, 'Why do you not offer sacrifices?' 'We have no suitable grain.' T'ang sent the people of Po to help in the ploughing and also sent the aged and young with gifts of food. The Earl of Ke led his people out and waylaid those who were bringing wine, food, millet and rice, trying to take these things from them by force. Those who resisted were killed. A boy bearing millet and meat was killed and the food taken. The *Book of History* says,

> > The Earl of Ke treated those who brought food as enemies.

> That is the incident to which this refers. When an army was sent to punish Ke for killing the boy, the whole Empire said, 'This is not coveting the Empire but avenging common men and women.'

> T'ang began his punitive expeditions with Ke.

> In eleven expeditions he became matchless in the Empire. When he marched on the east, the western barbarians complained, and when he

marched on the south, the northern barbarians complained. They all said, 'Why does he not come to us first?' The people longed for his coming as they longed for rain in time of severe drought. Those who were going to market did not stop; those who were weeding went on weeding. He punished the rulers and comforted the people, like a fall of timely rain, and the people rejoiced greatly. The *Book of History* says,

> We await our lord. When he comes we will suffer no more.

In the end T'ang attacked Chieh who fled to Ming T'iao and died in exile. Thus T'ang became the first Emperor of the Shang or Yin Dynasty which was said to have lasted for over six hundred years.

The man who was a key figure in the overthrow of Chieh was Yi Yin. Yi Yin is mentioned a number of times in the *Mencius*. As we shall see Yi Yin is particularly important for Mencius as an example of a good minister banishing a ruler who was bad.

There was a tradition that Yi Yin attracted the attention of T'ang by his culinary abilities. This is included in the *Shih chi* as, at least, one of the traditions. Mencius repudiates this as false and gives his own account of the matter:

Yi Yin worked in the fields in the outskirts of Yu Hsin, and delighted in the way of Yao and Shun. If it was contrary to what was right or to the Way, were he given the Empire he would have ignored it, and were he given a thousand teams of horses he would not have looked at them. If it was contrary to what was right or to the Way, he would neither give away a mite nor accept it. When T'ang sent a messenger with presents to invite him to court, he calmly said, 'What do I want T'ang's presents for? I much prefer working in the fields, delighting in the way of Yao and Shun.' Only after T'ang sent a messenger for the third time did he change his mind and say, 'Is it not better for me to make this prince a Yao or a Shun than to remain in the fields, delighting in the way of Yao and Shun? Is it not better for me to make the people subjects of a Yao or a Shun? Is it not better for me to see this with my own eyes? Heaven, in producing the people, has given to those who first attain understanding the duty of awakening those who are slow to understand; and to those who are the first to awaken, the duty of awakening those who are slow to awaken. I am amongst the first of Heaven's people to awaken. I shall awaken this people by means of this

Way. If I do not awaken them, who will do so?' When he saw a common man or woman who did not enjoy the benefit of the rule of Yao and Shun, Yi Yin felt as if he had pushed him or her into the gutter. This is the extent to which he considered the Empire his responsibility. So he went to T'ang and persuaded him to embark upon a punitive expedition against the Hsia to succour the people. (v. A. 7)

Mencius, however, did not seem to be consistent, for in another passage he said that Yi Yin 'went five times to T'ang and five times to Chieh' (VI. B. 6). This would seem to describe a man who was anxious to take office, rather than the man content to live in retirement depicted in the previous passage.

After Yi Yin went to T'ang, he was first treated as a teacher and only afterwards treated as a minister. It was for this reason, said Mencius, that T'ang was able to become a true King without much effort (II. B. 2). Yi Yin was, for Mencius, above all 'the sage who accepted responsibility' (V. B. 1).

When T'ang died, his eldest son T'ai Ting did not succeed to the throne as he, too, died soon afterwards. T'ai Ting's younger brother Wai Ping ruled for two years, and Wai Ping's younger brother, Chung Jen, ruled for four. T'ai Chia, the son of T'ai Ting, was then put on the throne by Yi Yin. According to Mencius,

T'ai Chia upset the laws of T'ang, and Yi Yin banished him to T'ung. After three years, T'ai Chia repented and reproached himself, and, while in T'ung, reformed and became a good and dutiful man. After another three years, since he heeded the instruction of Yi Yin, he was allowed to return to Po. (v. A. 6)

Mencius was asked by Kung-sun Ch'ou whether it was permissible for Yi Yin, a subject, to banish his Emperor, and his answer was that it was permissible only if he had the motive of a Yi Yin, otherwise it would have been usurpation (VII. A. 31).

Between T'ang and Tchou the only Emperor of the Yin to be mentioned in the *Mencius* is Wu Ting (II. B. 1). His minister, Fu Yüeh, who appeared to him in a dream, is also mentioned as having been raised from amongst the builders (VI. B. 15).

The name of Tchou, the last Emperor of the Yin, is always coupled with that of Chieh. His wicked deeds are, however, recorded in some detail in the *Shih chi*. He is said to have indulged excessively in drink and music. He, too, made a lake of wine and a forest of meat, and had all-night orgies in which men and women chased one another in the nude. He burned people over a charcoal grill. He killed Chiu Hou and E Hou, two of his three ducal ministers and imprisoned the third, Hsi Po (known to posterity as King Wen) who was only released when he made gifts of beautiful women, fine horses and rare objects to the tyrant.

Mencius mentions a number of good and wise men who assisted Tchou (II. A. 1). Of these, Ch'i, Viscount of Wei, an elder brother of Tchou, was the son of a concubine. He left after Tchou refused to listen to his advice on numerous occasions. Of Wei Chung, the younger brother of Ch'i, nothing is known. Prince Pi Kan angered Tchou by his insistent advice. Tchou had heard that sages had hearts with seven apertures, so he killed Prince Pi Kan to see if that was so. The Viscount of Chi was filled with fear, feigned madness and became a slave. Even then he was put in prison by Tchou. According to the *Kuo yü*, Chiao Ke went over to the Chou when Tchou showed excessive favour to Ta Chi, one of his concubines (7/2). It was during the time of Tchou that Po Yi fled to the edge of the North Sea and T'ai Kung to the edge of the East Sea (IV. A. 13, VII. A. 22). T'ai Kung subsequently played a very important part in helping King Wen towards winning the Empire.

The Chou were said to be descended from Ch'i who, as we have seen, was given the task by Shun of teaching the people the cultivation of the five grains. Kung Liu, who is mentioned by Mencius for his fondness for money (I. B. 5), marked the beginning of the rise to power of the Chou, but the first important Chou king was Ku Kung Tan Fu, the grandfather of King Wen. He is known to posterity as T'ai Wang. That he was a benevolent ruler is evident from the fact that he would rather abandon the territory he had than to cause misery to his people by fighting the barbarians. This incident is mentioned three times in the *Mencius*. In I. B. 3, his serving of the Hsün Yü was given as an example of a small state serving a large one. The most complete account is, however, given in I. B. 15:

In antiquity, when T'ai Wang was in Pin, the Ti tribes invaded the place. He tried to buy them off with skins and silks; he tried to buy them off with horses and hounds; he tried to buy them off with pearls and jade; but all to no avail. Then he assembled the elders and announced to them, 'What the Ti tribes want is our land. I have heard that a man in authority never turns what is meant for the benefit of men into a source of harm to them. It will not be difficult for you, my friends, to find another lord. I am leaving.' And he left Pin, crossed the Liang Mountains and built a city at the foot of Mount Ch'i and settled there. The men of Pin said, 'This is a benevolent man. We must not lose him.' They flocked after him as if to market.

In I. B. 14 Mencius again mentions this and comments, 'If a man does good deeds, then amongst his descendants in future generations there will rise one who will become a true King.' In other words, the eventual success of King Wu in winning the Empire was due, to no small extent, to the good that T'ai Wang did.

When King Wen succeeded to the throne, he was benevolent towards his people, treating them 'as if he were tending invalids' (IV. B. 20). The people, for their part, loved him so much that they named the terrace and pond they had built for him by their own sweat and toil as the 'Sacred Terrace' and the 'Sacred Pond' (I. A. 2). King Wen also showed great deference to good and wise men and they came flocking to him. Po Yi and T'ai Kung who had fled from Tchou to the edge of the sea came to him (IV. A. 13).

King Wen is said to have submitted to the K'un tribes whose state was smaller than his own, but he is also said to have shown his valour in stopping an invasion of Chü (I. B. 3).

In spite of his virtue, King Wen did not succeed in winning the Empire in his lifetime because, according to Mencius, 'the Empire was for long content to be ruled by the Yin', and what had gone on for long was difficult to change (II. A. 1).

After the death of King Wen, King Wu, aided by the Duke of Chou, made war on Tchou. According to the *Mencius*,

When King Wu marched on Yin, he had three hundred war chariots and three thousand brave warriors. He said, 'Do not be afraid. I come to bring you peace, not to wage war on the people.' And the sound

of the people knocking their heads on the ground was like the top-
pling of a mountain. (VII. B. 4)

According to the *Wu ch'eng* chapter of the *Book of History*, how-
ever, in this war 'the blood spilled was enough to carry staves along
with it'. Mencius expressed incredulity at this, for how could this
happen when the most benevolent waged war on the most cruel?
(VII. B. 3).

The Duke of Chou was the younger brother of King Wu. He
assisted King Wu in overthrowing Tchou. Then he made Kuan
Shu overlord of Yin and Kuan Shu used Yin as a base to stage a
rebellion against King Ch'eng, the son of King Wu. Ch'en Chia
asked Mencius whether the Duke of Chou knew this was going
to happen. Mencius answered that as the Duke of Chou was the
younger brother of Kuan Shu it was only natural for him to have
made such a mistake.

The Duke of Chou, according to Mencius, tried to combine
the achievements of the Three Dynasties and the administrations
of the Four Kings, i.e., Yü, T'ang, King Wen and King Wu.

Whenever there was anything he could not quite understand, he
would tilt his head back and reflect, if need be through the night as
well as the day. If he was fortunate enough to find the answer, he
would sit up to await the dawn. (IV. B. 20)

The Duke of Chou and, before him, Yi and Yi Yin were all
sages, and the question arises why they never became Emperor.
Mencius' answer to this is that 'he who inherits the Empire is only
put aside by Heaven if he is like Chieh and Tchou' (V. A. 6). It
was perhaps the misfortune of the Empire that these sages did not
live in the time of wicked tyrants.

Appendix 5

ON MENCIUS' USE OF THE
METHOD OF ANALOGY IN ARGUMENT

This paper first appeared in Asia Major, *N.S., Vol. X (1963). It is here reprinted with the kind permission of the Editor. As this was written some years ago, the translation given in it of passages from the* Mencius *differs occasionally from the present translation, but I have decided not to make any changes. I have, however, corrected one or two minor errors.*

It is not unusual for a reader of the *Mencius* to be left with the impression that in argument with his opponents Mencius was a sophist with little respect for logic. Not the least contributory factor to this impression is the type of argument which centres round an analogy. Yet it is difficult to believe that a thinker of Mencius' calibre and reputation could have indulged consistently in what appears to be pointless argument or that his opponents were always effectively silenced by *non sequiturs*. The fault, we suspect must lie with us. We must have somehow failed to understand these arguments. There are extenuating circumstances. In every case the bare bones of the argument alone are recorded, the background necessary to its understanding being tacitly assumed. There is no doubt that a good deal could be assumed to be familiar to the readers of Mencius' day, including assumptions accepted alike by Mencius and his opponents as well as the philosophical views peculiar to each side and also, of course, the method of analogy as used in argument. But for the modern reader, however, at least some of these things may be unfamiliar, and we can understand the difficulties he finds in these arguments. The purpose of this paper is to examine the passages containing such arguments afresh, making explicit as much of the available background as is useful, and then to see if we could gain a better understanding of the way the method of analogy works and judge whether, by the standards of the time, Mencius was not an honest and skilful exponent of the method. The passages we shall examine are 1-5 of Part A of Book VI and 17 of Book IV Part A.

Kao Tzu said, 'Human nature is like the willow. Yi[1] is like cups. To make morality[2] out of human nature is like making cups out of the willow.'

Mencius said, 'Can you make cups by following the nature of the willow? Or must you do violence to the willow before you can make it into cups? If the latter is the case, must you, then, also do violence to a man before you can make him moral? It is these words of yours that will lead men in this world in bringing disaster upon morality.' (VI. A. 1)

Kao Tzu said, 'Human nature is like whirling water. Give it an outlet in the east and it will flow east; give it an outlet in the west and it will flow west. That human nature shows no preference for either becoming good or becoming bad is like water showing no preference for either flowing east or flowing west.'

Mencius said, 'It is certainly the case that water shows no preference for either flowing east or flowing west, but does it show the same indifference to flowing upwards and flowing downwards?

1. I have deliberately left the word *yi* 義 untranslated in all these passages from the *Mencius*, because in some cases it is not possible to retain the continuity of the argument if the word is translated, as there is no one English equivalent which will do in all contexts. The reader can substitute 'right', 'righteous', 'rightness', 'duty' or 'dutiful', according to the demands of English usage in each case.

2. *Jen yi* has been translated as 'morality' and not as 'benevolence and *yi*' for two reasons. Firstly, by Mencius' time *jen yi* was almost always used as a single term meaning 'morality'. Secondly, in his opening statement Kao Tzu said only of *yi* that it was like cups; benevolence was not mentioned. In VI. A. 4, as we shall see, Kao Tzu was explicit on the point. 'Benevolence', he said, 'is internal, not external; *yi* is external, not internal.' This, as we shall also see, can only mean that in Kao Tzu's view benevolence was part of original human nature while *yi* was not. When he said that human nature was like the willow and that *yi* was like cups, he was making the same point. If, in the next sentence, he were to say that making 'benevolence and *yi*' out of human nature was like making cups out of the willow, he would not only be inconsistent with what he had just said, but also contradicting what he said in VI. A. 4.

Human nature being good is like water seeking low ground. There is no man who is not good just as there is no water that does not flow downwards.

'Now with water, by splashing it one can make it shoot up higher than one's forehead, and by forcing it one can make it stay on a hill. But can that be said to be the nature of water? It is the special circumstances that make it behave so. That man can be made bad shows that his nature is open to similar treatment.' (VI. A. 2)

These two arguments are best taken together as they constitute different attempts on the part of Kao Tzu at elucidating, by means of different analogies, a basic thesis which is capable of varying interpretations. In VI. A. 6, Kung-tu Tzu quotes Kao Tzu as saying, 'There is in human nature neither good nor bad.' In our first passage, the analogy put forth by Kao Tzu is that human nature is like the willow and morality like cups, and that to make morality out of human nature is like making cups out of the willow. The point of the analogy is this. The willow is the raw material out of which cups can be made, but this possibility has no basis in the original nature of the willow. It is no part of the nature of the willow to be made into cups. Similarly, not only is morality not in original human nature, it is something alien to it. Thus to make man moral is as arbitrary and artificial as making the willow into cups. By means of his analogy, Kao Tzu is interpreting his thesis as meaning that man is naturally a-moral.

Mencius' basic objection to this is that human beings are in fact not a-moral. They have a natural tendency towards moral behaviour, though this tendency is weak and often submerged by the habit of egoistic behaviour. This is a point to which we shall return. For the time being, let us concentrate on Mencius' objection to the analogy itself. On the one hand, it is obvious that we cannot make cups out of the willow by following its nature and that we have to do violence to its nature in order to do so. On the other hand, were we to draw the parallel conclusion that we cannot make man moral except by doing violence to his nature this would have disastrous consequences for the authority and prestige of morality.

There are two points which Mencius does not state but which

are implicit in his objection. It is perhaps legitimate to deal with
them as if they had been made by Mencius. Firstly, when we say
that it is necessary to do violence to man's nature in order to make
him moral, we are in fact making a moral judgement. We are saying
that it is bad to make man moral. But if man is by nature a-moral,
moral judgements are artificial and unnatural things for him to
make. Yet the paradox is that in stating this it is natural for us
to make it in the form of a moral judgement. This would seem to
show that the making of moral judgements is inescapable and so
cannot be artificial and unnatural. Hence given a position like Kao
Tzu's we have no right to say that it is bad to make man moral
and yet this seems the natural thing for us to say.

Secondly, if man is by nature a-moral, it is as much a violation
of his nature to make him immoral as to make him moral. Kao Tzu
should have said that to make man immoral, no less than to make
him moral, was like making cups out of the willow. As he omitted
to do this, it is very easy for anyone hostile to morality to draw
the one-sided and therefore wrong conclusion that it is only making
man moral which involved doing violence to his nature. The next
step would be to argue falsely that since it is unnatural for man to
be moral it must be natural for him to be immoral. That is why
Mencius said to Kao Tzu, 'It is these words of yours that will lead
men in this world in bringing disaster upon morality.'

As no comment by Kao Tzu on Mencius' objection to his analogy
is recorded and no linking passage between the two chapters is
supplied, we can only conjecture that Kao Tzu must have accepted
Mencius' objection as valid. He, then, puts forth a new analogy,
viz., that human nature is like whirling water which will flow in-
differently east or west as an outlet offers itself. In so doing Kao
Tzu is giving up his earlier interpretation of his thesis that there
is neither good nor bad in human nature, an interpretation capable
of being misrepresented as meaning that morality runs counter to
human nature, in other words, that man is naturally immoral. In-
stead, he accepts that morality is not alien to human nature, though
he still wishes to maintain that man shows no preference for either
the good or the bad. Man becomes good or bad as he happens to
be guided one way or the other.

This analogy is worth more serious consideration because it represented more accurately Kao Tzu's true position. Perhaps Kao Tzu never meant his first analogy with the willow to be taken seriously. It was simply an opening gambit which allows him to give some concessions to his opponent without retreating beyond his real position. Whether this conjecture as to Kao Tzu's motive is justified or not, Mencius certainly takes the new analogy seriously and gets down to providing an alternative analogy which represents his own position and, in his view, better fits the facts of the case.

In VI. A. 6, apart from quoting Kao Tzu's view on human nature, Kung-tu Tzu attributes to an unnamed person the view that human nature can become either good or bad. Now this is a view which was likely to have been accepted by both Kao Tzu and Mencius, because it is no more than a description of the undeniable fact that human beings sometimes become good and sometimes become bad. But just as the fact itself admits of different interpretations, so does the description. The views of both Kao Tzu and Mencius can be looked upon as different interpretations of the fact and so also of the description. At any rate, the way Mencius criticized Kao Tzu's second analogy shows that he at least looked upon it as an elucidation of this ambiguous thesis of anonymous authorship. What Kao Tzu was doing was to interpret the statement that human nature can become either good or bad as meaning that human nature shows no preference for becoming good or bad and so as meaning that it is equally easy for it to become good or bad. And this is, presumably, also the meaning to be given to his own thesis that there is neither good nor bad in human nature. Whether the analogy with the indifference water shows to flowing east or west is acceptable or not depends on whether one accepts or rejects the view of human nature it is meant to illustrate.

Mencius rejects the analogy because, for him, to say that man can be made either good or bad does not imply either that it is equally difficult to make him good or bad, or that it is equally natural for him to become moral or immoral. For Kao Tzu's analogy he substitutes one of his own. It is true, human nature is like water, but it is, in its preference for the good, like water in its tendency to flow downwards. This, in Mencius' view, was a better analogy, because though water shows a definite preference for low ground, it is possible to make it go upwards – say by splashing or forcing it – and it is certainly not the case that it is as easy to make it go up as to make it go down. It is more natural for water to flow downwards, and this means that it is more difficult to make it go upwards. Far from its being the case that to make man moral is to go against his nature, as Kao Tzu's first analogy with the willow can be taken to imply, Mencius wanted to say that the contrary is the case. It is more natural for man to be moral and so easier to make him good. 'There is no man who is not good just as there is no water that does not flow downwards.' Though Mencius does not produce arguments in support of his view here, elsewhere he does try to produce evidence for the goodness of human nature. Briefly it is this. We all have the beginnings of morality in us. We all feel pity, spontaneously and without ulterior motive, at the sight of a baby creeping towards a well. We all have the *shih fei chih hsin* 是 非 之 心 which distinguishes right from wrong and approves of the right, irrespective of what we in fact choose. If we happen to choose the wrong, we disapprove of our own action and feel a sense of shame.[1] In the argument under consideration Mencius is content to work Kao Tzu gradually round to his view. Firstly, he shows that the analogy with the willow is likely to be misrepresented as meaning that it is difficult to make man good because it is natural for him to be immoral and that this is unacceptable even to Kao Tzu and probably never intended by him. When Kao Tzu shifts his position to the analogy with whirling water, Mencius goes on to show that this is still not a satisfactory analogy because Kao Tzu was mistaken in thinking that this was based on the thesis that human nature can become either good or bad. The mistake lies in thinking that to say that man can become either good or bad implies that it is equally difficult or easy for him to become either. This is not the case. It is easier to make man good because it is, in a legitimate sense, more natural for him to be moral. What Mencius has done is, in fact, to turn Kao Tzu's first analogy upside

1. For a fuller treatment of Mencius' theory that human nature is good, see my 'Theories of human nature in *Mencius* and *Shyuntzyy*' (*Bulletin of the School of Oriental and African Studies*, 1953, Vol. XV, pp. 541–65).

down. It is making man immoral that is analogous to making cups out of the willow, because it is natural for man to become moral just as it is natural for water to flow downwards.

> Kao Tzu said, 'That which is inborn is what is meant by "nature".'[1]
>   Mencius said, 'Is that the same as "white is what is meant by 'white' "?'
>   'Yes.'
>   'Is the whiteness of white feathers the same as the whiteness of white snow and the whiteness of white snow the same as the whiteness of white jade?'
>   'Yes.'
>   'In that case is the nature of a dog the same as the nature of an ox and the nature of an ox the same as the nature of a man?' (VI. A. 3)

This is an interesting example of the use of analogy, because there are two features not met with in the examples we have seen. Firstly, it is not an analogy between two things but an analogy between two states of affairs which are described by statements of overtly identical form. 'That which is inborn is what is meant by "nature" ' and 'white is what is meant by "white" ' are both tautologous in form. The second feature is that the analogy was in fact suggested by Mencius in an attempt to elucidate Kao Tzu's initial statement. Kao Tzu accepted the suggestion, presumably not realizing that Mencius was going to show that the two statements were in fact not comparable. This meant that Kao Tzu was not, in the first instance, at all clear as to the implications of his own statement.

Mencius shows the difference between the two statements by saying that it follows that if white is what is meant by 'white' then the whiteness of white feathers is the same as the whiteness of white

---

1. Although the present text reads 'sheng chih wei hsing 生 之 謂 性', there is good reason to believe that originally 性 was simply written 生. (For a discussion of this point see Yü Yüeh 俞 樾 Ch'ün ching p'ing yi 羣 經 平 議, Huang Ch'ing ching chieh hsü pien 皇 清 經 解 續 編 chüan 1394, pp. 16b–17a.) The two words, though cognate, were most probably slightly different in pronunciation, but the statement 'sheng chih wei hsing' was at least tautologous in its written form and an exact parallel to 'pai chih wei pai'.

snow which in turn is the same as the whiteness of white jade. By the same token, it follows that if that which is inborn is what is meant by 'nature' then the nature of a dog is the same as the nature of an ox which in turn is the same as the nature of a man. But this was not acceptable, presumably even to Kao Tzu. What Kao Tzu's reaction was we are not told; neither are we given any explanation of why the analogy fails to hold. The former we can only conjecture, but towards making good the latter omission we can make some attempt.

The reason for the failure of the analogy is this. The term 'nature' is a formal, empty term. We cannot know, in specific terms, what precisely 'nature' is, unless the thing of which it is the nature is first specified. On the other hand, the term 'white' has a minimum specific content. We can know, up to a point, what white is without having to be told what it is the whiteness of. What is even more important is that when we specify the thing which is white – say, feathers or snow or jade – we may know more about its characteristics, but these must include the minimum specific content that we know from the term 'white' *per se*. If this condition is not fulfilled, then the thing is not really white. To put this whole point in another way. The 'nature' of a thing depends entirely on what the thing is, while whether a thing is 'white' or not depends on whether it includes the characteristic which we define as whiteness independently. In other words, in the expression 'the nature of x', the term 'nature' is a function of the term 'x', while in the expression 'the whiteness of white feathers', the term 'whiteness' is not a function of the term 'feathers' but has an independent value of its own.[1]

It is not indicated how Kao Tzu made use of his thesis that 'that which is inborn is what is meant by "nature".' One suspects that this may well be connected with his view that appetite for

---

[1]. There is also a formal difference between the two expressions which is a result of this distinction. In the expression 'the whiteness of white feathers', the term 'white' is a constituent of the term 'white feathers'. This is because whiteness is not included in the essence of feathers but is an independent character which has to be explicitly mentioned if it is 'white feathers' and not simply 'feathers' that we wish to mean. The same is not true of the expression 'the nature of a dog'.

food and sex is human nature (VI. A. 4). He might have argued that all living creatures are born with appetite for food and sex and that therefore this is 'nature' and so also 'human nature'. If he had argued thus, he would certainly have been helped by the practice, current by the time of Mencius, of using the word 'nature' to mean specifically 'human nature' when the context did not demand greater than usual precision. (When there was need for precision, the term 'the nature of man' was used, as we have seen in VI. A. 3 above.) If in meaning 'human nature' one says only 'nature', it is easy to assume that 'human nature' shares with the nature of other animals characteristics which go to make up the essence of 'nature' *sans phrase*.

Mencius' argument was designed to expose this unconscious assumption and to show that it was mistaken. He exposed it by explicitly asking the question, 'In that case is the nature of a dog the same as the nature of an ox and the nature of an ox the same as the nature of a man?' No one could return a positive answer who was not prepared to go all the way and say that the nature of all animals was identical in every respect. In this way, Mencius shows that what the nature of x is depends on what x is. That man shares with animals the appetite for food and sex is not sufficient grounds for equating this with the whole of 'nature', much less the whole of 'human nature'. There may be something else peculiar to human beings which is the essence of human nature, and in Mencius' view there is, and this is morality. Morality is peculiar to man, and distinguishes him from animals. It is worth mentioning that nowhere does Mencius deny that appetite for food and sex is human nature. All he asserts is that it is not the whole of human nature nor even the most important part, precisely because, being shared with all animals, it fails to mark him from the brutes. If we insist on saying that this constitutes the whole of human nature then we will have to accept the logical conclusion that the nature of a man is no different from that of a dog or an ox and this not even Kao Tzu was prepared to accept.

Ch'un-yü K'un said, 'Is it required by the rites that, in giving and receiving, man and woman should not touch each other?'

Mencius said, 'It is.'

'When one's sister-in-law is drowning, does one stretch out a hand to help her?'

'Not to help a sister-in-law who is drowning is to be a brute. It is required by the rites that, in giving and receiving, man and woman should not touch each other, but to stretch out a hand to help the drowning sister-in-law is to use one's discretion (*ch'üan* 權).'

'Now the Empire is drowning, why do you not help it?'

'When the Empire is drowning, one helps it with the Way; when a sister-in-law is drowning one helps her with one's hand. Would you have me help the Empire with my hand?' (IV. A. 17)

This argument is puzzling at first sight. Mencius' final question seems totally irrelevant. Yet one cannot help feeling that there is more to it than meets the eye. When we examine the analogy in detail, we find that this feeling is fully justified, for the argument turns out to be of considerable complexity, and it is this complexity that hides the point from us on a casual reading.

The question raised by Ch'un-yü K'un concerns the salvation of an Empire in disorder. He draws an analogy between this and the rescue of a drowning woman. The point Ch'un-yü K'un makes is that just as one ought to use one's hand to rescue a sister-in-law who is drowning, though this involves a breach of the rule that man and woman should not, in giving and receiving, touch each other, so ought one to be prepared to make some concessions in one's attempt to save a drowning Empire. The means for rescuing a drowning person is the hand, while the means for saving the Empire is, as Mencius points out, the Way. In either case the end is not in question; what is in question is whether one is justified in using any means that involves a breach of the ethical code in order to realize the end. To understand this argument, it is therefore necessary to say something about the nature of the means mentioned in each case.

Let us first take the case of the rescue of the drowning woman by the use of one's hand. The hand is useful purely as an instrument to the realization of the end, but does not affect its nature. After the person is rescued, we would not know, unless we are told, by what means the rescue was effected, and what is more, it does not matter.

We shall call this 'instrumental means'. If we turn to the salvation of the Empire, we find the case to be different. But first let us see how the salvation of an Empire in disorder was understood by Mencius and Ch'un-yü K'un. In their time, the common way of describing an Empire in disorder was to say that it lacked the Way (*wu tao* 無 道). Hence to save the Empire is to provide it with the Way. When the Empire has attained order it would be in possession of the Way (*yu tao* 有 道). We can see from this that the Way is a different kind of means. It becomes part of the end it helps to realize, and the end endures so long as the means remains a part of it. Remove the Way at any subsequent time, and the Empire will revert to disorder. We shall call this 'constitutive means'.[1]

There is another difference between the hand and the Way. The hand is only one of a number of possible means for rescuing a drowning person. One could equally use a stick or a rope. Furthermore, one's hand is as adequate a means for the purpose as any other. The Way, on the other hand, is a unique means for the realization of the desired end of saving the Empire. One could, of course, use a watered-down version of the Way instead, but then the end realized would be less perfect. This difference between the hand and the Way, though it does not follow from the distinction between them as instrumental and constitutive means, is not unconnected with it. The less any specific technique is required in the realization of an end, the less specific the instrumental means. For instance, few things other than a screw-driver will drive in a screw, but almost any blunt object can be used to hammer in a nail. The rescue of a drowning person involves no specific technique. Hence the variety of possible means. On the other hand, in a sense constitutive means are always unique. Vary the means and you vary the end as well. This is particularly true where the constitutive

1. I am aware that the distinction between instrumental and constitutive means is a crude one. Both form and matter would come under the latter term – and the Way is in fact form, as it furnishes the Empire with a regulative principle. I have not taken the discussion further, partly because this rough distinction is more or less adequate for my limited purpose of elucidating the argument we are considering, and partly because a more detailed discussion will take us too far afield.

means furnishes the principle of organization. For instance, if one varies a mould slightly the resulting shape will, accordingly, be different. The Way is a regulative principle, and as such it is unique.

Now the use of the hand is in itself morally neutral. In the case under consideration this is wrong only because there is a rule against man and woman touching each other and because the drowning person happens to be a woman and the rescuer a man. All the same we are faced with a dilemma. On the one hand we have a duty to save life. On the other we also have a duty to observe accepted rules of conduct. The situation is such that there is no way of saving the life of the drowning woman except by the breach of a rule of conduct. We weigh up (*ch'üan*) the relative stringency of the conflicting claims and come to the conclusion that the duty to save life far outweighs the duty to observe rules of conduct. This weighing up is possible because we can appeal to basic moral principle. The Way, however, is not morally neutral. It *is* basic moral principle. It is therefore impossible for the use of the Way to be wrong in the manner the use of the hand can be wrong. And even if, for argument's sake, we were to grant that in using the Way we may be breaking some rule of conduct, we cannot see how this is to be justified: there is no moral principle more basic to which we can appeal for justification.

We can now turn to the analogy. The main difficulty with this analogy is to see how it is meant to hold. For the moment let us leave aside the difference between instrumental and constitutive means and look upon both the Way and the hand simply as means. If we are to interpret the analogy exactly, we have to take it in the following way. Just as we have to use our hand to rescue our sister-in-law, though this involves the breach of a rule of conduct, so must we use the Way to save the Empire, though in so doing we err in a similar manner. This as we have just seen is both an impossibility and an absurdity. Moreover, this interpretation of the analogy renders it trivial, and was unlikely to have been what was intended by Ch'un-yü K'un.

A more likely interpretation is this. In using one's hand, when this involves the breach of a rule, one is resorting to a compromise.

In saving the Empire, if need be, we should also be prepared to compromise. If the Way is too lofty for the ruler, we should offer him a watered-down version of it. This, as we have seen, is different in kind from the compromise in using one's hand, for in adopting the use of the hand we have chosen a means perfectly adequate to the realization of the end, while in adopting a watered-down version of the Way we are compromising on the end as well. To the extent the Way is watered-down, to that extent the end we realize will fall short of the perfection we aimed at in the first place. Furthermore, this is a double compromise. Firstly, one is compromising on the Way. Secondly, one is compromising on one's own standards. On our analogy, the compromise on the Way is to be justified, as we have seen, paradoxically by an appeal to the Way itself. Even leaving this aside, Mencius shows clearly that in his view there can be no justification for compromising on the Way at all. He thinks that as soon as one realizes that what one has been doing is wrong one should rectify the wrong immediately and completely. Difficulty cannot be used as a pretext for allowing an injustice to go on unredressed.

> Tai Ying-chih said, 'In the present year we are unable to change over to a tax of one in ten and to abolish custom and market duty. What do you think if we were to make some reductions and wait for next year before we put the change fully into effect?'
>
> Mencius said, 'Here is a man who appropriates one of his neighbour's chickens every day. Someone tells him, "This is not the way of the gentleman." He answers, "May I reduce this to one chicken a month and wait for next year before stopping altogether?"
>
> 'If one realizes that something is morally wrong, one should stop doing it as soon as possible. Why wait for next year?' (III. B. 8)

This shows clearly that Mencius would not approve of watering down the Way in face of difficulties. Mencius feels equally strongly about not compromising on one's own standards, because he thinks that a man who is willing to do so is not the man to put others right. He says, 'One who is willing to bend himself will never be able to straighten others' (III. B. I), and again, 'I have never heard of anyone who can bend himself and rectify others' (V. A. 7).

If we take the compromise on the Way in this fashion, the analogy with the use of the hand is not an exact one. Firstly, in the case of the rescue of the drowning woman there is no constitutive means corresponding to the Way in the salvation of the Empire. Secondly, in deciding on the use of one's hand one is not accepting something less than the rescue of the drowning person. The hand is a perfectly adequate means for the realization of that end. But in using a watered-down version of the Way one is accepting as one's end something less than restoring the Empire to perfect order. If we wish to make the analogy more exact, we have to modify the facts of the situation concerning the rescue of the drowning person and to envisage something like this. We have no means of rescuing the drowning person outright and as a second best we decide to throw him a plank for him to hold on to for the time being. Even in this revised form the analogy does not hold completely. Whether we have the means to rescue a drowning person or not is a matter of fact, but whether we insist on the Way as means seems to be a matter of choice which depends more on our moral standards than on external circumstances.[1]

There is another way of revising the analogy to make it more exact, and that is by introducing the element of instrumental means into the case of the salvation of the Empire. In the time of Mencius, when philosophers travelled from one state to another, trying to gain a hearing, they had often to rely upon courtiers and favourites for access to princes. The temptation must have been at times great to enlist the help of those who were far from being men of honour. It is easy to argue that association with an unsavoury character was a cheap price to pay if in return a prince could be persuaded to adopt the Way in the government of his state. This would be parallel to the argument for using one's hand to rescue a drowning person though this involves the breach of a rule of conduct. We have seen that the general objection to this is that one can never

1. Mencius thinks that a prince should not look upon himself as incapable of adopting the Way in his government. This can be seen from his remark to King Hui of Liang, 'For this reason, that Your Majesty fails to become a true King is a case of not doing so and not a case of not being able to do so' (I. A. 7). Of the subject who thinks of his prince as incapable of becoming a good ruler, Mencius has this to say, 'To say "My prince will never be able to do it" is to do him harm' (IV. A. 1).

hope to straighten others by first bending oneself, but Mencius has in fact something more specific to say about this problem. There were certain traditions about Confucius' behaviour in just such circumstances. In the *Analects of Confucius* there is an account of Confucius having an audience with Nan Tzu, the notorious wife of the Duke of Wei. Tzu-lu did not hide his displeasure and to placate him Confucius had to swear that there was nothing improper in what he did (VI. 28). There must have been other traditions concerning incidents of a similar nature, for we find Mencius expressing incredulity at these traditions which he took to be totally unfounded.

Wan Chang asked, 'According to some, when he was in Wei Confucius had as host Yung Chü and in Ch'i he had the royal attendant Chi Huan. Is this true?

Mencius said, 'No. That is not so. These were fabrications by busybodies. In Wei Confucius had as host Yen Ch'ou-yu. The wife of Mi Tzu was a sister of the wife of Tzu-lu. Mi Tzu said to Tzu-lu, "If Confucius would have me for a host, he can attain high office." Tzu-lu reported this to Confucius who said, "There is the Decree." Confucius advances in accordance with the rites and withdraws in accordance with *yi*, and in matters of success or failure says, "There is the Decree." If in spite of this he had had as hosts Yung Chü and the royal attendant Chi Huan, then he would be ignoring both *yi* and the Decree. . . .

'I have heard that one judges courtiers who are natives of the state by the people to whom they play host, and those who have come to court from abroad by the hosts they choose. If Confucius had had as hosts Yung Chü and the royal attendant Chi Huan he would not be Confucius.' (V. A. 8)

We can see from this passage that to Mencius the choice of one's associates is a vital matter. One may deceive oneself and think that association with influential but disreputable courtiers is only a means to a worthy end, but what is likely to happen is simply the degradation of one's own moral character to no purpose, as such people will never permit the Way to prevail for should such a thing happen they would be the first to suffer.

This last interpretation of the analogy is most likely to be the one that Mencius had in mind, and we can see that Mencius' final question 'Would you have me help the Empire with my hand?' was an expression of exasperation. Ch'un-yü K'un, in suggesting that Mencius should make a compromise in order to save the Empire, did not realize that the price for such a compromise was so high as to defeat its very purpose.

Kao Tzu said, 'Appetite for food and sex is nature. Benevolence is internal, not external; *yi* is external, not internal.'

Mencius said, 'Why do you say that benevolence is internal and *yi* is external?'

'He is old and I treat him as elder. He owes nothing of his elderliness to me, just as in treating him as white because he is white I only do so because of his whiteness which is external to me. That is why I call it external.'

'The case of *yi* is different from that of whiteness. The 'treating as white' is the same whether one treats a horse as white[1] or a man as white. But I wonder if you would think that the "treating as old" is the same whether one is treating a horse as old or a man as elder? Furthermore, is it the one who is old that is *yi*, or is it the one who treats him as elder that is *yi*?'

'My brother I love, but the brother of a man from Ch'in I do not love. This means that the explanation lies in me. Hence I call it internal. Treating a man from Ch'u's elder as elder is no different from treating my own elder as elder. This means that the explanation[2] lies in their elderliness. Hence I call it external.'

1. Following Yü Yüeh I read 異 於 白 白 馬 之 白 也, repeating *pai*. See op. cit., pp. 17a–b. The same comment is also to be found in his *Ku shu yi yi chüli* 古 書 疑 義 舉 例 (*Ku shu yi yi chü li wu chung* 五 種, Shanghai, 1956, pp. 19–20).

2. In translating *yüeh* 悅 in both instances as 'explanation', I am reading it as *shuo* 說. In classical works the common form of the character was 說, whether the meaning is 'to please' or 'to explain'. The *Mencius* is exceptional in that the distinction between the two forms is generally observed in it. But even in the *Mencius*, the character is not always written 悅, when it means 'to please'. It is, therefore, reasonable to suppose that the form used in any passage reflects no more than the reading adopted by some editor in the course of the transmission of the text. There is no reason why we should not depart from the existing reading when the sense of the text demands it, as in the present case. Dr A. Waley has also expressed dissatisfaction with the reading. In his *Notes on Mencius*, he writes, 'The 悅 is unintelligible. The sense seems to be "make

'My relishing the roast provided by the man from Ch'in is no different from my relishing my own roast. Even with inanimate things, we can find cases similar to the one under discussion. Are we, then, to say that there is something external even in the relishing of roast?' (VI. A. 4)

Meng Chi Tzu asked Kung-tu Tzu, 'Why do you say that *yi* is internal?'

'It is the putting into practice of the respect that is in me. That is why I say it is internal.'

'If a man from your village is a year older than your eldest brother, which do you respect?'

'My brother.'

'In offering wine, which would you give precedence to?'

'The man from my village.'

'The one you respect is the former; the one you treat as elder is the latter. This shows that it is in fact external and not internal.'

Kung-tu Tzu was unable to find an answer to this and gave an account of the matter to Mencius.

Mencius said, '[Ask him,] "Which do you respect, your uncle or your younger brother?" He will say, "My uncle." "When your younger brother is acting the part of an ancestor at a sacrifice, then which do you respect?" He will say, "My younger brother." You ask him, "What has happened to your respect for your uncle?" He will say, "It is because of the position my younger brother occupies." You can then say, "[In the case of the man from my village] it is also because of the position he occupies. Normal respect is due to my elder brother; temporary respect is due to the man from my village." '

When Meng Chi Tzu heard this, he said, 'It is the same respect whether I am respecting my uncle or my younger brother. It is, as I have said, external and does not come from within.'

Kung-tu Tzu said, 'In winter one drinks hot water, in summer cold. Does that mean that even food and drink can be a matter of what is external?' (VI. A. 5)

As these two arguments deal with the same problem, whether *yi* is internal or external, they are best taken together. There are some

---

me the determining factor".' (*Asia Major*, New Series, Vol. I, p. 104). However, he made no suggestion as to the emendation of the reading of the character.

preliminary points which must be made if we are to understand these arguments.

Firstly, Kao Tzu begins by saying that appetite for food and sex is nature, and although this is not discussed in the sequel it is of some importance. The fact that Kao Tzu states this before raising the problem about *yi* shows that Kao Tzu looks upon the problem as one concerning human nature as well. To say that *yi* is external though benevolence is internal is to say that benevolence is part of human nature but *yi* is not. This implies that to say something is internal is to say that it is part of human nature. That this implication is accepted by Mencius can be seen from one remark he made in VI. A. 6. Mencius says there, 'Benevolence, *yi*, observance of the rites and wisdom, are not welded into me *from the outside*. I had them from the very beginning. It is simply that I never reflected upon the matter.' Here Mencius implies that if something is welded into me from the outside, then it is not inherent in my nature. Conversely, whatever is inherent in my nature is internal and not external to me. Another point worth remembering is that with Kao Tzu's statement that appetite for food and sex is nature and that benevolence is internal Mencius has no quarrel. What Mencius objects to specifically is the position that *yi* is external. Mencius' view is that *yi*, no less than benevolence, is internal.

Secondly, neither Kao Tzu nor Mencius liked arguing in the abstract about benevolence and *yi*. They preferred to deal with concrete acts and situations which exemplify these abstract qualities. Mencius says elsewhere, 'The content of benevolence is the serving of one's parents; the content of *yi* is obedience to one's elder brothers' (IV. A. 27), and again, 'There is no child who does not know love for his parents, and, when he grows up, respect for his elder brothers. The love for one's parents is benevolence; the respect for one's elder brother is *yi*' (VII. A. 15). We can paraphrase Mencius' words by saying that to love one's parents is the typical benevolent act, while to show respect for one's elders is the act which is typically *yi*. We can, then, understand why Kao Tzu and Mencius should choose to conduct their arguments in terms of the concrete examples they used.

Thirdly, when the word *yi* is translated, the argument may seem forced and artificial, for in Chinese the same word *yi* can be applied to an act which is right as well as to the agent who does the right act, while in English if we use the word 'right' for the act, some other word like 'righteous' or 'dutiful' has to be used for the agent. The use of two different words in translating a single word in the original destroys the apparent continuity of the argument.

Furthermore, the dichotomy between 'internal' and 'external' is too simple for the statement or the solution of the problem. Kao Tzu and Mencius both start from the position that benevolence is internal and part of human nature, because benevolence is the outward manifestation of love which, without any doubt, is part of the original make-up of man. The question is whether *yi* is equally well-rooted in human nature. In the case of benevolence, we can decide whether an act is benevolent or not by referring to the motive. If it is motivated by love, then it is benevolent. But in the case of *yi*, the facts of the situation are more complicated. Whether an act is *yi* does not depend only on the motive, but also on whether it is fitting in the situation.[1] What makes the position worse is that the very existence of a specific motive for acts that are *yi* is, at times, challenged.

This problem, however muddled it may seem to us, must have appeared to be of crucial importance to Mencius. By Mencius' day the opposition between *hsing* 性 'human nature' and *ming* 命 'the Decree of Heaven' must have become acute. The sort of view that Mencius was trying to combat must have been something like this. In human nature there are simply appetites – for food and sex, for instance – and emotions like love, and it is unnatural for man to do anything for which his nature does not equip him with a motive. It is all very well to say that it is the Decree of Heaven that man should be moral, but if it is unnatural for him to be moral it would be unreasonable to expect him to obey the Decree. For this reason the question whether *yi* was internal or external was a vital one for Mencius and his contemporaries.

1. In the *Chung yung* 中 庸 (chapter 14), '*yi*' is defined as 'fitting' (義 者 宜 也). This is more than just a meaning gloss by a near homophone, because the character was originally written 誼, thus showing that it was cognate with the character 宜.

Let us now examine the first argument. The starting point is the act which is typically *yi*, viz.,

(1) the act of treating someone old as elder.

The analogy is then drawn by Kao Tzu between this and

(2) the act of treating someone white as white.

It is argued that in (2) I treat someone white as white solely because of his whiteness which is external to me. That is to say, whether I treat him as white or not depends solely on external circumstances. There is nothing in my nature which can have any bearing on my act. Similarly, whether I treat someone old as elder depends solely on his age which is external to me. There is nothing in my nature which can have any bearing on this act of mine either. Therefore *yi*, of which (1) is a typical example, is external.

Mencius answers by pointing out that the analogy fails to hold. This he does by producing two parallel statements, one about (2) and one about (1), and showing that though both are true one is positive and the other negative:

(2.1) To treat a white horse as white is *no different* from treating a white man as white;

(1.1) To treat an old horse as old *is different* from treating an old man as elder.

The failure of the analogy rests on two points of difference. In treating an old man as elder, respect is evinced, but not in treating an old horse as old. In (2.1), the question of internality does not arise in either of the two cases because respect does not come in, but in (1.1) it is not true that nothing except circumstances external to the agent is relevant. Respect is relevant and respect is internal to the agent. Furthermore, the term *yi* applies to the agent as well as to the act. (In this respect *yi* is like benevolence.) Kao Tzu's position is unsatisfactory on two counts. Firstly, it is based on *yi* only as applied to an act. Secondly, even there, he has failed to take into account the fact that an act which is *yi* involves respect which is a quality of the agent.

Having failed in his analogy between an act which is *yi* and an act which is indubitably external, i.e., between (1) and (2), Kao Tzu then tries to show that there are differences between an act which is *yi* and a benevolent act. For this purpose he brings in

(3) the act of loving one's brother.

He makes two parallel statements, one about (3) and one about (1), and shows that though one is positive and the other negative both are true:

(3.2) I love my brother but I do not love the brother of a man from Ch'in;

(1.2) I treat the elder of a man from Ch'u as elder in the same way as I treat my own elder as elder.

Since (3) is agreed by both parties to be a typical benevolent act and benevolence is indubitably internal, this discrepancy between (1) and (3), in Kao Tzu's view, shows that *yi* is not internal. In fact, Kao Tzu goes on to say, it shows more. It shows positively that *yi* is external. Why do I love my brother and not the brother of a man from Ch'in? The explanation lies in his being *my* brother. In other words, I love him because of his relation to me. 'The explanation lies in me.' On the other hand, I treat the elder of a man from Ch'u as elder just as I treat an elder who is my own kith and kin as elder, because in either case my treatment is due to his age and this is a circumstance external to me. If my treatment of an elder as elder depends solely on external circumstances, then, it is concluded, *yi* is external.

Again, Mencius accepts what Kao Tzu has said about the facts as true but tries to show that it does not prove what Kao Tzu claims that it proves. In order to do this, Mencius brings in a fourth kind of act,

(4) the act of relishing roast.

Of this there can be no doubt as to its internality on the part of Kao Tzu, because he has said at the outset that appetite for food is nature. Yet of this one can make precisely the same statement as about (1), a statement which is supposed to prove that *yi* is external:

(4.2) I relish the roast provided by a man from Ch'in in the same way as I relish my own roast.

Thus Kao Tzu failed to establish the externality of *yi* either
through the similarities (1) shows to (2) or through the dis-
similarities (1) shows to (3). Mencius refuted the former by showing
that there are dissimilarities between (1) and (2) overlooked by
Kao Tzu, and the latter by showing that there are dissimilarities
between (4) and (3) of the same kind as between (1) and (3),
though there is no question of acts of relishing food being external.

The second argument opens with Kung-tu Tzu's statement that
he considered *yi* to be internal because in performing acts which
are *yi* he was putting into practice his respect. However, it consists
mainly of Meng Chi Tzu's attempt to establish the externality of
yi. Meng Chi Tzu's argument is as follows. There is a man from my
village who is a year senior to my eldest brother. Although under
normal circumstances I respect my brother, in offering wine I give
precedence to the man from my village. My treatment of the latter is
determined by external circumstances. As this is an act which is *yi*,
yi is external. Apart from this, there is a further point which Meng
Chi Tzu seems to be making by implication. By his careful wording
he seems to imply that there is a distinction between showing res-
pect and treating as elder: 'The one you *respect* is the former; the
one you *treat as elder* is the latter.' The line of reasoning appears
to be as follows. Respect is a quality of the agent and so any action
which evinces respect is internal. But whether I treat the man from
my village as elder depends on the occasion, and since this is the
case my treatment varies according to external circumstances. It,
therefore, cannot evince respect which is a permanent disposition.
If respect is not involved in all acts which are *yi* then it cannot be
the basis of the internality of *yi*.

Mencius replies by providing a new example. One respects one's
uncle, but when one's younger brother is acting the part of an
ancestor at a sacrifice then one respects one's younger brother. On
the surface, Mencius seems to be providing an example of his own
which reinforces Meng Chi Tzu's case, but in fact he was undermin-
ing the distinction between respecting and treating as elder that
Meng Chi Tzu was trying to establish. In his own example Mencius
has substituted the younger brother for the fellow villager. There
is no question of treating one's younger brother as elder, for even

when he is acting the part of an ancestor he is still one's junior. What is due to him in his special position is respect. Thus in Mencius' example, though one's act is still determined by external circumstances, it nevertheless evinces respect. This Mencius explains by the distinction between normal and temporary respect. That the act of treating the man from my village as elder is determined by external circumstances, instead of showing that it does not evince respect, shows only that it evinces temporary respect. Meng Chi Tzu seems willing to accept this distinction between normal and temporary respect but argues that, in that case, acts which are *yi* are external in spite of the fact that they evince respect because they depend on external circumstances. Mencius' reply is that even of

(5) the act of drinking

it is true that it is conditioned by external circumstances:

(5.3) In winter one drinks hot water, in summer cold.

Of (1) which is also conditioned by external circumstances we can equally say:

(1.3) Normally I respect my eldest brother, but in offering wine I give precedence to the man from my village.

Again, by showing that (5.3) can be said of (5) which is indubitably internal, Mencius argues that the fact that (1.3) can be said of (1) does not show that *yi* is external. Furthermore, by drawing an analogy between (1) and (5), Mencius is returning to Kung-tu Tzu's opening remark: 'I put into practice my respect.' As in an act which is *yi* one puts into practice one's respect, so in an act of drinking one is motivated by one's thirst.

The arguments are obviously not conclusive, but this is in part due to Mencius' limited purpose. All he set out to do, in both cases, was to show that his opponents failed to establish the externality of *yi*. He did not attempt to go beyond this and to establish positively that *yi* was internal. The main reason for the inconclusiveness is, however, one we have already touched upon. The dichotomy between internal and external was too simple for the facts of the situation. Such a dichotomy could only work if there was only one characteristic or one set of characteristics which is to be found in one kind of act but not in another. In the present case, there are a number of characteristics, some of which are sometimes present and sometimes absent in acts of the same kind. In the course of the arguments, three such characteristics are mentioned. (1) The motive. In the case of benevolent acts, it is assumed that this is love. In the case of eating and drinking it is assumed to be appetite. According to Mencius, the motive is respect in the case of all acts which are *yi*, and this his opponents either deny or deny to be significant. (2) There are the external circumstances. These are irrelevant to benevolent acts. But in the case of acts which are *yi* these determine the matter of precedence in particular situations. In the case of drink, these decide what we want in different seasons. (3) The relation which the object of respect has to the agent. In the case of benevolence, the patient is a relative of the agent. In the case of *yi*, there need be no special relationship at all. In the case of food, there is no special relationship either. As acts which stem indubitably from what is internal show no uniformity in the possession or otherwise of these characteristics, so acts which are *yi* display an ambivalence in the similarity and dissimilarity they show to these acts. The result is that no conclusion can be drawn from the success or failure of these analogies.

The problem whether *yi* is external in contrast to benevolence which is internal must have been an issue of some importance, as we find that the later Mohists were also interested in it. In the logical chapters of *Mo tzu*, viz., chapters 40 to 45, there are three places where this problem is discussed. I shall quote only the longer passage from the *Ching shuo hsia* chapter, because this is comparatively free from textual difficulties and is a lucid statement of the Mohist position:

> Benevolence is loving; *yi* is benefiting. He who loves and he who benefits are here; he who is loved and he who is benefited are there. Of the one who loves and the one who benefits we cannot say that one is internal and the other external. Neither can we say this of the one who is loved and the one who is benefited. To say[1] that benevolence

---

1. Read 為 as 謂.

is internal and *yi* is external is to select the one who loves and the one who is benefited. This is selection with no consistent basis. It is like saying that the left eye goes out and the right eye comes in. (*Ssu pu ts'ung k'an* 四 部 叢 刊 ed., 10.21a–b)

At first sight the Mohists seem to have brought order to an otherwise untidy problem, but on closer examination one sees that this is achieved only by ignoring certain factors that Kao Tzu and Mencius took into account. In defining *yi* in the way they do, the Mohists are looking upon it as exactly parallel to benevolence. As benevolence is a disposition to love, so is *yi* a disposition to benefit others. Both are relations obtaining between an agent and a patient. In respect of the agent both benevolence and *yi* are internal; in respect of the patient both are external. In the view of the Mohists, whoever says that *yi* is external though admitting that benevolence is internal must be guilty of inconsistent selection. He must be taking the patient in the case of *yi* and the agent in the case of benevolence. Though the Mohists were defending the same position as Mencius, the basis for their defence is certainly unacceptable to Mencius. Mencius was quite clear that *yi* was an attribute of the agent and could not possibly be applied to the patient. 'Is it the one who is old that is *yi* or is it the one who treats him as elder that is *yi*?' Mencius knew full well that when both benevolence and *yi* were applied to the agent there was no problem. But he was also aware of the fact ignored by the Mohists that *yi* applied equally to actions, and it was here that a case could be made out for challenging its internality. Part of the conditions for an action being *yi* is that it should be 'fitting', and this means that whether an action is *yi* depends, to no small measure, on external circumstances. It is from this that Kao Tzu and others argued that *yi* was external, and it is also with this that Mencius grappled when he defended the internality of *yi*. For the Mohists to say that the problem rested on the failure to distinguish between agent and patient is both to misrepresent Mencius and his opponents and to distort the usage of the word *yi*. This misrepresentation is due to the refusal on the part of the Mohists to take into account certain factors involved in the problem of *yi* and this refusal is, in turn, due to two features of the Mohist position. Firstly, they define *yi* as benefiting, and by so doing render it independent of the ethical code. A 'fitting' action depends on external circumstances in a way a 'benefiting' action does not. This definition of *yi* is certain to be unacceptable to either Mencius or Kao Tzu. Secondly, by rendering *yi* similar to benevolence, the Mohists were ignoring its applicability to actions and looked upon it solely as an attribute of agents. This emphasis on the agent to the exclusion of actions is a marked feature of Mohist moral thinking. Here are some passages from the logical chapters in which this feature can be clearly seen:

Canon: *Yi* is benefiting. (10. 1a. 6)
Explanation: The will takes the Empire as its responsibility[1] and the ability is capable of benefiting it. There is no need to be in office[2]. (10. 6b. 6)

Some live long, some die young, but they benefit the Empire to the same extent.[3] (11. 7a. 2)

Even when a man is in as exalted a position as that of an emperor, he does not benefit the Empire to a greater extent than a common man.[4] If two sons serve their parents and one meets with a good year while the other meets with a bad, then the one benefits[5] his parents to no greater extent than the other. As it is not through his action that more has resulted, this does not add to his merit.[6] External circumstances[7] are powerless to add to the benefit for which I am responsible (11. 6a. 2–5).

All these passages show that in the view of the later Mohists external circumstances are irrelevant to the moral assessment of the character of the agent. So long as a man has both the will and the capacity

1. Emend 芬 to 分.
2. Cf. Canon: To be filial is to benefit one's parents. (10. 1b. 1) Explanation: One takes one's parents as one's responsibility (see previous note), and one's ability is capable of benefiting them. There is no need to succeed. (10. 7a. 2–3)
3. Emend 指 若 to 相 若.
4. Emend 正 夫 to 匹 夫.
5. Emend 其 親 也 to 其 利 親 也.
6. This sentence is obscure, as the text is almost certainly corrupt.
7. Emend 執 to 埶.

to benefit the world or his parents, whether in fact he succeeds or not is immaterial, because success – and even opportunity – depends on favourable conditions over which he has no control and for which he can take no credit.[1] Thus *yi* is removed from the contaminating influence of external circumstances only through denying it application to action. In this way the problem with which Mencius and his opponents were concerned was by-passed by the Mohists. This hardly justifies their claim that the problem itself rested on confusion and inconsistency.

Not only is one of the problems discussed between Mencius and Kao Tzu also discussed by the later Mohists but the method of argument as well. In the *Hsiao ch'ü* chapter[2] we find logicians of the Mohist school writing on the different methods of argument amongst which is to be found the method of analogy:

> Analogy is to put forth another[3] thing in order to illuminate this thing. Parallel is to set [two] propositions side by side and show that they will both do. (11. 8a. 3–5)

Here an analogy drawn between two things is distinguished from one drawn between two statements. We have seen that both methods were used by Mencius. The analogy between 'That which is inborn is meant by "nature"' and 'White is what is meant by "white"' is an analogy between two statements and would come under "parallel" in the Mohist classification.

The Mohist chapter goes on to discuss the method:

1. The Mohist position that in moral assessment it is the agent and not the actions that should be emphasized seems to have some relevance to a problem concerning moral goodness in Western philosophy. If we define moral goodness as goodness which is realized only when an agent chooses to do his duty from the motive of dutifulness the question arises whether a man who acts dutifully more often than another necessarily realizes more moral goodness. Those who feel uneasy about returning an affirmative answer may find a certain appeal in the Mohist position.

2. For a more detailed discussion of the *Hsiao ch'ü* see my 'Some logical problems in ancient China' (*Proceedings of the Aristotelian Society*, Vol. LIII 1952–3, pp. 189–204).

3. Read 也 as 他.

Things may have similarities, but it does not follow that therefore
they are completely similar. When propositions are parallel, there is
a limit beyond which this cannot be pushed.[1] (11. 8a. 7–8)

This is a very good description of the method as it was used by
Mencius. In his hands the method of analogy was used to throw
light on things which were otherwise obscure. It is by proposing
analogies and showing in what way they broke down that this was
achieved. That the aim was to arrive at the truth can be seen from
the fact that it was not always analogies proposed by his opponents
that were shown to be inadequate in this way. We have seen a case
of Mencius suggesting an analogy to illustrate his opponent's thesis,
and this was criticized after his opponent accepted it.

It is perhaps worth pointing out that the use of analogy is often
the only helpful method in elucidating something which is, in its
nature, obscure. Two examples come readily to mind. Theories
about the mind are often presented through the medium of models,
and so are physical theories of the atom. In either case the models
are not only helpful in enabling us to see something of the 'struc-
ture' of the mind or the atom which is not open to inspection by
the senses, but also instructive in the way they break down.

I hope enough has been said to show that in the fourth and third
centuries B.C. in China the method of analogy, indispensable for
certain types of philosophical problems, was in wide use,[2] so much

1. Emend 正 to 止.

2. There is a story about the famous sophist Hui Shih in the *Shuo yüan* which
illustrates this point:

> Someone said to the King of Liang, 'Hui Tzu is very good at using
> analogies when putting forth his views. If your Majesty could stop him
> from using analogies he will be at a loss what to say.'
> The King said, 'Very well. I will do that'.
> The following day when he received Hui Tzu the King said to him,
> 'If you have anything to say, I wish you would say it plainly and not
> resort to analogies.'
> Hui Tzu said, 'Suppose there is a man here who does not know what a
> *tan* is, and you say to him, "A *tan* is like a *tan*," would he understand?'
> The King said, 'No.'
> 'Then were you to say to him, "A *tan* is like a bow, but has a strip of
> bamboo in place of the string," would he understand?'
> The King said, 'Yes. He would.'
> Hui Tzu said, 'A man who explains necessarily makes intelligible that

so that the only surviving treatise on the methods of argument deals with it in some detail. Seen in the light of the Mohist treatise, Mencius was, indeed, a very skilful user of this method, who never failed to throw light on philosophical issues that were discussed. This is an impression somewhat different from the ineffective debater that he is sometimes made out to be.

---

which is not known by comparing it with what is known. Now Your Majesty says, "Do not use analogies." This would make the task impossible.'

The King said, 'Well said.' (S.P.T.K. edition, 11. 6b–7a)

Hui Shih's explanation of the function of analogy can be seen to be similar to that given in the *Hsiao ch'ü*.

Textual Notes

1. Omit 欲

2. Omit 也 at the end of the sentence

3. Read 必 for 不

4. Take 正 心 as a corruption of 忘

5. Omit 國. Cf. 王 由 足 用 爲 善 (II. B. 13)

6. Read 與 as 舉

7. For this use of 責, cf. 言 責 in II. B. 5

8. Read 迎 for 迹

9. In all three cases read 呼 for 于

10. Read 如 何 as 而 何

11. Add 如 此 on the authority of the parallel in V. A. 7

12. Read 分 for 糞, following chapter 5 of the *Li chi*

13. Read 臺 as 始

14. Read 異 於 白 白 馬 之 白

15. In both cases read 悅 as 說

16. Read 予 for 子

Note. For a discussion of a number of textual points and problems of interpretation the reader is referred to D. C. Lau, 'Some Notes on the *Mencius*', *Asia Major*, N. S., Vol. XV, Part 1 (1969), pp. 62–81.

Glossary of Personal and Place Names

All dates given are B.C.

Bandit Chih, III. B. 10. The most famous name in banditry in ancient China. In chapter 29 of the *Chuang tzu*, he is said to be the brother of Liu Hsia Hui, a byword for scrupulous integrity, but this seems to be just an ironical touch which can hardly be taken seriously.

Blind Man, the, IV. A. 28, V. A. 2, 4, VI. A. 6, VII. A. 35. Father of Shun. See Appendix 4.

Chang Tzu, IV. B. 30, i.e., K'uang Chang.

Chang Yi, III. B. 2. A native of Wei, Chang Yi tried to persuade the six states to submit to Ch'in by joining the so-called 'horizontal alliance'. For his biography see *Shih chi*, 70.

Ch'ang Hsi, V. A. 1, V. B. 3. According to Chao Ch'i, disciple of Kung-ming Kao who was, in turn, disciple of Tseng Tzu.

Chao Meng, VI. A. 17. Because Chao Tun, a famous minister of the state of Chin, was also known as Chao Meng, his descendants are generally referred to as Chao Meng as well.

Ch'ao Wu, I. B. 4. A mountain in modern Shantung.

Chen, IV. B. 2. A river which arises in the north east of Mi Hsien in Honan and then joins the River Wei.

Ch'en, VII. B. 18, 37. A small state in the region east of Kaifeng in Honan and north of Po Hsien in Anhwei.

Ch'en Chen, II. B. 3, VII. B. 23. According to Chao Ch'i, disciple of Mencius. See also Ch'en Tzu.

Ch'en Chia, II. B. 9. According to Chao Ch'i, a Counsellor in Ch'i.

Ch'en Chung, VII. A. 34, i.e., Ch'en Chung-tzu.

Ch'en Chung-tzu, III. B. 10. Famous for his scrupulousness, but attacked by Confucians for contracting out of his obligations to society. Also known as T'ien Chung and Wu-ling Chung-tzu.

Ch'en Hsiang, III. A. 4.

Ch'en Liang, III. A. 4.

Ch'en Tai, III. B. 1. According to Chao Ch'i, disciple of Mencius.

Ch'en Tzu, II. B. 10, VI. B. 14. This is Ch'en Chen, according to Chao Ch'i.

Cheng, IV. B. 2, 24, V. A. 2, VII. B. 37. A small state comprising the central part of Honan.

Ch'eng Chien, III. A. I. A brave warrior of Ch'i.

Chi, III. A. 4. The River Chi, arising in the west of Chiyuan Hsien, flows south into the Yellow River today, but formerly it crossed the Yellow River to flow eastward into Shantung and then into the sea.

Chi, IV. B. 29, i.e., Hou Chi.

Chi family, the, IV. A. 14. A powerful noble family in the state of Lu.

Chi Huan, V. A. 8.

Chi Huan Tzu, V. B. 4. A member of the Chi family and a high minister who held the reins of government in the state of Lu from Duke Ting (reigned 509-495) to Duke Ai (reigned 494-477).

Chi Jen, VI. B. 5. According to Chao Ch'i, the younger brother of the Lord of Jen.

Chi Sun, II. B. 10.

Chi Tzu, VI. B. 5, i.e., Chi Jen.

Ch'i, V. A. 6. Son of Yü who founded the Hsia Dynasty. See Appendix 4.

Ch'i, I. B. 5. The area round Chishan Hsien in Shensi. See also Mount Ch'i.

Ch'i, I. A. 5, 7; I. B. 1, 10, 11, 13, 14; II. A. 1, 2; II. B. 1, 2, 3, 5, 6, 7, 8, 11, 12, 13, 14; III. B. 5, 6, 10; IV. A. 24; IV. B. 31, 33; V. A. 4, 8; V. B. 1; VI. B. 5, 6, 8; VII. A. 34, 36; VII. B. 17, 23, 29. A powerful state comprising the northern part of modern Shantung and the south-western part of Hopei.

Ch'i, VI. B. 6. A river in Honan.

Ch'i, Viscount of Wei, VI. A. 6. Elder brother of the tyrant Tchou. See Appendix 4. See also Viscount of Wei.

Ch'i Chou, IV. B. I. Ch'i is Mount Ch'i and Chou is the name of the state.

Ch'i Liang, VI. B. 6. Accounts of Ch'i Liang are to be found in the Tso chuan, Hsiang 23, the Shuo yüan, 11/9, and the Lieh nü chuan, chapter 4.

Chiao Ke, II. A. 1, VI. B. 15. An official at the court of the tyrant Tchou.

Chieh, I. B. 8, IV. A. 9, V. A. 6, VI. B. 2, 6, 9, 10. The tyrant Chieh was the last Emperor of the Hsia Dynasty. See Appendix 4.

Chih, VII. A. 25, i.e., Bandit Chih.

Ch'ih Wa, II. B. 5. According to Chao Ch'i, Counsellor in Ch'i.

Chin, I. A. 5, II. B. 2, III. B. 3, IV. B. 21, V. A. 9, VII. B. 23. A state in modern Shansi. With Duke Wen (reigned 636-628) assuming the leadership of the feudal lords, Chin became one of the most powerful states in the Spring and Autumn period. In 452, Chin was, in all but name, partitioned by the three noble families of Han, Chao and Wei, and in 403 the Chou emperor gave *de jure* recognition of the fact by formally making the three families feudatories. The three new states were commonly known as the Three Chin, but the people of Wei (or Liang) in particular often used the name of Chin when referring to their own state.

Ch'in, I. A. 5, 7, V. A. 9, VI. A. 4, 12, VI. B. 4. A powerful state in the north west, comprising the south east of Kansu, part of Shensi, and reaching to Honan.

Ch'in Chang, VII. B. 37.

Ching, III. A. 4, III. B. 9. Another name for the state of Ch'u.

Ching-ch'ou family, the, II. B. 2.

Ching Ch'un, III. B. 2. According to Chao Ch'i, a politician in the time of Mencius.

Ching Tzu, II. B. 2.

Chou, I. B. 3, II. A. 1, II. B. 13, III. A. 3, III. B. 5, IV. A. 7, V. A. 4, 6, V. B. 2, 4. After T'ai Wang moved to the region of Mount Ch'i (in modern Shensi), his state was known as Chou, and, when King Wu finally won the Empire, Chou became the name of the new Dynasty.

Chou, II. B. 11, 12. According to Chao Ch'i, Chou was to the south west of Lintzu, the capital of Ch'i.

Chou, Marquis of Ch'en, V. A. 8. According to Chao Ch'i, Chou was the son of Duke Huai of Ch'en and had no posthumous name because Ch'en was annexed by Ch'u. This is at variance with the *Shih chi* and the *Tso chuan*.

Chou Hsiao, III. B. 3. According to Chao ch'i, a native of Wei. He is mentioned in the *Chan kuo ts'e*, *Wei ts'e*, II.

Chu Feng, IV. B. 1. According to tradition, fifty *li* to the south of Hotse Hsien in Shantung.

Ch'u, I. A. 5, 7, 1 B. 6, 13, II. B. 2, III. A. 1, 4, III. B. 5, 6, IV. B. 21, VI. A. 4, 12, VI. B. 4. The largest state in the Warring States period, its territory comprising the eastern tip of Szechuan, the whole of Hupei, the north east of Hunan, the north of Kiangsi, the north of Anhwei, the north east of Shensi, the south of Honan and the central part of Kiangsu north of the Huai River.

Ch'u Tzu, IV. B. 32, VI. B. 5. Also mentioned in the *Chan kuo ts'e*, *Yen ts'e*, I.

Chuan Fu, I. B. 4. A mountain in Shantung.

Chuang, III. B. 6.

Chuang Pao, I. B. 1.

Chuang Tzu, I. B. 1, i.e., Chuang Pao.

Ch'ui Chi, V. A. 9. A place in Chin.

Ch'un-yü K'un, IV. A. 17, VI. B. 6. A man of humble origin who rose to high position by his quick wit, Ch'un-yü K'un was a prominent member of the group of thinkers gathered at Chi Hisa in Ch'i. For an account of his life see *Shih chi*, 126 and 74.

Chung Jen, V. A. 6. Son of T'ang. See Appendix 4.

Ch'ung, II. B. 14. Place name.

Ch'ung Yü, II. B. 7, 13. According to Chao Ch'i, disciple of Mencius.

Chü, I. B. 3. Name of a state.

Ch'ü, V. A. 9. Place name.

Confucius (551-479), I. A. 4, 7; II. A. 1, 2, 3, 4, 7; III. A. 2, 4; III. B. 1, 3, 7, 9; IV. A. 2, 7, 8, 14; IV. B. 10, 18, 21, 22, 29; V. A. 4, 6, 8; V. B. 1, 4, 5, 7; VI. A. 6, 8; VI. B. 3, 6; VII. A. 24; VII. B. 17, 19, 37, 38. See Introduction.

Duke Ching of Ch'i (reigned 547-490), I. B. 4, III. A. 1, III. B. 1, IV. A. 7, V. B. 7. A mediocre ruler whose only claim to fame was his good fortune in having Yen Tzu as prime minister.

Duke of Chou, II. A. 1, II. B. 9, III. A. 1, 4, III. B. 9, IV. B. 20, V. A. 6, VI. B. 8. Younger brother of King Wu. See Appendix 4.

Duke Hsiao of Wei, V. B. 4. There is no Duke Hsiao in Wei according to the *Tso chuan* and the *Shih chi*. He must be the same person as Che, the Ousted Duke (reigned 492-481).

Duke Huan of Ch'i (reigned 685-643), I. A. 7, II. B. 2, IV. B. 21, VI. B. 7. The most illustrious of the feudal lords in the Spring and Autumn period, Duke Huan of Ch'i was the first of the so-called Five Leaders of the feudal lords. He owed his position in no small measure to his prime minister, Kuan Chung.

Duke Hui of Pi, V. B. 3. Ruler of a small state.

Duke Ling of Wei (reigned 534-493), V. B. 4. A rather bad ruler, remembered mainly because Confucius stayed for some years in Wei during his reign.

Duke Mu of Ch'in (reigned 659-621), V. A. 9, VI. B. 6. Responsible for making Ch'in a powerful state, Duke Mu is counted amongst the Five Leaders of the feudal lords.

Duke Mu of Lu (reigned 415-383), II. B. 11, V. B. 6, 7, VI. B. 6.

Duke Mu of Tsou, I. B. 12.

Duke P'ing of Chin (reigned 557-532), V. B. 3.

Duke P'ing of Lu (reigned 322-303), I. B. 16. See Appendix 1.

Duke Ting of T'eng, III. A. 2.

Duke Wen of Chin (reigned 636-628), I. A. 7, IV. B. 21. Ch'ung-erh, the second son of Duke Hsien of Chin, fled the country when his elder brother committed suicide rather than expose the false accusation made by the favourite concubine of his father. After twenty years in exile, Ch'ung-erh returned to Chin to succeed to the throne and, during his short reign, became an illustrious ruler and is counted, after Duke Huan of Ch'i, as the second of the Five Leaders of the feudal lords.

Duke Wen of T'eng, I. B. 13, 14, 15, III. A. 1, 3.

Earl of Ke, III. B. 5.

East Sea, IV. A. 13, VII. A. 22. The modern Yellow Sea.

Eastern Mount, VII. A. 24. Situated to the south of Mengyin Hsien in Shantung.

Fan, VII. A. 36. South east of Fan Hsien in Shantung.

Fang Hsün, III. A. 4, V. A. 4, i.e., Yao.

Fei Lien, III. B. 9. A favourite of the tyrant Tchou's, said to be a fleet-footed runner.

Feng Fu, VII. B. 23.

Five Leaders of the feudal lords, VI. B. 7, VII. A. 30. There are various ways of counting the Five Leaders of the feudal lords: (1) Duke Huan of Ch'i (reigned 685-643), Duke Wen of Chin (reigned 636-628), Duke Mu of Ch'in (reigned 659-621), Duke Hsiang of Sung (reigned 650-637), King Chuang of Ch'u (reigned 613-591); (2) Duke Huan of Ch'i, Duke Wen of Chin, Duke Mu of Ch'in, King Chuang of Ch'u, He Lü, King of Wu (reigned 514-496); (3) Duke Huan of Ch'i, Duke Hsiang of Sung, Duke Wen of Chin, Duke Mu of Ch'in, Kou Chien, King of Yüeh (reigned 496-465); (4) Duke Huan of Ch'i, Duke Hsiang of Sung, Duke Wen of Chin, Duke Mu of Ch'in, Fu Ch'a, King of Wu (reigned 495-474).

Fu Ch'u, IV. B. 31.

Fu Hsia, IV. B. 1. Place name.

Fu Yüeh, VI. B. 15. See Appendix 4.

Hai T'ang, V. B. 3.

Han, VII. A. 11. One of the noble families in Chin in the Spring and Autumn period, Han eventually took part in the partition of Chin. See Chin.

Han, III. A. 4, III. B. 9. The River Han.

Hao-sheng Pu-hai, VII. B. 25.

Ho Nei, I. A. 3. The area in Liang to the north of the Yellow River, in the region of Chiyüan Hsien in modern Honan.

Ho Tung, I. A. 3. The area in Liang to the east of the Yellow River, in the region of Anyi Hsien in modern Shansi.

Hou Chi, III. A. 4. Ch'i was given the task by Shun of teaching the people the cultivation of the five grains. For this reason he is known to posterity as Hou Chi. See also Chi.

Hsi, III. B. I.

Hsi Po, IV. A. 13, VII. A. 22. King Wen was known as Hsi Po because he was the leader of the feudal lords in the west.

Hsi Shih, IV. B. 25. The most famous beauty in Chinese history, Hsi Shih lived in the time of Kou Chien, King of Yüeh (reigned 496-465).

Hsia, I. B. 4, II. A. I, III. A. 3, IV. A. 2, V. A. 6, 7, V. B. 4. The first of the Three Dynasties. See Appendix 4.

Hsiang, V. A. 2, 3 , VI. A. 6. Younger brother of Shun. See Appendix 4.

Hsieh, III. A. 4. See Appendix 4.

Hsieh Liu, II. B. 11, III. B. 7. See also Tzu-liu.

Hsien-ch'iu Meng, V. A. 4. According to Chao Ch'i, disciple of Mencius.

Hsin, III. A. 4.

Hsiu, II. B. 14. Just to the north of Teng Hsien, not very far from Mencius' home.

Hsü Hsing, III. A. 4. Ch'ien Mu identifies Hsü Hsing as the Hsü Fan mentioned in the *Tang jan* chapter of the *Lü shih ch'un ch'iu*, a disciple of Ch'in Ku-li who was, in turn, a disciple of Mo Tzu's. (See *Hsien Ch'in chu tzu hsi nien*, pp. 352-3.)

Hsü Pi, III. A. 5. According to Chao Ch'i, disciple of Mencius.

Hsü Tzu, III. A. 4, i.e., Hsü Hsing.

Hsü Tzu, III. A. 5, i.e., Hsü Pi.

Hsüeh, I. B. 14, II. B. 3. To the south east of Teng Hsien in Shantung.

Hsüeh Chü-chou, III. B. 6.

Hsün Yü, I. B. 3. Barbarian tribes in the north, also known as the Ti tribes.

Hu He, I. A. 7.

Hua Chou, VI. B. 6. Accounts of Hua Chou are to be found in the *Tso chuan*, Hsiang 23, the *Shuo yüan*, 11/9, and the *Lieh nü chuan*, chapter 4.

Huai, III. A. 4, III. B. 9. The River Huai.

Huan Ssu-ma, V. A. 8, i.e., Huan T'ui, the *ssu-ma* (Minister of War) of Sung who wanted to have Confucius murdered. See the *Analects of Confucius*, VII. 23.

Huan Tou, V. A. 3. An official in the time of Yao and Shun.

Jan Ch'iu, IV. A. 14. Disciple of Confucius.

Jan Niu, II. A. 2, i.e., Jan Keng, disciple of Confucius.

Jan Yu, III. A. 2.

Jen, VI. B. 1, 5. Region north of Chining in Shantung.

Ju, III. A. 4. The River Ju.

Kao T'ang, VI. B. 6. South west of Yücheng Hsien in Shantung.

Kao Tzu, II. A. 2, VI. A. 1, 2, 3, 4, 6. It has been suggested that this is the same as the Kao Tzu mentioned in the three sections at the end of chapter 48 of the *Mo tzu*, but this is very unlikely as it is difficult for the same person to span the time between Mo Tzu and Mencius. Although Kao Tzu is not mentioned by name, some ideas are to be found in chapter 26 of the *Kuan tzu* which are reminiscent of what he says in the *Mencius*. For a discussion of this point, see A. C. Graham, 'The Background of the Mencian theory of Human Nature', *The Tsing Hua Journal of Chinese Studies*, N.S. VI, 1 and 2, (December, 1967) pp. 215-71, particularly pp. 227-31.

Kao Yao, III. A. 4, VII. A. 35, VII. B. 38. Was made judge by Shun. See Appendix 4.

Kau Tzu, II. B. 12, VII. B. 21, 22. According to Chao Ch'i, disciple of Mencius.

Kau Tzu, VI. B. 3. Unlikely to be the same as the Kau Tzu mentioned in II. B. 12 and VII. B. 21, 22, as Mencius refers to him as 'old Master Kau'.

Ke, I. B. 3, 11, III. B. 5. A state to the north of Ningling Hsien in Honan. See also Earl of Ke.

Ke, II. B. 6. North west of Yishui Hsien in Shantung.

King of Ch'i, VII. A. 36, i.e., King Hsüan of Ch'i.

King of Sung, III. B. 6. This is most probably Yen, King of Sung (reigned 328-286). See Appendix 1.

King Hsiang of Liang (reigned 318-296), I. A. 6. See Appendix 1.

King Hsüan of Ch'i (reigned 319-301), I. A. 7, I. B. 2-11, IV. B. 3, V. B. 9, VII. A. 39. The usurpation by the T'ien family of the state of Ch'i was recognized by the Chou Emperor in 386. By the time of King Wei (reigned 357-320), Ch'i was a powerful state. It was King Wei who assembled a group of thinkers at Chi Hsia. This practice continued in the time of King Hsüan. Although few of the Chi Hsia thinkers are mentioned by name in the *Mencius*, there is little doubt that Mencius was aware of what was going on and in many respects made use of current ideas.

King Hui of Liang (reigned 370-319), I. A. 1-5, VII. B. 1. When Marquis

Wu died in 371, his son Ying succeeded him as Marquis of Wei. In 361, he moved his capital to Ta Liang (modern Kaifeng). It is for this reason that Wei is also known as Liang. In 334, Ying had a meeting with King Wei of Ch'i when they mutually recognized each other as king. On his death he was given the posthumous title of King Hui. When Mencius had his first meeting with him, King Hui was already an old man and his state had greatly declined in fortune, but he was still hoping, before he died, to be able 'to wash away' the shame of the defeats and humiliations he had suffered.

King Li (reigned 857-842), VI. A. 6. One of the tyrants of the Chou Dynasty.

King Wen (d. 1027), I. A. 2; I. B. 2, 3, 5, 10; II. A. 1, 3; III. A. 1, 3; III. B. 9; IV. A. 7, 13; IV. B. 1, 20; VI. A. 6; VI. B. 2; VII. A. 10, 22; VII. B. 19, 22, 38. Father of King Wu who founded the Chou Dynasty. See Appendix 4.

King Wu (reigned 1027-1005), I. B. 3, 8, 10, II. A. 1, II. B. 12, III. B. 9, IV. A. 9, IV. B. 20, VI. A. 6, VII. A. 30, VII. B. 4, 33. The founder of the Chou Dynasty. See Appendix 4.

King Yu (reigned 781–771), VI. A. 6. The tyrant under whose rule the Chou Dynasty came to its end.

Kou Chien, I. B. 3. King of Yüeh (reigned 496-465), sometimes counted as one of the Five Leaders of the feudal lords.

Ku Kung Tan Fu, I. B. 5, i.e., T'ai Wang.

Kuan Chung, II. A. 1, II. B. 2, VI. B. 15. The prime minister of Ch'i who was responsible for the power and prestige attained by Duke Huan of Ch'i. It is illuminating to contrast the admiration Confucius shows for Kuan Chung (see the *Analects of Confucius*, XIV. 16, 17) with the condescension with which Mencius treats him.

Kuan Shu, II. B. 9. Brother of the Duke of Chou.

K'uang Chang, III. B. 10, IV. B. 30. See Appendix 1.

K'uei Ch'iu, VI. B. 7. East of Kaocheng Hsien in Honan, known in history for the meeting of the feudal lords called by Duke Huan of Ch'i in 651.

K'ung Chü-hsin, II. B. 4.

Kun, V. A. 3. Father of Yü, put to death by Shun for his failure to put down the Flood. See Appendix 4.

K'un tribes, I. B. 3. Western barbarian tribes.

Kung chih Ch'i, V. A. 9. For an account of his advice against accepting the bribe offered by Chin, see the *Tso chuan*, Hsi 2.

Kung Kung, V. A. 3.

Kung Liu, I. B. 5. An ancestor of the Chou house. See Appendix 4.

Kung-hang Tzu, IV. B. 27. According to Chao Ch'i, a Counsellor of Ch'i.

Kung-ming Kao, V. A. 1. According to Chao Ch'i, disciple of Tseng Tzu.

Kung-ming Yi, III. A. 1, III. B. 3, 9, IV. B. 24. Also mentioned in the *T'an kung* and *Chi yi* chapters of the *Li chi*. Said by Cheng Hsüan to be Tseng Tzu's disciple.

Kung-shu Tzu, IV. A. 1. Kung-shu Pan, known also as Lu Pan, was a contemporary of Mo Tzu's and the most famous craftsman in Chinese history.

Kung-sun Ch'ou, II. A. 1, 2; II. B. 2, 6, 14; III. B. 7; IV. A. 18; VI. B. 3, 13; VII. A. 31, 32, 39, 41; VII. B. 1, 36. Disciple of Mencius.

Kung-sun Yen, III. B. 2, i.e., Hsi Shou, a native of Wei and a prominent itinerant politician. For his biography, see *Shih chi*, 70.

Kung-tu Tzu, II. B. 5, III. B. 9, IV. B. 30, VI. A. 5, 6, 15, VII. A. 43. According to Chao Ch'i, disciple of Mencius.

Kung-yi Tzu, VI. B. 6. This is, perhaps, Kung-yi Hsiu who was prime minister of Lu. See *Shih chi*, 119.

Kuo, V. A. 9. A small state in Pinglu Hsien in modern Shansi.

Lady Chiang, I. B. 5, i.e., T'ai Chiang, a concubine of T'ai Wang's.

Lai Chu, VII. B. 38.

Lang Yeh, I. B. 4. A mountain to the south of Chucheng Hsien in Shantung.

Li Lou, IV. A. 1. In the *Chuang tzu* (chapters 8, 10 and 12), Li Lou is known as Li Chu and said to be a man with keen eyesight in the time of the Yellow Emperor.

Liang Mountains, I. B. 15.

Ling Ch'iu, II. B. 5. Place name.

Liu Hsia Hui, II. A. 9, V. B. 1, VI. B. 6, VII. A. 28, VII. B. 15. Chan Ch'in, a Counsellor in Lu, is commonly known as Liu Hsia Hui, but there is no convincing explanation as to why he was so called.

Lu, I. B. 12; II. B. 7; III. A. 2; IV. B. 21; V. A. 8; V. B. 1, 4; VI. B. 6, 8, 13; VII. A. 24, 36; VII. B. 17, 37. A state comprising mainly the south eastern part of modern Shantung.

Lung Tzu, III. A. 3, VI. A. 7.

Meng Chi-tzu, VI. A. 5.

Meng Chung-tzu, II. B. 2. According to Chao Ch'i, cousin of Mencius.

Meng Hsien Tzu, V. B. 3. A Counsellor of Lu.

Meng K'e, I. B. 16, i.e., Mencius.

Meng Pin, II. A. 2. A famous brave warrior in antiquity.

Meng Shih-she, II. A. 2.

Mi Tzu, V. A. 8, i.e., Mi Tzu-hsia, a favourite of Duke Ling of Wei (reigned 534-493).

Mien Chü, VI. B. 6.

Min Tzu, II. A. 2, i.e., Min Tzu-ch'ien, disciple of Confucius.

Ming T'iao, IV. B. 1. Place name.

Mo, III. B. 9, VII. B. 26, i.e., Mo Ti.

Mo Chi, VII. B. 19.

Mo Ti, III. B. 9. A philosopher whose life falls within the 5th century B.C. He is best remembered for his doctrine of 'love without discrimination', a doctrine violently attacked by Mencius as denying the greater claim parents have on a son.

Mo Tzu, VII. A. 26, i.e., Mo Ti.

Mount Chi, V. A. 6. South east of Tengfeng Hisen in Honan.

Mount Ch'i, I. B. 5, 14, 15. The present Chankua Shan, to the north east of Chishan Hsien in Shensi.

Mount Ch'ung, V. A. 3. A region in the extreme south.

Mount T'ai, I. A. 7, II. A. 2, VII. A. 24. In Shantung and one of the most revered mountains in China.

Mount Yü, V. A. 3. A region in the extreme east.

Mu Chung, V. B. 3.

Mu Palace, V. A. 7. The palace of the tyrant Chieh.

Mu P'i, VII. B. 37.

Nan Ho, V.A.5. Place name.

Nan Yang, VI. B. 8. The same as Wen Yang which is south west of Mount T'ai and north of the River Wen.

North Sea, I. A. 7, IV. A. 13, V. B. 1, VII. A. 22, i.e., Po Hai or the Gulf of Chihli.

Ox Mountain, VI. A. 8. To the south of Lintzu Hsien in Shantung.

P'en-ch'eng K'uo, VII. B. 29.

P'eng Keng, III. B. 4. According to Chao Ch'i, disciple of Mencius.

P'eng Meng, IV. B. 24.

Pi Chan, III. A. 3.

Pi Ying, IV. B. 1. East of Hsienyang Hsien in Shensi.

Pin, I. B. 14, 15. West of Hsünyi Hsien in Shensi.

P'ing Lu, II. B. 4, VI. B. 5. In the region of Wenshang Hsien in Shantung.

Po, III. B. 5, V. A. 6, 7. North of Shangchiu Hsien in Honan.

Po Kuei, VI. B. 10, 11. Mentioned in many ancient works as an expert in water control.

Po Yi, II. A. 2, 9, III. B. 10, IV. A. 13, V. B. 1, VI. B. 6, VII. A. 22, VII. B. 15. Po Yi and Shu Ch'i were the sons of the lord of Ku Chu. The father intended Shu Ch'i, the younger son, to succeed him, but when he died neither of his sons was willing to deprive the other of the succession and they both fled the country and retired into the mountains.

Po-kung Ch'i, V. B. 2. According to Chao Ch'i, a native of Wei.

Po-kung Yu, II. A. 2. According to Kao Yu in his commentary to the *Huai nan tzu* (chapter 9), a native of Ch'i.

Po-li Hsi, V. A. 9, VI. B. 6, 15. There are divergencies in the tradition concerning Po-li Hsi. Even in the *Shih chi* alone, according to chapters 5, 39 and 63, he was taken prisoner by Chin when Yü was conquered, while according to chapter 68, he sold himself to a traveller in order to be taken to Ch'in so as to gain an opportunity of coming to the notice of Duke Mu.

Prince Pi Kan, II. A. 1, VI. A. 6. The uncle of the tyrant Tchou. See Appendix 4.

Prince Tien, VII. A. 33. According to Chao Ch'i, son of the King of Ch'i – presumably King Hsüan of Ch'i.

River, the, III. A. 4, i.e., the Yangtse River.

San Miao, V. A. 3. Name of a state.

San Wei, V. A. 3. A region in the extreme west.

San-yi Sheng, VII. B. 38. An official of Tchou's who went over to King Wu.

Shang, IV. A. 7. Another name for the Yin Dynasty.

Shang Kung, VII. B. 30.

Shen Hsiang, II. B. 11. According to Cheng Hsüan in his commentary to the *T'an kung* chapter of the *Li chi*, the son of Tzu-chang and son-in-law of Tzu-yu, both disciples of Confucius.

Shen Nung, III. A. 4. Legendary emperor credited with the discovery of agriculture.

Shen T'ung, II. B. 8.

Shen Tzu, VI. B. 8. Most unlikely to be the same person as Shen Tao, one of the philosophers at Chi Hsia.

Shen-yu Hsing, IV. B. 31.

Shih Ch'iu, VI. B. 4. Place name.

Shih K'uang, IV. A. 1, VI. A. 7. The court musician of Duke P'ing of

Chin (reigned 557-532), Shih K'uang is the most famous musician in Chinese history.

Shih Tzu, II. B. 10.

Shu, III. A. 4, III. B. 9. A small state to the west of Luchiang Hsien in Anhwei.

Shun, II. A. 2, 8; II. B. 2; III. A. 1, 4; III. B. 4, 9; IV. A. 1, 2, 26, 28; IV. B. 1, 19, 28, 32; V. A. 1, 2, 3, 4, 5, 6, 7; V. B. 1, 3, 6; VI. A. 6; VI. B. 2, 3, 8, 10, 15; VII. A. 16, 25, 30, 35, 46; VII. B. 6, 33, 37, 38. A sage king. See Appendix 4.

Snow Palace, I. B. 4.

Ssu, III. A. 4. A river.

Ssu-ch'eng Chen-tzu, V. A. 8.

Sun Shu-ao, VI. B. 15. A prime minister of Ch'u.

Sung, II. A. 2, II. B. 3, III. A. 1, 2, 4, III. B. 5, V. A. 8, VII. A. 36. A state comprising the eastern part of Honan and parts of Shantung, Kiangsu and Anhwei.

Sung K'eng, VI. B. 4. One of the philosophers at Chi Hsia, known for his strong anti-war position. He supported his position by the theory that men did not really desire much and that they could avoid fighting if only they could refuse to feel humiliated in face of insult.

Sung Kou-chien, VII. A. 9.

T'a, III. A. 4. A river.

Tai, III. B. 10.

Tai Pu-sheng, III. B. 6.

Tai Ying-chih, III. B. 8.

T'ai Chia, V. A. 6, VII. A. 31. Son of T'ang. See Appendix 4.

T'ai Kung, IV. A. 13, VI. B. 8, VII. A. 22, i.e., Lü Shang who first helped King Wen and then King Wu in winning the Empire. For his biography see Shih chi, 32.

T'ai Kung Wang, VII. B. 38, i.e., T'ai Kung.

T'ai Ting, V. A. 6. Son of T'ang.

T'ai Wang, I. B. 3, 5, 14, 15. Grandfather of King Wen. See Appendix 4.

Tan Chu, V. A. 6. Son of Yao.

T'ang, V. A. 6. The name of Yao's dynasty.

T'ang, I. B. 3, 8, 11; II. A. 1, 3; II. B. 2, 12; III. B. 5; IV. A. 9; IV. B. 20; V. A. 6, 7; VI. B. 2, 6; VII. A. 30; VII. B. 33, 38. Founder of the Yin Dynasty. See Appendix 4.

T'ang, VII. B. 23. To the south of Chimo Hsien in Shantung.

T'ao Ying, VII. A. 35. According to Chao Ch'i, disciple of Mencius.

Tchou, I. B. 8; II. A. 1; III. B. 9; IV. A. 9, 13; V. A. 6; V. B. 1; VI. A. 6;

VII. A. 22. The tyrant Tchou was the last Emperor of the Yin Dynasty. See Appendix 4.

T'eng, I. B. 13, 15, II. B. 6, III. A. 1, 3, 4, VII. B. 30. A small state in the region of Teng Hsien in modern Shantung.

T'eng Keng, VII. A. 43. According to Chao Ch'i, younger brother of the ruler of T'eng.

Ti tribes, I. B. 14, 15, i.e., Hsün Yü.

Three Dynasties, III. A. 2, 3, IV. A. 3, IV. B. 20. Hsia, Yin (or Shang) and Chou are known as the Three Dynasties. See Appendix 4.

Tieh Tse Gate, VII. A. 36.

Tsai Wo, II. A. 2. Disciple of Confucius.

Ts'ai, VII. B. 18. A small state to the south west of Shangtsai Hsien in Honan.

Tsang Ts'ang, I. B. 16. Favourite of Duke P'ing of Lu.

Ts'ao Chiao, VI. B. 2.

Tseng Hsi, II. A. 1. The younger son of Tseng Tzu.

Tseng Hsi, IV. A. 19, VII. B. 36, 37, i.e., Tseng Tien, father of Tseng Tzu.

Tseng Tzu, I. B. 12, II. A. 2, II. B. 2, III. A. 2, 4, III. B. 7, IV. A. 19, IV. B. 31, VII. B. 36, i.e., Tseng Ts'an, disciple of Confucius, largely responsible for the undue emphasis on filial dutifulness in later Confucianism.

Tseng Yüan, IV. A. 19. Son of Tseng Tzu.

Tsou, I. A. 7, I. B. 12, III. A. 2, VI. B. 1, 2, 5. Mencius' native state, in the region around Tsou Hsien in modern Shantung.

Tuan-kan Mu, III. B. 7. According to tradition, Tuan-kan Mu was a broker who became a man of distinction after he became a disciple of Tzu-hsia.

T'ung, V. A. 6, VII. A. 31. Generally thought to be south west of Yenshih Hsien in Honan.

Tung-kuo family, the, II. B. 2.

Tzu-ao, IV. A. 24, 25, IV. B. 27, i.e., Wang Huan.

Tzu-ch'an (d. 522), IV. B. 2, V. A. 2, i.e., Kung-sun Ch'iao, prime minister of Cheng, who was a most enlightened statesman with strong humanist leanings, greatly admired by Confucius.

Tzu-chang, II. A. 2, III. A. 4, i.e., Chuan-sun Shih, disciple of Confucius.

Tzu-chih, II. B. 8. Prime minister of Yen in the time of King K'uai.

Tzu-chuo Ju-tzu, IV. B. 24.

Tzu-hsia, II. A. 2, III. A. 4, i.e., Pu Shang, disciple of Confucius.

Tzu-hsiang, II. A. 2. According to Chao Ch'i, disciple of Tseng Tzu.

Tzu-k'uai, II. B. 8. King of Yen.

Tzu-kung, II. A. 2, III. A. 4, i.e., Tuan-mu Ssu, disciple of Confucius, famous for his eloquence.

Tzu-liu, VI. B. 6. According to Chao Ch'i, the same as Hsieh Liu.

Tzu-lu, II. A. 1, 8, III. B. 7, V. A. 8, i.e., Chung Yu, disciple of Confucius, known for his valour and impetuosity.

Tzu-mo, VII. A. 26.

Tzu-shu Yi, II. B. 10.

Tzu-ssu, II. B. 11, IV. B. 31, V. B. 3, 6, 7, VI. B. 6, i.e., K'ung Chi, grandson of Confucius. According to tradition, Mencius studied under a disciple of Tzu-ssu's.

Tzu-tu, VI. A. 7. A byword for a handsome man. Mentioned in Ode 85 in the *Book of Odes:*

Tzu-yu, II. A. 2, III. A. 4, i.e., Yen Yen, disciple of Confucius.

Viscount Chien of Chao (reigned 517-458), III. B. 1. Senior minister of Chin.

Viscount of Chi, II. A. 1. Uncle of the tyrant Tchou. See Appendix 4.

Viscount of Wei, II. A. 1. See also Ch'i, Viscount of Wei.

Wai Ping, V. A. 6. Son of T'ang.

Wan Chang, III. B. 5; V. A. 1, 2, 3, 5, 6, 7, 8, 9; V. B. 3, 4, 6, 7, 8; VII. B. 37. Disciple of Mencius.

Wang Huan, II. B. 6, IV. B. 27. See also Tzu-ao.

Wang Liang, III. B. 1. A famous charioteer.

Wang Pao, VI. B. 6.

Wang Shun, V. B. 3.

Wei, VII. A. 11. One of the noble families in Chin in the Spring and Autumn period, Wei eventually took part in the partition of Chin. See Chin, and King Hui of Liang.

Wei, IV. B. 24, 31, V. A. 8. A small estate comprising the northern part of the region where Honan and Shantung adjoin.

Wei, IV. B. 2. River which arises in the east of Tengfeng Hsien in Honan and flows eastwards through Mi Hsien to join the Chen.

Wei Chung, II. A. 1. Younger brother of Viscount of Wei.

Wu, I. B. 3, IV. A. 7. A powerful semi-barbarian state in the Spring and Autumn period, comprising parts of modern Kiangsu and Chekiang.

Wu-lu Tzu, VI. B. 1, 5. Disciple of Mencius.

Wu Ch'eng, IV. B. 31. South west of Picheng Hsien in Shantung.

Wu Huo, VI. B. 2.

Wu Ling, III. B. 10. South of Changshan Hsien in Shantung.

Wu Ting, II. A. 1. A Yin emperor.

Yang, III. B. 9, VII. B. 26, i.e., Yang Chu.

Yang Ch'eng, V. A. 6. Traditionally identified with the mountain north of Tengfeng Hsien in Honan.

Yang Chu, III. B. 9. Philosopher who advocated an egoism opposed to hedonism. See also Yang Tzu.

Yang Hu, III. A. 3, III. B. 7. Steward of the Chi family in Lu.

Yang Tzu, VII. A. 26. See also Yang Chu.

Yangtse River, III. B. 9, VII. A. 16. See also the River.

Yao, II. A. 2; II. B. 2; III. A. 1, 4; III. B. 4, 9; IV. A. 1, 2; IV. B. 32; V. A. 4, 5, 6, 7; V. B. 1, 6; VI. A. 6; VI. B. 2, 8, 10; VII. A. 30, 46; VII. B. 33, 37, 38. A sage king. See Appendix 4.

Yellow River, II. A. 2, III. B. 9, VI. B. 6, VII. A. 16.

Yen, I. B. 10, 11, II. B. 8, 9. A state comprising the north of Hopei and north east of Shansi.

Yen, III. B. 9. A state to the east of Chüfu Hsien in Shantung.

Yen Ch'ou-yu, V. A. 8.

Yen Hui, II. A. 2, III. A. 1, IV. B. 29. The most brilliant of Confucius' disciples who died at the early age of twenty-nine.

Yen Pan, V. B. 3.

Yen Tzu, I. B. 4, II. A. 1, i.e., Yen Ying, prime minister of Ch'i in the time of Duke Ching (reigned 547-490), who was a most distinguished statesman.

Yi, III. A. 4, V. A. 6. Assisted Yü in the government of the Empire. See Appendix 4.

Yi, IV. B. 24, VI. A. 20, VII. A. 41. Famous archer in antiquity.

Yi Chih, III. A. 5.

Yi Ch'iu, VI. A. 9.

Yi Tzu, III. A. 5, i.e., Yi Chih.

Yi Ya, VI. A. 7. Gained the favour of Duke Huan of Ch'i through his culinary art. According to tradition, he offered the Duke the cooked head of his own son so that the Duke could taste the ultimate delicacy.

Yi Yin, II. A. 2, II. B. 2, V. A. 6, 7, V. B. 1, VI. B. 6, VII. A. 31, VII. B. 38. Assisted T'ang in gaining the Empire. See Appendix 4.

Yin, II. A. 1, II. B. 9, III. A. 3, IV. A. 2, 7, V. A. 6, V. B. 4, VII. B. 4. Second of the Three Dynasties. See Appendix 4.

Yin Kung chih T'uo, IV. B. 24.

Yin Shih, II. B. 12.

Ying, II. B. 7. North west of Laiwu Hsien in Shantung.

Yu, III. B. 5. Name of a state.

Yu Chou, V. A. 3. A region in the extreme north.

Yu Hsin, V. A. 7. A state to the north east of Chenlin Hsien in Honan.

Yu Jo, II. A 2, III. A. 4. Disciple of Confucius.

Yu Pi, V. A. 3. Place name.

Yung Chü, V. A. 8.

Yü, V. A. 6. The name of Shun's dynasty.

Yü, II. A. 8, III. A. 4, III. B. 9, IV. B. 20, 26, 29, V. A. 6, VI. B. 11, VII. B. 22,
    38. Founder of the Hsia Dynasty. See Appendix 4.

Yü, III. B. 5. Name of a state.

Yü, V. A. 9, VI. B. 6. A small state north east of Pinglu Hsien in Shansi.

Yü Kung chih Ssu, IV. B. 24.

Yüeh, IV. B. 31, VI. B. 3. A state comprising the southern part of Shan-
    tung, a large part of Kiangsu, the northern part of Chekiang and
    parts of Anhwei and Kiangsi.

Yüeh, III. B. 6.

Yüeh-cheng Ch'iu, V. B. 3.

Yüeh-cheng Tzu, I. B. 16, IV. A. 24, 25, VI. B. 13, VII. B. 25, i.e., Yüeh-
    cheng K'e, disciple of Mencius.

FOR THE BEST IN PAPERBACKS, LOOK FOR THE

In every corner of the world, on every subject under the sun, Penguin represents quality and variety – the very best in publishing today.

For complete information about books available from Penguin – including Puffins, Penguin Classics and Arkana – and how to order them, write to us at the appropriate address below. Please note that for copyright reasons the selection of books varies from country to country.

In the United Kingdom: Please write to *Dept E.P., Penguin Books Ltd, Harmondsworth, Middlesex, UB7 0DA.*

If you have any difficulty in obtaining a title, please send your order with the correct money, plus ten per cent for postage and packaging, to *PO Box No 11, West Drayton, Middlesex*

In the United States: Please write to *Dept BA, Penguin, 299 Murray Hill Parkway, East Rutherford, New Jersey 07073*

In Canada: Please write to *Penguin Books Canada Ltd, 2801 John Street, Markham, Ontario L3R 1B4*

In Australia: Please write to the *Marketing Department, Penguin Books Australia Ltd, P.O. Box 257, Ringwood, Victoria 3134*

In New Zealand: Please write to the *Marketing Department, Penguin Books (NZ) Ltd, Private Bag, Takapuna, Auckland 9*

In India: Please write to *Penguin Overseas Ltd, 706 Eros Apartments, 56 Nehru Place, New Delhi, 110019*

In the Netherlands: Please write to *Penguin Books Netherlands B.V., Postbus 195, NL–1380AD Weesp*

In West Germany: Please write to *Penguin Books Ltd, Friedrichstrasse 10–12, D–6000 Frankfurt/Main 1*

In Spain: Please write to *Longman Penguin España, Calle San Nicolas 15, E–28013 Madrid*

In Italy: Please write to *Penguin Italia s.r.l., Via Como 4, I-20096 Pioltello (Milano)*

In France: Please write to *Penguin Books Ltd, 39 Rue de Montmorency, F-75003 Paris*

In Japan: Please write to *Longman Penguin Japan Co Ltd, Yamaguchi Building, 2–12–9 Kanda Jimbocho, Chiyoda-Ku, Tokyo 101*

FOR THE BEST IN PAPERBACKS, LOOK FOR THE 🐧

PENGUIN CLASSICS

Bashō	**The Narrow Road to the Deep North**
	On Love and Barley
Cao Xuequin	**The Story of the Stone** *also known as* **The Dream of the Red Chamber (in five volumes)**
Confucius	**The Analects**
Khayyam	**The Ruba'iyat of Omar Khayyam**
Lao Tzu	**Tao Te Ching**
Li Po/Tu Fu	**Li Po and Tu Fu**
Sei Shōnagon	**The Pillow Book of Sei Shōnagon**
Wang Wei	**Poems**

ANTHOLOGIES AND ANONYMOUS WORKS

The Bhagavad Gita
Buddhist Scriptures
The Dhammapada
Hindu Myths
The Koran
New Songs from a Jade Terrace
The Rig Veda
Six Yuan Plays
Speaking of Śiva
Tales from the Thousand and One Nights
The Upanishads

FOR THE BEST IN PAPERBACKS, LOOK FOR THE 🐧

PENGUIN CLASSICS

Pedro de Alarcón	**The Three-Cornered Hat and Other Stories**
Leopoldo Alas	**La Regenta**
Ludovico Ariosto	**Orlando Furioso**
Giovanni Boccaccio	**The Decameron**
Baldassar Castiglione	**The Book of the Courtier**
Benvenuto Cellini	**Autobiography**
Miguel de Cervantes	**Don Quixote**
	Exemplary Stories
Dante	**The Divine Comedy** (in 3 volumes)
	La Vita Nuova
Bernal Diaz	**The Conquest of New Spain**
Carlo Goldoni	**Four Comedies (The Venetian Twins/The Artful Widow/Mirandolina/The Superior Residence)**
Niccolò Machiavelli	**The Discourses**
	The Prince
Alessandro Manzoni	**The Betrothed**
Benito Pérez Galdós	**Fortunata and Jacinta**
Giorgio Vasari	**Lives of the Artists** (in 2 volumes)

and

Five Italian Renaissance Comedies (Machiavelli/**The Mandragola;** Ariosto/**Lena**; Aretino/**The Stablemaster;** Gl'Intronati/**The Deceived**; Guarini/**The Faithful Shepherd**)
The Jewish Poets of Spain
The Poem of the Cid
Two Spanish Picaresque Novels (Anon/**Lazarillo de Tormes;** de Quevedo/**The Swindler**)

FOR THE BEST IN PAPERBACKS, LOOK FOR THE

PENGUIN CLASSICS

ANTHOLOGIES AND ANONYMOUS WORKS

The Age of Bede
Alfred the Great
Beowulf
A Celtic Miscellany
The Cloud of Unknowing and Other Works
The Death of King Arthur
The Earliest English Poems
Early Christian Writings
Early Irish Myths and Sagas
Egil's Saga
King Arthur's Death
The Letters of Abelard and Heloise
Medieval English Verse
Njal's Saga
Seven Viking Romances
Sir Gawain and the Green Knight
The Song of Roland

PENGUIN CLASSICS

Aeschylus	**The Oresteian Trilogy** (Agamemnon/The Choephori/The Eumenides) **Prometheus Bound/The Suppliants/Seven** **Against Thebes/The Persians**
Aesop	**Fables**
Ammianus Marcellinus	**The Later Roman Empire (AD 353–378)**
Apollonius of Rhodes	**The Voyage of Argo**
Apuleius	**The Golden Ass**
Aristophanes	**The Knights/Peace/The Birds/The Assembly** **Women/Wealth** **Lysistrata/The Acharnians/The Clouds/** **The Wasps/The Poet and the Women/The Frogs**
Aristotle	**The Athenian Constitution** **The Ethics** **The Politics** **De Anima**
Arrian	**The Campaigns of Alexander**
Saint Augustine	**City of God** **Confessions**
Boethius	**The Consolation of Philosophy**
Caesar	**The Civil War** **The Conquest of Gaul**
Catullus	**Poems**
Cicero	**The Murder Trials** **The Nature of the Gods** **On the Good Life** **Selected Letters** **Selected Political Speeches** **Selected Works**
Euripides	**Alcestis/Iphigenia in Tauris/Hippolytus** **The Bacchae/Ion/The Women of Troy/Helen** **Medea/Hecabe/Electra/Heracles** **Orestes/The Children of Heracles/** **Andromache/The Suppliant Women/** **The Phoenician Women/Iphigenia in Aulis**

FOR THE BEST IN PAPERBACKS, LOOK FOR THE 🐧

PENGUIN CLASSICS

FOR THE BEST IN PAPERBACKS, LOOK FOR THE

PENGUIN CLASSICS

Pliny	**The Letters of the Younger Pliny**
Plutarch	**The Age of Alexander** (Nine Greek Lives)
	The Fall of the Roman Republic (Six Lives)
	The Makers of Rome (Nine Lives)
	The Rise and Fall of Athens (Nine Greek Lives)
	On Sparta
Polybius	**The Rise of the Roman Empire**
Procopius	**The Secret History**
Propertius	**The Poems**
Quintus Curtius Rufus	**The History of Alexander**
Sallust	**The Jugurthine War** and **The Conspiracy of Cataline**
Seneca	**Four Tragedies** and **Octavia**
	Letters from a Stoic
Sophocles	**Electra/Women of Trachis/Philoctetes/Ajax**
	The Theban Plays (King Oedipus/Oedipus at Colonus/Antigone)
Suetonius	**The Twelve Caesars**
Tacitus	**The Agricola** and **The Germania**
	The Annals of Imperial Rome
	The Histories
Terence	**The Comedies** (The Girl from Andros/The Self-Tormentor/The Eunuch/Phormio/The Mother-in-Law/The Brothers)
Thucydides	**The History of the Peloponnesian War**
Tibullus	**The Poems** and **The Tibullan Collection**
Virgil	**The Aeneid**
	The Eclogues
	The Georgics
Xenophon	**A History of My Times**
	The Persian Expedition